DRAGON'S TRIANGLE

DRAGON'S TRIANGLE

CHRISTINE KLING

THOMAS & MERCER

This is a work of fiction. Names, characters, organizations, places, events, and incidents are either products of the author's imagination or are used fictitiously.

Published by Thomas & Mercer, Seattle
www.apub.com

Amazon, the Amazon logo, and Thomas & Mercer are trademarks of Amazon.com, Inc., or its affiliates.

Cover Design by The Book Designers

ISBN-13: 9781477823132
ISBN-10: 1477823131
Library of Congress Control Number: 2013958063

Printed in the United States of America

To Irv Kaine and his brothers in arms,
the veterans of World War II

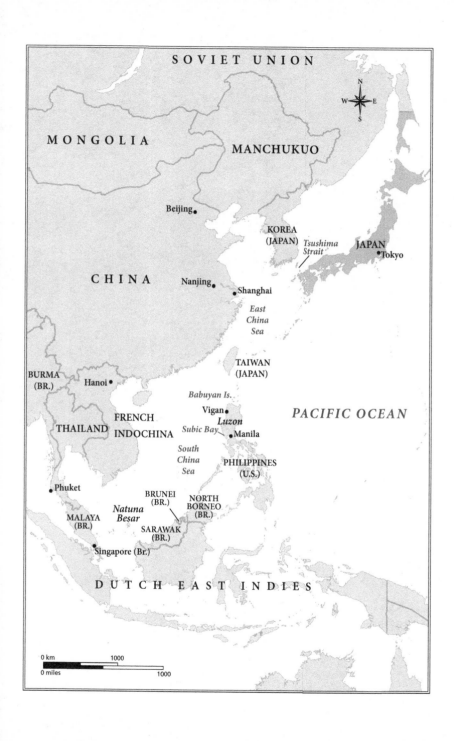

All that is necessary for the triumph of evil is that good men do nothing.

—Edmund Burke

AUTHOR'S NOTE

The real USS *Bonefish* (SS-223) was a Gato-class diesel-electric submarine launched in March of 1943. On her eight patrols, she sank a total of twelve Japanese ships, five of those under her last captain, Commander Lawrence Edge. Her story, and that of the other eight Hellcat subs, is a tale of one of the most daring submarine raids in the history of World War II. Called Operation Barney, this effort at the end of the war saw a wolf pack of American subs enter the Sea of Japan in June of 1945, using the very new technology of FM sonar to map the minefields that had protected that piece of water. These subs delivered a final blow to both Japan's merchant and military shipping.

Tragically, the *Bonefish* did not return from her final mission and her wreck has never been found. Japanese records released after the war have led the US Navy to assume she was sunk by Japanese vessels in Toyama Wan, Honshu, on June 18, 1945.

My novel, *Dragon's Triangle,* is a work of fiction and the characters herein bear no resemblance or relation to the real eighty-five men who lost their lives defending their country, nor does my imaginary story reflect the true respect I have for the men and women of the United States and the Philippines whose devotion to country and service put an end to that war. This book is dedicated to the veterans of World War II.

Christine Kling

CHAPTER ONE

Ao Chalong Anchorage
Phuket, Thailand

November 15, 2012

When the voice erupted from the VHF radio, Riley jumped. The sandpaper in her hand slid off the teak handrail and scratched the boat's gel coat.

"*Bonefish, Bonefish,* this is *Merlin II.*"

Eerie to hear this call just when she was thinking about him—as though he were reading her mind. She wanted to talk to him, too. His wet swimsuit lay on the cabin sole where he had stepped out of it, and his iPad and sheet music covered the main salon table. He had been sitting below playing guitar and crooning his Carolina bluegrass while she sanded and put another coat of varnish on the starboard handrail. Okay, it wasn't his boat, so she couldn't expect him to do the maintenance, but before he hopped into that dinghy and raced off to the yacht club, he might have cleaned up after himself. He now spent so much of his life with the 1 percent he often forgot how the rest got by.

In two steps she was at the chart table, and she grabbed the microphone.

"This is *Bonefish*. Up one?"

He started speaking immediately on the new frequency. "Riley, glad you were listening. I think you'll want to come ashore."

"Okay, what's up?"

"There's something here you're going to want to see right away."

She climbed up the steps and peered across the still, flat water of the bay. She spotted the lighthouse and then looked right until she could make out the low structure of the Ao Chalong Yacht Club.

"What's going on? Are you at the club?"

"Yeah, I played one set, and when I went to the bar for a cold one, Roger told me he had something for you."

Riley cocked her head to one side and stared at the mike in her hand as though it could explain what he was talking about. When it didn't, she pressed the button and said, "Go on."

"It's a letter, babe. Postmark is Bangkok. No return address. Funny-looking handwriting. Kinda looks weird, nervous-like. Anyway, I figured you'd want to know."

A letter for her? Addressed to the Ao Chalong Yacht Club? Who even knew she was here? When she communicated with her employers at Mercury Security or with her best friend, Hazel, it was always by email. Snail mail was about as relevant to her as a vinyl record.

Still, someone had sent her a letter. Who the hell wrote letters anymore?

There was one very remote possibility. She shook her head. No way. She was done chasing after that dream.

Only one way to find out. She keyed the mike. "Thanks, Billy. I'm on my way in."

The oars struck bottom, and with one last pull she drove the flat-hulled dinghy onto the beach. Riley hopped out and pulled the boat a few feet up the sand. She ran her cable around a palm tree and through the dinghy pad eye, then snapped on the big combination lock. Security was never far from her thoughts, just as when she set her alarm system before leaving the boat. The sun had already set behind the island's mountaintop Big Buddha statue. Even with the sun gone, the sweat dripped from her brow and upper lip. She'd rowed as if there were some hurry, and harder still when her old Marine Corps shoulder injury began complaining. Somehow it felt right to punish herself for even considering that *remote possibility*. After chasing shadows from Martinique to Venezuela to Panama and across the Pacific for more than three years, she had moved on. Billy was proof of that, wasn't he? She dug her grapnel anchor into the sand and started up the beach toward the lights of the Ao Chalong Yacht Club.

A big white awning covered the deck, protecting the dark wood tables and wicker chairs from the effects of both Thai seasons—wet and dry. At one end of the deck, Billy Barber sat on a stool picking his guitar and nearly swallowing the microphone as he wailed "Honey, let me be your salty dog" to the three occupied tables. Riley stood next to a palm tree out in the dusky darkness. She knew he couldn't see her yet.

Damn, he looked good. When it came time for them to part, and she reckoned that time wasn't far off, she would miss him. His deep tan and the almost-white blond hair falling into his eyes made him look like the quintessential surfer dude. In fact, he was a Grand Prix–level professional racing sailor conditioning here in Phuket and preparing for the King's Cup Regatta in December.

They'd met at a bar that belonged to an Aussie, a former sailor. The bar was sort of a yachtie hangout, and Billy had been telling stories about his racing success as bowman on *Merlin II*, the custom eighty-footer that belonged to some gazillionaire. Billy's North Carolina twang brought back bittersweet memories, and Riley had been smiling as she listened to him regaling the crowd with tales of a spinnaker run on the Route du Rhum race that finishes at Pointe-à-Pitre on the Caribbean island of Guadeloupe. He must have thought she was smiling at him because when he finished his story, Billy Barber came over and introduced himself. And after all the lonely, abstinent years, she'd given in to him.

It had been four years ago, back in the spring of 2008, that Riley had learned of her father's terrible secrets and witnessed his murder. She and Cole Thatcher had gone on to share an adventure like nothing she had ever experienced—up until that day when Cole disappeared at sea while diving in the wreck of the World War II submarine *Surcouf* off Guadeloupe. Believing she might still find the love of her life alive, she raced halfway around the world trying to decipher the clues Cole had left for her: a Spanish lullaby and those engraved numbers on the French Angel coin. She'd tried every combination she could think of to break the cipher. But nothing worked. She couldn't find him in Venezuela or the Cayman Islands. He'd mentioned the Dragon's Triangle, but it turned out to be a big stretch of empty ocean between the Philippines and Japan made infamous by strange disappearances of ships and planes—on the exact opposite side of the world from the Bermuda Triangle, where the *Surcouf* had first disappeared.

Thailand had been her last hope.

She'd never found Cole Thatcher or his boat, the *Shadow Chaser*. The US Coast Guard no longer listed the vessel in their documentation records. It was as though the Dragon's Triangle had swallowed Cole and his first mate, Theo, and the *Shadow Chaser*, and there was no proof left they had ever existed.

But sailing single-handed was lonely and chasing never-ending dead ends was frustrating.

And then along came Billy. Just like that song. There was no romantic pretense between them—it was pure, no-strings-attached sex. She and Billy both knew the connection would last only until one boat or the other hoisted anchor and sailed away. And lately, she'd been itching to do just that.

The problem wasn't that he was boring or messy and certainly not that he didn't please her as a lover. The problem was that Billy Barber couldn't compete with a dead man.

When Billy finished his song, Riley stepped up onto the concrete slab and crossed between the tables. He saw her and smiled. Then he turned and spoke to Roger, who walked to the other end of the bar and grabbed something next to the cash register. By the time she reached him, Billy was holding out an envelope.

"Here you go. Your letter."

"Thanks."

"Why don't you stay for a drink?" he said. "My set will be over after a couple more songs."

Riley nodded, though she wasn't certain what he had said. She was staring at the handwriting on the crumpled envelope. Her throat tightened. Of course she knew better, but still she had allowed herself to hope. The address was printed in block letters by what looked like a shaky hand.

She slid onto a stool and placed the letter on the bar. With her elbows planted at either end of the envelope, she rested her forehead on the heels of her hands and stared at the handwritten address. It was all wrong: the handwriting, the postmark, and the name *Marguerite Riley*. No one called her that. Least of all Cole.

Roger set down an icy Singha beer next to her. Ignoring it, she slid a finger under the flap and tore the envelope open. She slid out one sheet of paper and unfolded it. The words were written in the same squiggly block letters.

Dear Marguerite Riley,

You do not know me, but I was a friend of your grandfather, Lieutenant Oswald Riley, during WWII. We were in the OSS together. I have an antique trinket he gave to me back in '45, the last time I saw him. I should like very much to meet you, to tell you about my friend Ozzie, and to give you this remembrance of your grandfather. I promised him I'd give this to his family, and too much time has passed. Now, I don't have much time left and I'd like to fulfill this promise to an old friend.

I apologize for this abrupt request, but I hope you can meet me at noon on Saturday in the Chatuchak Weekend Market in Bangkok. A friend has a booth called Land of Smiles Antiques on Soi 3. I work there sometimes.

I hope you can make it. I will tell you what happened to your grandfather.

Regards,
Peewee

When her eyes got to the end of the page, they bounced back to the beginning and she read it again. And then again.

Riley was not aware the music had stopped until Billy slid onto the stool next to her.

"So what's in the letter?"

She looked up and handed him the paper. As he read she did some quick calculations. This Peewee would certainly be in his nineties, just like Henri Michaut, that other World War II survivor she and Cole had met back in the Caribbean.

Billy chuckled when he got to the end of the page. "Peewee?" he said. "Doesn't that sound just like a character right out of an old World War II movie? He'd be the sidekick guy you'd know was going to die before the end."

Riley took the letter back from him and read it again. She looked up at Billy and shook her head. "I don't get it. How did this guy find me?"

Billy shrugged. "It's getting to be a pretty damn small world." He waved his hand to take in the crowded anchorage. "At least half those boats out there have websites and blogs, and they're always writing about the other boaters they meet."

"Most ninety-year-olds aren't reading blogs, though. You'd think he'd explain a little more. Like what does he mean—a trinket?"

"Don't know." He rested a hand on her bare knee.

Riley looked at the hand and quashed the impulse to brush it aside. "I wonder what he really wants from me."

Billy shrugged. "So what do you know about this granddad?"

She shook her head. "Not much. He died long before I was born—in the Second World War."

"Surely your dad must have said something."

"My dad—" She coughed as though to clear her throat. Even four years after his death, she still had difficulty talking about her father. "My father didn't talk about my grandfather much, and I was five when my grandma died. I barely remember her."

"No family photos or anything?"

She lifted her aching shoulder, leaned her head into the pain, and then stretched her neck by looking up at the patio's white awning. She drew in a deep breath. "My dad had one photo album with a few old black-and-white pictures in it, but he never said much about it. The only thing he ever said about the war was that my grandfather joined the Coast Guard before Pearl Harbor, then got recruited into the OSS."

"What's that?"

"The Office of Strategic Services. Military intelligence. My brother Mikey tried one time to find out more about our grandpa, but the records were still sealed."

"So no idea what happened to him?"

Riley shrugged. "Dad said the military never told his mother any details. Only that Grandpa was transferred to the Pacific after the Germans surrendered in May of 1945, and then—he just disappeared."

CHAPTER TWO

Aboard the USS *Bonefish*
Sea of Japan

June 18, 1945

"Radar contact!"

Lieutenant Junior Grade Harold Oswald "Ozzie" Riley glanced up at the bulkhead clock in the officers' wardroom: 0100 hours. Shit. Not again. *Lunch will have to wait,* he thought as he heard the call to battle stations. Now, the acid would go back to work on his stomach lining. Damned radar man.

It was their second radar contact today. Just over two hours ago, they had sunk a small transport. Ozzie's job was coastal surveillance and the interrogation of any prisoners, but through the periscope he'd seen no survivors in the thick morning haze. Fortunately. At this point, he just wanted it all to be over. He was done with this war.

"Stand by tubes forward," the skipper said. This skipper didn't want to go home with any fish left in his arsenal. If you looked up *gung ho* in the encyclopedia, you'd see a picture of Commander Elmer Johnson.

After all he'd seen in the last four years, Ozzie thought such enthusiasm was not only ill-advised, but it was downright stupid, for God's sake. The Krauts were done and the Japs were on the run. It was over. The Yanks knew it and so did the Japanese, especially now that US subs had penetrated into the Sea of Japan. The problem was their damned samurai honor code. They wouldn't give up. They had to go down in flames. As an American, he didn't get it. The point now was just to survive.

The USS *Bonefish* was due to rendezvous with the other eight Hellcat subs on the twenty-fourth—in six days—at which time they had orders to exit out of what the crew now called "Lake Hirohito," via the La Pérouse Strait. But Johnson had only racked up two kills thus far, and he was determined to increase that number before they had to skedaddle back to Guam. Ozzie couldn't quite believe that there was still a rah-rah patriot around at this point in the war. Not after all they'd seen.

Admiral Lockwood, ComSubPac, had dubbed this adventure Operation Barney. Nine American subs loose in the virgin hunting grounds of the Sea of Japan thanks to this newfangled invention called FM sonar. Ozzie didn't understand exactly how it worked, but when he, a Coast Guard officer and member of the OSS Maritime Unit, had been assigned to this boat back in Guam his superiors told him the sub would be able to thread its way through the lethal minefields and enter through Tsushima Strait. Once inside, their mission was simple: Sink as many Japanese ships as possible.

Ozzie covered the few steps from the wardroom aft to the control room. Commander Elmer Johnson stood stooped over, one arm slung over a fold-down handle, his eye pressed to the periscope lens.

"Steady on one-two-zero," he said.

Six torpedo-ready lights glowed below the firing plungers.

The executive officer repeated the range and bearing.

"Fire one!"

At the captain's order, the sub lurched as the blast of compressed air sent the first torpedo on its way.

"Fire two!"

No one spoke until the sonar operator raised his fist over his head; then they felt and heard the distant explosion through the hull. There were smiles all round.

"Oh, shit," Johnson said.

Now what? Ozzie thought. He tried not to flinch at the pinch of searing pain in his gut.

The skipper straightened up to his full six foot four height, stepping aside to dodge around some low-hanging piping. Again Ozzie wondered how the hell a man of his height had ended up in submarines.

The skipper slapped the side of the periscope tube. "Down scope." He turned to the chart table, reached out straight-armed, and placed his hands on either side of the chart. "All ahead flank. Take her down to one-nine-zero."

The diving officer repeated Johnson's orders and the sub rattled and groaned as she started the fast descent. All eyes were on the skipper, wondering what he had seen at the surface.

"What is it?" Ozzie asked. He was a guest aboard this boat, and he had no business questioning the captain, but military discipline had never been his strongpoint—a fact that had served him well in the OSS.

"Sank that transport, all right, about eight hundred tons. First one missed, went too deep, but the second hit amidships—broke her back. What I didn't see through the haze at first was the goddamn destroyer escort on the other side of her."

The skipper's words were greeted by silence in the control room. All but Ozzie were experienced submariners, and it was clear they all knew what was coming, and it wasn't good. Ozzie had survived this war from the start, and had every intention of making it to the end.

Back in Guam, they'd told him there was no better commander than Johnson. Now if only he could convince his stomach.

"Rig for depth charges," the skipper said.

For the next several minutes, the sub descended and the skipper took them away from the position they'd fired from. Their strategy had shifted from that of predator to prey—hide and live to fight another day. Johnson issued the order for silent running. In the quiet that followed, they heard the distant pings from the destroyer's search at the surface.

The first depth charges went off not long after. It started as three distant booms, but over the course of the next half hour, the explosions grew closer and louder as the destroyer zeroed in on their location. One of the planesmen crossed himself after every boom. It was warm inside the sub, but the sweat that beaded up on every man's face was due more to the bone-jarring explosions just outside the hull than the heat.

BOOM.

It was the waiting between explosions, Ozzie thought, that was likely to drive men mad. The trick was going somewhere else in your head, because there was nothing you could do to change the situation. If your time was up, it was up.

BOOM.

Ozzie imagined he was at the helm of a sleek racing yacht headed across the sunlit sound for Block Island.

He could handle his fear, but not his stomach. It wasn't seasickness—not him, the dinghy-racer kid who'd used the sailing team to get admitted to Yale. But life on this submarine was going to give him an ulcer before he hit his twenty-eighth birthday. Just when you started to hope the depth charges were over, when around the room men's lips were moving with prayers of thanks, they would start again with a huge *kaboom* that made the whole boat shudder and creak.

Ozzie remained standing with one arm wrapped around the ladder that led up to the conning tower.

Then two depth charges blasted so close by, the skipper staggered and had to grab at the chart table to keep from falling. Several light-bulbs exploded and patches of cork used to insulate the hull hung down from the overhead.

BOOM.

Ozzie's ears were ringing. He saw the CO's lips moving next to the ear of his exec. The young man tore off forward at a run and soon returned, heading back through the control room with two seamen. They carried chairs and the small writing desk from the captain's cabin.

Curious, Ozzie followed them through the engine rooms to the aft torpedo room. There a couple of machinists were pushing a wood barrel into a torpedo tube. The place stank even worse than usual with the odor of hot diesel oil. The sailors smashed the furniture up into small pieces and shoved clothing and bags of trash from the galley in alongside the leaking barrel of diesel. The exec slammed the door to the torpedo tube and flashed a thumbs-up sign that was relayed forward to the control room.

Moments later another depth charge exploded so close Ozzie felt as if his teeth were rattling in his head. Seconds after the explosion, the sub shuddered as the blast of compressed air flushed into the torpedo tube and sent the bubbles, oil, and debris out toward the surface.

Clothing, bits of wood, oil. That was all that made it to the surface when one of those depth charges broke open a sub.

Ozzie smiled. *Brilliant.*

CHAPTER THREE

Hua Lamphong Station
Bangkok, Thailand

November 17, 2012

The train's conductor stopped outside Riley's berth and indicated with sign language that he was there to strip the bedding and rearrange the sleeper into the two-seat configuration it had been in when she boarded. On this second-class train, there were no private compartments, only curtains to close off the fold-down bunk beds.

She nodded, then swung her feet over the side of the berth and slipped them into her sandals. She hadn't slept much on the overnight train from Surat Thani. The AC was freezing and the thin blanket they provided hadn't done much good.

The train was moving at a crawl as they entered the outskirts of the city, and she stretched her arms and yawned. She could have *walked* faster. There had better be coffee at the station. She needed it. A quick glance at her watch showed that it was only 7:30 a.m.—she had plenty of time before the noon meeting with Peewee—but she felt antsy. Once she had made the decision to travel the nearly five hundred miles to meet this mystery character, she wanted to see it through. She still had so many unanswered questions about her family.

Grabbing her small backpack, she headed to the toilet compartment. She'd packed light, hoping to keep this Bangkok trip brief. After a quick wash and change into her only clean khaki capris and a polo, Riley returned to her seat to watch the slow parade of dark wood shacks slip by. Close by the tracks and constructed out of bits of trash and debris, the shanties were squeezed between the traffic-clogged streets and the trains. Sometimes, a few banana or papaya trees grew among the weeds, and lazy-looking dogs glanced with disinterest as the train clanked past. Just beyond, rising through the smog stood the metal and glass high-rise hotels and office buildings of downtown Bangkok.

She unzipped her backpack, removed her iPhone, and opened the web browser. Billy was right when he said all the folks on cruising boats were blogging these days, but her site was different. Her single WordPress page offered her services as a security consultant and system designer and referred any inquiries to her current employer, Mercury Security. On the header was a tab with the name *Bonefish*. She clicked on the tab and typed the password *tombolo* into the box that appeared. This led to a blog page where she posted her latitude and longitude and a few words in the comments section. She reread her notes about taking the train to Bangkok. Then she lifted her head and turned toward the window, but her eyes were not focused on the scene outside.

Six days.

It was hard to believe that was all the time she and Cole had spent together from the time she plucked him out of the Caribbean Sea until that terrible Monday when the earth shook and he'd disappeared.

She looked back at the screen on her phone. Still no comments there other than her own. She was certain that if Cole were alive, that *Bonefish* tab would lead him to this blog. But she was not the only one looking for Cole Thatcher, and she didn't want to facilitate *their* efforts. When the authorities don't recover a body, friends *and foes* stay alert to all possibilities. She'd set it up so that he could leave an encrypted comment on the page, and she'd been checking it every day for more than three years. To date there'd been nothing.

Here in Thailand, Riley had studied the Buddhist idea of karma. She wanted answers but she only found more questions. Were daughters responsible for the sins of their fathers? She had done something long ago, and she'd never had the opportunity to tell Cole before he was gone. As the Buddha said, "We are the heirs of our own actions." Perhaps the deaths of her brother Michael, her father, Cole, even Diggory Priest were all karmically related to that day down in Lima when she had carried that package into the Marine House.

At least her work for Mercury Security gave her life some purpose. She sailed her boat from island to island and worked for Mercury as an independent consultant designing custom security systems. They emailed her blueprints; she designed the systems and emailed them back. She was helping people, keeping them safe.

She slid her phone back into the backpack and her fingers touched the envelope. She pulled it out and unfolded the single sheet of paper.

Now, here was this letter from a stranger claiming he knew her grandfather. Her father's father. She wasn't sure she believed a word of it, but the letter had lit a spark of something inside her. Of what? Hope?

Outside the train window the buildings grew more dense. Plain, featureless concrete block buildings backed onto the train tracks, while between them stood a few traditional Thai stilt houses, their steep roofs distinguished by the curving points at the gable ends. Tangled webs of electrical wires sagged from pole to pole. The occasional streets that crossed the tracks showed bumper-to-bumper cars, motorbikes, and *tuk-tuk* tricycles crammed together waiting for the train to pass.

On a clear patch of dirt, a couple of little kids sat cross-legged playing tug-of-war with a stick while a man she assumed was their father leaned against a rusty car body smoking a cigarette and watching them with a bemused look on his face.

Riley pressed her forehead to the window, trying to keep them in view, but they disappeared as the train climbed onto a bridge over a wide brown river. Compact little tugboats pulled strings of barges piled high with cargo while long-tail boats buzzed around them. In the distance tall golden spires glittered in the sunlight where a *wat*, or temple, stood a few blocks from the water's edge.

How her brother would have loved this scene. "I miss you, Mikey," she whispered and her breath fogged the glass. She felt the familiar ache, and her throat tightened as it always did when she thought of him. The river disappeared as she conjured up a vision of her brother's face, his snaggle-toothed smile, his thick glasses making his eyes look even bigger than they already were. "What do you make of this weirdness? Our *grandfather?*"

Even now, more than fifteen years after Michael's death, she often talked to her brother's ghost—although they never discussed the truth about her father. Had her grandfather been a better man than his son? Had he been a member of Skull and Bones? He had been the first Riley to go to Yale, after all.

"Mikey, I feel like I'm poking a sore tooth. Like maybe if I can learn something about Grandpa, I'll be able to understand what Dad did. I keep thinking, *I've got his blood in my veins.* I wish I could let it go."

Her brother had been that rare breed of human who was both a math whiz and socially and emotionally intelligent. In spite of his odd appearance, people found him so sweet and empathetic, they soon felt as though they had known him all their lives. People told him their secrets. Or he found them out on his own.

Riley shook her head. "Mikey, I have to see this thing through, but I don't have a good feeling about it," she said. Secrets had been the death of too many in her family.

The station was crowded, even at that early hour, but Riley stopped in the midst of the throng to take in the high, arched ceiling, the curving designs of the floor tiles, and the shuttered restaurants on the second-floor terraces on either side of the huge terminal. She hooked her thumbs under the straps for her backpack and slowly turned around, taking it all in. Around her rushed families, uniformed school kids with white wires snaking into their ears, men in suits and jeans, and women all dressed more elegantly than Riley in her khakis. In spite of the heat and humidity, the Thai people never seemed to sweat. Looking around, she saw a sea of dark-colored hair. She reached up and tucked a loose strand of hair behind her ear, knowing the sun had streaked her brown hair even lighter. And even at her meager five foot seven, she felt tall in the Thai crowd.

And that was when she felt it—that prickly, tingling sensation that creeps up the back of the neck. That feeling of being watched. Riley turned in a slow circle, surveying the station from the crowded lower floor to the elevated terraces. No one appeared to be paying any special attention to her. But she trusted her intuition.

She sniffed the air. Over the stench of train and traffic exhaust, she smelled coffee. One place did look open. The sign read BLACK MOUNTAIN COFFEE. She headed for the stairs.

She had no appetite, so she ordered a café au lait and sat at a table next to the railing overlooking the crowds below. The few Westerners certainly stood out, clustered in little knots of backpacks around unfolded maps. Riley couldn't tell whether they were Americans, Canadians, or Europeans, but they all fell into the category of tourist. As did she. In Phuket, she'd learned the Thai word was *farang.* The word embodied the constant feeling of "otherness" she felt in this country. Maybe that was what had triggered that feeling of being watched earlier.

The hot, rich coffee tasted so good. She took another big gulp and held it in her mouth a few seconds, knowing the heat would make her sweat more, dampening the clean clothes she'd changed into on the train.

Riley reached up and rubbed at the scar tissue beneath the fabric of her shirt, then she rotated her arm and shoulder to loosen it up. It had been more than seven years since she'd been injured while serving as a Marine Security Guard at the embassy in Lima. When they'd told her at the Bethesda Burn Unit that it would be slow to heal, she had never imagined feeling pain all these years later.

As she stretched, she noticed a man who'd appeared at the top of the stairs. He paused and looked around the tables before he walked to the counter to order. His eyes had remained trained on her a few seconds longer than any of the others sitting around her. She was not unaccustomed to men noticing her, but there were several younger, and in her view, far more beautiful Thai women at another table, but his eyes had not lingered there at all. Perhaps it was only because she was a *farang*.

Riley looked back out across the crowds and processed the information. She went through the details she had observed as he paused at the top of the stairs. Flat nose, sharp cheekbones, and a Fu Manchu mustache. He was Southeast Asian of some sort, but she did not think he was Thai. Most men here were small, but there was something more solid about this man. He wasn't tall—only about her height—but he seemed to take up more space. Broad shoulders, narrow waist. Long hair, mostly gray with black streaks, pulled up into an odd knot at the top of his head. She put him in his late forties. Blue jeans, leather sandals, a denim shirt with sleeves rolled partway up his forearms showing the blue ink of tattoos. And he carried a tooled leather satchel embossed with an exotic primitive design slung over his shoulder.

She was pleased with the number of details she had been able to recall. It was important to her to keep in training. After two tours as an MSG, some behaviors were so ingrained, she would probably not be able to give them up if she wanted to. She didn't really think he was any threat, but her training had taught her not to make that judgment too soon.

Turning her head away from the lower terminal, she pretended to check the time on her watch. He was sitting at a table off to her left and slightly behind her. An unopened bottle of water stood on the table in front of him.

She stood and walked toward the stairs. As she passed him, the man looked up and their eyes met. His eyes looked hard and flat as black glass. Riley walked on and continued down the stairs.

As she crossed the terminal floor, following the signs that directed her to the Metro, Riley took one last glance at the second-floor coffee shop. The man was standing at the rail watching her. When she reached the top of the stairs leading into the tunnel, he still had not moved.

CHAPTER FOUR

The Red Dog Ranch
Virginia City, Nevada

November 15, 2012

During the last mile of their walk, Tess had been running off, nose to the ground, hackles raised, and disappearing into the pinyon and juniper woods on either side of the trail. Elijah Hawkes hoped his dog hadn't found herself a bear or a bobcat. He had his boot knife, as always, but he hadn't brought his bow, and he'd damn himself for that if the opportunity presented itself. Elijah had always wanted to bag a bear—he'd even reserved a spot for the head on the wall in his game room.

The shadow of the ridge was already upon them. It was only late afternoon but night came on early here deep in the basin. Elijah whistled for his dog and heard her trotting through the underbrush before he saw her.

"Heel, Tess."

She fell in line, just off his left boot. Tess was a great dog. All German wire-haired pointers were smart, and they were good hunters, too, but few matched this one. At age four, she was seventy-five pounds of pure muscle under her white and liver-spotted coat. Her face was what gave her character, though, with her reddish-blond bushy eyebrows and beard and her golden-yellow eyes.

Those eyes looked up at him now as she whined softly.

He was about to ask her what was wrong when he heard the *yip-yip* from the mountain far above them.

Coyotes.

Elijah stopped and swung his head around to pinpoint the direction of the pack. He knew it would be that pack. There were four coyotes he recognized who roamed the hills around his ranch, and one of these days he was going to send his hired man Caleb out to shoot them. They were pests who stole his chickens and spooked the horses.

"Come on, Tess. You pay them no mind. Let's get home."

When Elijah started up the trail this time his pace was quicker. It was no good slowing down and getting lost in thought when this walk was a cornerstone in his daily regimen to keep his body in top shape. That was a requirement of his business—at least of what his business had evolved into. And he was very good at everything he did. Now, it would be best to get Tess inside away from that damn pack. He took his hands from his pockets and swung his arms at his sides as he lengthened his strides. The cold air stung his lungs and the bare flesh of his fingers. It would certainly dip below freezing tonight.

Soon the trees thinned and he could see the two-story wood-framed ranch house in the clearing halfway up the side of the ridge, smoke puffing from the stone chimney and the yellow lights in the windows welcoming them back. The house, *his* house, nestled into the hillside like it belonged there, like a God-made natural part of the ridge. Caleb would be setting the table for his evening meal. Elijah could see his own breath now as he climbed the hillside. He slowed his pace when he rounded the barn and the empty horse paddock. Tess trotted ahead and sat by the kitchen door. All of this belonged to him. He'd come a long way from that troubled kid getting into fights on the streets of Reno, running away from his older sister and guardian. He'd done all right for himself.

Elijah settled into his comfortable leather chair in front of the fire in the game room that doubled as his study. Elijah found that when he needed to write reports or read difficult mining texts, the heads of the deer, wild boar, mountain lion, and all the others calmed him, put him into a sort of transcendental state. There were times when he even talked out loud, though he'd not admit to anyone that he was in fact talking to the animals. He'd done his best work in here.

He stretched out his legs and admired his new boots. They were handmade black Lucchese American-alligator boots, and they'd cost him over four grand. Right now they looked pretty much like any pair of dusty cowboy boots, and that thought made him smile. Caleb would clean them later. Yes, he thought, looking around the walls of his favorite room, the good Lord had favored him.

Tess trotted in and placed her wet muzzle on his knee. He didn't scold her. Caleb would have filled her water bowl after the long walk, and she deserved the drink. Elijah reached for the scotch he'd poured himself earlier, and thought, *We've both earned our drinks after that trek.* Tess would eat her evening meal later when he did—though hers would be out in the kitchen with Caleb. He scratched her ears, and she closed her eyes in bliss. Though his servant might feed her and care for her while Elijah traveled, it was clear to him that the dog recognized and revered her master. She was a purebred animal, after all.

"All right," he said. "That's enough." She turned for the door, then stopped, ears up, head cocked to one side, staring at the black window. Elijah didn't hear a thing, but he had grown accustomed to his dog's supersonic hearing. If it was a serious threat, she would let him know. Most of the time, she was just being curious about the night sounds of the wilderness.

"Tess, go on. Go lie down."

From the end table next to his chair, he retrieved a folded-back copy of *Western Miner Magazine*, and he returned to studying the advertisement for the double-layer trommel with submersible water pumps and a hydraulic-powered belt for the hopper and sluicing box. It was for sale up in the Yukon. They were asking half a million, and he wondered what they'd really take for it.

His phone pinged and vibrated. He straightened out one of his long legs and pulled the phone out of his jeans pocket.

It was a text message from the Brightstone Security Group, the corporate front for his real employers. *Problems at the Benguet Mine in Baguio. Booked you on 11:30 a.m. flight San Francisco to Manila.*

He leaned back into the soft leather and a small smile lifted the corner of his mouth. Back to the Philippines. This was good. He'd wanted to go back for several months now. Much as he loved the ranch, winter was setting in and Caleb wasn't the best company. He closed his eyes and pictured Esmerelda, the young girl he'd met the last time he was in Manila. She was fascinated with the dragon tattoo on Elijah's back. It had that effect on Asian girls—his preference. Esmerelda was a tiny little thing who barely spoke more than a few sentences in English. But what a body. Much better company than Caleb.

Elijah looked up when he heard a long mournful howl not far from the house. The *yip-yipping* started up again—more excited now, it sounded almost like screaming. Then he heard Tess's deep warning bark, also from outside the house.

Elijah flew up out of the chair and stormed into the kitchen. "Goddammit, man, why did you let the dog out?"

Caleb Penn stood at the kitchen sink washing lettuce. He wore a black apron over his blue work shirt. As he stepped to turn, his right shoulder dropped and he hitched his body around, swinging his artificial leg with it. "She was scratching at the door. I figured she had to pee."

"What kind of a moron are you? Are you deaf as well as crippled?" Elijah yanked opened a drawer and rummaged around until he found his LED flashlight.

"Tess can handle herself against a coyote, I reckon."

Elijah grabbed his coat off the peg. "But not against a pack."

When Elijah stepped outside, his eyes weren't yet accustomed to the dark. The night was pitch-black, but he knew his way around the ranch blindfolded, so he took off at a trot. Tess's barking sounded close; he figured they had her surrounded in the woods on the other side of the paddock. He'd heard that a lone coyote would often come into the yard acting all doggy-friendly-like to lure the domestic dog off to the spot where the pack waited. It sounded like that spot hadn't been very far away this time.

When the barking stopped, he slowed down. He didn't want to come on them so fast they'd turn on him—he hadn't brought a gun. He had only his boot knife with him, but in his hands the blade was all that would be needed. He was at the tree line anyway, and he couldn't hit a target he couldn't see, regardless of the weapon. Though his eyes had adjusted to the night's darkness, it was darker still inside the woods.

Ahead of him he heard low growling. It was Tess. They must be closing in, and she didn't like it one bit.

At once the night exploded with yipping, growling, and cackling that sounded like maniacal laughter. The coyotes had moved in for the kill.

He clicked on the powerful flashlight. More than a hundred feet ahead, through the trees, the beam reflected off a pair of sly eyes that glanced in his direction for a second. Then the animal's head turned away from the light, and the beast lunged forward. In the shadows he saw a blur of moving fur.

The beam of light bounced as Elijah ran yelling at the snarling pack. He heard Tess yelp once and then growl and snarl. He figured she was giving as good as she got. When he was about fifteen feet away from them he saw one animal slink off into the darkness. Another followed after.

He was surprised the other two hadn't fled also. They seemed not to notice him in their bloodlust. Tess was standing her ground, teeth bared and hackles raised. She was bigger than both of the coyotes and was swinging her head from one to the other, daring either of them to attack.

Elijah reached into his boot. When one animal stepped forward to nip at Tess, Elijah drew back, aimed, and let the knife fly at the other. He felt satisfaction from the sharp cry. There weren't many men who possessed his strength or skill with knives. The knife had plunged deep into the fur at the base of the coyote's neck, and the beast's legs collapsed. The blade must have injured the spinal cord.

The last coyote fled into the trees.

Tess limped toward the downed animal, her low growls loud in the suddenly still night. In the light from his flashlight, Elijah saw her ear was torn and bleeding.

He called her name. When he reached her side, his dog gave his hand a single lick, then she turned back, lowered her head, and growled again at the injured coyote.

Elijah patted her side, then passed the light over her body, checking for damage. He saw numerous blood spots in the wiry hair on her back. Closer inspection showed them to be puncture wounds. One of her back legs had a bone-deep gash. He waved her back and told her to stay.

He knelt next to the downed animal and saw the white-rimmed eyes and flared nostrils as the coyote struggled to move his paralyzed body. The tongue hung out the side of his mouth and clouds of foul-smelling steam puffed out from his labored breathing. Elijah reached his arm out slowly, not sure how much movement that head and mouth were still capable of. Then in a single, quick movement, he pulled the knife out of the flesh. He heard the animal's breath catch as the head twitched and blood oozed out across the matted fur.

Tess whined. Elijah stood and swung the flashlight around. In the beam of light he saw his dog lying in the dirt, licking at the gash on her leg. He heard a low animal-like noise and realized it was coming from deep inside him.

Elijah turned back to the filthy beast and felt his jaw muscles tighten. The flashlight fell from his hand.

He grabbed the bloody fur at the nape of the coyote's neck, then yanked up the head and pulled his blade across the taut throat. Blood sprayed over the ground. Elijah grunted and shook the head. The body, attached only by the bones of the spine, appeared to dance in the dirt. Then he dropped the carcass and stood still, breathing in the cold night air through his nose, smelling the overpowering scent of fresh blood.

"Caleb!" he shouted when he burst through the back door after carrying Tess half the way home. She could walk on her own, but not fast enough for his taste. He wanted the gash on that leg seen to sooner rather than later. Coyotes were foul creatures.

There was no one in the kitchen. "Caleb! Where the fuck are you?" He set Tess down on the floor.

"I'm right here," Caleb said as he limped through the doorway from the dining room. "I had to take a piss." He reached for the dog. "Shit. What happened to Tess?"

Elijah grimaced as he shrugged off his coat. Caleb was efficient, but the man's missing leg and Godless foul manners infuriated him. "What do you think happened? She'd be fine if you had one iota of intelligence in that heathen head of yours. The coyotes got her and that's on you. Now get your first aid box and fix her up or I'll kick your no-good drunk ass back to that rehab center where I found you."

When Caleb returned with his medical kit, Elijah lifted the dog onto the butcher block island in the center of the kitchen. Caleb cleaned the wounds and Tess watched him with unflinching eyes.

"Bring her to me when you're finished cleaning up your mess here," Elijah said. As he left the kitchen, he took a rawhide bone from the cupboard. He would reward the dog when she was cleaned up. With all his recent travel, Tess was spending too much time with Caleb.

Back in his game room, Elijah drank off the rest of the whiskey and moved to the bar to wash up. He pulled the bloody knife from his leather boot sheath and set it on the bar. He squirted some dish soap onto his hands and scrubbed his wrists and forearms hard. As he rinsed the suds out of the black hairs on his arms, the pink foam swirled in the water at the bottom of the stainless sink. Drying his hands, Elijah turned and admired his reflection in the mirror behind the bar. He reached up and ran his fingers through his black hair, pushing the stiff hairs back into the short upswept curl over his widow's peak.

He heard the buzz as his phone vibrated on the end table. He folded the bar towel, crossed the room, and picked up the phone. He read the new text message from his contact at Brightstone.

Come armed.

Elijah nodded and set down the phone. He walked across the room and stood in front of the large glass cabinet that displayed his collection of knives and swords. The three samurai katana were among his favorites. One was a thirteenth-century Kamakura blade and it had cost him nearly half a million. He rubbed his hand over the dark stubble on his chin, then returned to the bar and picked up the bloody boot knife. He ran his finger through the coagulating blood. Then he carefully cleaned the four-inch double-edged steel blade and slid it back into its sheath.

CHAPTER FIVE

Aboard the USS *Bonefish*
Sea of Japan

June 18, 1945

The sonar man pulled off one side of his big headphones. Although it had been more than ten minutes since the last depth charge exploded, he spoke in a voice barely above a whisper. "It worked, sir. They're leaving."

Several men in the control room sighed audibly. Ozzie checked his watch. They'd been down listening to those damn *kabooms* for more than two hours.

The Japs hadn't bought their ruse right away. When the bits of wood and the oil popped to the surface, it seemed they weren't sure whether the sub was really gone or not. They had continued dropping their cans of hell. But now it looked like the waiting game was over. After no more sign of life, the destroyer was finally moving on.

It was nearly four o'clock. Ozzie was starved. He never did get that lunch, but he decided to wait and see what happened once they reached periscope depth.

"Up scope," the skipper said.

The old man made a quick check around the horizon, then stopped.

"Destroyer bears zero-one-three, range three miles." He stood back and folded up the handles. "Down scope."

"You don't mean to chase her, do you?" Ozzie asked.

"No. I don't. Day's almost done. We need to surface and recharge. I just want to know where to go hunting tomorrow." He spread his arms, grasped the sides of the chart table, and looked thoughtfully at the chart. "Let's get out of Toyama Wan for now. Put her on a heading of three-five-zero."

Ozzie was finishing off a ham sandwich in the wardroom a couple of hours later when a crewman appeared in the doorway. "Skipper wants you on the bridge, sir."

He nodded, then shoved the last bite in his mouth and followed it with the dregs from his coffee cup. He was tired of this war, tired of orders, and sick of the men who still believed in it. He'd joined up back in 1940 after working for his old man at the bank for a couple of years. Some of his buddies from university had suggested getting in before the rush, and he'd thought being an officer would mean he could give the orders for a change. Rah-rah guys like Commander Johnson hadn't seen the sort of action Ozzie had, first with the Signals Intelligence Service and then the OSS. Now he just had to survive until the damned Japanese figured out they'd already lost this war.

He headed topsides.

The sky was clear and there was no land to be seen anywhere. The sun was about to kiss the horizon. When Johnson noticed him, the old man handed Ozzie the binoculars and pointed slightly right of the setting sun. "Look over there."

Ozzie raised the glasses to his eyes. It was one lone life raft and what looked like only two men inside. One man was waving while the other, his head shaved bald and dressed all in white, sat up straight, his back rigid. The heading of the sub was swinging around to aim for the raft.

"It looks like there are only two of them," Ozzie said.

"Yup," the skipper said. "I don't like it."

"What do you mean? You think it's some kind of trap?"

"I don't know exactly. My gut's giving me warning signs, and I've learned to trust my gut."

After a couple of seamen pulled the two survivors aboard, they led them up to Ozzie and the skipper atop the conning tower. The man in white was a Japanese officer. On the left breast pocket of his tunic was a bright red circular emblem trimmed in gold thread in the shape of a chrysanthemum flower. The design caught his eye, and Ozzie wondered if he had seen it somewhere before. Above that was a wide row of colorful medals. At his waist, he wore a sword. Ozzie could see that he was some high officer, but he had no idea in what branch. He'd never seen this uniform, and the insignia on his epaulettes was just as baffling.

The other one was just a boy, no more than fifteen years old, and clearly not Japanese, nor was he in military dress. Ozzie thought he looked Filipino.

The Japanese officer reached down to his belt and released his sword and scabbard. He held it out horizontally at arm's length and offered it to Commander Johnson.

The old man coughed, took the sword, then turned back to the horizon without a word.

"They're all yours, H2O." The captain had nicknames for all the officers, and when Ozzie had first come aboard and introduced himself as Harold Oswald "Ozzie" Riley, the skipper had dubbed him H2O.

Ozzie looked at the two prisoners. The officer wore a hint of a smile, but the boy looked terrified. "Do either of you speak English?"

The man said, "I speak little English." He turned and put his hand on the boy's shoulder. "I teach Ben here."

"You are a naval officer?"

The Japanese man glanced at Commander Johnson, who kept the binoculars to his eyes, scanning the horizon. The man dipped his head for such a quick second, Ozzie wasn't sure if it was a nod.

"*Hai,*" the Japanese officer said.

"Your ship?"

The skipper lowered the binoculars and interrupted them. "Lieutenant, will you take our guests down below and offer them something to eat or drink? You can finish your interrogations there."

"Yes, sir."

Ozzie ushered the prisoners down to the officers' wardroom and told them to sit. "You must be hungry or thirsty. Can I get you a cup of coffee?"

Again that slight head bob. "Please. Water for the boy."

Once he had set the drinks out, Ozzie sat across the table from the two of them. He always carried a notebook in his hip pocket, and he took it out now with a stub of a pencil. "So, why don't you start at the beginning and tell me who you are; then we'll get to what you were doing out there."

The bald officer reached inside his tunic, removed a pair of gold spectacles, and slowly slid the pieces behind his ears. He adjusted the fit, then spoke. "I am Lieutenant Colonel Miyata." He turned to indicate the boy, who had already emptied the water glass. "This is Ben."

Ozzie scribbled the names in the notebook. "Does Ben here have a last name?"

"If he does, I do not know it."

"Is Ben in the military?"

"No. He is my valet."

Ozzie raised his eyebrows and looked at his prisoner. A valet, huh? *Must be nice,* he thought. Well, this fancy-pants Jap officer was about to learn about life on a sub.

"Where are you stationed, Lieutenant Colonel?"

"We were at Manila. Since that city has fallen to your people, we are in the mountains in the north of Luzon."

Ozzie lifted his pencil off the paper and stared at the little man. Manila. Just hearing the name brought back a flood of memories from his time there in forty-one.

He gave his head a tight shake to throw off the distraction. "So, how'd you end up out there in a raft in the Sea of Japan?" Ozzie stared at him, waiting. Again he saw that little hint of a smile travel across the man's face.

"My mother was ill. I return home to be with her. After she die, I board a cargo ship to return to Philippines. The captain was not taking precautions. We are unaccustomed to seeing American submarines in the Sea of Japan."

"And what was the name of this ship?"

"The *Nanshin Maru.*"

Ozzie wrote the name in the upper right corner of the page. "The two of you were the only survivors?"

"There was only one raft."

"Okay, only one raft. But why only two guys in it?"

He'd learned to look for certain signs when interrogating prisoners to determine if they were lying or telling the truth. Ozzie tried to concentrate on the man's face, but his eyes kept being drawn down to that bright red chrysanthemum embroidered on his tunic. He was certain he had seen that somewhere before.

"When a captain loses his ship, honor dictates that he must go down with it."

"And the crew?"

"They would not get into the lifeboat."

"Why not?"

The prisoner reached for his coffee mug and took a drink. As the sleeve to his tunic rode up his arm, Ozzie saw what looked like a very expensive gold watch on the man's wrist. If he was not mistaken, that was a diamond on the face. Ozzie took in the well-manicured hands, the crisply ironed pleats on his sleeves and trousers. This guy reeked of money.

"Lieutenant," the Japanese officer said. "My people and your people are very different, are they not?"

"Yeah, but I don't see what you're getting at."

"The American ideals do not exist in Japan. We have *bushidō*. The men who permitted the enemy to sink my ship were disgraced. They regained some honor in death."

"So what makes you better than those other guys off your ship who died?"

"I am Prince Kaya Masako. Cousin to the emperor."

CHAPTER SIX

Metro Station
Bangkok, Thailand

November 17, 2012

That prickly feeling around her collar was back. Riley stood in front of the ticket machine trying to make sense of the station names. She retrieved her wallet from a zippered pocket in her daypack and bought her ticket. When she turned away from the machine, she searched the faces of the crowd. She didn't see anyone she recognized. There was no sign of the man with the Fu Manchu mustache, but the feeling persisted. What was she missing?

Riley made her way down to the platform and joined the long queue of people waiting along the painted lines that showed where the train doors would open. She couldn't imagine Americans lining up so politely in any subway station back home.

When the train arrived, it was standing room only inside her car. She made her way to the back and got one hand onto a pole. Bending her knees slightly so she could get a good look through the windows at the crowd on the platform, Riley scanned the faces of the people scurrying by. What was setting off her internal alarms?

The doors hissed closed, and as Riley turned her attention from the platform to the inside of the car, she felt a sudden sense of déjà vu. Again, it was that glimpse of something familiar that didn't register right away. She'd felt this sensation dozens of times over the past four years.

She swung her head back and saw a nearly empty station. Then the view vanished as the train passed into a dark tunnel. She closed her eyes and reached back into her memory, trying to recall that fleeting glimpse of something familiar. In her mind's eye, she saw the image of a hoodie sliding off a head of brown hair with strands of sun-bleached gold, a *farang* man whose head stood above the crowd with only a small fraction of his face visible in profile.

She reconstructed the memory of what she had not paid attention to the first time around. He had been sitting on the platform, along the far side of a large round concrete bench area opposite the car ahead of hers. She'd noticed him only because when he'd straightened up, his hood had slid off his head. He was walking against the flow of people exiting the train. A flash glimpse of the side of his face caused her breath to catch in her throat. But then the image was gone and the harder she tried to retrieve the memory, the farther it receded.

"Cole?" she whispered.

Just saying his name caused that familiar hollow ache beneath her breastbone. She crossed her left arm over her chest, grabbing onto her right shoulder, and squeezed. Now that was real pain, not some phantom.

All the same, she felt the flush of heat spreading through her abdomen. She clenched her insides tight, and a shiver traveled up her neck and set her nipples tingling. Her eyes snapped open as the train drew to a fast stop and the doors opened. She looked around her to see if anyone was watching. All eyes were averted, but embarrassment that someone *might* have noticed made her face redden.

It was happening again. She'd think she saw him, then she'd have this physical reaction like she felt his presence. It was all in her head, and if she didn't keep herself grounded in what was real, she was going to go mad.

It had been three or four months since her last vision. Just because she talked to her dead brother's ghost and imagined she felt Michael's touch at times didn't mean she was some kind of conduit to the limbo spirit world. She was no Demi Moore shivering at the touch of her Patrick Swayze on the other side. Cole was either dead or he was alive—there was no in between. Time had shown her it didn't matter how much she wanted him alive. Wanting it wouldn't make it so.

But sometimes she made up little stories to make herself feel better. In these made-up tales, some evil force was keeping him prisoner and Cole would escape. Then he would appear on some terribly romantic street corner or at the top of a flower-covered hill and they would race into each other's arms. Riley felt these dreams made her weak and she was more than a little ashamed of them—especially about their similarity to American shampoo or perfume commercials.

She squeezed her shoulder again and a jolt of pain coursed down her arm. Concentrate. She had to concentrate. She was about to meet a man who could tell her more about her mysterious grandfather and the history of the Riley clan. Maybe he could help her understand what had turned her father into a monster.

CHAPTER SEVEN

The Caribbean Sea
Off Îles de la Petite Terre

March 31, 2008

Cole Thatcher pushed his shoulders up off the wet sand and his stomach contracted. He vomited up yellow watery bile, but a wave rushed in and the water swirled around his body, carrying all the sick away. His arms gave out and he collapsed facedown in the sand again. When the next wave surged in he took a mouthful of salt water to rinse away the acid taste. He spit it out. The water was cool as it washed some sand off his face. The sun burned his back through his wetsuit and the bright light hurt his eyes if he tried to open them.

An inner voice was telling him he should move, but he didn't know where he was. And his head—oh, God, his head was throbbing. And that sun was so bright.

Something about this situation was wrong. He knew that. He wasn't supposed to be lying on the beach in his wetsuit. He was supposed to be somewhere else, but he couldn't remember where. It hurt his head to think about it.

What he wanted to do was sleep.

So he shushed that inner voice.

And let the cool waves stroke his skin.

Whatever it was that he couldn't remember could wait.

He was too tired.

When he heard the outboard engine it was already very close. He had no idea how long he had been lying there. He should sit up. People were coming and they would think it odd to see a man lying down in the surf. They might know what had happened to him.

A voice called out, "Hallo? Hallo?" Then he heard splashing and the engine stopped.

He tried to roll over. A hand touched his shoulder and helped him to sit up. The hand was a light coffee color and he looked up into the dark eyes of a young woman. Her face was pretty, but her forehead was creased with worry lines. She was saying something to him.

He blinked, trying to get his eyes to focus. The woman wore a baseball cap and men's clothing. He couldn't make sense of her words.

"Something happened to me," he said. "Was I in an accident?"

Two dark-skinned men stood on the sand behind the woman. The three of them were dressed alike. Cole wondered if they were fishermen.

"Monsieur," she said. "Do you know who I am?"

Cole shook his head and the pain exploded in a white-hot burst behind his eyes. He squeezed his eyes shut, then opened them. He looked past the men at the long white beach. "Where's my dinghy?" he said. "Have you seen my dinghy?"

"Do you know your name?"

"Yes. It's Cole."

"Monsieur, you've been injured. Your head is bleeding."

He reached up and touched his scalp above the eyebrow. Blood. He pressed his eyes shut and watched the wild lights playing off the insides of his eyelids. He breathed in slowly through his nose, waiting for the pain to pass.

"I'm here to help you. Get you to a doctor."

Cole let go of his eyes and looked up at the woman. "Where's my dinghy? Something happened to me."

"Yes, you've been hurt. I don't know how you survived."

"I don't remember." A small wave broke onto the beach, and Cole watched the sea foam in around his wetsuit.

"Don't you remember me?" the woman asked.

He looked up at her face again and squinted.

"We met at my grandfather's house," she said. "My name is Monique Jules."

He looked from her to the two men with her. He didn't recognize any of them.

"I don't remember."

"My grandfather. You know him as Henri Michaut."

An image flashed in his head. Three people sitting on chairs. He could not see the woman's face. "I think I know that name."

"Yes, my grandfather sent me to help you. We've been fishing nearby and watching your boat."

The young woman signaled to the two men with her. They helped him to his feet. One of the men picked up a backpack with two diving cylinders that lay on the beach not far from him.

"Do you see my dinghy?"

"No, monsieur, you did not come by dinghy. You've been in an accident."

They helped him climb into their open fishing boat. A couple of rods in holders at the stern were rigged for trolling. One of the men started the engine while the other lifted the anchor out of the shallows and waded out to the boat. That man hopped aboard, and with the engine in reverse they turned around and headed out to sea.

In the distance, through what looked almost like fog, he saw a big island. *Yes,* he thought. *I know that island.* He had been diving off Guadeloupe. A huge bulbous cloud loomed over the island. Cole had never seen anything like it. As their boat moved out into deep water, the strange cloud covered the sun and the day darkened. Several boats speckled the horizon, including one cluster of boats with flashing colored lights. They were too far away for him to see what was happening, and besides, he couldn't clear the salt haze out of his eyes.

CHAPTER EIGHT

The Cordillera Mountains
Baguio, Philippines

November 17, 2012

Elijah Hawkes awoke after the limousine had started the familiar climb into the mountains. He'd slept poorly on the eleven-hour Philippine Airlines flight, and he was attempting to make up for it on the long drive from Manila up to Baguio. He could have flown, but the wait for a flight was longer than the five-hour drive, and the Manila Airport wasn't air-conditioned. He'd decided he could catch up on sleep in the limo.

He sat up, smoothed the wrinkles out of his shirt sleeves, and straightened his bolo tie. The gold and silver star emblem on his bolo matched the one on his belt buckle. It was important to make the right impression from the first moment he stepped out of the car. In case the big man was there. Elijah rolled his head around to stretch his neck and then reached for the bottle of water the driver had provided. The air was dry already at this elevation, and by the time they reached Baguio, they would be at forty-eight hundred feet. After a long drink, he leaned back and admired the pine trees clinging to the craggy stone cliffs as the driver downshifted on the twisting steep grade.

Hawkes had always enjoyed the time he got to spend up in the Cordillera. He thought of it as cowboy country, and he felt at home there. The geology and the terrain reminded him of his home in Nevada, and it was not surprising that both regions were rich in gold. The gold-mining industry up here in Benguet province had started at the end of the Spanish-American War when many American soldiers stayed on to pan for gold. Through the years, the mining had grown more sophisticated, and they'd pulled tons of gold out of these mountains. Like many mines in the region, though, the Benguet Mine was nearing the end of its days for pulling new shiny out of the ground. Twenty years ago when his organization had bought the mine, he'd told them as much. That doesn't matter, the big man had said. Mining new gold is not our primary concern.

When the big car pulled into the gravel parking lot outside the Benguet Mining offices, Jaime Belmonte stood on the big porch watching. Elijah supposed he'd seen the car enter the grounds on the video monitors. The headquarters building, made from rough-hewn logs and set back in the pines, looked like a tourist lodge. Belmonte was smoking, and when the car pulled to a stop, he strolled down the steps and ground out the butt under the heel of his black leather shoe. He brushed off the sleeves of his corduroy jacket and ran his fingers around his ears, making certain his hair was in place.

Belmonte was Brightstone's man in charge of the Benguet Mining facilities, but he was not the man who had texted Elijah. Was the big man here, or would Belmonte deliver a message for him? If so, Belmonte would never know the true origin of the message. He had no idea that the corporation he worked for was nothing more than a front. Belmonte lived in his little "need to know" world.

Once the car door opened, the strong wind blew cold air inside and Elijah breathed deeply. At this elevation, it didn't feel a bit like the tropics. And the piney air smelled so much better than that canned air-conditioning he'd been breathing ever since he left San Francisco. He needed the clean air to clear his head. When he climbed out of the car, the noise of the mining operations drifted over the low hill to the south. The clanking of railcars, the shrieking of metal on metal, the roaring of both diesel and electric motors made the mine sound far more productive than he knew it to be.

Belmonte shook his hand. "Good to see you, Mr. Hawkes. Please, come inside where we can talk."

The mine manager led him through the front office, past his elderly secretary who smiled and nodded at Hawkes, and back to a conference room where a small fire burned in a stone fireplace. He motioned toward one of the chairs in front of the fire.

"I trust you had a good trip?"

"As good as one can expect from eleven hours cooped up in an aluminum tube with several hundred coughing, sneezing strangers and their crying babies."

Belmonte smiled. "You do always look on the bright side of things, don't you, Mr. Hawkes? Could I get you something to drink? Are you hungry?"

"Just a mineral water. I tried to eat the food out here at the mine once. I won't make that mistake again."

After the secretary had served them bottled mineral water and ice-filled glasses, Belmonte pulled his pack of Marlboros out of his jacket pocket.

Elijah raised his hand like a traffic cop. "Please, I've inhaled enough poison today."

"Pardon me," Belmonte said, slipping the pack back into his pocket. He walked over to the window and looked out over the mine facilities. "You must be certain to visit Wolfgang before you leave today. He always asks after you."

Elijah had had about enough of the man's stalling tactics. "The news must be bad if you're doing all this crap to postpone telling me. Just spit it out. Why did he bring me all the way out here?"

"Well," Belmonte said after a long exhale of air. "You do jump right to the point, I see."

"So spit it out. I need to get into town, have a decent meal, and check into my room."

"I'm afraid you may not have the chance to do that, sir."

"Why? Explain."

"Last week we sent the last shipment out to Hong Kong. There's nothing left, except the small volume of new gold we still get out of the mine."

"We knew that was coming. How are things progressing on the Dragon's Triangle situation?"

Belmonte sighed again. "That's where the problem is."

"I don't understand. You located those artifacts at the Tuguegarao site that mentioned the *Teiyō Maru*."

Belmonte nodded. "We think the documents might show the site where the ship went down."

"And you hired the old man."

"Yes, that's right. That was all in my last report. He's worked for us for years. In fact, the organization has never used anyone else as a cryptographer." Belmonte paused for effect, then clutched at his chest as though it pained him to have to speak. "What wasn't in the report was that the old man disappeared with the artifacts."

Elijah was on his feet in a second. "You allowed that to happen?" he shouted. "What kind of a cretin would give a stranger unfettered access?"

Belmonte threw his hands in the air. "It wasn't *unfettered*, as you say. There was a guard. And the cryptographer, he's not a stranger. He's worked for us for what, fifty years?"

"My God, you incompetent half-wit." Elijah grabbed Belmonte by the front of his jacket, pulled him out of his chair, and held him so close their noses were nearly touching. "You do realize that the Dragon's Triangle may be the most lucrative find yet. There's much more than gold at stake here. What if your cryptographer is shopping it around? Did you consider that possibility?"

"He's an old man and he's always been loyal." Belmonte's voice had risen in pitch. "I don't know what's got into him."

"He's ninety-three fucking years old and you let him get away. How fast can he move? He probably shits his pants and can't remember his own name. But because you don't have either the brains or the cojones to deal with an old man, they've had to call me in. That's it, isn't it?"

Belmonte stuttered, "I—I . . ."

Elijah shoved him down into the soft chair. "You disgust me."

The mine manager straightened his jacket and sat up. When he ran his fingers through his hair, Elijah saw that his hands were shaking. The little pig had good reason to be afraid.

"How do I know you didn't put him up to it?" Elijah said quietly.

The man shook his head and his eyes grew large. "I swear to God, I had nothing to do with it."

Elijah swung his hand into the air, then stopped. He spoke in a soft, tense voice. "Don't use the Lord's name in vain."

Belmonte had half turned his face away from the impending blow. From the corner of his eye, he looked up at Elijah. "I had him here at the mine, and I kept him under guard. If I am guilty of anything, it is in my choice of the guard. For that I take full responsibility, Mr. Hawkes. The guard fell asleep, and the old man escaped in the night. We didn't know he was gone until morning."

"Were you able to track him?"

"Yes, through my connections at the airport, we found his face on a surveillance video. He used a different name, of course. Very professional-looking passport. He left for Bangkok two days ago."

"And?"

"I sent Benny, Mr. Hawkes. Benny Salim. He'll find him. We had the old man under video surveillance here, too, and we examined the computer he had been using. I gave Benny some leads based on the old man's correspondence. I'm certain Benny will locate him."

Elijah stepped closer to the fire and spread his fingers toward the flames. "And the guard?"

"We told his wife that he did not report to work that day. She has reported him missing to the police. It won't be any further problem for us."

"I see."

"You know Benny is the best. He will find him."

"You'd better hope so, Jaime."

CHAPTER NINE

Chatuchak Weekend Market
Bangkok, Thailand

November 17, 2012

By the time the MRT approached Chatuchak Station, the train car was jammed full with people and Riley had forced herself to put away thoughts about her imagined Cole sighting. It had to have been her imagination, just like all the other times, so she stored the vision in that compartment in her head and moved on. It was time now to think more about the upcoming meeting with Peewee.

Before she'd left Phuket, she'd done her research on this market she was about to visit. It was supposed to be the world's largest weekend market, with around five thousand stalls on over thirty-five acres, so her first order of business was to walk the grounds and get her bearings. While this Peewee character might very well be on the up-and-up, he could just as well have chosen a restaurant or a coffee bar for their meeting. The only reason to choose this market was because it was so easy to get lost in here. Until she met this guy face-to-face, she could not walk into this meet-up assuming he was a friendly. It was standard operating procedure to go over the terrain first.

When the train stopped, the crowd compressed to fit through the doors and surged forward like one big multi-legged insect. It wasn't until she reached the stairs that Riley finally had enough space around her to breathe normally.

The aroma of meat cooking over a charcoal fire was tainted by the stench of stagnant water that wafted up from a grate at her feet.

Riley paused before descending the steps to take a look around. The place looked even bigger than it had in the online photos. She saw a clock tower in the middle of the grounds, which must have been well over a quarter mile away. It stood in the center of a permanent structure full of stalls. She turned right and followed a wide asphalt walkway with vendors on both sides selling everything from handbags to housewares, clothing to fresh coconut ice cream.

The song "Gangnam Style" blared from speakers overhead. The crowd was mostly Thai. Bands of girls walked arm in arm, giggling and sneaking looks at the loose groups of boys who pushed one another and shouted over the music. Families herded their children in and out of booths and the occasional orange-robed monk passed on his way out, clutching his alms bowl to his chest.

Though it was only ten thirty in the morning, the sun blazed down on Riley's head. She should have brought a hat. After about a hundred yards, she came to another entrance gate where "schoolgirls" wearing low-cut white blouses, pleated plaid miniskirts, and knee socks were handing out maps to the market. Riley took one and stepped into the shade of a big umbrella spread above a bin of bootleg DVDs. The movies looked like the real thing, but she'd been in Thailand long enough to know they never were.

As Riley unfolded the map, a tiny woman wearing an apron with huge pockets stepped out from behind a glass case containing cell phones.

"Movies?" she asked. "You like Clin Easwood?"

Riley raised her head and squinted. "No, thanks. Do you sell bottled water, by any chance?"

The woman's wrinkled face broke into a big smile. She walked over to a cooler and grabbed one of the bottles floating in the icy slush. She handed it to Riley.

"Fifty baht."

Riley thanked the woman, paid her, and gulped the water so fast her chest ached. She then poured some into the palm of her hand and splashed it onto her cheeks.

The woman stepped around the DVD bin and handed Riley a small hand towel. She smiled again and Riley saw several gaps where teeth should be.

"You first time Bangkok?"

Riley wiped her face and returned the towel with her own smile. "Yes. I came up from Phuket."

"Where you stay?"

"I don't know yet."

The old woman reached into one of the big pockets of her apron and handed Riley a card the size of a postcard, but made of rough-looking artisan paper. On it was printed the name "Napa Place" and an address. The woman pointed to the address. "My family owns. Very nice place for lady."

"Thank you so much for your kindness."

Riley slipped the half-full bottle and the card into the mesh side pocket of her backpack. She hoisted the pack onto her back, and when she had walked half a dozen steps she turned and waved good-bye to the woman.

According to the map, the layout of the market was fairly straightforward. Riley spent the next hour walking the main road around the perimeter before she plunged into the center aisles. She'd visited the weekend markets and night markets down in the south, but she had never seen the variety of goods they had here in Bangkok. The stalls were divided into areas where goods of a certain sort were offered. There was an entire section on pets and accessories where little baby bunnies wearing gingham dresses were for sale next to pen after pen of adorable purebred-looking puppies: pugs, beagles, shih tzus, and Pomeranians. In the dried-food section there were huge sacks of colorful spices and herbs, and dried fish, squid, prawns, and octopus. Aisle after aisle of teak and wicker furniture, clothing of all sorts, ceramics, appliances, gardening equipment.

Since she was meeting Peewee at the Land of Smiles Antiques, Riley saved the antiquities section for last. The aisles that penetrated into the main building were called *sois*, or alleys, and there were more than sixty of them. They were like the spokes of a wheel that started at the center hub where the clock tower stood and then radiated outward. They were crossed by the fifteen or twenty aisles that ran all around the building from the center all the way out to the Main Road. She'd been counting down the *sois*, and now finally, Sois 2, 3, and 4 comprised the area where antiques and collectibles were offered. Here, Riley found Buddhas in all shapes and sizes, temple bells, masks, statues of Hindu goddesses, ceremonial swords, and incense-burning pots. The more valuable items, like those made of ivory, silver, and gold, were kept inside glass cases.

Many of the stalls in this section were really more like shops, with hard walls, doors, and signs hanging overhead. The bright yellow sign for Land of Smiles Antiques was visible about a third of the way in down Soi 3. The sign promised Thai Buddhas, Khmer bronze, Lopburi pots. Riley checked her watch. She was about ten minutes early, but since the guy said he would be working there, she supposed early would be all right.

The booth had no front wall, unlike its neighbors on either side that were enclosed shops. As she neared, Riley didn't see anyone inside at first, but the stall was overflowing with furniture pieces, glass cases full of trinkets, and very lifelike, creepy-looking statues of wrinkly-faced monks in their saffron robes. Merchandise was piled in the center of the booth so that the walkway through it was essentially a U shape. Along the bottom of the U was the counter at the back of the shop. Riley had no idea what was valuable and what wasn't, but the overfilled shop made her nervous, afraid she might break something. She slid off her backpack, tucked it under her arm, and stepped into one side of the booth. She walked back to the counter.

"Hello?" she called out.

A head popped up from behind the glass case. It was a young Thai girl, maybe ten years old. She offered a shy smile and a nod, then disappeared through a curtain into the back of the stall.

A few seconds later, the curtain was swept aside and an elderly *farang* man walked out. He stood only a couple of inches over five feet tall, and he was wearing a US Army garrison cap, the fore and aft cloth hat that could be folded and tucked into a back pocket. The olive-drab cap was covered with colorful ribbons, medals, and patches. Emblazoned down one side were the words *Military Order Purple Heart.*

Riley's first impression was that he was certainly old enough to be a World War II vet. He looked like he was in his nineties but he moved with a lightness that belied his age. The left side of his face was disfigured with old scars that caused his features to droop, and even on the good side of his face his skin was mottled with age spots. On the ear that was visible she saw a bulky hearing aid, and he was working his lips like she'd seen older people do who wear dentures. There was something odd about the way he was looking at her—it was a hungry look, like he wanted something from her. Then his face broke into a wrinkled smile showing a lineup of too-perfect, artificial-looking teeth.

He stepped around the counter, pulled up his pants that were already well above his waistline, and extended his hand. "You must be Miss Riley." His voice was strong, but the enunciation sounded mushy, like that of a person who could no longer hear himself speak.

She reached out and found his grip surprisingly strong. "Hello," she said. "And you are?"

"Irving Weinstein, but all my friends call me Peewee. Or you can call me Irv."

She smiled. "Nice to meet you, Irv."

"Come here, we got a couple of chairs."

The young girl pushed a teak chair out from behind the counter. Riley sat and perched her backpack on her lap. Peewee sat on a similar chair that was part of a display. The girl disappeared through the curtain, and Riley sat staring at her own entwined fingers resting on top of her backpack. The silence stretched out. She could feel Peewee's eyes on her, but she wasn't about to speak first. He was the one who called this meeting. Let him figure out how to get started.

"You've got your grandmother's eyes," he said at last.

"You knew her?"

"Oh yeah, I was best man at the wedding. Is it all right if I call you Maggie?"

"Actually, Irv, most people just call me Riley." Only Cole had called her Miss Maggie Magee, then shortened it just to Magee. She'd found it both irritating and charming.

Irv chuckled. "Riley. That's what I called your grandpa when we were kids. Most folks called him Ozzie later on, though."

"You knew my grandfather as a kid?"

"Hell yeah." He bunched his hands into fists and made like he was throwing a couple of pretend punches. "They called us the trouble twins. Everyone thought we were brothers. We even looked alike. Grew up together in Middletown, Rhode Island. It was the Depression, but we were just kids, and when we weren't in school we were playing in the woods or building sailing dinghies. My pops was a jeweler—he learned the trade in Europe and then did real well for himself when he immigrated to the US, so they let the Jews into the neighborhood." His eyes met hers and he winked.

"So, what did you want to see me about? And how did you find me?" Riley noticed he watched her mouth as she spoke.

"I thought you'd want to know about your granddad. Especially after losing your pops the way you did, may he rest in peace. I read about that in the papers, and that's when I learned Richie had a daughter. My condolences on your loss, Miss Riley."

"Just Riley."

He looked at her for a long time, working his lips over his teeth. Riley decided it was an unconscious thing. He'd probably be surprised to see a video of himself doing it.

"Okay, then. *Fine feathers do not make fine birds.* Even with a man's name, you are still the *crème de ma café.*" He winked at her again.

Riley didn't know what to make of him. Was he flirting with her? "About my grandfather," she said. "What can you tell me?"

"Let me show you," he said. He slid one hand into the inside breast pocket of his blue canvas jacket. He removed something small wrapped in what looked like a white silk handkerchief, then just held it without unwrapping the cloth. "When we graduated high school, Ozzie left for university down in New Haven, and my pops wanted me in the family business. Wasn't what I wanted, though. So, in July of forty-one, I enlisted in the infantry. I knew we'd be in the war soon, and I wanted to see Europe. Imagine my surprise when after boot camp, they shipped me out to a place called Manila."

The Pacific. That was where her grandfather had disappeared.

"Are you saying you met up with my grandfather again during the war?"

"Yes, ma'am. See, in Manila, I trained with the Philippine Scouts. Went on expeditions all over Luzon. Most of those Filipino boys couldn't drive, so I became a jeep driver. Next thing you know, I'm driving General MacArthur's chief of staff, General Sutherland. Moved out to Corregidor with him, too, when the Japs invaded. After the brass and the SIS guys hightailed it out of there, me and the rest of those boys hung on as long as we could. We surrendered after four months of hell."

"SIS?"

"Signals Intelligence Service. Those were the code-breaker boys who were listening in on the Japs' chatter."

"I've read about the siege of Corregidor and the Bataan Death March. I can't believe I'm speaking to someone who was actually there."

"Not for long. I escaped in Bataan. Spent the rest of the war in the mountains with some of my buddies from the Scouts. Guerrillas. We captured a Jap radio and caused a little mayhem with the help of the OSS. Then long about the end of the war, who shows up but my old friend, Ozzie."

"What was he doing in the Philippines?"

"It's hard to say what their mission was. But he arrived on a US submarine."

"A submarine," Riley said slowly. She shook her head. *Not another submarine,* she thought.

"Yup. Last time I saw him alive was in the Philippines. He said if anything happened to him, I was to give this to his son." The old man folded back the layers of silk cloth to expose an ornate gold tube just over two inches long, with pointed caps on both ends.

"It's beautiful."

"And old. Real gold, too. Ozzie said he got it off a Jap officer. He said the guy claimed he was a prince or something. So that's called a Tibetan prayer gau. See this little end to the tube here? It slides off and inside are some small scrolls inscribed by monks. They're prayers, so that's why they call it a prayer gau. People are supposed to wear these on a chain around the neck to keep the prayers close to the heart."

"What was a Japanese officer doing with a Tibetan artifact?"

Peewee chuckled. "Listen, sweetheart, the Japs looted every place they went. I saw things you would not believe when I was with the guerrillas."

"Like what?"

"Let me put it this way. You know how people dream of finding a pirate treasure chest full of gold and jewels? What I saw wasn't just a chest. It was truck convoys and every truck full of crates."

"Crates of stuff like this?" She held up the gau.

"That's right. Anyway, Ozzie's boy Richie was maybe six years old at the time. Ozzie carried a picture of him he showed to everyone he met. I always meant to go back, find Richie, and tell him his dad was thinking of him right at the end. But the army makes you sign these papers promising never to tell about the secret stuff we did. And you know what they say, *Never trouble trouble till trouble troubles you.* Always thought I had time. Never thought I'd outlive the boy." The old man reached up and dabbed at a moist eye.

"Do you know how my grandfather died?"

He coughed, then glanced behind her, apparently at a new customer who had just entered the stall. He sat up straighter. "Listen, you've heard enough of my stories today." He reached for her hand, placed the silk-wrapped prayer gau in her palm, and then folded her fingers over it, making her hand into a fist. "Ozzie thought there was something special written inside this, and I think you're a smart enough cookie to figure it out."

Riley was surprised at how heavy the small gold object was.

"This is the closest I can come to fulfilling that promise I made," he said quietly.

"Irv, do you know what happened to him or the submarine?"

He wasn't looking at her. His lips were working his dentures furiously as he watched something over her shoulder and behind her. "Both are listed as missing," he said quietly.

"What was the name of the sub?"

"The USS *Bonefish*," he whispered.

CHAPTER TEN

**Aboard the USS *Bonefish*
Sea of Japan**

June 18, 1945

Ozzie stared at the man for several seconds. *Holy shit,* he thought, *that's where I've seen that flower before.* Then he drew a pencil line in his notebook under the name Lieutenant Colonel Miyata and beneath it wrote "Prince Kaya Masako."

"So the other men drowned rather than get into a boat with you?"

"That was their duty."

Ozzie shook his head. "So what should I call you?" He knew a little about diplomacy from the years working for his father at the bank back home in Newport, Rhode Island. The rich were America's royalty.

"Colonel Miyata is fine." The man lifted his mug and took a small sip. His lips compressed as he swallowed, then the corners of his mouth turned up in a small smile. "We are not encouraged to reveal our identity to the enemy."

"Then why tell me?"

"Because I think you and I might be able to reach an agreement. You look like a man who has seen much and now is interested in a better life than this." The prince waved a hand through the air to indicate the submarine.

Ozzie leaned back and stretched his arm out along the back of the chair next to him. He looked from the prince to the boy and back to the prince again. "Are you saying you think I can be bought?"

"Lieutenant, every man has his price. It is no insult to say I will find yours. Japan has been building her empire for more than fifty years. From Korea to China to the countries of Southeast Asia, Thailand, Malaysia, Vietnam, and yes, the Philippines. We have dealt with many enemies."

Ozzie noted that this guy's grasp of English was improving the more he talked. He'd started out playing dumb. Now he had shifted his game.

"Yeah, yeah, but things aren't going so well for you now. Germany's surrendered. Won't be much longer until your cousin's got to do the same thing."

The prince's dark eyes were fixed on Ozzie's, unblinking behind the round gold-rimmed glass lenses. He continued speaking as though Ozzie hadn't said a word.

"These countries once had enormous wealth. From the noble citizens to the temples, the banks to the museums, Japan has been acquiring the riches of all she has conquered."

"We call that looting, Colonel. When you guys surrender, and we march on Tokyo, it will be ours."

The officer's mouth stretched wide into a toothy grin. Ozzie could see the high cheekbones, the skull beneath the bald head, and the ridges under the gums that held his teeth in place. He thought of the grinning death heads they painted in Mexico to celebrate the Day of the Dead.

"Not if you can't find it, Lieutenant."

"Oh, we'll find it all right," Ozzie said.

That grin. Ozzie really wanted to punch him just to make him shut his mouth. That grin was giving him the creeps.

"Not if you're looking in Japan, you won't."

"What do you mean?" Ozzie said.

"Lieutenant, I see from your uniform that you are not a regular American naval officer. May I ask what is your position aboard this ship?"

"I'm asking the questions here, Colonel Miyata."

"I thought perhaps if you are involved with your intelligence services"—the man paused and lowered his voice—"you might be interested in Operation Golden Lily."

Ozzie took a drink of his coffee before answering. It was already cold and acidic. Just what he needed. He forced himself to swallow. It pissed him off that the prince had manipulated him like this, but there wasn't any way of pretending he wasn't interested. "What is it?"

The prince grinned again.

Ozzie looked away.

"Operation Golden Lily has been under way for many years. Prince Chichibu was tasked by the emperor himself with collecting the valuables from the countries that have joined our empire. Three years ago, it became more difficult to transport this cargo back to Japan. Several ships carrying Golden Lily cargo were sunk by your submarines."

The steward stepped into the wardroom and asked if there was anything more they needed. Ozzie asked him for a glass of water, then told him to feel free to go take a smoke topsides. After the man left, the prince continued.

"Since it was no longer safe to transport these goods to Japan, the emperor decided to store them in the Philippines."

Ozzie removed a small bottle of white powder from his pants pocket and shook some into the water. He noticed Miyata was watching him with a questioning look on his face. "Sodium bicarbonate. It's for my stomach," Ozzie said. "Helps with the acid. If this war doesn't end soon, I'm not going to have a stomach left."

"You have been fighting a long time, Lieutenant?"

"Since before Pearl."

"I see. You have seen many terrible things then. Do you think your country is going to appreciate all you have suffered?"

"I'm not the only guy who's been in this mess a long time. Sometimes, though, it does seem like I've outlived most of them."

"Lieutenant, when this war is over, Japan will surely keep the islands of the Philippines. It has been my job to turn many of the natural caves in those islands into vaults for these valuables. I know all of the Golden Lily locations, Lieutenant."

"You're saying you know where all this looted treasure is hidden."

"I do not like this word *loot*. The word implies that we are stealing. It is not stealing if we already own it. These countries are Japan's possessions, part of our empire."

"Why are you telling me all this?"

"It is no accident that I am here and your ship has picked me up. This was meant to happen."

"What the hell are you talking about?"

"Ben and I would be happy to show you."

The prince looked at the boy, Ben, and the young man smiled for the first time.

"Show me what? You're not making sense."

"Lieutenant, imagine a treasure more vast than anything man has ever assembled in one location. Think about so much gold that it would take a navy of ships to remove it."

Ozzie didn't say anything.

"It is imperative that I return to the Philippines."

Reluctantly, Ozzie forced his mind to turn away from the visions the prince's words had evoked. "Good luck with that. MacArthur kept his promise and he's pushing your guys out."

"You are correct when you say this war will be ending soon."

"And until that happens, you're gonna be a guest of Uncle Sam."

The prince shrugged as if to say, *Maybe, or maybe not.* "When the war ends, the smart men will be very rich." He stared into Ozzie's eyes once again. "Those not so smart will return home to the same lives they had before the war."

Ozzie felt the burn crawling back up his throat. He thought about the tiny apartment where his wife lived with their son, little Richie, and the job waiting for him working for his father at the bank. He'd watched his father handling the money of the residents of Newport's mansions all his life, never making enough of his own to be anywhere near in their league. After all Ozzie had done for *them* in this war, no one was suggesting he'd go home to anything different. He coughed and then swallowed. His gut tensed for the pain he knew was coming.

"I do not have the luxury of time, Lieutenant. I have very important information I need to return to the Philippines."

Ozzie told himself to snap out of it. This was what he was supposed to be after: information.

"What kind of information?"

The prince lifted both his hands into the air with his fingers spread wide. "Do I have your permission to reach for something in my tunic?"

Ozzie shrugged. He knew the sailors who had brought these prisoners aboard the sub had already patted him down. "Sure. Just take it slow."

"On my honor, it is not a weapon."

The prince reached inside his tunic and Ozzie saw him pull apart some small stitches. He reached inside the lining of the upper end of his sleeve and withdrew a small gold cylinder about three inches long. It had caps on both ends. The fine gold filigree work around the tube looked like some sort of Eastern lettering like Hebrew or Arabic. In gold alone, it was worth more than Ozzie made in a year.

So much for the capabilities of the sailors who searched this guy, he thought.

"What is that?"

"It is called a prayer gau, or prayer box. It was made in Tibet more than one hundred years ago. Their monks would use these to carry small prayers close to their hearts." The prince held up the gau and showed Ozzie that there were tiny scrolls of paper inside.

"So, I take it that this one doesn't have prayers in it."

"You are correct." The prince flashed his creepy grin again.

"So, what is this? Some kind of coded message?"

"It is the key to a map."

"What sort of map?"

"It is an encrypted map that represents my work over the last three years."

"You mean this Golden Lily?"

"Yes, the map shows the locations of all the Golden Lily vaults located in the islands of the Philippines. It is located in Luzon and I know where."

CHAPTER ELEVEN

Chatuchak Weekend Market
Bangkok, Thailand

November 17, 2012

Riley couldn't believe what she'd just heard. "The USS *Bonefish*?" she said, her voice sounding loud after Peewee's whisper.

Was this one more instance where her father had lied to her? She thought of all the boats he had owned in the many places her family had lived. Whenever the State Department posted him to an embassy close to a body of water, her father always found and purchased some sailing boat and named her *Bonefish*. And now Riley's own boat carried the same name. Yet her father always swore that he never knew anything about his own father's time in the Pacific.

Peewee leaned in close, focused his eyes on hers, and said, "*Shhhh.*" He inclined his head toward the customer over her left shoulder and folded both his hands over hers. "Keep this safe. There are others who want it."

She started to turn her head, but he made that shushing noise again. Then she felt his hot breath on her ear, and she barely heard him when he said, "Meet me at the Temple of the Reclining Buddha in three hours. When I say so, you run."

Peewee leaned back in his chair, still watching the customer behind her. Riley wrapped the handkerchief around the heavy metal object and slowly slid it through the zipper on the side of her backpack.

"So how long have you been in Thailand, miss?" Peewee asked in a loud voice.

She slid her right arm through one of the straps. "A little over a month," she said. "But this is my first trip to Bangkok."

Peewee stood. "I see. Well, I think it's time for you to *go*. Now."

When Riley bolted out of the chair, she turned just enough to get a look at the man who had walked into the stall behind her. The Fu Manchu mustache and gray-streaked hair of the Asian man from the train station coffee shop.

Peewee was surprisingly fast for such an old man.

When the stranger lunged for her, somehow Peewee kicked her empty chair into his path and the mustache man disappeared behind the pile of merchandise in the center of the store. The last she saw of him, Peewee had darted around the fallen man and was headed for the curtain at the back of the shop.

Riley took off, her sandals slapping the asphalt as she dodged around all the shoppers. The crowd seemed to have multiplied three-fold in the time she had been talking to Peewee. Her backpack bounced against her side, and she slowed for a moment to get her other arm through its strap. She didn't have a chance to see whether the strange man had followed her or Peewee, but soon she heard footsteps and people crying out as her pursuer shoved them aside in the aisles behind her.

She was headed back the way she had come, following Soi 3 out to the perimeter Main Road, when she decided it would be smarter to stay inside the crowded market for cover. She darted to her right and followed an aisle lined with clothing boutiques. She pushed her way through throngs of Thai teenagers clad in skintight jeans and wearing huge sunglasses on the tops of their heads. They were giggling and pushing one another and blocking the aisle.

Riley dropped down onto her hands and knees and dove between the hems of a rack of hanging sundresses. The cloth brushed aside and she emerged on the other side of the rack with a clear space ahead of her. She leapt up and heard a scream. A quick glance over her shoulder showed a young girl, her head hanging forward, glasses gone, dark hair covering her face. The stranger had his arm raised to strike again, and in his hand she saw what looked like a thin yellow stick or bamboo pipe. The other terrified teens were running and screaming, scrambling to get out of his way.

She turned right again at the next intersection and was now heading for the center of the building. At the end of the long aisle, she saw sacks of grain, herbs, and dried fish. She smelled the hot grease and pungent spices and saw the yellow heat lights. Food stalls. Behind her, more screams. She didn't dare take the time to look.

Going left this time, she found herself among mountains of shiny aluminum pots and tier after tier of plastic bowls and boxes with bright-colored plastic lids. She swerved to avoid a stroller and ran into a tightly balanced display of huge cook pots. The pile caved in and crashed to the ground. An old Thai man wearing a *Notre Dame Irish* T-shirt came running out yelling at her.

Ahead was another restaurant stall with a cooking island out front and a man in a bloody apron hacking at what looked like a chicken carcass with a meat cleaver. Riley dodged around the man and cut through the tables packed with diners. There was a swinging saloon-style door at the back of the stall, and she was certain there had to be a back door. Through the swinging door, she found herself in a packed room with a stove on one side and a dishwashing sink on the other. In between, seven or eight startled people stared at her.

"Out?" she said.

A woman pointed to the curtain that covered the back wall. Riley swept it aside and found herself in a small passageway behind the stalls. When the curtain dropped it was dark back there. The hard concrete wall to her left must be the building exterior. The various booths on her right used this space for storage and to dump their garbage during the day. She felt her way forward. She heard a man shouting behind her, back in the kitchen. She was moving away from the sound, carefully stepping over cardboard boxes and pieces of cellophane packaging, trying not to make any noise yet trying to cover as much ground as possible. Water on the ground soaked her feet, and her toes slid around in her sandals as she climbed over the piles of trash. Her nose told her she was moving away from the cooking stalls.

Then she heard noises behind her. Someone else moving down the passage. She heard crashing and what sounded like cursing as he kicked at the trash blocking his route.

Riley's eyes were getting more accustomed to the darkness. Her arms reached out in front of her, feeling for obstructions. Pushing aside a bucket and mop, she turned to look over her left shoulder. Her back was to the booths on her right, and it was then she felt arms close around her. There was cloth between her and the person, as well as her backpack. A flap of the heavy fabric fell over her head, blinding her.

The arms yanked her out of the alley into a stall. She coughed and choked on the odor of wet wool. Even through the blanket, she heard the sound change. More noise, distant music. She squirmed and struggled against that strong grip. Swinging her head, she tried to throw off the heavy fabric. Her feet kicked at the ground as she tried to get purchase. It grew harder to breathe and her heart hammered as she beat with all her fury at the body pressed against hers.

Then the arms lifted her feet off the ground and turned her. Something caught against the backs of her knees and she started to fall backward. She landed on her butt but the blanket cushioned her fall.

Before she could try to stand, someone picked up her feet, tucked them inside, pushed down her head, and closed some sort of lid.

The sounds outside were muffled. Riley hated small, tight spaces, and she fought to get her rising panic under control. The smelly wool was suffocating her, and finally she pulled the cover off her head. Slow your breathing, she told herself. Still she couldn't see anything in the darkness. She felt around, walls and floors of rough-hewn wood. A domed lid. Trying to push up on the lid that held her inside was no good. It wouldn't budge. She tried pounding on the wood sides, but she couldn't pull her fist back far enough to make much noise. She was about to start screaming when outside she heard hammering feet and hard breathing.

She froze. A man's voice was shouting in Thai. A woman was whimpering, then she spoke very fast. Riley heard the man's voice move from one side of the box to the other, then she heard nothing.

CHAPTER TWELVE

Chatuchak Park
Bangkok, Thailand

November 17, 2012

Benny Salim could not believe his luck. The woman had somehow vanished right in front of him, so he was leaning against a tree in the park smoking a cigarette, thinking about how he was going to pick up the trail again, when the geezer walked out of the market gate into Chatuchak Park not twenty meters away. Benny would not have recognized the old man if he had not been wearing that stupid hat that looked like an army-green tent covered with medals. There were not many men wearing those around Bangkok these days.

He had underestimated the old man earlier. He would not do so again. The old man was walking at a brisk pace across the grass, headed for the underground train station. Benny ground out the butt of his cigarette and fell in behind him. He closed the gap between them with his longer strides and when they were still about one hundred meters from the entrance to the MRT, he grabbed him by the shoulder and spun the old man around.

"Jesus!" the old man said, clutching his chest. "You almost gave me a heart attack."

Benny looked into the distance over the top of the old man's head. The scars on the old guy's face made him uncomfortable. "You know why I'm here."

"Yeah, but I can't help you, Benny. Go back home to Borneo or wherever you're from." Peewee pointed to the slender leather satchel Benny had slung over his shoulder. "And take that pipe with you. Besides"—he smiled with the good half of his face, lifted his hands palms upward, and shook his head—"I don't have it anymore."

"You gave it to her, didn't you? That's what Belmonte said you were going to do."

"How the hell would he know what I intended to do?"

"You don't think he was watching your every move while you were working at the mine? Tracking every site you visited on the computer? You're an old fool. I used the girl to find you, Peewee."

"Well, shit."

"I found her once and I'll find her again. All this would be so much easier, though, if you would just tell me where she is."

Peewee hung his head and didn't say anything. His lips were moving over his teeth. Then he looked up. "Or what?"

Benny touched the strap of the leather bag. "You know what's in here. Don't think our past history's gonna make any difference to me."

"Benny, I'm ninety-three years old. You really think I'm afraid of dying? I've had a long time to get used to the idea."

"And what about the girl? You brought her into this. What's she to you? What's she going to do with Enterprise property?"

"Maybe you'd understand better if you knew exactly what it is you're looking for. I know how they work. They only told you enough to recognize it. You're supposed to track it down and retrieve it. Can't you just forget about this one? Let her go."

"No can do. You know that."

Peewee looked away, rubbed his hand over his chin, and squinted his good eye toward a line of trees across the park. Benny wondered what the old man was really seeing. Probably some memory from years back, something about how he was connected to the girl.

"Okay, look," Peewee said. "I'll get it back from her. I'll meet you somewhere and bring it to you."

Benny laughed out loud. "No, you are not getting out of my sight. We'll go find her together. You get what I came for, and I'll leave the girl out of it. But you, Peewee, Belmonte's going to want to talk to you." *And,* Benny thought, *you will learn soon enough what Belmonte really told me to do with you.*

Then the old man shrugged again and pulled his belt even higher. "Okay, then. Let's do it." He looked at his watch. "We're running out of time. I'm supposed to meet her at Wat Arun at five o'clock. A boat will be faster than the traffic in this town."

Benny grabbed the old man by the arm and steered him down the path toward the park exit. "Let's get out of here," he said.

When they got to the street, Benny flagged down a *tuk-tuk*, shoved the old man in first, and then climbed in after him. He held on to Peewee's upper arm in case he got some idea about jumping out. Then he told the driver to take them to the Bang Pho pier.

CHAPTER THIRTEEN

Chatuchak Weekend Market
Bangkok, Thailand

November 17, 2012

Riley wasn't aware she'd been holding her breath until she began to feel dizzy. After a quick exhale, she drew in a long breath. She was trembling.

She strained to hear something beyond her own breathing, but there was nothing. No footsteps, no voices. The air smelled of old wood and dust. Her neck ached from the cramped position she was in, but her backpack was wedged under her, and there was nothing to support her head. She put one hand on the lid above her to help her shift her body, and to her surprise it was the lid that moved instead of her body. When she'd tried earlier, the lid wouldn't budge, but now it lifted a crack and light flooded into the box.

She peeked out and blinked at the brightness. As her eyes adjusted, she saw row after row of wood and ceramic Buddha heads. Beyond that were some cabinets and furniture. She didn't see any people, so she raised the lid higher, until she was able to get her other hand up on the side of the box. She stood. Around her trunk were several others, all with leather straps holding the lids onto them. She was standing inside the largest trunk of all.

Outside the shop, people walked up and down the aisle. Some of them glanced in at her, but their eyes moved on. No one was paying any attention to her. She stepped out of the trunk and lowered the lid back down. She stepped to the back and swept aside the curtain. It opened directly onto the dark passageway behind the shops. There was no one there.

When she dropped the curtain and started for the door, an elegantly dressed woman turned into the shop carrying a white Styrofoam cup. "Hello," she said and ducked her head in a small bow. "May I help you?"

Riley looked around the small space again. There was no one there but her. "Is this *your* shop?"

The woman smiled. "Yes. Is there something special you're looking for?"

"Were you in here just now?"

"No, I just went out for a cup of coffee."

"Did you see . . . ?"

"Are you all right? My neighbor across the way came to find me at the restaurant. He said a strange man had run into my shop."

"And this man, did he have tattoos on his arms here?" Riley pointed to her forearms.

"He didn't say. All he said was that he had light brown hair and a beard."

Riley opened her mouth to say something else, but she stopped with her mouth hanging open. *No,* she thought, *not possible. No way.*

She tried to smile at the shop owner. "Thank you," she said, and she spun around and started walking. At first, she wasn't even aware of what direction she was going. She didn't see the stalls or the merchandise or the people. Some sort of autopilot kicked on and was navigating her body through the crowds for her. Her mind was going back over what it had felt like when those arms closed around her and her pulse had skyrocketed. She'd thought it had been fear—fear that her pursuer had caught her. Had it been something else?

There was only one way she could think of to start finding answers and that was to go find Peewee.

Riley came to an intersection and saw that the perimeter Main Road was only a few aisles away. She turned and started toward the bright light.

When she'd first arrived in Phuket, she had downloaded the Lonely Planet's guide to Thailand on her iPhone and she used it now to locate the Temple of the Reclining Buddha. There were so many different temples in Bangkok, it was difficult to keep them straight. The one she was looking for, she discovered, was called Wat Pho. It was down along the Chao Phraya River, and she decided the safest and probably the fastest way to get there would be via the SkyTrain to Surasak and then a ferry to Tha Tien. She'd heard about Bangkok traffic.

After the air-conditioning inside the elevated train, the heat felt good when Riley descended the stairs from the platform and started for the river. She'd missed both breakfast and lunch and the food carts along the street were making her stomach growl. The old man had said to meet in three hours, so she had time to kill. She stopped at a cart with a smoking grill and pointed to the pork satay skewers, then raised two fingers. The man behind the grill placed the skewers in a square of waxy paper and handed it to her. She paid him and thanked him and hurried over to the water's edge, where several people were gathered outside what she assumed was the ticket booth. When she got to the window, she said, "Wat Pho?" and the young woman punched holes in a ticket and handed it to her.

Riley found an open space on the concrete bench and settled herself to eat a quick meal and wait for the ferry. She slid the still-warm chunks of meat off the sticks with her teeth and chewed thoughtfully.

Back at the market, she had simply reacted when this Peewee guy had told her to run. She wasn't sure why she had just taken him at his word, except for the fact that the man he wanted her to run from had obviously been following her.

Why hadn't she seen him earlier as she walked around the market? She had been keeping her eyes open for a tail. The only logical conclusion was that he was very good at following someone and remaining undetected, meaning he was a pro. But what did that mean? Was he police, military, a private contractor? And what was his interest in her?

She pulled the half bottle of water out of the side pocket of her backpack and washed down the rest of the food. The people around her started getting up and moving toward a man who now stood at the entrance to the dock. He held them back as the boat approached. A boy jumped off the ferry as it neared the dock, and he blew a loud whistle when he got the spring line on the bollard. The dock man lifted his arm and let the crowd surge forward. Riley followed, wondering how they were all going to fit when only two passengers got off the already-crowded ferry.

Riley couldn't stand to be on a boat and not be able to watch the water, so she squirmed her way through the hard-packed humanity until she got one hand on the wooden rail at the edge of the boat. She was facing the side of the river where she had boarded so she was able to watch the techniques of the captain and crew each time they docked at a new ferry station.

The river was busy. She saw all sorts of boats both tied along the river's edge and charging up and down, churning the garbage-filled water into a mass of confused wakes. She loved the colorful long-tail boats with the big automotive engines on a pivot. Out the back of the engine was a twelve- to sixteen-foot shaft with the prop way out on the end. That was how they got their long-tail name. A tiller-like rod jutted out of the forward end so that the driver could press down on the rod and lift the prop out of the water, alleviating the need for a transmission. The sheer of the long wooden boats rose forward into these high curving bows, and often they were draped with what looked like garlands of flowers. Riley wondered how the drivers squatting in the stern could see anything directly ahead of them.

There was such a stark contrast between the stilt houses at the river's edge, built of dark bits of wood and flotsam, and the glittering high-rise towers. It looked as though class in this city could be determined by elevation.

After several stops along the western bank, the ferry turned to cross the river. They would be docking on the opposite shore now. By bending her knees to see under the coach roof and peering over the heads of the other passengers, she saw a cluster of spires on the opposite riverbank. She consulted the map on her phone, and decided it must be Wat Arun, otherwise known as the Temple of Dawn. The *prang* towers were encrusted with bits of broken porcelain and they were supposed to glitter when reflecting the first morning light.

The boat emptied half the passengers at that stop, and Riley was relieved that, at last, she no longer had people pressing against her. She was able to walk across to the opposite side of the boat to check out the scenery on that riverbank for a while. The boat was crossing back to the other shoreline, dodging around the front of a tug with a string of four barges and loads of colorful laundry flapping in the breeze, when Riley saw a long-tail boat approach them headed upriver. The boat was really moving and the prop was throwing a rooster tail of water several feet into the air. That was the first reason she took note of the boat, but as they grew closer, she focused on the two men sitting amidships.

Riley wouldn't have recognized Peewee if he'd been alone. Without that medal-covered garrison cap on his head, he looked like a generic little old white man with long wisps of hair blowing back in the wind. His hands were below the level of the gunwale, and Riley suspected he was clutching the cap on his lap. But the guy from the market was there, too. Him she would recognize anywhere, with or without the blue work shirt. His flat face and mustache, the full head of salt-and-pepper hair pulled back into a knot that looked like a lady's bun, the ink on the forearms. And he was still carrying the tooled leather satchel.

Standing at the rail a few feet from her was a German family with two strapping sons in their late teens. She stepped to her right to place the tourists between herself and the passing boat. Through them she could see the topknot man was standing with one hand clutching a support post that held up the long narrow roof over the boat. He didn't have a gun and as far as she could tell, he wasn't threatening Peewee. In fact, as the boat passed about fifty feet abeam of the ferry, she saw the topknot guy was talking on a cell phone. It looked like the old man was just enjoying the ride.

She walked back to the stern and watched as the long-tail boat pulled up to the dock at Wat Arun. Peewee was first off the boat, and he turned to wait for the other man. What sort of game was he playing?

CHAPTER FOURTEEN

Benguet Gold Mine
Baguio, Philippines

November 17, 2012

Elijah was halfway across the yard to the limo when he stopped and turned. Belmonte was still standing in the doorway of the office.

"Jaime, while I'm here, I am going to visit the lab and talk to Wolf. I'd like to take a look at the work he's been doing. If you're right and Benny finds the old man, we could be up and operating again within the week."

"Yes, sir. I'll call down and have him come up to meet you right now."

Belmonte turned and spoke to his secretary inside the office.

"Tell him I'll meet him halfway," Elijah said. "Meanwhile, book me on the next flight from here to Manila." He took off down the gravel path toward the lab, pleased that he would be able to see Esmerelda's smile even sooner than he had anticipated.

He had almost arrived at the prefab building when the back door swung open and Wolfgang, dressed in his usual white lab coat, stepped outside. Elijah had hired the chemist six years ago and brought both

Wolf and his wife, Ulrika, to the Philippines. Today Wolf was very good at his job only because Elijah had spent so much time in the Philippines teaching him. The German crossed the gap between them and extended his hand.

"Elijah. Come inside." He turned and extended his arm toward the door to the lab.

Once inside the lab, Elijah walked over to the mass spectrometer and rested his hands on the table next to the instrument. "I expected to hear from you, Wolf."

"You mean about that sample?"

Elijah turned and faced the German. He examined him for several long seconds before he answered. "Of course. Are you stalling for some reason?" He no longer trusted Wolfgang. Ever since his wife had taken her own life a little over a year ago, the man had changed.

"No, not at all. My findings aren't conclusive. I wanted to pin it down to the exact mine."

"And what have you found?"

"It's been more than two weeks, and I can't even determine the country, much less the mine."

Elijah's face broke into a broad smile. "Excellent! If you can't, no one can."

"I don't know what you did differently this time, but if you can replicate that, we can pass off gold mined anywhere in the world. No one will be able to fingerprint it."

Elijah patted Wolf's forearm and crossed to the door. The big man would be pleased. "I'll report your findings to Brightstone," he said as he pushed the door open.

He was halfway out when he turned to face the German. "On the phone last week, you said you had something you wanted to ask me."

Wolfgang dropped his head like a dog being scolded by his master.

"Wasn't it something about your wife?" Elijah could see the man's chin quivering. It was little wonder Ulrika had needed the attentions of a real man. And Wolfgang had made it so easy, since he liked to watch.

"I have something to show you," the German said.

Elijah stepped back inside and eyed his friend. He wondered what sort of secrets Wolf was keeping from him.

Wolf stepped past Elijah and activated the electronic lock on the door. They had installed fingerprint-activated locks six months earlier. Elijah knew because he had made the request and signed the orders. Not only did they often have millions in gold in the lab, but there was also more than a million dollars' worth of equipment in that room.

"So what have you been up to, Wolf?"

"I get bored and my mind wanders. I don't want to have too much time on my hands. You know what I mean. They won't let me leave this mountain, and there is nothing more for me to do here until they bring me more gold. But this," he said, squatting down and opening a cabinet, "this has been one of my greatest pleasures these days."

Wolfgang removed what looked like a rolled-up swath of dark velvet fabric. He carried it over to one of the tables in the lab and carefully unrolled then folded back the fabric.

When he saw it, Elijah drew in a quick breath. The detail in the metalwork was exquisite.

"I remembered the design on your back, you see, when Belmonte brought it in from the same site where they located those documents. It was that last dig up near Tuguegarao. He told me to destroy it because we had no way to prove its provenance. He said we aren't in this business to sell to private collectors, so I was to extract whatever I could." Wolf lifted the sword from the table and handed it to Elijah. "I couldn't do it—and I thought you would understand."

The heft of the blade felt balanced across his palms. "Hmm. Yes."

Wolfgang would not look directly at Elijah. When he spoke, his face was turned away. "Ah, I was right. I knew you would see it that way. I'm not an expert, but I have spent some time doing research since

I've had little else to do. It's an eighteenth-century Chinese ceremonial sword—more of a broadsword than a saber. The Qianlong emperor had many swords made with that dragon along the dorsal edge during that period. Much of the gold on the hilt there is only gold leaf, but the scales on the dragon's back are all solid droplets. And then there are the jewels. That was all that Belmonte saw. But I knew you would appreciate that is not where the value is."

"Quite right," Elijah said. "You know me well, Wolf. I appreciate beautiful things." He wrapped both hands around the hilt and lifted the sword, stepping back from the table. The blade was only about twenty inches long, but it felt perfectly balanced. This was not only a ceremonial sword. This blade was a true weapon. Elijah closed his eyes and he was certain it wasn't his imagination. He really did feel the tingling of a force flowing from the dragon sword in his hands to the ink on his back.

He'd once been a lost kid on the streets of Reno being raised by his older sister. Then he had discovered that he had been born in the Chinese year of the Wood Dragon. He'd found his way to a dojo, and between reading about Asia and studying martial arts he had become a different young man. God meant for him to find his path, and now the Good Lord meant this sword for him.

The sword's blade was a mess right now, but he would bring back the edge in time. He lifted it over his head, then brought it down from right to left and the sound of the wind whistling past the blade sounded like a wing in flight.

The phone on the desk rang. Wolfgang hurried over to answer it.

Elijah set the sword on the velvet cloth. It would be a crime to destroy such a weapon merely for the gold, but most of the men in the Enterprise lacked vision.

"Right," Wolfgang said. "I'll tell him." He hung up the phone. "That was Belmonte."

Elijah ran his fingers over the dragon's scales from the head to the tip of the tail.

"He said to tell you that Benny's got the old man, but he doesn't have the artifact anymore. The old man gave it or sold it to someone else. They want you to go to Bangkok."

The sheer incompetence of them all ignited his need to cause pain. In a flash, he saw a vision of himself grasping the jeweled hilt and swinging the sword at Wolfgang's neck like a crusader beheading an infidel.

Elijah drew a deep breath. He folded the ends of the fabric toward the center, then rolled up the sword. He slid his palms under the package, lifted it, and extended it to Wolfgang.

He knew the German wanted the sword for himself, but the man had decided to confess his disobedience so he would not risk being accused of stealing. He was offering it to Elijah just as he had offered his little blond wife.

"You will keep this safe for me," Elijah said.

The skin around the German's left eye twitched. "Of course. Whatever you say."

CHAPTER FIFTEEN

**Aboard the USS *Bonefish*
Sea of Japan**

June 18, 1945

It took some finagling to find berths for the boy and Lieutenant Colonel Miyata—as Ozzie had promised to call him. With the extra technicians for the FM sonar aboard, the sub was already overcrowded, and many of the men were hot-bunking three to a bunk as it was. At last he managed to get them eight hours each of sleep time in a couple of berths in the compartment just forward of his quarters.

On any other ship as a junior officer, he would have had his own cabin, but not on a sub. He shared a cabin with two other officers. Since one of the three was always asleep in there, it wasn't as though having a cabin afforded him any privacy. But he did have a small compartment in the cabin where he kept his personal effects, clothes, and a few books.

Ozzie was thinking about what was stored in his kit that night as he stood atop the conning tower smoking a cigarette with the sub's second in command, Lieutenant Commander Dustin Westbrooke, Jr. Ozzie hadn't been able to stop thinking about that gold all evening, and when an outlandish scheme popped into this head, he couldn't let that go either.

Westbrooke was a weak executive officer—the sort who had risen in the Navy on the coattails of his father, Admiral Westbrooke. Dustin was twenty-four years old, only three years younger than Ozzie, but he was young for his age and not very bright. He was a perfect example of a guy who was nervous in the service—and he had no combat experience to account for it. He had no rapport with the men, most of whom were older than he was. Westbrooke had been flown out to Guam to join the *Bonefish* when Commander Johnson's previous executive officer had suffered a burst appendix during training maneuvers with the new sonar. It had been Johnson's bad luck to get stuck with Westbrooke on this trip. Now, it might turn out to be something Ozzie could work to his own favor.

"So, Westbrooke," he said, "what are your plans when this thing is all over?"

"You mean the war?"

"Of course I mean the war. You got a girl at home?"

"No. I haven't got much luck with girls."

"I'm going to let you in on a secret, okay? Do you want to know what the trick is to getting girls?"

"Why, sure."

"Girls like the guys with dough. Heck, your old man's an admiral. You should be able to get yourself a nice new sports car when you get home. Get yourself an expensive haircut, fancy clothes, the best money can buy. Then you'll have all the girls you want."

Westbrooke laughed. "Right. My old man's so tight with his money he squeaks every time he gives me a dollar."

Ozzie shook his head and tossed his cigarette butt into the sea. "Now that's a downright shame. Young officer like you risking your life for God and country. You deserve better than that."

"Try telling my old man."

They stood in silence for the next several minutes watching the horizon and listening to the soft sound of the water sliding past the hull. The wind had died at sunset and the boat was now slicing through an almost mirrorlike sea. They could see the reflection of the Milky Way like a pale gauzy arc across the water.

"You know, there was a girl once."

Ozzie kept his face stern but he felt the smile behind his eyes. "What happened?"

"Nothing. That's the point. Like I said, I've never had luck with girls. But this one—Susan Mulligan was her name. She came to a party at our house. She didn't even know I was alive."

"It's like I said, Westbrooke. Women are attracted to rich and powerful men. And, of course, brave men who aren't afraid to take risks. I think that's the sort you are. You just need the car and clothes to attract their attention."

CHAPTER SIXTEEN

Wat Pho
Bangkok, Thailand

November 17, 2012

After she paid the entrance fee, the man in the booth handed Riley a pamphlet that explained some of the history of the temple and showed a map of the grounds. Peewee had said three hours. She was about fifteen minutes early, and given that she had just seen him exiting a boat on the other side of the river, she assumed she had beat him to their rendezvous location.

Again, she decided to walk around and familiarize herself with the layout of the compound. Either the old man was going to show, and he'd have some logical explanation for what he was doing fraternizing with the man he'd identified as the enemy, or there was something else going on here, some whole other story she knew nothing about. She was worried that it was the latter.

But as she walked around admiring the huge stone statues of funny-looking old men, some with long beards, others in weird derby hats, she kept coming back to the one word *Bonefish*. If this was all some kind of scam and this Irv guy really never knew her grandfather, but he had some other goal in getting her up to Bangkok, then how did she explain him coming up with the USS *Bonefish*? Was it coincidence? She doubted it. Obviously, there was some truth in what he had to say. If there was some, there might be more. She was already here in Bangkok. She might as well learn all she could.

Riley took note of the three exits and the relationship of Wat Pho to the river and the main streets where she could catch a taxi if necessary. All the while she stayed close to buildings, out of the open whenever possible, and stayed alert, checking out every person she encountered. She did not want to be taken by surprise, and now she knew just how good her adversary was.

When she finally got to the chapel that housed the Reclining Buddha, Riley took off her sandals, and rather than leave them on the rack outside she stuffed them into her backpack. She didn't want to end up running around Bangkok in her bare feet.

It took a few moments for her eyes to adjust to the low light inside, but when she could finally see down the full length of the statue, she was aghast at the size of it. The statue barely fit inside the building that housed it, and according to her brochure it was almost one hundred and fifty feet long. You couldn't step back far enough to take it all in. In other circumstances, she would have enjoyed playing tourist, but on this day, she searched the chapel for a shadowy alcove where she could keep her back to the wall and stand watch. She found her spot down by the mother-of-pearl-inlaid feet of the statue.

Riley slid the backpack off and reached inside for the artifact Peewee had given her. She had not had time to examine it. He'd said it was a Tibetan prayer gau. She supposed it weighed eight to ten ounces, and assuming it was pure gold and that gold was selling at around fifteen hundred dollars an ounce, it had significant value beyond any historical value. But was twelve to fifteen thousand dollars enough to make a big fuss over? To some people, yes, but not, she thought, to the sort of people who hire men like the one who had chased her.

. . .

Riley thought again about her father and the organization he had belonged to most of his adult life: Skull and Bones. They *were* the sort of people who could hire a man like that, and it was time she stopped avoiding the issue and considered that possibility.

Skull and Bones was a Yale secret society whose members pledged loyalty to Bones until their deaths. When she had first met Cole, Riley didn't want to believe his wild conspiracy theory about how the Patriarchs, an inner circle of Bonesmen, had orchestrated the murder of Cole's father, James Thatcher. Cole claimed his father had somehow learned that evidence was hidden aboard the wreck of the submarine *Surcouf* that proved how those monsters had been perpetuating the business of war for profit.

Then that fall day back in DC, Riley began to believe Cole wasn't crazy after all. In a matter of hours, she learned that her own father was one of the monsters, and he had sat idly by as his fellow Patriarchs ordered her brother Michael's murder. Then, when that rogue Bonesman Diggory Priest had murdered her father before her eyes, Riley and Cole had escaped and returned to the Caribbean, determined to find the *Surcouf* and expose them all.

Only it had not quite turned out that way. Thanks to old Henri Michaut, Cole located the *Surcouf* down in the Caribbean, but he was diving inside the wreck when the volcano on Montserrat erupted, causing an undersea earthquake that rocked the Leeward Islands and sent the submarine's wreck sliding into deeper water. Cole never surfaced. The madman Diggory Priest died in a boat explosion that same day, and Cole's first mate, Theo, and Riley were left to try to make sense of what happened. As the police boat approached, they had agreed to report that Cole too had died in the explosion and fire.

She had not gone back to Washington for her father's funeral. She just wanted to find a quiet cove to anchor her boat and give in to her grief. Eventually, Riley had returned to France, where she had lived as a child. She visited her mother, who had remarried a French national, but found only a woman intent upon distancing herself from her first marriage and the daughter who had been its result.

Thankfully, that bruising discovery wasn't all that she found in France. It was there that she'd last seen Theo, who'd hinted not only that Cole might still be alive, but also that the two of them had found the *Surcouf*, along with its secrets. Riley had so wanted it to be true, wanted to believe that the Patriarchs were through.

Then Theo too had disappeared.

It was crazy to think that this business with Peewee and the strange Asian mustache guy could have anything to do with Cole or the Patriarchs. But then again, if there was one thing Cole had taught her, it was to be careful about calling anything crazy.

After thirty minutes of waiting and watching all the people who passed through the chapel admiring the huge Buddha, Riley decided that Peewee was not coming. She realized she was still holding the gold tube in her hand. She'd been rolling it across her palm with her thumb, then pushing it back with her fingers like a devotee counting prayer beads. Flattening her palm, she held the object close to her face and tried to examine it in the dim light. She shook her head, hiked her pack higher up her shoulder, and walked to the closest door to the exterior.

The ground was paved with cut stone, and the single bench was already occupied by a monk sliding on his sandals, so Riley continued barefoot. She found a shady spot down a walkway between two buildings. Off the walkway, she leaned against the column and opened her palm again. The light there was much better. The goldsmith work was exquisite, with tiny beads placed around the caps on both ends and on several strips around the middle. This divided the tube into three bands, each decorated with intricate curling designs forming letters or pictographs, she assumed. Not being an expert on the Tibetan alphabet or language, she couldn't be sure, but that was what it looked like.

The top had a loop so that the tube could be worn around the neck on a string, and the bottom was a removable cap. It took some tugging, but she pulled the cap free and slid out one of the rolled scrolls of paper. The paper was very thin and the ink had bled through, so though the writing was on the inner side, she could see the designs. The figures looked very different from the writing in the gold-work on the tube.

From the corner of her eye, Riley noted movement, and when she turned to look, she saw the monk wrapped in his orangish-yellow robes and wearing wire-rimmed glasses. He smiled at her and pointed at the gau in her hand.

She smiled back, not sure if she was supposed to speak to him or not.

"Excuse me," he said, and he stepped closer to her. "Do you speak English?"

"Yes. I'm American. Your English sounds very good."

"Thank you. You are very kind." He nodded at the object she was holding. "Do you know what that is?"

"I was told it is a Tibetan prayer gau."

He nodded again. "Yes. I studied in Tibet, and I speak and write the language. A wonderful country. I have seen many of these prayer gaus. They are worn around the neck to keep the prayer close to the heart."

"So this is writing on the outside?"

"Yes, it is the Tibetan Buddhist mantra, *om mani padme hum*, which translates to 'hail to the jewel in the lotus.'"

Riley sighed. "That's really lovely."

"But the scroll you hold looks very strange. May I see it?"

Riley knew that monks were not allowed to touch women or take objects directly from them, so she slid the gold pieces into her pants pocket and unrolled part of the scroll. She held it up for him to see. Each figure was like a little drawing.

"It almost looks like hieroglyphics to me," she said.

"Hmm. Yes, you are correct. This is not Tibetan writing, and it is not Egyptian either. I study languages, and I have never seen writing like this. It may be a code."

"Code, huh? I've had a little experience with that." She rolled the scroll back up and pulled the pieces of the gau out of her pocket. She slid the paper back inside and closed the cap. Then she held the object in her palm for him to examine. "Is there any way to know how old this is or when the scroll was written?"

"I am not an expert in objects of antiquity. I cannot say. But there are many places here in Bangkok where you could find people to help you."

Riley pulled her backpack around to her side and slid the gau through the zipper. "Well, you have been very helpful. Thank you." She placed her hands together in front of her chest, then bowed her head until her thumbs touched her forehead in the traditional *wai*, or Thai greeting.

The monk looked down at her bare feet, then smiled.

CHAPTER SEVENTEEN

Wat Arun
Bangkok, Thailand

November 17, 2012

When they arrived at the entrance gate to Wat Arun, the old man told Benny he didn't have any money for the entrance fee, so Benny paid for them both. But he wondered if the old man was lying to him about the girl's location. Why choose the *wat* as a meeting place if he didn't have the money to get in? They walked around the gardens, looked into a few chapels, and Benny even climbed halfway up one of the *prang* spires to get a better look across the entire compound. The view of the river was great up there, but there was no sign of a young white woman alone. Benny had had enough.

When he got to the bottom of the stone steps, the old man could probably tell from the look on Benny's face that he wasn't happy.

"I swear this is where she was supposed to meet me," Peewee said. The side of his face with the scars didn't move much, while the good side was trying too hard to look believable.

"You think you are a clever trickster, old man, but you are going to end up dead."

"We all will, Benny. But you know what they say, *It's the bad plow-man who quarrels with his ox.* You want this girl? I can find her for you, but not with you hanging in my shadow and threatening to kill me."

"Peewee, I wouldn't fit in your shadow."

"Are all Malay people that literal?" Peewee whacked himself on the side of the head. "What am I thinking? You're headhunters. It doesn't get much more literal than that." His cap had slid down over one eye, and he reached up and centered it on his head.

"Let's get out of here, old man. She's not going to show. It's almost six o'clock."

"I've got to drain my lizard."

"What did you say?"

Peewee rolled his eyes. "Aw," he groaned. "You know, I've got to point Percy at the porcelain?" He turned his head sideways and looked at Benny out of the corner of his eye. "I'm going to free Willy?" He shook his head. "Still nothing, huh? How about, can you find me the little boys' room?"

"Are you saying you've got to take a piss?"

"That's the idea."

"I'm sure there's a toilet around here somewhere."

"Yeah, I saw it up close to the exit. You know, where we saw those two big demon statues? This way."

Several vendors had parked their carts around the exit gates. They were selling food and trinkets. Off to one side, a slender man in a broad straw hat led a young elephant around by soft touches to the animal's ear. Over his shoulder was slung a cloth bag. He reached in and handed out handfuls of elephant food to a group of children. They giggled as the trunk vacuumed up the grain.

"I'll be right back," Peewee said as he hurried past another group of children who were playing a game of tag in and around the bushes. The old man turned and called over his shoulder, "Sometimes at my age, this can take a while, though."

Benny followed the old man down the path to the concrete slab outside the latrine. Along the edge of the concrete, a cluster of vendors was selling bottled water and food. One woman had a blue plastic tub filled with eight- to twelve-inch live eels. He recoiled at the sight of the slithering animals. When he was a young boy, Benny had lived in his grandfather's stilt house on a river in Borneo. His people were the Dayak and he remembered eating fish, but he had no memory of eating anything that looked like these nearly colorless worms. But Benny didn't remember much of his boyhood. His mother had taken him to the city of Kuching when he was ten years old, and he had fallen in with a group of boys who ran wild in the streets. By the time he was eighteen, he had already killed two men.

Later, when he was much older, he went back and tried to find his grandfather's house. There weren't many Dayak still living on the river. They said his grandfather had died shortly after they left the village. That was when Benny decided it was time to learn more about his heritage.

His thoughts were interrupted by a child's scream. Benny turned his head. A little girl lay on the grass and the elephant had his foot on her abdomen. The man in the straw hat was screaming at the beast and pointing at the girl.

Benny ran over and scooped the child up off the ground. He was surprised at how easy it was to slide her tiny body out from under that big gray foot. It seemed the elephant's foot had just been hovering over her. He knelt in front of her and brushed off the girl's dress. She smiled at him and looked as though she expected praise for something. When she turned to look up at the elephant, she reached out her tiny fingers toward the trunk. He saw no fear in her face at all. There were no tears on her cheeks.

Benny looked up at the man in the straw hat and saw the shadow of a smile on his face, too.

"Is this some kind of game?" he asked them in Thai.

The man in the straw hat shrugged and looked away. Benny realized the man was looking in the direction of the toilet.

He jumped to his feet and started to run.

CHAPTER EIGHTEEN

Chao Phraya Express
Bangkok, Thailand

November 17, 2012

The woman who had sold her a ticket on the Chao Phraya Express boat had looked at the address on the card and told her to get off at stop number thirteen. As the boat churned its way upriver, Riley found a seat and pulled out her phone. She had a good connection, so she checked her email and was happy to see a note from Billy telling her everything was fine with her boat and offering any other help she might need. Then she pulled up a web browser window and went to her blog page and logged in with the password *tombolo*. It was her habit to post the latitude and longitude of her position, but whenever she was off the boat, she posted her address for the night. After she'd typed the date and the information for Napa Place into a new comment post, a familiar window popped up with a message written in Thai. She couldn't read it, but it had happened once before, so she knew it said she had nearly used up the data she had purchased. She would need to find a Wi-Fi connection soon to access the website where instructions for purchasing more were written in English.

The crowd on the ferry was mostly Thai with the usual smattering of young Caucasian backpackers, girls in long skirts or wide-legged cotton pants, and guys with their beards, braids, and dreadlocks. None of them were paying her any undue attention, nor did anyone look out of place. The backpackers all headed for the exit at the back of the boat as they approached her stop.

Riley followed the crowd through an alleyway to the street, Thanon Phra Arthit, where traffic was bumper-to-bumper, tourists jostled with Thai hustlers for sidewalk space, and the many lighted signs for hostels, hotels, travel agencies, and restaurants lit the street despite the gathering dusk. The smell of curry and grilling meats mixed with exhaust fumes. Riley stepped into the doorway of a clothing shop and pretended to admire a dress in the window as she scanned the street. She was certain no one had followed her from the temple to the river ferry, but in this crowd, it would be much more difficult to tell if anyone was watching her. Again, she saw no one, but now that she was aware of the skill of this guy, she kept checking every few minutes.

Her directions were to cross the street here and go right for several blocks. The Napa Place was on a side street barely wide enough for a small car. A sign directed her up the one hundred yards or so off the main street to the narrow door to the hotel. To the left just inside the entry the wall was covered with a honeycomb of little cubbyholes, several of which were filled with shoes. Riley removed her sandals, placed them inside her backpack, and passed through into the lobby. The reception desk was at the back. Through a pair of French doors to her right, she saw a lovely open courtyard with tables scattered among the greenery and a stone fountain with a Buddha head on the far wall.

The petite woman behind the desk gave her a *wai* and said *"Sawadee ka."* Riley returned the greeting and made arrangements for a room for the night. She was disappointed to learn there was no Wi-Fi in the rooms, only in the common areas, so after freshening up, she grabbed her backpack that held her phone and wallet, and returned downstairs to order dinner and use the Internet access in the restaurant.

After ordering her food, and purchasing more data minutes to keep her iPhone working, the first thing on her list was to learn more about the USS *Bonefish*. Between *Wikipedia* and several sites maintained by naval historians, she discovered there had been two subs with that name. The one she was interested in was a Gato-class diesel-electric submarine 319 feet long. Peewee had said that her grandfather supposedly arrived in the Philippines in 1945, but what Riley learned was that the *Bonefish* was in San Diego for a refit in the early part of that year. Then it went on a war patrol in the South China Sea, and from May onward was involved in something called Operation Barney.

The *Bonefish* entered the Sea of Japan in June 1945, along with eight other American subs, but they had been in training on how to use the relatively new invention of sonar in Guam before that. The wolfpack of subs sank a whole bunch of unsuspecting enemy ships inside what the Japanese thought were protected waters, but when they rendezvoused at the end of the month up near the Strait of La Pérouse, the *Bonefish* was a no-show. The eight other subs waited as long as they dared, then they returned to Guam, and the *Bonefish* was declared missing and presumed lost.

After the war, Japanese records showed an anti-submarine attack on June 18 in an area called Toyama Wan, where the *Bonefish* had last been seen. During the attack, a great many depth charges were dropped and finally some wood chips and oil came to the surface. The Japanese claimed to have destroyed an enemy submarine, and the US Navy, she read, then recorded that as the attack which sank the USS *Bonefish*.

The USS *Bonefish* had never gone anywhere near the Philippines in 1945.

CHAPTER NINETEEN

Aboard the USS *Bonefish*
Sea of Japan

June 19, 1945

Ozzie's watch ended at 0400. He stopped outside the wardroom when he saw Colonel Miyata sitting ramrod straight in front of a cup of tea.

"Can't sleep, Colonel?" he said.

When the man looked up, the round lenses in his glasses reflected the overhead lighting. The opaque lenses made him look blind. "I was hoping to speak to you."

"Stick around a minute," Ozzie said.

He walked to his cabin and looked fore and aft before stepping inside. There was no privacy in a submarine. In the forward torpedo room, fourteen men slept over and around the sixteen torpedoes. Here in officers' country, curtains served as cabin doors. At least all the men he saw were sleeping, and with engine noise no one would overhear a conversation. Ozzie woke Lieutenant Flores, who rubbed his face, then staggered off to hit the latrine before going topsides for his watch. For the moment, Ozzie had the tiny cabin to himself.

He returned to the wardroom and tapped Colonel Miyata on the shoulder. "You can bring your tea if you want." He tipped his head toward the officers' quarters forward.

If anyone saw them, no one would think it odd that the OSS man was trying to buddy up with the Jap prisoner.

When he got to his cabin, he turned and motioned for Colonel Miyata to enter. The Japanese prince looked around for somewhere to sit, then perched on the edge of the bunk Flores had just exited.

Ozzie closed the curtain. The heavy cloth blocked some of the noise from outside the cabin.

He stood and looked down at the strange man in the white uniform. Lieutenant JG Harold Oswald Riley was at a crossroads, and he knew it. Even for him. In the last five years with the OSS, he had killed, even tortured men to death. He had decided what information would be passed on to his military higher-ups, and what would be subverted. His world had long ago stopped being a place of black and white, right and wrong.

He thought back to their last day before departing Guam. The skipper assembled the ship's company and read to them from the *Articles for the Government of the Navy*. The words outlined the penalties for such offenses as disobedience, attending to an enemy, desertion, mutiny. The penalty? Death. Ozzie had restrained himself from chuckling at the time. If that were the case, he thought, he'd be dead several times over.

But this? Making this kind of a deal with Hirohito's cousin? Even for him, this was big.

But this war had taught him over and over that the life of one man weighed little in the broad view. Ozzie was certain the men he ultimately answered to would be very interested in Golden Lily, and if he played this right, Ozzie could please them and enrich himself in the process.

"So Colonel Miyata, you want to get to the Philippines and you want this submarine to take you there."

The colonel's mouth stretched wide in a toothy grin. "You Americans are so direct. Yes. This is correct."

"And how do you propose I go about this?"

"I won't tell you your business, Lieutenant. I think you will come up with something. Especially if the reward is great."

"What kind of reward are you talking about?"

The man reached into the pocket of his jacket and brought out the gold prayer gau. "I told you that this contains the key to the map of all the Golden Lily locations. I can offer you gold and jewels."

"You'll give me that gold tube with the key in it if I figure out a way to turn this sub around and take you to the Philippines?"

Again the grin. "No, Lieutenant. But I will give you more gold than you have ever seen."

"I'd be committing mutiny—at least."

"General MacArthur has taken Manila. Yamashita cannot hold out forever in the mountains of northern Luzon. I know this. I hold the key, but the only complete map of Golden Lily is there in Luzon. My men are waiting for my return. I will pay you very well for this service. When we arrive, you can go ashore with me and when you rejoin the American Army in the Philippines, you can say you were taken prisoner."

The gold alone was tempting, but the opportunity to get his hands on that map and the key, that was what would make the operation worth it. There would be casualties, yes, but one thing he'd learned in this war was that life was cheap.

Once Colonel Miyata had slipped out the curtain and headed back to his bunk, Ozzie opened the compartment where he kept his things and pulled out a small canvas satchel. Inside were his sidearm in its holster, his one-time pad for encoding messages to be sent to headquarters, a pocketknife, cigarettes and matches, extra pencils, and, inside a metal box, his suicide pill. It was a small glass ampoule coated in rubber so that he could hold it in his cheek without fear of it breaking. In the event that capture was imminent, he was to crush the glass with his teeth. With all that he knew, his orders were to avoid capture by the Japanese at all cost.

Just before 0500 hours on June 19, Ozzie opened that box for the first time. He slipped the capsule into his pocket and headed for the radio room.

CHAPTER TWENTY

Napa Place
Bangkok, Thailand

November 17, 2012

When her meal arrived, Riley set her research aside and slipped her phone into the backpack hanging on her chair. She wanted to savor the enormous prawns in green curry sauce served with rice and an icy Singha beer. She thanked the young girl who was the only one working there and doing an excellent job of handling the entire dining room on her own. Riley's table was in the corner close to the kitchen door, but in a spot where she could have her back to the wall and keep her eye on everyone who entered. Thus far, she had not seen anyone questionable—most of the other diners were tourists—and she turned her attention to her meal. She had grown to love Thai food in the months since she had arrived, and she found the food at this small hotel restaurant was as good as any she had tasted in Phuket.

While she ate, she tried to sort through what she had learned about the *Bonefish* and what it meant. She supposed it was possible that during that March to May patrol in the South China Sea, the sub had detoured to the Philippines. But suppose it hadn't. Suppose Peewee or Irv or whoever he was, was lying to her. She certainly needed to consider the possibility and then, the question was, what was his motivation? He had given her an object that certainly appeared to be made of several ounces of solid gold. That's not something you'd hand over without a very good reason. The object contained some kind of odd scrolls inside that were not the typical contents for a Tibetan prayer gau. They were not in the Tibetan language, but rather appeared to be in some kind of code.

She and Cole had dealt with codes four years earlier when they were searching for the submarine *Surcouf*, but that certainly didn't make them cryptologists. But it was a connection, so she needed to think it through. Who knew about that? Obviously Theo—Cole's first mate—did, but he had disappeared as effectively as Cole. When Riley saw him last in Cherbourg, he told her he had become the head man for Full Fathom Five Maritime Explorations and the captain of the *Shadow Chaser*, formerly Cole's boat. Six months later, when Riley tried to contact Theo again, the organization had folded, and the boat was no longer listed as a federally documented boat.

So, if all the talk about the *Bonefish* was just a ruse to bring her to Bangkok, and what Peewee really wanted was to get someone to crack this code, why choose her? Where was the connection from Peewee to Riley the code breaker?

Riley's thoughts were brought back to the present when she saw movement in the hotel lobby. Though the lighting wasn't terrific, she recognized the peaked military cap on the short man's head. Peewee passed through the French doors and marched across the dining room to her table. Without a word, he pulled out a chair and sat next to her.

"So how did you find me?" she asked.

"Back at the market, I noticed a business card stuffed in a pocket of your backpack. I could read the name. Easy enough to find the address."

"You sure get around for an old guy in his nineties."

"I work at it, sweetheart."

"What were you doing at Wat Arun with that man—"

He interrupted her. "So you saw us. Listen. We don't have much time. The item I gave you earlier. I need it back."

"What?"

"Please." He rubbed his hands on his pants legs under the table as though to dry off wet palms. "Don't ask questions. I'm doing this to protect you. That man you saw me with? He is very dangerous. I didn't realize I would lead him to you, but I should have known. He's a hell of a tracker. I'm sorry." As soon as he stopped talking, his lips and tongue started working at his teeth.

"Irv, explain. You look frightened."

"This is no joke, sweetheart. Give it to me and you'll be out of this."

"So, it wasn't a gift meant for my father, and you never knew my grandfather." She grabbed her backpack off the back of her chair and reached inside.

"No, Riley, I knew Ozzie. But that's a long story and Benny's following me. I gave him the slip this afternoon, but my guess is he's no more than ten minutes behind me. *It is too late to prepare for danger when our enemies are upon us.* If I don't give him that thing back, he'll kill us both."

"Benny, huh. Kill us?" Riley rummaged around inside the pack. "You're serious?"

She pulled out her wallet and Peewee stopped working his teeth long enough to stare at her.

"I'm dead serious," he said. "Give it to me."

Riley threw several hundred baht onto the table, then zipped her pack closed and threaded her arms through the straps.

"Riley, this is no game. We've already used five minutes."

"I guess we shouldn't waste our lead time then." Riley pushed back her chair and stepped around the old man.

"You don't understand," he said.

"You're right. Explain it to me while we get out of here. I'm willing to listen." She opened the door to the kitchen. "After you."

"Oh, shit."

"Suit yourself," she said, and she stepped through the door.

The kitchen was tiny. The only person back there was an old woman who was standing over a stove. She looked up in surprise as Riley crossed toward the back door. Pausing, Riley stuck her head out and checked the alley in both directions. Nothing but trash cans as far as she could see—which wasn't far in the pitch-black night. From the corner of her eye, she saw the old woman's head swing back toward the dining room. Riley turned around and Peewee came trotting through the kitchen, looking like he was about to piss himself.

"Come on, old man," she said. "Follow me."

CHAPTER TWENTY-ONE

Mandarin Oriental Hotel
Bangkok, Thailand

November 17, 2012

Elijah swirled the ice in his glass and then drank the last sip of his watery scotch. The flimsy paper on the table in front of him was printed in multiple languages, but the print was tiny. There wasn't enough light at his table out on the Riverside Terrace to read the instructions for the little twenty-dollar disposable cell phone he'd purchased at a 7-Eleven on the way in from the airport. He signaled the waiter to bring him a second drink. When the man arrived, Elijah asked him if he could provide him with a flashlight so he could read the activation instructions for his phone.

"I would be happy to assist you with that if you would like, sir."

Elijah liked that about this hotel. They knew how to treat a man. And unlike some of the less exclusive hotels, they never made "cowboy" comments about the way he dressed.

"I'd appreciate that." He handed the man the phone and the cards with the pass codes for adding the minutes he had purchased.

The waiter walked over to the bar and held the phone under the light. He pressed buttons and checked the numbers on the cards.

Elijah liked the fact that the man stayed where he could keep an eye on him so he'd know if the waiter dropped the phone or something.

Unfortunately, that was his reality. He could not count on anyone to do things as well as he could do them himself. God alone knew what was happening back on the ranch with Caleb left to his own devices. Or take Belmonte. It made no difference that the man didn't even know who he really worked for or the stakes involved. He was a Filipino, so how could he understand what the Enterprise was truly all about? From the moment of her birth America has had her enemies. It was only once they found the gold here in the Philippines that men like Elijah had acquired the resources to fight those enemies without government interference. His predecessors had successfully fought the communist threat through all those Cold War years, and now the Enterprise would deal with the Global War on Terror just as well. Even if Belmonte couldn't appreciate *why*, resmelting the gold for export was his job, and the old man was the key to their new supply. Belmonte never should have let him escape.

After a couple of minutes, the waiter returned.

"Here you are, sir." He set the phone down on the table.

"Thanks. I'll let you know when I'm ready to order."

Elijah had selected this table because it was off in an isolated corner and there were no other diners nearby. He could have made this call from the room, but he wanted a drink and the opportunity to admire the great view of the river and the city skyline.

He liked Bangkok but he didn't get to come here often enough. Maybe he'd stick around this time once he'd finished his business here. Meet a nice Thai girl. He understood they were even better than the Filipinas when it came to knowing how to treat a man right. He deserved it after all he'd done for the Enterprise lately.

Before he'd left Baguio, Belmonte gave him Benny's Bangkok number, and Elijah had committed it to memory. He dialed the number and it only rang twice.

"Yeah?"

"Benny, it's Mr. Hawkes."

"Hey."

"So, what do you have to report?"

He didn't answer for several seconds. Elijah knew it wasn't going to be good. When the news was good, guys from the field couldn't wait to tell you.

"I saw the old man pass something off to a woman. She's American. I assume it's what you're looking for. No one gives me those details. The woman got away."

Elijah tried to insert a comment, but Benny kept right on talking.

"I got my hands on the old man and convinced him to take me to her. I don't trust him so I let him go, and I've been following him. He'll take me to her. I'm standing outside a hotel now and I'm certain they're both inside."

"Describe her."

"She's about five foot six, light brown hair down to her shoulders. Midthirties but still looks good—like an athlete. She can run."

Benny might find her attractive, but Elijah knew he wouldn't. American women disgusted him. So many of them were strident feminists and man-haters with ridiculous ideas about equality. They had no respect for the natural order that God intended. Not like Asian women. "How'd you let her get away in the first place?"

"I think she had help."

"Really." Elijah wondered if she represented competing buyers. "Any idea who she is?"

"Not yet. But I will."

"That's what I want to hear. You usually do better work than this."

"What do you want me to do when I have her in hand?"

"Bring both of them to me. I'm staying at the Oriental. And if she had help, we need to know who she's working for."

"Anything else?"

It was the way he said it, like he, Benny, was dismissing *him*.

Elijah clicked the red button to disconnect. One of these days he was going to teach that savage some manners.

CHAPTER TWENTY-TWO

Thanon Phra Arthit
Bangkok, Thailand

November 17, 2012

Benny heard the phone disconnect. He pulled it away from his ear and looked at the small screen. The man had just hung up without a word. He hated working with Hawkes. He'd only done it a couple of times before, but every time, he did weird shit like this. He had some inflated sense of self-importance, and he went out of his way to demand respect. Demanding it didn't work. You had to earn it.

He stood at the corner of Phra Arthit and a narrow alley where he could keep an eye on the door to the Napa Place hotel about a hundred meters away. Benny knew the old man he was after was over ninety years old. He must have a strong heart to have lived this long. Benny hoped it would stay strong so he would last awhile under Benny's attentions—when he got his hands on him. He intended to make the old guy suffer for what he did today. It was too bad that Hawkes wanted him to bring both the woman and the old man back to him alive. That made his job more difficult. But also more valuable.

When he'd found the men's room empty at Wat Arun, Benny had run for the docks. The ferry had just pulled out, and he saw the old man's cap in the middle of the Thai passengers. There was a long-tail boat tied to the far side of the dock, but the driver was nowhere to be seen. Benny jumped into the boat and began searching for how to start the engine himself. The driver, who was sitting under a tree on the temple grounds, shouted at him and came running down a ramp. By the time the boatman arrived and Benny had struck a deal for passage across the river, the ferry was almost to the dock on the opposite bank.

Benny had some luck on his side. On the far side of the river when he jumped out of the long-tail boat, there was a loudmouthed woman in the ticket booth who called out to him when he started asking people on the dock about the old man. She remembered (after he'd showed her one hundred baht) hearing Peewee asking if anyone had heard of a place called Napa House.

When Benny got to the street, he hailed a taxi. The first driver was very young, and he had never heard of Napa anything, but on his second try he found an old man who said he knew of a Napa Place. Benny told him to hurry.

Now he was wondering if the old man had beat him there or if he was still asking for directions. If they were in a hotel room, he couldn't go room to room opening doors. Then he had an idea, and he pulled out his cell phone. He got the number from the information service and dialed the hotel.

"Hello, I'm trying to find my sister. Do you have a Marguerite Riley registered there?"

"Just a moment please."

Benny stared down the narrow street and began inching his way closer to the front of the hotel. Every time the door opened, he tried to see inside.

The voice came back on the phone. "Hello? Are you still there?"

"I'm here," he said.

"Yes, your sister is registered at this hotel."

Benny picked up his pace. He reached for the door.

"I believe she is in the restaurant right now."

Benny clicked the phone off and thrust it into his jeans pocket. When he yanked open the door, he saw the double doors leading to the restaurant across the lobby. He ran across the lobby and stopped at the threshold. All the tables were occupied by diners except one. A single dirty plate and a half-finished glass of beer were all that was left. A slender girl was taking an order from a large family of European tourists. Benny grabbed her arm and she let out a cry of surprise.

Benny pointed at the empty table. "Was an American girl sitting there?"

She nodded her head.

"Where is she?"

The girl looked confused. She obviously had not seen her customer disappear.

The father of the family spoke in English with a heavy German accent. "They went into the kitchen."

He spun around to face the big blond man. "They?"

"Yes. An older American man joined her and they left a few minutes ago."

Benny didn't bother with thanks. He ran for the kitchen door.

CHAPTER TWENTY-THREE

Thanon Phra Arthit
Bangkok, Thailand

November 17, 2012

The first thing Riley did was make Peewee take his damn hat off. He pulled it off his head, folded it flat, and handed it to her. Without it, he could get lost even in a crowd of Thai people—with it, he was unmistakable.

"Don't call me old man," Peewee said. "I can keep up. I still go to the gym every day."

"Good," Riley said. "I'll remember that when we have to start running."

They were making their way up the dark alley, deeper in the Banglamphu district, away from the river and the main road along the waterfront. The narrow passage was filled with garbage from the back doors of all the shops and restaurants on either side. But the doors were all closed—not surprising, given the stench from the rotting food and the sound of scurrying feet, which she assumed belonged to rats. Riley still hadn't stopped to put her sandals on—something she wanted to do before she injured herself in the dark.

On the left, she saw a door that was propped open with a block of wood. She poked her head into the crack and saw an empty musical instrument shop. The lights were off, but the shop was lit from the neon sign outside the front window. Guitars and ukuleles hung from the ceiling, while drums and percussion instruments she did not recognize littered the floor.

"Come on. Inside." She swung the door wide and they stepped inside. Off to their right, she heard the sound of a toilet flushing. "Make sure the front door's open. I'm going to put my shoes on," she whispered.

It only took a couple of seconds to pull the sandals out of her backpack, but she had trouble sliding her dirty feet along the soles and under the straps.

Riley was bent over, tugging at the heel strap of her shoe, when she heard a door open close by in the darkness. She wiggled her toes to slide them in, and just as her heel at last slid through the strap the straw end of a broom whacked her across her back.

"Ow!"

Riley stood up and blocked the next blow from the broom. The lady was screeching in Thai at her. Holding her hands in the universal sign of surrender, Riley backed toward the front of the shop. She heard Peewee open the shop's front door behind her.

Then beyond the woman, close to the back of the shop, she saw movement. The back door swung inward and the light from the street lit the pale blue work shirt and reflected off the threads of silver in his hair.

"Go, Irv!"

Just as Riley made it out the door, she heard a loud *crack* as the broom handle hit something hard and the shop owner started screaming again.

This street wasn't much wider than the back alley, but it was full of nighttime tourists out to have a good time in Bangkok. While the crowd would slow them down, that was a good thing for Peewee. She heard him struggling to get his breath. But it would also slow the man behind them. Riley was certain the shopkeeper and her broom would not hold him back for long.

She turned left and herded Peewee past the restaurants with couches and burning tiki torches, the tattoo parlors, and the clothing stores selling knockoff designer labels, back down in the direction of the river. She couldn't have explained why, but the streets of the city seemed to pose a greater danger. She always sought refuge on the water.

They reached Thanon Phra Arthit sooner than she thought they would. It seemed they had not really gone so far in that dark, garbage-filled alley. The traffic was jam-packed and a skinny, white-gloved Thai traffic cop was trying to move the cars along. He held his palm up toward the pedestrians as he waved the cars along.

When Riley stepped off the curb in front of a bright pink taxi, the cop blew his whistle at her. Placing one hand on Peewee's shoulder, she steered him across the street with her. The taxi screeched to a stop and the driver poked his head out the window and began yelling at her in Thai. She continued at a brisk pace, dodging between and around vehicles as though she were deaf, despite the traffic cop who was blowing that damn whistle and sounding like a tea kettle in hell.

As she reached the far sidewalk, Riley heard a woman scream and risked a quick glance over her shoulder. The traffic cop had his wood baton out trying to stop the guy Peewee had called Benny. On the sidewalk behind them, a crowd was gathering around someone who was on the ground.

She grabbed Peewee's hand and said, "In here," and pulled him into the lobby of the Hotel New Siam Riverside. In the window she had noticed a sign about riverside dining, so she figured they could cut through and get off the street.

Irv's breaths were wheezing in and out and his shoulders slumped. She hoped he wasn't going to collapse on her. Yeah, he worked out, as he'd said, but still, he was ninety-three. Then again, there weren't many ninety-three-year-olds who would have made it this far.

The concierge stepped out from behind a podium with a broad smile on his face. "May I help—"

Riley brushed him aside and kept moving. Over her shoulder, she said, "My grandfather wants to see the river. Which way?"

The man pointed to the dark bar, and he began extolling the virtues of the menu in their restaurant. He didn't make it past the first course before they were out of earshot.

Behind the center bar, floor-to-ceiling windows showcased the colored lights of a bridge and the high-rise buildings on the opposite bank. There was a surprising amount of traffic out in the middle of the river.

At first she couldn't see any way out of the bar. Then, far over to her left, she saw a sliding glass door that stood open. When she got to the opening, she saw a broad cement deck and the turquoise water of a large swimming pool. Two handsome young men in hotel uniforms stood on either side of the door. When Riley and Peewee started through, the young men both put their arms out to stop them.

"Sorry, the swimming pool is closed."

"We don't want to swim. My grandfather wants—" Riley began to explain, but Peewee just bulldozed his way through the young men. He seemed to be counting on their courtesy toward their elders, and it was working. She hurried to catch up to him.

On the far side of the pool was a concrete wall about four feet high that separated the hotel pool deck from the riverfront. When Riley leaned over the wall to look down at the wooden public walkway, she saw that the planking was another five to six feet lower than the pool deck. A ten-foot drop wasn't a big deal for her, but for old bones, she wasn't so sure.

They both looked back at the windows that fronted on the pool deck. Across the bar, they had a clear view of the black-and-silver-haired man speaking to the concierge.

"Benny," Peewee whispered.

Riley saw Benny reach into that leather satchel he carried and pull out a long stick. She remembered him using it to hit people at the market.

Peewee said, "You go on. Jump." She turned to look at him and the expression on his face looked like a combination of fear and resignation. "I'll deal with Benny."

"I'm not leaving you, Irv."

"If you give me the prayer gau, he'll have no reason to hurt you."

Benny had started through the bar, but he hadn't seen them yet.

At the base of the wall at their feet, Riley noticed a long aluminum pole with a pool skimmer net on the end. She reached down and grabbed it. "Watch out, Irv." She swung it up and over the wall and rested the end against a solid wood piling on the far side of the walkway.

She laced the fingers of her hands together and lowered them in front of Peewee. "Put your hand on my shoulder and one foot here." He shook his head, but put a foot into her makeshift step. She hoisted him up until his butt slid onto the wall. "Swing your feet over to the other side," she said as she placed her palms on the wall and jumped up. In a second, she had vaulted over and landed on the boardwalk with a jolt. She had flexed her knees and managed not to fall. The aluminum pole had stopped a couple walking hand in hand. The man reached out to Riley and offered her a hand to steady herself.

"No, help him." She pointed at the old man above, who was wrapping one leg around the pole. The man grabbed Peewee's knees and eased him down the pole to the walkway. When the tourist let go of him, Peewee stood and smiled up at the couple, but Riley grabbed his hand and jerked before he had time to open his mouth. They dodged around another couple of tourists and began running down the walkway toward the ferry landing. Seconds later, she heard a loud thud as someone jumped onto the planks behind them.

At the ferry dock ahead, there were several clothing vendors as well as a small shop that sold sweets, cold drinks, and cigarettes. A cluster of tourists milled around looking at the goods as they waited for a boat. When Riley plunged into the middle of them, she thought she heard someone call her name.

She looked around. The ferries used the T end of the dock along the outside of the pier, but there were several boats tied to an inside finger pier off the main dock. One of them was a long-tail that looked like it had been there for a while. The other boat looked like a smaller ferryboat, with a forward helm station and a deck built over the upswept bow. A cover ran the length of the boat, blocking her view of the inside. The boat was backed into the dock and there was water chugging out the stern exhaust. There was a dark silhouette of a Thai man who stood at the stern rail waving at her with one hand as he held the dock with the other.

Running footsteps closed in on them from behind, and Peewee's breathing was audible over the sound of the boat's engine.

According to Peewee, the man behind them was a killer. From her one close-up look into the man's eyes, she believed it. She yanked and pulled him left. They ran down the dock.

"Riley!" the boatman called. His English was accented, but it was clearly her name. He waved again.

She turned down a short finger pier and pulled Peewee up even with her.

The boatman stepped back from the bulwark and reached out both arms. She gave Peewee a push. He fell into the man's arms and the man eased him down to a sitting position in the bottom of the boat. The boat wasn't tied to the dock and the gap was widening. Riley took several steps backward, then ran and jumped.

Her arms windmilled as she flew through the air. One foot caught on the side of the hull and she landed with a crash on her side in the bottom of the hull just aft of the boxlike structure that covered the engine and only a couple of feet from Peewee.

The boatman had disappeared forward and the engine was already revving up as the boat slid out onto the dark river.

From where she lay on the floorboards, she could see Benny standing on the dock. She started to sit up to see what he was doing. He was lifting that stick of his up to his face and putting it by his mouth.

"Get down!" Peewee shouted, and he threw himself across her upper body and flattened her.

She heard a thud.

The boat was gaining speed and the bow was rising out of the water.

"Get off me," she said.

Breathing hard, the old man pushed himself up and rolled off her. He sat up and pointed at the side of the engine cover. There was something sticking out of the wood.

Riley reached out to touch it, but Peewee's hand clamped onto her arm.

"Don't touch it," he said.

"What is it?"

Before Peewee could answer, she heard a familiar voice behind her.

"Nice landing, Magee."

She twisted around so fast she nearly knocked Peewee down again.

There, standing on the far side of the engine cover, was Cole Thatcher.

CHAPTER TWENTY-FOUR

Aboard the USS *Bonefish*
Sea of Japan

June 19, 1945

"Skipper! Oh my God! Skipper!"

Ozzie heard Westbrooke shouting, but waited several seconds listening to what the others were doing before he rose from his bunk. He stood in the doorway and tried to look over the crowd of men in the companionway. Up around the skipper's cabin someone was shouting for the medic and the man was pushing through the crowd from the forward torpedo room where he bunked.

"What's happening?" Ozzie asked the men who were craning their necks to see the skipper's cabin.

"Don't know," Ensign Bates said. "I think the skipper's sick."

Westbrooke yelled at the men to get back to work, but his voice sounded shaky and unsure. When the companionway cleared, Ozzie went to the door of the skipper's cabin. The door was closed. Ozzie knocked. The door opened and the medic slipped out, so Ozzie took the opportunity to slip in.

Inside he found Westbrooke hyperventilating, his eyes wide with fear. "My God, man, he's dead."

Ozzie looked at Commander Johnson's body. His mouth was open and his lips were curled back in a snarl. There was a bit of blue in his lips and hands, but not so as to be noticeable if one didn't know what to look for. Clearly, death had come hard. "What happened?"

"We don't know. The pharmacy mate said it could have been a heart attack, but the guy's only got a couple of weeks of first aid training. He tried to revive the old man, but it was pointless. Must have happened several hours ago. The body was already cool to the touch." Westbrooke bashed his fist against the bulkhead. "Shit, shit, shit."

"Pull yourself together, man. You're in charge now."

"Skipper wasn't sick or anything. How does something like this happen?"

"Listen, Westbrooke. You'll need to tell the men."

"Oh, God." He bent at the waist and buried his head in his arms. "I think I'm going to be sick." Westbrooke leaned over the tiny stainless-steel basin in the captain's cabin and vomited.

Afterward, neither man said a word. Westbrooke sat on his haunches and leaned against the bulkhead. Ozzie didn't think a man could look so white.

Westbrooke rubbed his hand across his mouth for the third or fourth time and then said, "What the hell are we going to do with him?"

"Burial at sea, I should think."

"No, can't. I'll have them put him in the freezer. We've eaten through half our rations. There should be room."

Ozzie frowned. He didn't like that idea, but there would be time to change those arrangements. "Fine. Westbrooke, I need to speak to you. Skipper received new orders last night." Ozzie went to the desk, where he had placed the message decrypt sheets several hours earlier. He handed the papers to Westbrooke. "Based on intelligence I got from our Japanese prisoner, we've been ordered to proceed to the Tsushima Strait and exit through the minefields there. Then we are to make way to that position off the Philippines." He pointed to the latitude and longitude on the message sheet. "And we're to maintain absolute radio silence."

"What about Operation Barney?"

"The other Hellcats are continuing north to La Pérouse Strait. We're the only boat on this mission. As you can see, it's top secret."

"What's this about?"

"I'm not at liberty to say."

Westbrooke stood up. "Christ, Ozzie, how the hell am I going to command this fucking submarine on some top-secret mission when I don't even know what we're doing?"

"Listen, Westbrooke, you've got me." He patted the younger man on the back. "Make me your executive officer. You can do that. I'll see you through this. Together, we'll manage, and I'll have you home driving that sports car before the summer's over."

CHAPTER TWENTY-FIVE

Chao Phraya River
Bangkok, Thailand

November 17, 2012

"Cole?"

The note of disbelief in her voice made Cole's chest constrict like a big fist was in there squeezing his heart and lungs. How could she not know him? Maybe she didn't recognize him now that he had grown a beard and the troubles of these past years had etched new wrinkles on his face.

She hadn't changed a bit. Of course, this wasn't the first time he'd seen her in the last four years, but he'd never been this close. She'd grown her hair out, and he wondered if it still smelled like citrus. He wanted to take her in his arms and explain everything, but there wasn't time.

Then Cole realized what was stuck in the wood engine box.

"Both of you, lie down, flat as you can make yourselves," he said to her and the old man. Cole stayed aft and squatted behind the engine cover. He raised his head just enough to peer over the top. He didn't like the way the pack on her back stuck up into the air, making it easy to spot her location. He wanted to go to her and protect her.

Ashore, a dark figure was running full tilt down the riverside walkway, knocking pedestrians aside.

Cole glanced up at his new Thai friend, Rak, who stood up at the helm forward. After getting Riley and the old man aboard, Rak had maneuvered the boat away from the dock, but they were still running close to the riverbank. Cole called out, "Faster, Rak! That guy on shore's gaining on us and he's got a weapon."

Rak turned his head to look, then Cole saw him flinch and reach up to the collar of his shirt. He yanked something out of the side of his neck and threw it into the river.

"Uh-oh," the old man said from where he lay next to Riley. "That's not good."

"What is it?" Cole asked.

"Blowpipe. And poison-tipped darts."

"What?" Riley started to sit up.

Cole dashed out, pushed her back down, then ducked back behind the engine compartment. Rak's knees had just given way, and he'd slumped over the wheel. The boat was starting a wide turn toward shore.

Cole saw that the walkway along the river had come to an end. The dark figure had stopped almost even with them, and he was lifting something to his face. Half-scared and half-fascinated, Cole watched. Then he heard a hiss as something passed through the air next to his right ear. He ducked down out of instinct, but he knew that he was just lucky the man had missed.

Where the shoreside walkway ended, a wooden wall stopped the tourists. The man had disappeared behind that wall as their boat executed the slow turn and closed with the shore. They had to be out of range of the blowpipe now, but their boat was heading straight for a collection of dark, ragged-looking shanties built on stilts over the river.

Cole rushed forward, eased Rak off the wheel, and spun it to put the ferryboat back on course. He heard their wake breaking against the rocks under the shanties. It had been close.

He smelled her before he saw her. She was there, right next to him, citrus scent and all. He looked all around. They'd left the man with the blowpipe far behind. But what had he done? Were there others coming? Focus, he told himself. One step at a time. Right now, he had to see to the driver.

"Riley. Can you take the wheel?"

He was thankful she stepped behind the helm without bombarding him with questions. He knew that would come later.

Cole felt Rak's neck and a weak pulse throbbed under his fingers. He hoisted the boat driver onto his shoulder and carried him back to the flat top of the box that covered the engine. The old man was using one of the seats along the side of the boat to pull himself upright. He grunted with effort, but waved Cole off.

"Don't worry about me. Take care of him first," the old guy said.

Cole set the unconscious man down on the warm wood where Rak had been working that afternoon. Cole had introduced himself and asked if he could rent the boat. The boatman had looked so happy to have a *farang* rent his boat for a couple of days.

The old guy made it to his feet and came over to help. He moved a collection of greasy engine parts aside so they could stretch out Rak's legs.

"So what do you know about this?" Cole asked. Then he realized that he didn't even know this guy's name. "I'm Cole Thatcher, by the way."

"Yeah, I know," the old guy said. He put his hand out. "My name's Irv Weinstein, but everybody calls me Peewee."

Cole turned away and didn't take the old man's hand. What did he mean, *Yeah, I know?* Other than Theo, nobody had called him by that name in four years. He'd used a string of aliases. Cole Thatcher was dead. And he intended for it to stay that way. But right now he had to deal with the situation at hand.

"So what's this poison we're dealing with?"

"It comes from a tree called the upas tree. They cook up the sap and tip their darts with it."

"They?"

"The Dayak. That guy's Benny Salim. He's from Borneo. Used to be headhunters, and Benny, he likes doing things the old-fashioned way."

"So, what's happening to this guy?"

"He's gonna die from heart failure unless you can get him to a hospital."

"Why is this guy after Riley?"

"How do you know she's the one he wants?"

Cole looked up at the old man. His voice sounded different all of a sudden. And the guy's eyes were dark and flat. Cole had the sense that he'd just got a peek past the man's cover. No doubt about it. He was one of *them.*

"Let's just say I keep an eye on her," Cole said. "And this isn't the first time I've seen that guy around."

Peewee turned away and Cole wondered why he'd answered a question with a question. Who was he? Cole only knew what Riley had written in that blog of hers. This old guy claimed to be a friend of her grandfather's. She had no idea what she was dealing with.

"Look," Cole said. "Watch him, and if he stops breathing, start CPR. You do know how to do that?"

"Yeah, go on." Peewee put two fingers on the man's throat to check his pulse. He pulled at the man's collar and leaned down to examine it.

"Looks like it passed through his shirt before it stuck him. That might save him."

Cole made his way forward to the helm. He had been concentrating on Rak, and he hadn't noticed that the scenery had changed. He was surprised to see that they were speeding up a canal and approaching a very low bridge.

"Riley, I want to explain—" he said when he reached her.

She held up an iPhone. "I checked the web for the closest hospital. Bumrungrad Hospital is up ahead off this canal. I called for an ambulance." She inclined her head toward the back of the boat. "How bad is he?"

"Your friend says he's likely to go into cardiac arrest at any minute."

She looked again at the glowing face of her phone. He recognized what was on the screen—it was a small nautical chart. She was using the phone's GPS to navigate their way to wherever she was taking them. Cole stared at her profile as she turned the wheel to pass a slower vessel on the narrow canal. She didn't return his gaze. He wanted to touch her, to hold her, to tell her how much he'd missed her, but it was like there was this wide, cold canyon separating them.

"Poor guy," she said. "This had nothing to do with him."

"Did you know that guy back there on the dock?"

She shook her head.

"He does." Cole inclined his head toward Peewee. "Your friend back there."

She glanced back at the old man. "Yeah, I know."

"You'd seen him before, too."

She nodded and turned the wheel to edge around a long-tail boat idling in the middle of the canal. "In the market today. That trunk. That was you?"

"Yeah."

She said nothing for several minutes. He kept trying out words in his head, but he couldn't find any that worked.

"Listen," she said at last. "We're going to be docking on the starboard side in a couple of minutes. You want to make sure there are lines or something?"

"Yeah." He meant to move immediately, but he paused, hoping she would look at him. When she didn't, he turned away and started for the starboard side of the boat.

"And Cole?"

He spun around.

"Once we get this guy into the ambulance, you've got a hell of a lot of explaining to do."

That fist in his chest went all white-knuckled on him.

CHAPTER TWENTY-SIX

Khlong Saen Saeb
Bangkok, Thailand

November 17, 2012

By the time the navigation program on Riley's phone told her she was approaching the Nana Nua ferry dock, Peewee had started doing CPR on the boat driver. No way she could miss the covered dock that was tucked up right next to the bridge. The flashing colored lights of the ambulance parked at the base of the bridge lit up the sides of the buildings on both sides of the street.

Cole was alive! She kept repeating it over and over to herself but she still wasn't sure she believed it. He was alive and she didn't know whether she wanted to kiss him or beat him to a bloody pulp.

When he'd started to talk to her, to explain or apologize, she couldn't deal with it. There was a man dying on this boat because of her. She'd met up with Peewee and started this chain of events, and now it was taking all her reserves of strength to continue to function. Her one priority was to get the boat driver to the hospital. She had to let her training take over. She could not afford to get emotional right now.

She came in to the dock a little too hot and threw it into reverse. Fortunately, the big diesel slowed her down and the boat nudged up against the black tires that lined the dock. Cole jumped ashore and tied off the lines while Riley helped the paramedics aboard with their gurney. These guys were good. It was only a matter of seconds before they had him on the board, breathing bag on his mouth and one attendant continuing the heart pumps as they carried him toward the ambulance. One of the guys spoke excellent English, and Cole followed them to the ambulance, telling them what little he knew about the fellow's identity.

"I hope he makes it," Peewee said.

She turned to face him. "You've got some explaining to do, too," she said.

"First I want my hat back."

Riley rolled her eyes. When she went to grab her backpack off the engine compartment, she saw the other poisonous dart stuck into the wood.

She tossed the backpack to Peewee and said, "Front zipper pocket." Then she grabbed an oily rag and pulled the dart out of the wood. "I'll be right back." She ran out to the ambulance and gave the dart to the attendant who was closing up the back door.

"This has got some of the poison on it," she said.

The man nodded, then stepped around to the front and climbed in. Then with a belch of exhaust and a screeching siren, they were gone.

She turned back and walked through the passage along the side of the bridge that led back out to the river. Cole was leaning against one of the supports that held the roof up. She paused for a minute to just look at him. There was nothing more she could do for that boat driver. Perhaps she could allow herself to let her guard down, to allow herself to feel.

He looked so different with the beard—and the last four years showed on his face. He had aged. He was still fit, though. If anything, he probably weighed less than he had back in the Caribbean. He was almost too thin.

She thought about the times she had imagined their first meeting. Not one of those scenarios included the stink of a Bangkok canal, the sound of horns honking and sirens, and a guy dying from being hit with a dart from a blowpipe.

But now, there he stood. She opened her mouth, wanting to say something to him, but no words came to her. She had trusted him so completely once, but so much had changed since then. How could he have lied to her for four years?

That was when she noticed who was missing.

"Irv's gone," she said.

Cole turned around and a small smile lifted one corner of his mouth. In spite of her worries, her body reacted as though he had touched her.

"Good riddance," he said. "I don't trust that guy."

"Oh, no." Riley ran over and jumped aboard the boat, but her backpack was right there on top of the engine box. The front pocket hung open and Irv's hat was gone. She felt a flush of panic as she reached into the other pocket and rummaged around. There. The Tibetan prayer gau was still there.

It wouldn't have been a crime if he had taken it. It was his, after all. She wasn't at all sure she believed the story about her grandfather wanting his son to have it. But she wanted it to be true.

So why hadn't he taken it? And why had he really given it to her in the first place?

Riley stepped off the boat and approached Cole. She should show him the trinket, as Irv had called it, and see what he thought about it. His head swung from right to left. He was watching the traffic passing on the bridge above them.

"There's something I want to show you," she said.

"Okay, but I feel like a sitting duck here."

She followed his eyes and saw all the pedestrians flowing across the bridge. "You're right. Irv said this Benny has an uncanny ability to track people. If Irv took off, we'd better get out of here, too."

"Then let's go." The engine was still running on the canal boat, and when Cole stepped aboard, she expected him to shut it down. Instead he turned and looked at her expectantly.

"You coming?"

"That's not our boat."

"The hell it isn't. I paid the man to charter his boat for twenty-four hours. It's my boat until, oh, about four o'clock tomorrow. Let's get the hell out of here. Throw off those lines."

Riley shrugged. She couldn't argue with that logic.

CHAPTER TWENTY-SEVEN

Saphan Taksin SkyTrain Station
Bangkok, Thailand

November 17, 2012

Elijah arrived at the SkyTrain station early and staked out his corner of the structure far from the turnstiles, where a few straggling passengers passed in and out of the arrivals and departure area. It was too late for the working people, and perhaps too early for the denizens of the night. He leaned on the concrete barrier and looked down on the pedestrians walking beneath the elevated platform. Assorted carts selling everything from barbecued skewers of meat and cold drinks to jewelry and T-shirts lined the sidewalk beneath him. The people hurried past, ignoring the bored-looking vendors, most of whom sat on upended plastic buckets and avoided making eye contact with their prospects.

After an exquisite meal at the Oriental, along with several whiskies, he felt sleepy and irked at getting called out for a meeting at this hour. Benny had better have good news for him.

"Mr. Hawkes?"

Elijah turned around and the moment he saw the hesitance in the man's manner, he knew it had all gone to shit.

"So you lost them again?"

"Yes, sir."

Elijah swung around and slammed the palm of his hand on the top of the concrete wall. "Fuck!" He dropped his head back as though he were staring at the roof over them, but in fact, what he was seeing was his longed-for interlude with a lovely little Thai girl slipping out of his grasp.

And he had so been looking forward to the next meeting in San Francisco, where he would announce his success with his methods for defeating gold fingerprinting. It would all be for naught if there wasn't any gold.

He turned and leveled his eyes on Benny. "How difficult could it be to find a ninety-three-year-old man and a woman?"

Benny said nothing.

"I should know better than to rely on some little Malay faggot with his fucking blowpipe."

Benny still didn't say a word. He stared back at Elijah.

So he was going for the inscrutable Oriental thing, was he? Elijah considered pulling out his boot knife to see if that would make the gook widen his eyes a little.

Elijah stepped in closer, then leaned in until their eyes were six inches apart. His voice was soft but tight. "The old man outrun you? The girl outsmart you?" He shoved Benny back against the railing and shouted, "Say something for yourself! What the fuck happened, asshole?"

"They had help."

"You're sure this time?"

Benny nodded.

Elijah stepped back. "What happened?"

"When I went into the hotel restaurant, they had already gone out the back door. Both of them. The old man and the girl. I followed them to the docks but before I could get to them, someone offered them a ride on a canal boat. They disappeared down the river."

"Did you shoot?"

He nodded. "I hit the driver."

"Any idea who this is who's helping them?"

Benny shook his head. "There were two of them on the boat. The driver and another man. The other one is the one who is helping. He's Caucasian."

"Does the old man know him?"

"I don't know."

"Where do you think they'll head?"

"That's why I asked to speak to you. It was no use following anymore. She is a sailor and she will want to return to her boat. It's down in Phuket. The old man, I don't know. I believe he will stay with her. I still don't know what he stole or what skin he's got in this game. It makes more sense for me to go to Phuket and intercept the girl there. Assuming she still has what you want."

Elijah looked out over the rooftops of the city at the crazy web of tangled electric and telephone lines. The man was right. There were dozens of ways they could travel to Phuket. Better to jump to the other end and not try to follow their trail. He nodded. "Okay."

"Mr. Hawkes, I could do a better job if I knew exactly what I was looking for."

Elijah sighed. Benny was getting out of line. He didn't know his place anymore. His part in this operation was strictly on a need-to-know basis. On the other hand, he didn't want Benny bringing back the wrong goods. And a tattooed heathen was expendable. In fact, that would give Elijah something to look forward to.

"The old man was working on certain documents. As usual, old stuff from the Second World War. They were found at a historical site in the Philippines. The first one was a typed letter written in Japanese. The second was a hand-drawn document with some pictograms. Both of these were wrapped in a piece of silk. The old man stole the lot, and now we're going to get them back."

"Yes, Mr. Hawkes."

"Good. Go down there and get our property back. These are old and fragile artifacts. Don't let them get damaged. The girl, you can get rid of, but bring the old man to me. We need him alive. Unfortunately, he's the only one who can figure out these damn Japanese codes."

CHAPTER TWENTY-EIGHT

The Chao Phraya River
Bangkok, Thailand

November 17, 2012

After Riley pushed the bow of the boat off the dock, Cole let the current do the rest to turn the boat around. He shoved up the throttle and headed back down to the river. There was plenty of traffic on the canal, even past nine. If anything, it seemed like the city was just coming to life.

She was right that it wouldn't take too much guessing for that guy to figure out where they'd headed—that they would try to get their man to a hospital. If Riley had figured out this was the closest hospital, someone else could do the same math. The only thing they had in their favor was that traffic on the streets of Bangkok was in a constant state of gridlock. Even if the guy took one of the motorbike taxis, he'd still be working his way across town.

When they started down the canal, Riley stayed at the back of the boat, looking at something in a piece of cloth. The damn canal boat had no autopilot so he couldn't leave the helm to go talk to her.

"What's that you're looking at?" he shouted over the noise of the engine.

She walked up to the bow and held out a small, tubelike container made of lacy gold filigree.

"That's beautiful. Where'd you get it?"

She didn't say anything right away. He waited.

When she did speak, it was to answer his question with one of her own. "How'd you know where to find me?"

Keeping his eyes on the narrow canal ahead, he reached into his pocket and pulled out a cheap disposable phone. "Theo called me. He's got an alert set so he knows every time you post something online. He told me you were going to a hotel called the Napa House down by the river. I decided to charter a boat in case I needed to make a fast getaway. I sure didn't expect to see you come running down the dock an hour later."

"How is Theo?"

Cole stared at the dark water of the canal ahead. Now wasn't the time. "He's fine."

"Where is he?"

"On the boat. In Subic Bay. That's in the Philippines."

"I used all my State Department connections to search for your boat. How'd you make her disappear?"

"Well, you wouldn't recognize her today. We made some big changes in Guatemala a few years ago."

"A new name, I guess."

He nodded. "We all got new names. And we fly under the Cayman Islands flag now."

"When I couldn't find either one of you, I really worried about Theo. I'm glad to hear you say he's okay."

He looked away from their course and stole a quick glance at her face. He'd heard something in her voice, and for a minute he thought maybe she knew somehow. But that was impossible.

"Theo's doing fine." He couldn't tell her the rest now. She'd see for herself—soon, he hoped, assuming he could talk her into going back to the Philippines with him. That he had to do. It was the only way to keep her safe now.

She walked to the side of the boat and looked up at the sky. She was still clutching that gold thing in her fist, but she hadn't offered to tell him about it. He felt as though she were slipping away from him.

When he'd first spoken to her, she'd been surprised, but still glad to see him. The longer this craziness went on, though, the longer she had to think about the last four years. He didn't blame her. He thought about how much he would have suffered if she'd made him believe she was dead. But he'd had to do it. He had to protect her. When he'd seen what they'd done to Theo, he knew it was no longer possible to contact her. And yet somehow, as stubbornly independent as she was, he had a feeling she wasn't going to buy that. Well, buy it or not, it was the truth.

And now it appeared as though what he had feared all along had happened. *They* had used her to find him.

When the canal ended at the Chao Phraya River, he turned right toward the sea. He had no charts, and while he knew it was quite a distance, he figured it was time they developed a plan. She'd had a navigation program on that little phone of hers with charts.

He looked over his shoulder. She was still standing with her back turned to him on the port side, bent forward at the waist, her forearms resting on the thick wood rail. The wind was blowing the hair back from her face. Even in the dim glow cast from the city lights she was a glass of ice water to a man dying of thirst. He wanted to stand there all night drinking in every detail of her.

But if these guys, both Peewee and Benny, worked for the men he thought they did—then he'd better stop mooning over the girl and come up with a plan.

"Riley, have you got charts and GPS on that phone of yours?"

She turned to look at him and smiled, and he almost forgot his name, much less a plan. She straightened up and strolled across the deck. She picked up her backpack, reached into a zippered pocket, and pulled out her phone.

"Where do you want to go?" she said.

"I want you to come back to the Philippines with me."

She smiled again. "Not in this boat. It's probably eighteen hundred miles down around Singapore and across the South China Sea."

"I like it when you smile."

"I assumed you were joking."

"I'm serious. Theo and I, we're on to something really big. This is bigger than those Skull and Bones Patriarchs, bigger than *Surcouf*. These guys have been behind false-flag attacks, buying elections, assassinations, Iran–Contra. You name some kind of black-ops deal in the last fifty years, and these guys were the ones."

She sighed. "Oh, Cole. You might look a bit different, but you haven't changed that much."

"Come back with me. There's no other way I can protect you now."

"Protect me?" She laughed. "Really?"

"You don't know what they're capable of."

"Cole, where the hell have you been for the last four years? I've done a pretty damn fine job of taking care of myself, thank you. I sailed my boat single-handed halfway around the world chasing after dead-end clues you left me, and suddenly you think I need you to protect me? Besides, I can't go to the Philippines. My boat's down in Phuket."

"Then let's go get it."

She stood with her arms crossed and didn't answer him.

He tried again. "We could sail it to Subic Bay together. It would take us what, a couple of weeks?"

"Yeah. But right now we're a long way from Phuket. What are we going to do with this boat?"

"At first I thought we'd just leave it at one of the ferry docks on the outskirts of Bangkok, but then I thought it through a little more."

"Yeah?"

"If we fly or take a train, you are going to have to show your passport."

"Right, but this is Thailand. It's not like they have supercomputers in their transportation industry here."

"Don't underestimate these guys, Riley."

"What guys? Cole, I've been standing over there at the rail trying to figure out what the hell is going on. Do you know who's behind this Benny guy? Because I sure don't. The last thirty-six hours or so have been . . . interesting, shall we say? A grandfather who was supposed to have gone missing in World War II supposedly showed up in the Philippines, a dead boyfriend turns up alive, and somebody is shooting poison darts at us with a blowpipe. And mixed up in the middle of it all is this ninety-three-year-old elf with loose dentures and an apparently endless supply of fortune-cookie wisdom. And now you're going to try to link what happened today to your crazy conspiracy theories. It's a lot to take in."

He nudged the helm a little to port to miss a tug with a long string of barges, then stroked the whiskers on his neck. "I know. And I know I have a lot of explaining to do."

She shot him a look that felt like she had laser vision. The kind of lasers they use to do surgery.

"But Riley, first, we'd better figure out where the hell we're going now. I say we take the river all the way to the Gulf of Thailand."

"What about that poor guy back in the hospital? I have to believe he'll live. How will he find his boat?"

"I've got his name. We'll call the hospital and leave a message explaining where his boat is. Let's pick a small place just south of the river mouth. Can you show me how to use that nav program?"

She sighed and pulled her lips in over her teeth. Then she rubbed the phone on her pants leg to polish the screen. She lifted it into his field of vision so he could watch the screen and the river at the same time.

"This app is called iNavX. I bought charts for all of Thailand. See that little blue boat on the screen? That's us. The GPS is amazingly accurate." She swiped her fingers across the screen. "See. This is how you zoom in and out. And at the top of the screen here, it shows that our speed over ground right now is 9.6 knots."

Cole took a sneak peek at her profile. Amazing. Ninety-nine percent of the women he knew would be flaying him up one side and down the other for deserting her. Riley was teaching him how to use her GPS. God, he loved her.

CHAPTER TWENTY-NINE

**Aboard the USS *Bonefish*
Sea of Japan**

June 19, 1945

Westbrooke made the announcement to the ship's company at 0900. Ozzie thought he would have problems with at least one of the four other officers. They all held the same rank, and while Ozzie had the most years of service, they were regular Navy submariners while he was Coast Guard on his first sub patrol. Turned out, though, that the others were all reservists, not career sailors, and not one of them was excited about getting any closer to Westbrooke. They took Ozzie's elevation to second in command with looks that said, *Better you than me.*

When Westbrooke set the boat's course for the Korean coastline along Tsushima Strait, there were raised eyebrows, but the new skipper settled it when he explained they had new orders for a top-secret mission. The thing that delighted Ozzie about these regular Navy boys was their allegiance to orders. If there were doubts, none were voiced.

In the late afternoon, Ozzie saw Ben and Colonel Miyata approaching from their quarters.

"Good afternoon, Lieutenant," Colonel Miyata said.

Ozzie nodded.

"I would like to express my sadness at the death of your captain," he said. Ozzie saw that hint of humor around the man's eyes.

They were standing only a few steps away from the captain's cabin.

"Perhaps we could find someplace to continue your questioning," Ozzie said.

The colonel nodded.

Ozzie turned and knocked on the bulkhead by the captain's door. He was almost certain Westbrooke was topsides, but he checked to make sure. They wouldn't be bothered in there. He opened the curtain and indicated that the two prisoners should join him. Ozzie closed the curtain and pointed to the bunk. "Sit," he said.

The cabin was barely six feet long. Ozzie paced the short section of floor. Neither Ben nor the prince said a word.

Finally Ozzie spoke. "I assume you are aware we have changed course."

"Lieutenant, I know nothing about the operations of this ship."

Ozzie barked a laugh. "Right. You know, Colonel Miyata, we are not as different as you might think."

The eyes behind the lenses opened wider. "You surprise me with your insight."

"The way I see it, we have each decided to use the other for our own purposes."

"It is possible you are correct, Lieutenant."

"So, what I need to know is, what are your purposes? What are you really up to?"

"I am just a sailor in this war like you are, and I am trying to get back to my men."

"Bullshit. There's more to it than that."

"It is as I told you. I am charged with Golden Lily. We have completed many of our projects, but the last one was not yet complete when I had to return to Japan. Just as it is very difficult to get our treasure back to our homeland, it is equally difficult for me to get myself back to the Philippines."

"That's why you were on a *maru* cargo vessel."

"Yes, by keeping close to the Korean and Chinese coasts, we hoped to make Hong Kong and then cross to the Philippines from there. We did not expect an attack here in the Sea of Japan. However, I have come to realize the potential benefit of my current situation."

Ozzie nodded. "A US submarine is one of the best and fastest ways for you to get back to your post." Ozzie had calculated that it would take them roughly four days to get to the coast of northern Luzon.

"Indeed."

"So, tell me more about these projects of yours. These Golden Lily caves."

When Colonel Miyata began to talk freely about the wonders he had buried underground, Ozzie knew the prince had marked him for death. Otherwise he would not be speaking so freely.

"So how many of these underground sites have you built?"

"Throughout the Philippines, there are one hundred and seventy-five sites."

"You're kidding. So many?"

"Yes, we had so much material. This represents two years of work and hundreds of thousands of man-hours of engineers and prison laborers. The majority are on the island of Luzon in the mountains known as the Cordillera."

"What kind of material are you talking about?"

"Much of it is gold bullion, but there are other treasures as well. Gems, priceless artifacts, artworks. But as I said, Lieutenant, if you do not have the locations, you will not find them."

"But you say there is a map."

"Yes, in order to prevent anyone outside the royal family from knowing the locations of these sites, the map and the key to deciphering the map have not been kept at the same location. However, now that the Americans are fighting my countrymen and pushing them back into the mountains, there is a real concern that the Philippines will fall into American hands. I must retrieve the map. If you return me to the Philippines, I will pay you very well—in gold."

"That's your offer?"

"I know you want more. You think you can get your hands on the map and the key. I would advise you to be satisfied with the gold, Lieutenant. The gold and your life."

"That's daring talk for a prisoner."

Colonel Miyata smiled that ghoulish smile. "Yes, but that situation could change."

"You're quite the optimist."

"I know my people."

"Speaking of which, where are we taking you, exactly? I gave Westbrooke some general coordinates, but I need—"

"I will give you the coordinates."

Ozzie took out his notebook and pencil and handed them to the colonel. The man wrote the latitude and longitude and handed the book back to Ozzie.

"Is this a port?"

Colonel Miyata showed all his teeth this time in a broad smile. "It is one we have made. You will see."

Ozzie opened the door. The little man stood and Ben followed him out. At the door, the colonel paused. "It's been a pleasure speaking to you, Lieutenant."

Watching the two of them return to their bunk area, Ozzie wondered, not for the first time, if the whole thing was a hoax. Did Golden Lily exist? Even if it was only a remote possibility that there were one hundred and seventy-five caves full of treasure, Ozzie knew the men he worked for would be pleased with his initiative.

CHAPTER THIRTY

Aboard the Ferryboat
Gulf of Thailand

November 18, 2012

Riley hadn't seen another vessel in a couple of hours, not since they'd left the mouth of the river and cruised out into the Gulf of Thailand. She checked her watch. It was past four in the morning. She hadn't slept all night. Hadn't slept much on the train the night before, either. This had been one of the longest days of her life. Although technically it was Sunday morning, it wouldn't feel like a new day until the sun came up.

She'd spent the first few hours stretched out on one of the benches at the stern of the boat watching the lights pass by on the banks of the river and trying to sleep. She couldn't silence her mind. Not that her thoughts were coherent. She'd spent four years hoping to find him alive and now that she had, she didn't know what to say to him. Maybe four years was just too long. Or maybe a part of her knew that if they did get back together, she'd have to tell him what she'd learned about that day in Lima and her part in it all.

Finally she'd walked forward and told Cole she would take the helm, and he should try to get some sleep. He'd spread out on the box over the engine compartment and then nodded right off like a good seaman. She envied him that. Sleeping while under way on overnight passages was always a struggle for her. On her single-handed crossings, she got most of her sleep during the daylight hours.

Cole had to know she was waiting to hear his story. And she figured he wasn't exactly eager for the opportunity. Why hadn't he contacted her? So much time had passed, and she had so many questions. Or maybe he knew more about *her* past than he was letting on. Perhaps the reason he'd stayed away was because he knew the truth about Lima, and now he was finding it difficult to tell her so.

After going over the charts on her iPhone a few hours earlier, they had decided to head for the Mae Klong River. If they kept this speed up, they should arrive around sunup. There were a few fishing boats and squid boats out on the gulf, but nothing that had come within half a mile of them. Keeping a lookout wasn't hard, just boring. She wished this boat had an autopilot. She wanted to go back and watch him sleep.

"Hey, Magee."

She jumped. She hadn't heard him approach.

"How are you doing?" He leaned on the dash at the front of the boat and looked out over the bow. They were running with the wind and there wasn't much breeze over the boat.

"Too much time to think on night watches," she said.

"Yeah. I know what you mean."

They both stared out into the black night. There was no moon and they were too far away from land to see any lights there. The sky was ablaze with stars. She was awkward with him, while he looked rested and relaxed.

"Riley, remember that first time you and I sailed your boat at night around the island down in the Saintes?"

She couldn't hold the smile back. She loved hearing him speak her name. "Yeah. We saw dolphins."

"I knew that night that I was falling in love with you."

She didn't know what to say to that. They were on a boat alone at sea, and he hadn't touched her. She felt her stomach muscles tense. Maybe now he would tell her why he had kept his distance all these years.

"So what changed?"

His head whipped around and the worry lines in his forehead were etched deep. "Nothing changed." Then he looked away. "Well, I didn't change. The world did."

"Cole, where the hell have you been for the last four years?"

She hated his silence. After what felt like forever, he said, "I had to keep you safe."

She didn't realize she'd been holding her breath until she heard the long exhale. "That was you that day in Cherbourg, wasn't it? Dressed up like a homeless Vietnam vet?"

One corner of his mouth turned up, and she wished she could see the dimple beneath the beard. "You didn't recognize me. It was a hell of a disguise to fool you."

He made it sound like a game. It hadn't seemed fun to her. "I followed the clues. I went back to my boat and took off down to Puerto La Cruz in Venezuela. From there to the Cayman Islands. I crossed the Pacific looking for the Dragon's Triangle. Even after four years, *you* are what brought me to Thailand. You gave me that damned recording. Let me know you were alive, and then it was like you broke your promise." She felt her chin trembling, and she bit her lower lip to regain control. "I solved all the puzzles you gave me, but you weren't there."

"I know. I'm sorry."

She turned her back to him. It was his turn now. The silence dragged on, and she could feel him watching her. She kept her eyes forward on the inky blackness beyond the glow of the boat's red and green running lights.

"It's hard to know where to start."

She nodded, but said nothing.

"I still don't know how I got out of that sub. I remember putting the box I'd found into the cargo net on the *Enigma*. While I was out of sight of the video camera, I opened the box. The lock had rusted and it broke after one punch from my fist. I grabbed the pouch and stuffed it inside my wetsuit. I checked my dive computer, and I knew I was running short on time. Then when I was back in front of the video cam, I felt the sub shudder and something hit me. I remember trying to find the camera again and signing to you as the water got all cloudy. I partially inflated my buoyancy compensator, and then that's it. Nothing more."

She turned around and the look on his face made her chest ache. "I saw your sign," she said. She held up her hand with the thumb and pinkie raised in the sign for *I love you*.

He looked at her hand and then his eyes locked on hers. She rocked back on her heels, then turned away.

"I washed up on the beach at Îles de la Petite Terre," he said. "I guess I must have swum part of it. Like I said, I don't remember."

He had been so close by. "Just like Henri Michaut did when *Surcouf* first sank. I should have thought of that. I should have searched there."

"No. I wasn't there long. Our old friend Henri had sent some of his family to pretend they were fishing off Petite Terre while we searched for the *Surcouf*. They saw me crawl onto the beach. I couldn't remember anything. They helped me into their boat and took me to the Princess Margaret Hospital in Dominica."

"I called all the area hospitals."

"They had me admitted under a false name. You remember how paranoid Henri was. There was a hyperbaric chamber there. The doctor said in addition to decompression sickness, I had a severe concussion. He told me the amnesia wasn't unusual with that kind of traumatic brain injury and diving accident. A few days later when I started remembering about the *Surcouf* and you and Theo, Henri told me about what had happened. There'd been a boat collision, a volcanic eruption on Montserrat, and an earthquake—hell of a trifecta. Then he said the authorities in Guadeloupe had declared me dead."

"And you decided to just go with that." *Without giving me a second thought.*

He winced, catching her tone. "No, it wasn't like that."

"Like what? What did I say?"

"Riley, I'm sorry. I know I've caused you pain. But it was about what I'd found. When they got me to the hospital and stripped me, they found the diplomatic bag I'd tucked inside my wetsuit. It was rubberized canvas and weighted with lead—but the documents inside were dry."

"Operation Magic."

"That's right. The hospital staff gave it to Michaut's granddaughter, and we opened it when I was released. I did a little research on the web while I was recuperating in Dominica, and what I discovered scared the crap out of me. I knew there were men out there who would kill for what was in those documents. I wanted to keep you safe."

"You were protecting me."

"Right! And I have been ever since. I've kept an eye on you. That disguise in Cherbourg? That wasn't the only time. I had to see you."

"So, all those times when I thought I was going crazy, when I thought I saw you—sometimes I was right?"

He grinned. "Nah, you never spotted me. I mean, *they* never found me either, so don't feel bad."

Riley expelled her breath like something between a cough and a groan. She shook her head. "So who the hell appointed you my protector? Why would I trust you with my life when you couldn't trust me with yours?" She handed him her iPhone. "Here are the charts. Here's the wheel." She stepped back and he grabbed the helm. "It's your watch. I'm going to get some sleep."

She heard him calling her name as she walked aft to the engine cover and stretched out. She didn't answer.

CHAPTER THIRTY-ONE

Sea Gypsy Village
Phuket, Thailand

November 18, 2012

Benny paid the cabdriver the ridiculous fare for the trip from the Phuket airport to the Sea Gypsy Village south of Ao Chalong. When the vehicle pulled away, he joined the tourists strolling down the road browsing the fish market stalls selling brightly colored reef fish, prawns, spotted crabs, squid, and green mussels. In clear plastic bags shelled oysters, clams, and dozens of other sorts of shellfish floated in seawater like flesh-filled water balloons displayed atop plastic bins filled with ice. Shoppers haggled in loud voices and tourists tried on shell necklaces.

Benny's destination was on the other side of the touristy section of the village, so he walked at a brisk pace. Where the road plunged down the hill to sea level, a mud and sand beach was crisscrossed with the stern lines of the dozens of wooden fishing boats anchored just a few feet offshore, their upturned prows pointing out to the bay. The road turned to dirt at the bottom of the hill and there under the trees, the boat builders worked repairing old leaking planks and crafting new vessels. They applied new coats of brilliant-colored paint and sparkling clear varnish.

His people, the Dayak, were waterborne folk. They had lived on rivers before immigrating to the city, and boatbuilding was taught from one generation to the next. One group from his clan had emigrated and settled here in Phuket. They now built boats in the distinctive Thai style. As he walked down the hill, he saw the characteristic red headband and the tattoos covering the back and arms of the man squatting next to a half-finished hull. One of the other workers nodded at his clansman, then pointed at Benny.

The man stood and turned. Benny saw the hand-rolled marijuana cigarette dangling from his lip. The man smiled, lips tight, eyes squinting, and the end of the cigarette flared red.

"Good to see you, Iban," Benny said.

"And you, Benjamin."

They shook hands.

Benny explained what he needed and Iban took him down to the water's edge to show him a selection of boats.

"I will need to anchor, perhaps for a few days, so I would like some nets to sleep on and a tarp. If you could have one of the women bring me two days' food, I will pay."

Iban shouted orders to a young boy playing with the shavings under the hull. The boy took off running toward the village.

A couple of hours later, Benny was motoring north in a bright blue fishing boat, the bow piled high with provisions. Iban's woman had sent enough food for him to live for a week. He hoped it wouldn't take that long. In the stern of the boat was a small charcoal cooker. The engine was an air-cooled automotive engine on a pivot with the prop at the end of a long shaft. Iban had shown him how to operate it. Benny preferred the old ways. Back home when he was a boy and they lived with his grandfather, his people poled their canoes on the river. He recognized the necessity of the big engine but he didn't like the noise and smell, and he did not feel proficient in its use.

His contact at the Enterprise had been able to provide him with the name of the woman's boat and a general description, but there were many white sailboats anchored off the Ao Chalong Yacht Club. He had a tourist map of the area and the yacht club was marked on the shore. That was where the old man had contacted her. He would watch for her to arrive from that direction once he located the boat.

Benny worked out a search pattern and traveled throughout the anchorage for thirty minutes before finding the one boat with the name *Bonefish* on the transom. Homeport Annapolis, Maryland.

He throttled the engine down and approached slowly. The sun had just set, but there was still enough light for him to see that the sailboat was boarded up and padlocked. He had beat her here, and that pleased him. He motored several hundred feet away from her boat and dropped his anchor over the side. He opened up the bundle of provisions to discover what he would eat for his evening meal, then settled down to wait for the woman to return to her boat.

CHAPTER THIRTY-TWO

Ao Chalong Pier
Phuket, Thailand

November 18, 2012

When the taxi dropped them off at the curb, Riley knew they were going to have to talk at some point. From the time they'd tied up their borrowed boat before dawn on the Mae Klong River to their all-day ordeal on buses, they had spoken only when necessary. The tension between them was so palpable, even the usually friendly Thai people on the express bus had whispered around them. But the time for talk would come later. For now, she simply wanted to make sure her boat was safe.

She hiked her pack onto her back. "Come on. We can see my boat from the end of the pier."

Cole was carrying a small duffel bag he had collected when they left the Bangkok canal boat on the Klong River. He tossed it over his shoulder and looked up and down the street. "I don't like it, Riley. It wouldn't be difficult for them to locate your boat. That guy with the blowgun could have flown down. He could be standing around here anywhere waiting for us."

"If he knows that my boat is here, he probably knows that my dinghy is at the Ao Chalong Yacht Club. That's way up there." She pointed up the coast. "My boat is what he would focus on. I don't think anyone would be looking for us on the pier."

"That's a marina right there."

"True, but there aren't many cruising boats in it. The cruising boats are in the anchorage."

"I think you might be attributing too much local knowledge to these guys."

"Look, Cole, the fact is, they could be anywhere. I can't let that fear paralyze me. Yeah, we can take some precautions, but a good first step is to go out on that pier and take a look at my boat while there's still enough light."

He looked around the streets. She could see that he really didn't want to give in on this. "Okay," he said. "Let's go."

When they moved out into the open area at the base of the pier, Cole kept turning around so he could watch the restaurant and the shops along the waterfront. She thought it was very unlikely that anyone would be waiting here, but she knew better than to try to stop Cole from doing his paranoid thing, his "protecting her" thing. She ignored him. She just wanted to see if there were any strange boats anchored too close to hers.

Before they were halfway out the pier she was able to spot her boat in the crowded anchorage, but what really drew her attention was a fishing boat that seemed to be milling about the cruising boats. It was an unusual sight. They usually kept clear of the yachts. She saw the boat reach the far edge of the anchored boats, and instead of continuing on it turned around and started back through the fleet. She saw him pass the huge *Merlin II*, the gold-plated racing sailboat that Billy Barber lived on. She wondered if Billy was aboard right then, but already it seemed like she had known him in another life.

When the fishing boat approached her boat, *Bonefish*, it slowed.

"Cole, look out there." She reached over his shoulder and pointed so he could follow her finger. She felt the jolt she always did when he touched her hand. "See that open Thai fishing boat way out there?"

"Yeah. Wait. That white sailboat he's circling—"

"Uh-huh, that's mine."

"I'd need binoculars to see the guy from here, but what do you want to bet that's our friend with the blowpipe?"

"Yeah, that's my guess, too."

They continued walking and watched as the boat motored away from the *Bonefish* around a big catamaran, then doubled back toward the far side of *Merlin II*. The small figure in the boat moved up forward.

"Looks like he's anchoring right there," Cole said.

"Shit," Riley said. "I was hoping to sleep in my own bunk tonight."

"I don't think that would be a good idea."

CHAPTER THIRTY-THREE

**Ao Chalong
Phuket, Thailand**

November 18, 2012

They took a table in the rear of the bar owned by her Aussie friend where they could keep a close eye on the entrance but where the other patrons couldn't eavesdrop on their conversation. After the waitress set down their frosty Singha beers, they sat in silence.

Finally when his beer was nearly gone, Cole said, "I have so much to tell you, I don't know where to begin."

Riley nodded. "How about starting with the Philippines. What are you doing there?"

He examined her face. Those intelligent gray eyes were studying him. So that was how this was going to go. He was being interrogated. "It started with what was in that pouch I told you about. From the *Surcouf.* Remember when Henri said he'd seen those papers?"

"Yeah," she said. "He saw the words 'Operation Magic.'"

"That's right. The documents were decrypts of intercepted Japanese messages from November and December of 1942. Some were done by the Brits, but most were by the American naval code-breaker division called OP-20-G. Operation Magic had to do with breaking the Japanese military code JN-25. Riley, the guy who decoded those messages knew about the Japanese plan to bomb Pearl Harbor and didn't pass the information on. He kept quiet and let all those men die."

"Oh my God."

"Yeah. There've been all sorts of theories about Pearl Harbor, but there I was on Dominica holding the actual messages in my hands. Proof that they had known about the attack and let it happen out of pure greed. All the deciphered intercepts had the same initials on them: A. K. They had numbers, too, and I worked out that the numbering corresponded to the station that picked up the signal. It took some work, but I finally connected those numbers to Station CAST on Corregidor."

Riley's head jerked up. "Corregidor?"

"Yeah. It's an island in the Philippines inside Manila Harbor."

"I know. It's just that's the second time I've heard Corregidor mentioned today."

"What?"

She waved her hand in the air. "I'll tell you later. You finish."

"Okay." He would make sure she did explain later. "Like I said, I matched those initials to this guy, Andrew Ketcham. He was a super-smart mathematician who graduated from Yale."

Riley froze, her beer bottle halfway to her mouth. "Aw geez, not again."

"Yeah, that got my attention, too. I'm not as good at this online research stuff as Theo is, but I found a list of all the members of Skull and Bones up to the 1990s, and I found Ketcham in the class of thirty-eight."

Riley sat back in her chair. "So that's why Diggory wanted to get his hands on those documents from the *Surcouf*. He knew what kind of power that proof would give him, along with a direct link to Skull and Bones."

"Yeah. And I knew what the Patriarchs would do if they knew *I'd* found those documents. Eisenhower had warned America about the rise of the military–industrial complex after the war, but I had proof they had engineered our entry into that war. I *had* to stay dead, Riley. Can you see that? I knew I was in way over my head, and I just couldn't bring you into it. I wasn't sure I could keep myself alive. But I also knew I couldn't do it alone. That was when I made a very tough decision—I contacted Theo. It was selfish and I'm to blame for everything that's happened since."

"What do you mean?"

He waved his hand and took a long slug of beer. He wiped his mouth on the back of his hand. "I'm getting ahead of myself. I'll get to that in a minute. Since Dominica was Theo's home, we knew no one would think it odd when he brought *Shadow Chaser* down to Scotts Head Bay. We used his family's connections in the government of Dominica to get those documents into the right hands in the US. And Theo and I set about designing a new and better ROV for deep-water salvage while learning everything we could about Andrew Ketcham."

"I can't believe you were able to get deep enough to reach the *Surcouf.*"

"We didn't get all the gold. But we got enough to finance the next stage."

"What do you mean?"

"I wanted my life back. I wanted to be able to contact you, to be with you. I thought all I had to do was bring all these secrets out into the light, and then there would be no more reason for anyone to want me or you dead."

Riley's face softened. "Still battling those windmills, huh?"

"When I made this plan I had no idea how far the tentacles of this octopus reached. I might have done things differently had I known. Scratch that. I *know* I would have."

She smiled and lowered her eyes.

"You think I'm exaggerating, don't you? You think I'm always seeing conspiracies everywhere. I was right about the *Surcouf*, wasn't I?"

"Yes, but Cole, it's not that I don't believe you, but I'm having trouble wrapping my head around the idea that the tentacles of your so-called octopus have reached us here in Thailand. That what is happening now is somehow connected to the *Surcouf*."

"Riley, finding the *Surcouf* wasn't the end of that story. I needed to know more about how those decrypts got on that sub in the first place. Once I had Theo's help we put together a better picture of the life of Andrew Ketcham. We found out that while the US claims they didn't break the JN-25 code until much later, there was our mathematical wonder boy in Corregidor reading all the messages between Tokyo and Yamamoto. Messages that never made it to anyone else in the government. Henri said while he was on *Surcouf*, they met a Canadian frigate at sea and that diplomatic pouch was transferred to the Brit officer on the *Surcouf*. Henri said the Brit Woolsey had planned to take those message intercepts to New Haven."

"To the Patriarchs," she said.

"Yeah. So how did they get on that Canadian boat? It wasn't Ketcham. He went to Australia with MacArthur when the Japanese took the Philippines."

"So the Patriarchs had a network."

"Then get this. After the war most of those code-breaker guys went to work for the NSA. But not Ketcham. He went back to the Philippines, where he worked under Captain Edward G. Lansdale, a guy who was quite the spook during the postwar years. Then Ketcham suddenly died in a car crash in the Philippines in 1948."

"What's so weird about that?"

"Lansdale had nothing to do with Skull and Bones or the Patriarchs, near as I could tell, so I started looking at what he was into. The deeper I dug, the more I started to see that the Patriarchs were just one small group in a much larger structure. It's like this worldwide web of loosely connected covert extreme right-wing organizations whose mandate seems to be to fight all enemies of capitalism—whether that's in the form of communists or Muslim extremists. The guys working in the Philippines are part of a PIO—a private intelligence organization. They fancy themselves a sort of shadow CIA and they call themselves the Enterprise."

"Shadow CIA called the Enterprise? This does get wilder the more you talk."

He shrugged. "Maybe. But you haven't heard the best part. Have you ever heard of the Legend of Yamashita's Gold?"

CHAPTER THIRTY-FOUR

Aboard the USS *Bonefish*
Sea of Japan

June 21, 1945

After the navigator's evening star sights showed them to be ten miles from the minefields in Tsushima Strait, the new skipper issued the order for them to submerge. Afterward, Westbrooke asked Ozzie to meet him in the wardroom. They each grabbed a cup of coffee and sat.

"It's going to be a hell of a night," Westbrooke said.

"We made it in this way. We'll make it out."

"We're taking the western channel. Last time through here, the skipper took us through at a keel depth of one hundred twenty feet. He reckoned the deepest they set their mines was seventy-five feet, but the anchor cables go all the way to the bottom. Still, since it worked for us last time, I'm planning to do the same thing. We threaded our way between the cables, but at least didn't see a single mine at that depth."

Ozzie had not taken the con during their last transit. That task had fallen only to the skipper and his executive officer, along with the secondary officers of the deck. "And we hope they haven't moved any of the mines while we've been playing in the Sea of Japan."

"Exactly. So we can't even go up to periscope depth."

"It would be a helluva thing to set off a mine with the periscope."

"Lieutenant Flores will be your assistant officer of the deck. I know you don't have much experience in submarines."

"I'll be fine," Ozzie said. "Nothing to worry about. Like you said, last time, we didn't even come close to a mine."

Westbrooke looked down into his coffee. "I wish I felt as confident as you."

"Look, man, you can't let the men see your doubts."

"I know." Westbrooke looked up at the overhead, then closed his eyes and rubbed his palm across his mouth. "I just can't get over my bad luck. I get the chance to serve under one of the best skippers in submarines, and he suddenly dies of a heart attack."

"Some men would see the opportunity to take command as good luck."

Westbrooke sat up straighter. "Right."

Ozzie noted that he didn't sound convinced.

Westbrooke stood the first watch, so when Ozzie came on at midnight, he walked into a tense conning tower. They'd been traveling at three knots for four hours, knowing that at any moment, the sub could come in contact with a spiked mine. One touch and they would all be dead. The FMS sonar rang out with a bell-like sound every time it made contact with a fish or a rock. Since the transducer was on the bottom of the hull, it made contact with many different objects. While the crew had spent several months training in the use of the equipment, and learning to recognize the difference between the sound and the appearance on screen of mines as opposed to fish, it was still very new and untested equipment. He could tell by looking at the faces of the men in the control room that they had lost their faith in the sonar.

Ozzie remembered how different the situation had been when they had passed through the minefields the first time. For the most part, the men aboard the USS *Bonefish* were, like him, battle-hardened sailors. For months they had lived day to day with the knowledge that each day could be their last. They'd learned not to focus on that—instead they did their duty, knowing that it was out of their hands, and put their trust in their officers. They believed in the sonar because their captain did.

That situation had changed with the loss of their skipper. They didn't trust Ozzie and Westbrooke the way they had trusted Commander Johnson. Ozzie hoped they could all hold it together long enough to get him to the Philippines—he only wanted this sub for the ride that far. He intended to leave them there, but for now, he had to make sure they arrived.

For the first couple of hours of Ozzie's watch, they saw nothing. No bells rang out. But just past 0200 hours all that changed. The bell sounded loud in the early-morning quiet. Ozzie glanced at the screen and saw the mine about one point off the port bow.

"Right full rudder!" he said. He kept his voice calm. He didn't need to shout. The helmsman had plenty of motivation to be quick about it.

Even if Ozzie had not wanted the whole ship to witness this drama, it would not have been possible. It was tradition in submarines to have a talker stationed in the conning tower with a microphone to report to the rest of the ship just exactly what was going on. The talker described the situation.

"The contact on the screen looks like a big blob. The bow is starting to swing away. The blob is out of sight now alongside."

The men in the forward compartments heard it first. It sounded like a banshee. The loud screech of metal on metal traveled back through the submarine as the anchor cable for the mine they had just seen on screen came in contact with the hull. How far above them was the mine? They did not know. And there were so many places, from the antennas to the stern planes to the propellers, that could catch and hold onto the cable. If the cable caught on any one of a dozen obstructions on their exterior, it would reel the mine down like a fish on a hook until it touched their hull. The scraping and screeching seemed to go on forever, but Ozzie kept his face expressionless. He knew the men were looking to him for their cues. Ozzie didn't pray, and he did his best not to look worried. If it happened, it happened. At this moment, there was nothing he could do to change that.

The screeching was past the control room now, growing more and more faint as the cables neared the stern.

And then it stopped.

Ozzie gave orders to resume their course and asked the navigator to plot their current position.

He wasn't about to let a few Japanese mines come between him and his treasure.

CHAPTER THIRTY-FIVE

Ao Chalong
Phuket, Thailand

November 18, 2012

The waitress came to their table and asked if they wanted another beer.

"Cole, much as I want to hear about your gold legend, I'm going to fall asleep right here on the table if I have another beer," she said.

After the waitress was out of earshot, Cole said, "Let's find someplace safe where you can get some sleep."

And plan how to get rid of the crazy guy watching my boat, she thought.

She went to the bathroom while Cole paid the bill. Before returning, she splashed water on her face and examined herself in the mirror. She saw the dark circles under her red-rimmed eyes. It had been two nights now with almost no sleep and hundreds of miles of travel. This was not how she imagined it would be when she and Cole took a hotel room together. None of this was playing out how she had imagined. And what was she to make of Cole's story about how he had come to be in the Philippines? Accepting the existence of an organization like the Patriarchs had required a massive shift in Riley's pragmatic world view. Now he was asking her to believe they were but one cell in a massive worldwide organization.

She heard Cole outside. "Are you okay in there?"

"Yeah." She dried her face, unlocked the door, and opened it. "I'm about to pass out on my feet."

"I know. I can see that. I had the bartender call us a cab, and then he called ahead to a guest house that belongs to a friend of his. It's owned by a South African woman who came here on a boat and never left. I'm beginning to see that as a theme in Phuket."

Riley laughed as he led her through the tables. "Yeah, I've noticed that myself."

The Shanti Lodge was one block off a big urban highway, but once inside the compound, it looked like they'd found a tranquil oasis. The combined dining room and lobby was open on three sides overlooking the swimming pool and the various other buildings surrounding it. Lazy ceiling fans kept the air moving and the tropical plants kept it cool. Comfortable furnishings made it seem more like a home than a commercial establishment. One set of steps led up to a platform where guests could get Thai massages, and the rooms were all dark wood, straw mats and bright fabric. The owner, Kim, showed them how to operate the room key to turn on the lights and ceiling fan, and she pointed out the common toilet and shower area.

Cole set his duffel bag down on one of the chairs in their room. "I'll go down and get us registered. Mr. and Mrs. John Jones."

"I'm headed straight to the shower," Riley said as she grabbed one of the towels off the bed.

She stood under the hot water for a good ten minutes. There wasn't much water pressure, but slowly she felt the knots of tension around her neck, back, and shoulders start to untie themselves. When she turned off the water and opened the shower curtain, she saw herself in the full-length mirror. *Not bad for thirty-six years old,* she thought. Her belly was flat and she could see the muscles in her arms and legs. There were mornings she didn't feel like rolling out of her bunk before daylight to exercise before the heat made it impossible, but she followed her exercise routine with twenty laps around her boat. The discipline paid off. Fitness to Riley was less about appearances than it was about a Marine Corps mindset. She had to be prepared for whatever came her way.

She frowned at the mirror when she pivoted around on one foot and examined the scar tissue that reached from the top of her shoulder to halfway down her back. It was difficult to believe it had been six, almost seven years now since that day the bomb went off in the Marine House in Lima. The scarring didn't look as fresh as it had the first time Cole had seen it, but it hadn't exactly gone away, either. And never would.

Unwilling to put on her sweaty, salty, filthy clothes, she rinsed them out in the sink, then wrapped herself in her towel and returned to their room. Cole hadn't returned yet. She hung her damp clothes across the chair backs, then discovered that the light cotton bedspread worked as a sarong with a long end to throw over her shoulder. She was standing in front of the mirror examining herself when Cole came through the door carrying a big tray with food, two more cold beers, and a bottle of water.

"Anybody hungry?" he asked.

"That smells fantastic."

Cole set the tray down on the big bed and Riley joined him. "I got us three different dishes to try," he said. "That's cashew chicken, shrimp fried rice, and green curry fish. Those are the names Kim told me, anyway. I couldn't pronounce the Thai names." He handed her a lovely pottery bowl and a fork. "Dig in."

"Is this your first time in Thailand?"

He nodded as he mounded rice in his bowl.

"But on that recording you made for me, you specifically mentioned Thailand. That's the reason I'm here."

He handed her the spoon for the rice. "Those were early days in our research. Everything changed when we learned about Yamashita's Gold."

"Okay, so what is it?"

"Hmm." He finished chewing and swallowed. "That green curry sauce is unbelievable."

"Cole!"

He grinned and for the first time she felt the intervening years fall away. The beard and awkwardness didn't matter in the least. He was still the crazy man with whom she had fallen in love.

"You do understand you are asking me, I might even say begging me, to explain a conspiracy theory to you."

"And you understand that I've been trained to kill men twice my own size with my bare hands?"

He took a big bite of his food and then stared at her as he chewed. He swallowed finally. "You have no idea how sexy you are when you talk like that."

She started to put her bowl aside.

"Okay, okay," he said, raising his hands, one holding his fork over his head. "I surrender. I'll tell you everything." He took a deep breath, shoveled another bite into his mouth, and began talking as he chewed. "The theory is that the Japanese amassed tons of loot both before and during World War II by systematically plundering all the countries they conquered. We're talking robbing temples, museums, the wealthy families' homes of paintings, statues, jewelry, gold bullion, you name it. Once the Americans took control of the waters around Japan, the Japanese began hiding their stolen treasure in Luzon in the Philippines, deep in caves and the many additional tunnels they dug. The Japanese called it Operation Golden Lily. General Yamashita was in charge of the land-based forces in the Philippines. When the war ended, some OSS guys under General Douglas MacArthur tortured Yamashita's driver until he spilled what he knew."

"OSS?"

"Yeah, it's—"

"I know what it is. It's just that I've heard some of this recently, too."

"Yeah? That's probably not good. But let me get to a stopping place: The short version of the rest of the story is that when the driver broke, he told them of the sites he had driven the general to, and these guys dug up tons of gold and priceless artifacts. The 'them' we're talking about here were the OSS guys, some of whom became CIA while others formed the Enterprise. They've kept the stash a secret—off the books—deposited in offshore banks under something called the Black Eagle Trust. They've been melting down these national treasures and the proceeds have been used to finance black ops ever since."

"Cole, don't tell me you're looking for the rest of this mythical treasure."

He grabbed a napkin off the tray and wiped the sauce off his mouth. "Not *exactly*. There's more to it. But before I go any further, why don't you tell me what you've been hearing about Corregidor and the OSS."

She told him the story about how she got the letter and what Peewee had told her about her grandfather. When she'd finished, she retrieved her backpack from where she'd set it on the floor, and she pulled out the bundle of wrapped silk. She sat back down on the bed and folded back the corners of the cloth to reveal the gold artifact.

"This is what Peewee gave me." She held it out to him.

Cole picked it up and turned it around, looking at the fancy filigree writing. "Amazing workmanship."

"Peewee said it's called a Tibetan prayer gau and he said my grandfather, who was OSS, got it from a Japanese prince."

At the word *prince*, Cole's head jerked up and he looked at her, his eyes wide with surprise.

"What is it?" she asked.

"It's just that Operation Golden Lily was overseen by several Japanese princes."

"According to Peewee, my grandfather had made him promise to give this prayer gau to his son, my dad. But, as you know, my dad's dead, so he was giving it to me."

"Is it okay if I open it?" he asked.

Riley nodded. "Yesterday afternoon, when I was at the Temple of the Reclining Buddha to meet Peewee—who never showed—I opened it myself. A monk there told me that the writing on the papers inside isn't in the Tibetan language at all. It looks like a bunch of symbols or hieroglyphs. He said he thought it looked like some kind of code."

Cole slid the papers out of the tube. There were three small sheets and he spread them out on the bed. Then he saw that the third sheet was folded in half. He unfolded it and spread it out next to the others. He let out a long, low whistle. "That monk was right. But this one looks like Japanese writing," Cole said.

She picked up the thin paper and looked at the characters. She held it one way, then rotated it. "I didn't see this one. How do you know it's not Chinese or some other language?"

He took the letter from her. "I've been looking at lots of Japanese documents lately. Military letters and orders."

She pointed to the two sheets on the bed. "It's odd that these two are the right size to fit in the gau, but that one needed to be folded."

Cole looked up from his study of the Japanese document. "Does that phone of yours take pictures?"

"Sure."

"Okay. Take a quick picture of this and we'll send it to Theo. Kim said we've got Internet here. She wrote the password down on my receipt." Cole stood up and reached into his back pocket while Riley dug her phone out of her backpack.

She snapped the photo and checked to make sure it was legible. Cole handed her the receipt. As she typed in the password to access the Wi-Fi network, she noticed that the room had been purchased by a Mr. John Jones.

"So, Mr. Jones. To what email address should I send this photo?"

"You're going to like this. Send it to MVBonhommeRichard at Gmail dot com."

"Seriously?" She laughed out loud as she typed the email address into her phone.

"Do you have any other email address you could send it from in case someone is monitoring your account?"

She stared at him, started to say something, then just shrugged. He really was the old Cole. Just as paranoid as ever. She sent the email from an account she'd only used once before.

"So that's the name of *Shadow Chaser* now," she said when the email went through.

"Yup. Can you use that phone to make a Skype call?"

When she nodded, he wrote a number down in the margin of the receipt. "Okay, then dial this number." Once it started to ring, he took the phone from her.

"Hey, Theo. It's me. I just sent you a photo of a document."

Riley watched his mouth as he listened to his friend. She really wanted to kiss that mouth, but she would need to rest for just a minute first.

"Yes," Cole said, "I know it came from a different email address. That's because Riley sent it." Cole held the phone away from his ear, and even from the other side of the bed she could hear the enthusiastic whoops that erupted from the phone. "Okay already. It was unexpected, but now that we're sitting in a hotel room in Phuket, I'm finding it a very pleasant surprise."

Cole held the phone to his ear for a second, then grabbed a pillow, put it over the phone, and smiled at her. "That Theo," he said. When he pulled the phone out, he said, "She's right here, you know. She can hear you. Keep it clean. Listen, can you run that document through your translator?"

Riley felt the exhaustion creeping up to her head. She set her bowl back on the tray and eased back onto the pillow Cole had just been using.

"Already? That was fast. It's Riley's. It's a long story."

Riley closed her eyes and she felt like she was floating.

"You're kidding me! Holy shit! After all this time! Right. Paste it into an email and send it back to the same address. I'll call you later."

She opened her eyes. "What is it?"

"Theo and I came to the Philippines looking for the Dragon's Triangle."

"But Cole, I looked it up and the Dragon's Triangle is just a big empty piece of ocean."

"I know. But it's also the Enterprise code name for their project to find the wreck of a Japanese hospital ship called the *Teiyō Maru*. The cargo she carried was top secret. They believe she sank sometime in April of 1945, but in Japan and in the US, there are almost no records of this vessel." He held up the letter. "This letter is from a Japanese Lieutenant Colonel Miyata. And he says she sank in the Babuyan Islands."

"You sure look excited about this ship."

"You bet. I've got to get back right away. Listen, we can put your boat into a marina where she'll be safe. Then we'll fly to the Philippines. This could be the breakthrough I've been waiting for."

"What breakthrough?"

"Obviously, this Peewee guy is with the Enterprise. Sorry, Riley, but he probably never knew your grandfather. My guess is they were using you to smoke me out. You're not safe here anymore. You've got to come with me."

She opened her eyes and propped herself up on her elbows. "Got to? So, now it's all about you?"

"Surely you don't think it's a coincidence that he gave you these documents when I happen to be searching for this wreck?" He held up the letter.

"I don't know what I think right now. I'm exhausted. But I can't leave my boat. I've got my work. I need my computer, my books."

"Bring 'em with you. I can't afford to wait two weeks or longer now while we sail your boat to the Philippines."

She flopped back down on the pillows. "And I can't leave her."

"I'll hire a delivery skipper. She'll arrive safe and sound. You don't have to worry about it."

She rolled onto her side and supported her head in the palm of her hand. "What's so important about that *Maru* ship?"

Cole smiled. "In addition to the gold?"

"Shoulda known." She wasn't sure she could keep her eyes open much longer. "Yeah, in addition to the gold."

"Well, not much. Just a map to the mother of all treasure sites in the Philippines."

"Oh," she said. "That's all." Her head fell back on the pillow and she gave in to the welcome darkness.

CHAPTER THIRTY-SIX

Ao Chalong
Phuket, Thailand

November 19, 2012

When Riley opened her eyes the room was pitch-black, and she didn't know where she was. Her heart rate kicked straight into high gear. The ceiling fan turning overhead groaned in a regular rhythm, and she tried to prevent herself from hyperventilating. Then she heard a long snore. Moving only her eyes, she took in the lump of a body lying next to hers on the bed. The odor of soap and warm male skin jogged her fully awake. Cole. Shanti Lodge. She must have fallen asleep while he was talking to her. More like passed out. *Oh, God,* she thought. Why was she so inept at romance?

The air from the overhead fan was quite cool, and he had covered them both with a light sheet. He was sleeping on his side, facing her. The bedspread was gone and she lay there naked under the sheet.

The tray of food was gone, and he smelled like he had showered. This, their first night back together, hadn't exactly been the passionate night of lovemaking she'd imagined it would be.

He could have awakened her if he'd really wanted her. But then he had been able to get a good look at her scars when he removed the bedspread and covered her with the sheet. Billy had never had a problem with shaking her awake when he wanted sex. With Billy, though, she'd always insisted on wearing a T-shirt to bed. She had no problem with him reaching under the cloth to touch her breasts, but he didn't need to see the scars on her back.

Cole was the only man—other than her doctors—who had ever seen her shoulder and back, who had touched her scars.

Riley rolled onto her side, facing him, and studied his face in the shadows. She began to remember what they had been talking about the night before. He'd been so excited about the letter in the prayer gau, and he'd been certain Peewee had never met her grandfather and the whole story had just been a ruse so that she would lead Peewee and the Enterprise back to Cole.

It didn't fit. Either that old man was one of the world's best actors or he really had known her grandfather. Cole was wrong on this one, she was sure.

He said he wanted her to go back to the Philippines with him. But, of course, she was the one who had these documents Cole wanted-ed. His idea was for her to go back to his boat in the Philippines with him, to leave her boat there in Phuket, and then have some professional delivery skipper take *Bonefish* to Subic Bay later. She knew she was supposed to find it sweet that he wanted to protect her. But there really was something demeaning about the fact that, after all these years, he suddenly didn't think she could take care of herself. And she had her own mystery to solve in the Philippines. Riley wanted to find out the truth about what happened to the USS *Bonefish* and Ozzie Riley, her grandfather. She needed to understand how her father had known to name all his sailboats *Bonefish*.

Besides, she couldn't imagine anyone else sailing her boat. She was the only one who really knew all the little idiosyncrasies of her

Bonefish. She had made so many upgrades to all the boat's systems, including security. It was no longer a standard Caliber 40.

And then there was her work. She had recently received the blueprints of a mega-mansion some country singer was having built outside Nashville and Mercury Security was waiting for her plans for the state-of-the art electronic security system she was supposed to be designing for them. She could be in Singapore in a week, get the work done en route, and email them the preliminary plans from there. She was accustomed to being alone on the boat, and she doubted she could work with Cole around, anyway. He would just be a distraction.

He would fuss at her, saying he just wanted to protect her. Now that she thought about it, the main emotion he felt toward her seemed to be pity—like he thought she needed to be looked after. He'd been off having adventures while this poor damaged woman was sailing around mooning about him. No wonder he'd kept his distance.

If he really felt he had to get back to Theo and his boat immediately, he could just go, as far as she was concerned. Hop a plane and leave her to get her boat there on her own. She'd sailed her boat solo more than halfway around the world. A few hundred miles more wouldn't make much difference to her at this point. And she wanted to find out the answers to what happened to her grandfather on her own.

Very slowly she eased back the covers and slipped her legs over the side of the bed as she rose to a sitting position. Other than a little hitch in his breathing, he didn't react at all. He was deep in sleep.

It would be easier this way. And at this hour, she hoped Benny would be sleeping out there in his fishing boat, too.

Her clothes were still damp and it was uncomfortable slipping on the bra and panties as they stuck to her skin. It took some adjusting to get things to fit right. She pulled on her khakis and the polo shirt, collected her backpack, and checked all the surfaces in the room for anything else that belonged to her. She almost missed her phone on the floor. He had plugged it in to charge overnight.

When she eased open the door, she dangled her backpack from the tips of her fingers. If he woke up, she planned to tell him she had an upset stomach and needed to go to the bathroom. But the opening door didn't even register. He slept like a man who hadn't a worry in the world. She paused, wondering if she should leave a note, but decided not to risk it. With her satellite phone she could access the Internet and leave him a message on her blog. She eased the door closed and winced at the light click.

Her sandals were outside the door, and she picked them up so she could get away without waking any of the other customers as she crossed the creaking wood floors.

A low light burned in the lobby area, but the grounds were deserted. She stopped in to the downstairs toilet and brushed her teeth, combed her hair. She stared into her own eyes in the mirror above the sink. *Are you sure you know what you're doing?* she thought. Feeling unsure of herself was not something she was accustomed to.

When she crossed the parking lot, she was almost away, but she found a locked, solid wooden gate barred her from getting out onto the street. Riley swore under her breath. The chain was beefy and the padlock was bigger than her fist. But when she pulled on the lock it clicked open.

There wouldn't be any way she could replace the padlock once she'd exited. She didn't want to leave them all vulnerable to thieves. She checked her watch. It was 3:25 a.m. The sun would rise in little more than two hours. She arranged the gate so that it looked like it was still locked on the inside. She hoped that would suffice.

No one was around on the small side street, but she could see the occasional car passing on the highway beyond. She'd ridden her bicycle this way before. The waterfront was about a mile and a half away. She would need to walk fast to beat the approaching dawn.

• • •

Her dinghy was where she had left it on the beach, upside down on the sand and chained to a coconut tree. The oars were still there, too. Riley trotted over to the building that housed the Yacht Club lockers and restrooms, and she searched the grounds around the dinghies, anchors, and bits of broken gear that decorated the back of the shed. She found what she was looking for attached to a deflated dinghy with a rotted-out transom. She pulled her small Leatherman tool from her backpack and cut away the length of old polypropylene rope that was tied to the towing ring. After wadding up the line and stuffing it in her pack, she headed back to the beach.

She dragged her boat down to the water's edge, pushed off, and jumped in. The water was shallow for nearly the first quarter mile, too shallow for sailboat moorings. The night was very dark but a tiny sliver of a moon had just peeked over the island of Ko Lon out in the bay. The moon provided little light but it did make it easier to be certain she was headed in the right direction. Since the wind had chosen this night to quit entirely, she rowed slowly. Sound travels far over the water, especially when it is still.

After so many months on her mooring out in Ao Chalong Bay, Riley had made friends with most of the boaters around her. She knew the Aussie couple on the big catamaran *Incommunigato* had flown home for a month of visiting family and no one was aboard their boat. Their mooring was on the opposite side of her boat from where Benny's boat was anchored. She had been watching his boat as she neared, and so far there had been no sign of movement there. She shipped the oars when she pulled up to the aft swim step on one of the big cat's hulls, then climbed out and tied up her dinghy. She took off her sandals and put them in the backpack after she pulled out the line she'd collected. She tied the line around her waist so she wouldn't lose it. She slipped into the water via the ladder off the cat's swim platform and started swimming a gentle side stroke toward her own boat, holding her backpack above the water and keeping *Bonefish* between herself and the fishing boat on the other side.

When she came alongside *Bonefish*, she tucked her backpack under the swim ladder and then kept swimming even more slowly. Her breathing sounded loud in her ears, but she hoped it was just her imagination.

The fishing boat's engine was angled forward so the propeller rested just out of the water at the end of the long shaft. She untied the line around her waist and wrapped it around the prop. She was about to start back to her boat when she looked at the engine. Unlike most marine engines, these were air-cooled automobile engines and she just might be able to reach the air intake manifold. She liked hedging her bets, so she reached around behind her back, under her polo shirt, and undid the clasp on her bra. She threaded the straps around her elbows and the bra floated free. She grabbed the bra and she couldn't resist running her hand over her breasts. It felt so much better in the water without it.

At the stern of the wooden boat she placed one hand on the side of the engine well. She knew what came next would rock the boat a bit, but she hoped he wouldn't notice. She took a deep breath and pulled herself partway out of the water. Just as her hand reached the gaping air intake, she heard a cough from inside the boat. She froze half out of the water and watched for movement at the other end of the boat, where she could just make out the mound of a figure under a tarp. With two fingers, she pushed the bra as far as she could, then lowered herself back into the water. The boat rocked even more as he shifted position and coughed again.

Riley realized her polo shirt was white and it would glow in the water if he happened to sit up and look. She pulled the shirt over her head and pushed it under his boat. Holding her breath, she started to swim.

All the way back to her boat, she was expecting a dart to hit her in the back of the neck. But a few minutes later, she was pulling herself up on her swim step and climbing into her cockpit. She unlocked the boat, turned off her alarm, and went below to change into some dry clothes.

Once dressed she looked around the familiar cabin and thought about putting to sea for such a long voyage. She always carried a good supply of canned and dry goods, so she was fine on food. Her Caliber 40 sailboat had tankage for just over two hundred gallons of diesel fuel, and she liked to keep her tanks topped off so she didn't have to worry about too much condensation in her fuel. And as for water, her reverse-osmosis water maker could make twenty gallons of fresh water out of salt—per hour. She was ready to go. As always.

She went through the rest of her pre-departure routine, throwing switches for instruments, autopilot, radar, and radios. While swimming, she had noticed the outgoing tide, and now she reckoned that she could use that current. At the bow, she paused briefly to note the faint light in the eastern sky, then threw off her mooring lines and let her boat drift free. The tide would carry her south past the fishing boat, and once she was far enough away, she could start her engine, set her course for Langkawi in Malaysia. Hopefully, by the time he awoke, she would be out of sight.

Her plan looked like it was going to work perfectly until she realized that the current was carrying her boat directly toward the eighty-foot-long gleaming navy-blue hull of the *Merlin II*, the exorbitantly expensive ocean-racing greyhound that Billy Barber called home. *Merlin II* was moored about two hundred feet from where Benny had dropped his anchor. She knew what the paint job on that hull cost. Billy had told her. Several times. There was no way she could let her white hull collide with that perfect navy-blue hull. When it was clear that there was no way she could avoid it, she turned the key and fired up her engine.

CHAPTER THIRTY-SEVEN

Ao Chalong
Phuket, Thailand

November 19, 2012

The noise of an engine starting jolted him awake. Benny threw off the tarp, sat up, and looked for the woman's boat. The mooring ball was floating alone; the boat was gone. He jumped to his feet and turned. He didn't expect to see the white sailboat so close to his boat and even closer to the fancy blue one. He heard the engine revs increase as her boat swung away from the blue boat and began to pick up speed. The sky was a bluish gray but there was already enough light for him to see the woman's face when she turned and stared at him over her shoulder. She wasn't afraid and that surprised him.

Benny reached for his bag. This woman had been too much trouble to him already and now she was disrespecting him. He untied the top of his bag, reached inside for his blowpipe, then stopped. He could kill her easily enough. The distance was not too great, but Hawkes wanted her alive. Where were the other two? If the old man had the artifact now, and he wasn't aboard, how would he locate him? No, he couldn't kill the girl, no matter how much he wanted to.

He stepped to the back of the boat and thought back to the lessons that his cousin had taught him for starting the engine. He went through each step, and he was thankful when the engine roared to life on his first try. It sounded very loud in the still morning air. The next step was to pivot it by lifting the front tiller and then lower the prop into the water. When he bent down he heard the engine noise change. He knew from driving cars that when an engine sounded like it was coughing, it was not good. Then the sound died altogether. He could no longer even hear the sound of the woman's boat.

Benny swore. He knew nothing about mechanics. He stepped to the side and looked at all the metal parts and hoses and wires. Then he saw something that looked like white fabric dangling out from a hole. He reached down and grabbed it. When he pulled, it would not come at first. He pulled harder and something tore. It came free. He saw he was holding a white, lacy woman's bra.

He saw from the corner of his eye that her boat was widening the gap very quickly. Sailboats were not supposed to be fast, he thought. Benny tried to start the engine again and this time he had the throttle so far open, the engine seemed to scream. He lowered the revs down to idle speed.

Then he remembered the anchor. He could not put the boat into gear with the anchor on the bottom. He hurried to the front of the boat and pulled the rope in hand over hand. When he got to the chain it was heavy, but there was only about twenty feet of it. He piled it on top of the nets he'd been using as a mattress. The anchor was muddy, but he didn't have time to clean it.

Benny ran to the back of the boat, lifted the engine to put the prop in the water, and shifted it into gear. Not more than five seconds after he put it into gear, the engine stopped again. The sun was just peeking over the top of the island. Benny lowered the front end of the engine and the first rays of sunlight lit the ball of bright orange rope wrapped in a tight ball around the propeller.

The white sailboat had cleared the anchorage, and it was heading for the mouth of Ao Chalong Bay. The woman stepped away from the steering wheel and walked to the side of her boat. He saw her raise a hand and wave.

CHAPTER THIRTY-EIGHT

Shanti Lodge
Phuket, Thailand

Cole wondered what was taking her so long. He guessed by the angle of the sun out the window that it was perhaps 6:30 a.m. When he awoke to find Riley's side of the bed empty, he assumed she had gone to the head. After all, she had fallen asleep very early the night before.

He tried to fall back asleep, but once he'd started thinking about her, that was the only thing that filled his mind—and other parts of his body. As he waited for her in all his morning glory, he thought back over the recent hours he had spent with her. He pictured her running down that dock in Bangkok and taking that flying leap onto their boat as it was pulling away from the dock, frowning as she drove the boat, staring out the bus window as they made their way south, and snoring softly as he covered her with a sheet the night before. For more than twenty-four hours he'd been wanting to take her in his arms and kiss every inch of her. This morning, finally he would get that chance.

If only she would come back from the head. Suddenly, it occurred to him that she might be sick. He threw off the sheet and swung his legs over the side of the bed. He reached for his clothes on the chair next to the bed. That was when he noticed her phone was no longer plugged in where he'd left it the night before. She probably wanted to check her email and had taken it with her. But her backpack and clothes were gone, too. Perhaps she'd wanted to shower. He wanted to believe that but the two towels slung over the other chair back made that difficult.

Breakfast. That was it. She'd gone down to breakfast without him. He pulled on his clothes. He was in no hurry. For the moment, he could not be sure she had left without saying good-bye. He could believe she was downstairs eating, chatting with Kim, waiting for him to come down. Or try to.

As he descended the stairs, he could see into the dining room. A slender Thai girl was placing sugar bowls and cream pitchers on the tables. She was the only person he could see.

"Good morning," he said. He saw from the clock over the bar that it was actually after 8:00 a.m.

The girl placed her hands together almost as though she were praying. *"Sawadee ka,"* she said in a lovely singsong voice.

Cole nodded in return. "Have you seen an American woman with brownish-blond hair to here?" He touched his own shoulder to indicate the length of her hair.

She shook her head. "Sorry."

Cole gave her an order for his breakfast and said he would be back downstairs in about ten minutes. He returned to the room and went to the bed stand where he had emptied his pockets the night before. The cheap little Thai phone he had bought on arrival in the country was there. He picked it up and dialed.

"Hey. It's me," he said.

"So," Theo said, "did she rock your world?"

"She's gone."

"Say what?"

"I can't believe it either," Cole said. The truth was he didn't want to.

"She didn't like leave a note or anything?"

"No. I woke up and she was gone."

"Mon, what did you say to her?"

"Me? Why is everything always my fault?"

"Because you're the crazy one, that's why."

"Are you checking her website? I don't have any way to get on the Internet here."

"Of course I am. As we speak. And yes, there is something there. Listen—"

A robotic voice came through the cell phone: "Dear Cole, I'm sorry to leave in the night like this without waking you, but I didn't want to argue with you. I can't leave my boat. It's my home and office. So I'm on my way—just south of Ao Chalong Bay. I took care of Benny. Suffice to say he should not be a problem for me now. You need to keep your eyes open for him, though. He wants the Tibetan prayer gau (and its contents), and he doesn't know who has it. He will go after you if necessary.

"I plan to sail to the Philippines direct. No stopping. It will be roughly eighteen hundred miles. I hope to do it in two to three weeks. I have my single-sideband radio and satellite phone. I'll be in touch."

"That's it? That's all she wrote?"

"Yeah, mon. That's it. Well, at least you got to spend one night together."

"We *slept* together."

"You dog, you. Was it as good as you remembered? I mean, you've been fixated on getting this woman back into your life all these years."

"You didn't hear me. I said we *slept*. That's all we did. Sleep."

"Oh no you didn't."

"She hadn't slept in two nights. She ate and she virtually passed out. Listen, I don't want to talk about it."

"Okay, what now? Are you going after her?"

"No. I'm not going where I'm not wanted. I'm going to catch the first plane I can find back to the Philippines."

"We do have our work cut out for us now."

"Did you get the other two documents I sent last night?"

"You sent? I thought Riley sent them."

"Well, when she fell asleep, I kinda used her phone to take snapshots and send them on to you. She doesn't have to know."

"Did you erase them from her sent mail?"

"What?"

"Listen, you need to leave the tech stuff to me. She's going to know. Do you think she'll be okay with you taking copies without her permission? Does she even have any idea what it is she has—how valuable those documents are?"

"You mean how valuable the documents *we have* are? No, this is Riley we're talking about. She won't mind."

"Okay," Theo said. "So says the man who *slept* with her last night."

CHAPTER THIRTY-NINE

Aboard the USS *Bonefish*
South China Sea

June 25, 1945

They'd been lucky so far. Ozzie knew he couldn't count on that luck continuing, but so far, the lady had favored him. They had not encountered a single other warship on their entire trek across the South China Sea.

SubComPac would soon declare the USS *Bonefish* missing in action since she had not shown up for her rendezvous with the rest of the Hellcats on June 24. Ozzie had told the sub's radio operator to expect this—that it was all part of their orders for their whereabouts to remain unknown. If any other US ship saw them and identified them, they'd send out a search party the likes of which he did not want to deal with. Ozzie had a plan, and being missing in action suited him just fine. He intended to send the boys on the USS *Bonefish* off to make their reappearance later. For now, he needed the ride to the Philippines for himself and Prince Masako. If the treasure really was as vast as the prince claimed, it would not be possible for one man to handle tons of material. He knew there were plenty of his OSS mates on the ground in Luzon, and once he had located the treasure sites, he reckoned he could call on them to overpower the few Japs who remained.

The sticky part was going to be that moment of the arrival of the sub. Presumably, the prince had a loyal army waiting for his return. How many men? There was no way to know for sure, but given that all the word out of Luzon was that the core of Yamashita's men who had retreated into the mountains of Luzon were starving, weak, and low on ammunition, Ozzie believed their odds of overpowering them were pretty good.

Ozzie was going to have to give both Westbrooke and Prince Masako just enough information to think they each knew the whole score. He would like to avoid a shoot-out when they first arrived, but in the end, they would have the firepower of those deck guns and any shoreside installation would be a sitting duck for the nimble submarine.

As it turned out, Ozzie and Westbrooke were both standing atop the conning tower when the lookout called out that he could see land. It was late afternoon and the winds were down. The sea surface mirrored the crisp cumulous clouds, and the usual humid haze had taken a breather. The bluish mountains of Luzon's Cordillera range were visible over twenty miles away.

"I hear these are beautiful islands," Westbrooke said as he surveyed the distant coast through the binoculars.

"Oh yeah. I spent a good bit of time here before Pearl Harbor."

Westbrooke lowered the binoculars and turned to face Ozzie. "Really? I didn't know you'd been stationed in the Philippines."

"Yeah, lucky me. I was on Corregidor before the Japanese showed up. Used to work in SIS. I made it out of there just in time, too."

"I guess you've been a part of all this from the start, then."

"Yes, sir. It seems a lot longer than four and a half years ago."

"I was still in school when it started." Westbrooke turned back to look on the faint image of the coast ahead of them.

"Skipper," Ozzie said. "I think we need to talk about the details of a plan."

Without turning, Westbrooke said, "So I'm finally going to be told the details of this mission. It's about time."

"I'm just following my orders, sir."

"I hate this damn secrecy, but let's hear it now."

"As you know, MacArthur has taken Manila, but General Yamashita has withdrawn into those mountains we see over there." Ozzie pointed to the coast. "He has about fifty thousand troops with him and they are being supplied by Japanese submarines making drops at the port we are about to visit. Our mission is to get in there and take out the ground forces. We need to close this off as a supply line for Yamashita."

"Okay. What do we know about the shoreside installation?"

"Very little. We got these orders due to information I got from our prisoner, Lieutenant Colonel Miyata. He says it is a very small harbor, barely big enough for this sub to enter. But they don't have any big guns installed, so we'll only be looking at small-arms fire. It shouldn't be a problem to take it. Based on Miyata's intel, I suggest a night entry. He's given me the radio frequency and code that will make their guys think a Jap sub is coming in. They'll light up a range. They won't know who we are until it's too late."

"Our Japanese colonel seems to be uncharacteristically cooperative."

"Well, it's the end of the war. We know it and they know it."

Like all the officers on the USS *Bonefish*, Ozzie had been issued a sidearm, but on the boat he never wore it. But this evening, he and Westbrooke both wore their sidearms. As the USS *Bonefish* approached the coast, Westbrooke called for full battle stations. The crew manned the deck guns. After he had the radioman send the signal, Ozzie had the chief of the boat bring their two prisoners up to the top of the conning tower.

The moon was hidden behind a layer of clouds that had moved in after sunset, but the scent of land, that mixture of earthy vegetation and the sweet smell of rotting organisms, tingled in the noses of every man on deck. The night was so black Ozzie began to feel dizzy. It was difficult to know which way was up and he braced himself in a corner of the deck. He could not see the prince's face, but he felt him smiling.

"Dammit, Lieutenant Colonel, you'd better not be leading this submarine into dangerous waters. You know a grounded sub is no good to you."

"Don't worry, Lieutenant. Your submarine will be safe. I give you my word."

Then ahead of them two white lights appeared out of the blackness, one high and the other almost at water level. Westbrooke called for a course adjustment and slowly the range lights aligned one over the other.

The skipper ordered a man to the spotlight.

"Sir," Ozzie said, "if we light up this boat at all they will know it's not a Jap sub." He spoke quietly, knowing well how far voices carry across the water. "They might see our guys on the guns."

Westbrooke told the man to stay ready on the spot awaiting his orders. He dropped the speed to three knots and called for a constant depth.

"Fifty-two feet," a soft voice called.

"Forty-nine feet."

Every man on deck from the gunners to the officers was straining to see something in the dark, but all they saw were the two range lights aligned one over the other. It was impossible to tell how far away they were.

"Forty-eight feet.

"Forty-five feet.

"Forty feet."

"Ozzie," Westbrooke said. "Tell me I should keep on this heading. Tell me you can see something out there in the darkness."

"Thirty-eight feet."

They heard the whispers from the men on the bow first. They saw the cliffs. But even as slow as they were moving, there was nothing they could do at that point. Then the men on top of the conning tower saw the rock walls on either side emerge out of the darkness. The sub passed under a rock arch.

Westbrooke called for all engines hard astern. All the men on the sub braced themselves for a hard grounding. Ozzie pulled his gun out of his holster and grabbed Prince Masako. He put the gun to the prince's head.

"Depth is forty-five feet."

Everything sounded different, close, echoey. Ozzie strained his eyes to try to make out what was out there.

The range lights blinked out as the sub's engines drew the big boat to a stop.

Westbrooke called for the searchlight. When the brilliant light turned on, it was like turning on the sun. The light bounced off the walls around them and everything was illuminated.

Ozzie felt his mouth open even as he heard the prince chuckling.

"Welcome to the Philippines," Prince Masako said.

The sub was floating in a pale aquamarine pool under a dome several hundred feet above them. Around the sides of the chamber, long, slender stalactites reached down from the high dome, throwing shadows like witches' craggy fingers. On their port side was a long stone quay twice the length of their boat, with big black tires strung along the face to act as fenders. Two lone Japanese sailors in white uniforms were holding up their arms to shield their eyes from the bright light and waving at them, ready to take their lines.

"What the hell?" Westbrooke said.

"I guess we're docking here," Ozzie said. "Inside a cave."

CHAPTER FORTY

Ao Chalong
Phuket, Thailand

November 19, 2012

This was new. Benny Salim was not accustomed to failure. He didn't have a knife in his bag, so he had searched every inch of the boat until he found a small, rusty eating knife in the bottom of the boat. He'd stripped down to his underwear and slid into the water. He worked for nearly half an hour but he could not cut through the rope. It was stretched into a tight ball around the propeller and though he sawed his little knife back and forth, it barely made a dent.

Benny climbed back into the boat and sat on the nets. He could no longer see the woman's boat. Even her tall white sail had disappeared around the point. He pulled his bag to him and took out his phone. His cousin answered finally after many rings.

"Yes, I know it is early," Benny said.

His cousin groaned and mumbled something unintelligible. Benny didn't know if he was simply groggy from sleep or already high.

After he'd explained the situation, his cousin said he would come in another of his boats and bring a good knife.

"You aren't thinking of going after her, are you?" his cousin asked.

"I have to. That is my job."

"You'll never find her unless you know where she's going. Do you know where?"

"No," Benny answered. "But your boats are much faster."

"Yes, but I know these waters, and I would not search for such a boat. There are too many places to go, too many to hide. Maybe she is going around the southern tip of Phuket Island and up to Patong. Or she might continue north in the Andaman Sea to Burma or to the islands offshore. Or maybe she's going down to Langkawi, or on to Singapore or down to Australia. Chasing her would be no good. Find out where she is going."

Benny nodded, and at the same time he saw a large inflatable dinghy start up behind the very big blue boat. A suntanned young man was driving. Benny waved at him and then motioned to the shore. The young man turned the dinghy and began to head toward Benny.

"Thank you, cousin. You can send someone to get the boat."

His cousin started speaking and Benny disconnected the call. He grabbed his pants and pulled them on. By the time the dinghy pulled alongside, he was dressed again.

"You need a lift to shore, buddy?"

"Yes, thank you." Benny sat on the edge of the fishing boat and swung his legs into the dinghy. He could tell from the man's voice he was an American.

"Glad to be of help." The young man nodded. "My name's Billy, by the way."

"Nice to meet you. My name is Rafi."

"Is it okay if I drop you off at the Yacht Club? That's where I'm headed."

"Yes. That would be fine."

Billy revved the engine up and the big inflatable dinghy jumped onto a plane. For the next several minutes the boat dodged between the moored boats and the engine noise was too loud for them to speak. He throttled down as they approached the beach, and with a flick of a switch the outboard tilted up so the prop wouldn't hit the bottom. Billy tossed an anchor over the side.

"Sorry, man, we've got to wade in from here. It's not deep."

Benny followed the American when he slid out of the boat and started walking through the shallows. The young man crossed the sand beach and tied a rope from the dinghy to a palm tree.

Benny shook his hand. "Thank you for the lift."

"No problem. Want to join me for a cold one? I've got a nasty chore to do. Came in to borrow Roger's phone to call the cops. I think my girlfriend's sailboat was stolen last night."

"Really?"

"Yeah. I'm so pissed because I told her I'd watch it for her." They crossed the concrete slab, dodging between the tables, and sat down on benches at the bar. Benny didn't say anything. Billy was the sort of man who would keep talking as long as there was silence.

"The boat was right there when I hit the rack around three in the morning. I'd been partying pretty hard, but I wasn't so drunk I didn't check. It was there. But I didn't wake up till almost eight. I couldn't believe it when I looked outside. Gone." Billy held up two fingers when the bartender approached. "Beer okay with you?"

"Fine, thanks."

The bartender set the two cold bottles on the bar and Billy drained half of his right away.

"Hey, you were pretty close by. You didn't see anything, did you?"

"Maybe," Benny said.

"Really?"

"I woke up in the dark when I heard the sound of an engine. I saw a white sailboat go by, but it was a woman driving it."

Billy swung around on his stool and faced Benny. "Really? You're shittin' me. She took it out herself?"

"I don't know who it was," Benny said. He hoped his new friend Billy would provide him with more information.

"Well, I'll call her and find out. Hey, Roger, can I borrow your phone?"

The bartender walked toward them and pulled a small cell phone out of his pocket. "Here you go, you cheap bastard. When're you gonna get your own damn phone?"

"On the salary the owner of that boat pays me? Not likely." Billy took the phone and punched in a number. He held the phone to his ear and said, "Besides, I'd rather borrow yours and use *my* money for beer."

Billy frowned. "Hmm." He punched at the off button. "It went straight to voice mail." He handed the phone back to the bartender.

Roger said, "You trying to reach Riley?"

"Yeah, I got up this morning and her boat's gone. I thought it had been stolen. Nearly had a heart attack when I got up."

"When she rented the mooring here, I think she left the number of her satellite phone, too. Let me look."

Roger disappeared for a few minutes and when he returned, he had a scrap of paper. He handed it to Billy.

"Thanks, man."

Roger started toward the other end of the bar, halted, and retraced his steps. He sighed as he handed Billy his phone again.

"I'll leave you a big tip. I promise."

The bartender rolled his eyes.

Benny held his breath while Billy dialed the number. The man waited, then his eyes lit up. "Riley! I'm so glad you answered."

He listened for several seconds. Then he said, "Hey, that's cool. I'm just glad it was you. I thought your boat had been stolen at first."

He paused again. "Man, that's a long trip to make all by yourself."

Billy nodded as he listened. "I understand. He was your grand-father. I liked it there. I've done several races out of the Manila Yacht Club. Listen, this must be costing good beer money. Drop me an email if you ever need me. And I'm sure we'll cross paths again. The world of boats is like that. Bye."

Billy dropped the phone onto the bar. "Shit," he said.

"What's wrong?"

"That's a hell of a way to break up with a guy. I'm going to miss that one. Roger! Another round."

Benny held up his hand. "Not for me. I've got to get going. Sorry about your girlfriend."

Billy reached out and shook Benny's hand. "Thanks. I'll be fine. She was a fine woman, but a little weird, too. She was kinda secretive. Like just now, she made me promise not to tell anyone where she's headed." Billy shook his head, but then a broad grin split his face. "But it's not so bad being a single guy again in Thailand."

Billy high-fived Roger as Benny turned away and started walking out of the Yacht Club.

CHAPTER FORTY-ONE

**Patpong
Bangkok, Thailand**

November 20, 2012

The taxi dropped Elijah off at the corner of Silom and Patpong Roads. The night market vendors had set up their booths in the street selling T-shirts, jewelry, and knockoff perfume brands. Like in so much of Thailand, even this red-light district didn't have a clear identity.

Elijah did not understand why the man had asked to meet in such a degenerate part of the city. Patpong—the name alone made him feel nauseous. From the ladyboys to the BJ bars to the promises of a ping-pong show—Elijah knew better than to ask for details on that one—the place was a cross between a third-world Walmart and a modern-day Sodom and Gomorrah.

Though it was not yet ten o'clock, the street was crowded with Thai tourists and *farang* men who looked a sickly white in the light from the neon signs.

The mamasan out in front of the Thigh Bar was particularly obnoxious as Elijah approached the door. The old woman grabbed hold of his arm and screeched so she could be heard over the sound of the hip-hop music pulsating from the speakers overhead.

"Come have a look. You like!"

Elijah wrenched his arm free, but entered anyway, which pleased the old broad. She shouted something at him, but he didn't understand the words. He didn't want to, either.

Inside the bar, he saw the usual layout of dancers on poles in the center of the room and the tables for customers around them. The dancers were well lit by spotlights, but the customers were deliberately seated in the shadows. He was there to meet Mr. Black. While Elijah was head of the Philippines section, Black headed up the entire Asia section. Elijah tried not to allow himself to be distracted by the go-go girls.

He felt a tug at his sleeve and turned to see a girl no more than five foot two standing next to him. She wore a fluorescent pink bikini and her unnaturally huge breasts bulged out of the small triangles of cloth.

"Mr. Hawkes?"

"Yes," he said, but Elijah could not take his eyes off her breasts.

"Follow me."

She turned and slipped past the crowd of men who had just arrived and were arranging a table close to the dancers. Elijah hurried to catch up with her. As she led him up the stairs his face was mere inches from those smooth, hypnotically swaying cheeks, and he nearly ran into her when she paused at the top. Then she crossed the floor to a black leather booth back in the shadows away from the bar.

Mr. Black sat alone wearing his usual black Nike jogging suit and sneakers. That was all Elijah had ever seen him wear.

"Good evening, Elijah," he said. "Sit down. Suzie, take his drink order."

Elijah asked for a scotch on the rocks and watched the girl as she crossed to the bar.

"She's something, eh? I paid for those tits."

The man's words snapped him out of it. The girl, her body—both were less interesting, knowing that God had not made them.

"You said on the phone that we needed to talk," Elijah said.

"Yeah." The man drank off the last of the amber liquid and set his glass down hard. "I want to know what the fuck is going on."

Suzie returned with Elijah's drink and both men grew silent as they watched her approach. She stood farther away from the table than was necessary just so she had to bend over and reach to place the glass in front of Elijah. When she turned to leave, Elijah took a mouthful of the drink. The whiskey was already watery.

"We've run into a few problems," Elijah said.

"I don't care about your problems. What I want is results."

"I understand that."

"Do you?"

Elijah didn't answer.

"I've set up a meeting for next Monday."

"With who?"

"It's our buyer. He's intrigued by you."

"Me?"

"You know these foreigners. They're intrigued by the mystique of the American West, the Gold Rush. He wants to meet you, so I've set the meeting at your ranch."

"Okay."

"That's only six days off. Our man from the Company wants to sit in. They like to keep tabs on what we're up to. You know those Clandestine Services guys don't like surprises. They expect our guy to report on this Dragon's Triangle deal. We'll decide what we want them to know. How close are you?"

Elijah considered the option of telling the truth about losing the documents, then rejected it. "The translation is proving to be more difficult than we expected. It's wiser to get an exact latitude and longitude before sending a team up to Aparri. It will save us time and money in the long run."

"We're having to dip into our reserves right now, Hawkes. That damn Karzai expects us to show up every week with a bigger and bigger payoff and the whole Arab Spring mess is costing us a fortune."

"I understand that."

"I hope you do. You've done good work. Until you figured it out, we had plenty of gold in the Philippines, but it took forever to introduce it into the world market. We couldn't risk having any of these Asian countries asking for their gold back. It was brilliant. When you brought this Dragon's Triangle thing to us, you made it sound like a sure thing. A win-win. People have made financial and political decisions based on our belief that you, Hawkes, are a sure thing. You've always paid off for us in the past, and you've made yourself rich in the process."

"Yes, thank you, sir."

"Don't make us regret our confidence in you."

"I won't. You can count on that."

Black slid out of the booth and stood. "I'll see you at your place, then. I'll text you the details. Good night."

"Good night, Mr. Black."

CHAPTER FORTY-TWO

Subic Bay, Luzon
The Philippines

November 19, 2012

Cole's taxi pulled up to the gates of the Subic Bay Freeport Zone and the guard on the gate waved them through like the guards always did. Cole wondered for the umpteenth time what purpose the gate served. It seemed that after all those years of having the US Navy operating a massive base here, when it reverted to the Philippines in 1992, they didn't know how to stop guarding the place. Since lots of expat Americans lived inside the Zone, Cole figured they'd lobbied to turn it into a very large gated community to keep the local riffraff out.

The taxi turned in to the parking lot outside Gama's Resort and Dive Center. Cole hopped out and paid the driver. His only luggage was the small duffel he had thrown in the backseat.

Walking into Gama's through the arched colonial-style doors, past the cannons and figureheads and glass cases full of marine artifacts, felt like coming home. He had used the site as his home base for almost two years now, and Cole was delighted he had been able to stop running at last and get back to work. And at Gama's, he had found kindred spirits.

Brian, the owner, was sitting in his usual spot at the end of the bar. Behind him, across the terrace covered with dining tables, was a view of the deep blue waters of Subic Bay, where several freighters rested at anchor. Brian raised his right hand with his signature cigarette clutched between two fingers. "John, my boy! I knew you'd make it in time for happy hour!"

The other fellows round the bar laughed. They were mostly American expats, Vietnam vets who'd spent time in and out of Subic or Clark, then came back after the war, married Filipinas, and settled here.

For the first time in a long time, his alias name sounded odd to him. For two days with Riley, he had been Cole again and it felt good. He nodded to the group of regulars and patted Brian on the back. "A cold beer sounds good. It's taken me all day to get home."

"Theo told us you were coming back today."

The bartender set a bottle of San Miguel in front of Cole. The cold beer washed away some of the dust from the long bus ride up from Manila. "You seen Theo around much while I was gone?"

"Yeah, he's ashore now, helping Greg out back in the dive shop."

"Greg?" Cole said. He thought he knew everyone who worked in the dive center.

"New hire. I had to let Jack go. It's a problem finding sober help here in Subic. Lucked out this time. Great mechanic."

"You got that right. I lucked out with Theo, that's for sure. He knows engines and electronics."

"Yeah, well I think Greg's pulling a Tom Sawyer number on your friend. I asked Greg to build us an ROV of our own, but I think Theo's the one doing most of the work."

Cole smiled. "That's all right. He loves it."

"You have a good trip?"

Cole paused before answering. These men knew him only as John Jones, an American entrepreneur who had made a living in the dive shop business and sold out to dive his way around the world. He had to watch what he said. "You could say that. It was certainly full of surprises."

"Hope that doesn't mean you're going to be moving on to better diving grounds soon." Brian ground out his cigarette in the full ashtray on the bar. "Leastwise not until Greg's finished the ROV."

The men round the bar all laughed again. Brian offered drinks on the house often enough to be sure of a good reception for all his jokes.

Cole stood and fished out his wallet. Brian waved his hand in the air. "No, no. Theo's paid for that one." He winked.

"Thanks," Cole said. "I'll head out to the dive shop and see what the boys're up to." The guys at the bar roared with laughter again. Cole reckoned they were all way past happy hour.

He didn't have to go far to find Theo. Gama's was part hotel, part wreck-diving museum, part restaurant and bar—but the heart of the place was in the dive shop. When Brian arrived in Subic Bay just after the Americans pulled out, he'd bought this property and moved his diving business up from Puerto Galera. In the past twenty years, he'd been a part of all the most successful underwater archaeological finds, including the wreck of the galleon *San Diego*, lost in 1600, whose artifacts were in a spectacular display at the Philippines National Museum.

Cole paused in the doorway of the dive shop and watched. Theo was seated on a stool alongside the workbench, which ran the length of the shop. His laptop was on the bench to his left and on the right was a pile of parts—circuit boards, pumps, batteries, and motors. Several of those tiny new HD video cameras in their waterproof housings all the divers were using these days were scattered on the workbench.

Theo was alone, except for Princess Leia, his three-year-old yellow Lab. She rested on the cool concrete floor at the base of his stool. The metal handle of her guide dog harness was folded down across her back.

Theo raised his chin and half turned toward the door. He wore dark Ray-Ban shades. "Is that you John-Boy?" he said.

"If you're supposed to be Jim-Bob Walton, your skin's the wrong color."

"Hey mon, skin color means nothing to me." Theo started rocking back and forth on the bench. "Just call me BB Spencer. That's Black and Blind."

Cole chuckled. "You are a trip, Theo."

Theo said, "Welcome back, boss. We're just finishing up here." He swung back around to face the workbench and rested his hand on his Braille reader.

Whenever he had time to watch Theo work, Cole was amazed at how well his friend had adapted to his situation. He was always so upbeat and positive. During that first year, he had jumped right in, using his computers and all these adaptive technologies to teach himself Braille and get himself onto the list for a guide dog. Theo had told Cole close to a hundred times that his blindness wasn't Cole's fault. But hearing him say that didn't take away the guilt. If Cole hadn't sent him to the bank that day in Grand Cayman, Theo would not be blind today.

It appeared the world had accepted the death of Cole Thatcher. Theo had become the captain of *Shadow Chaser* and Cole posed as the ship's deckhand. They stayed off the radar as much as possible, anchoring in remote locations.

About six months after *Surcouf* had slid into the trench, they had recovered more than two thousand French Angel coins from the wreck, thanks to Henri Michaut's knowledge of the sub, and Theo's incredible design of a deepwater ROV. Theo had concocted a cover story about shooting videos of dolphins with the ROV off the islands. That was how they found themselves cruising around with, at current market value, more than a million and a half in gold aboard *Shadow Chaser*.

It had seemed like a good idea at the time. Cole decided the safest place for the gold would be in one of the offshore banks located in the Cayman Islands. Theo had just returned from France, where he had left Riley with the clues that they hoped would direct her to Grand Cayman. The plan was to meet up there.

Cole didn't want to risk entering a major bank where video cameras were the norm. That was why he sent Theo into Georgetown with two hundred coins to test out the situation. The bank welcomed him with open arms. Theo returned to the boat with a gold bearer bond for $188,000. Two days later, Theo returned to the bank with the intention of opening a safety deposit box, but the same banker who had taken his gold now claimed he'd never seen Theo before. When Theo insisted, the banker grew belligerent. Theo showed him the certificate and the banker claimed it was a forgery. After making quite a scene, Theo left and it was when he was walking in front of an alley on his way back to the harbor that someone pulled him into the shadows.

He never got a look at them. They almost beat him to death. They had clubs of some sort. He knew the blows weren't coming from fists.

A passerby noticed the dark form on the ground in the shadows. As the Good Samaritan approached, he stepped in blood. The man used his cell phone to call the police and they rushed Theo to the Cayman Islands Hospital in Georgetown. He had a broken arm, several broken ribs, a broken nose, but worst of all was the swelling on his brain. He was in a coma for four days. When he finally awoke, he could not see.

At first there was hope that once the swelling subsided, Theo would get his sight back. The doctors wanted to keep him in the hospital for several weeks. But the problem was the local police kept coming around and questioning him, trying to get more information about his attackers. Cole wasn't certain the police were really investigating the crime, or whether they were in cahoots with the bank that had just stolen their gold. They wanted to know what Theo remembered of the incident, and Cole told Theo to remember nothing. Four days after he awoke, Cole slipped Theo out of the hospital in the wee hours of the morning. He had a cab waiting outside and he told the driver to take them to the Barcadere Marina. Within the hour, *Shadow Chaser* put to sea and Cole vowed he would find out who was behind the attack on Theo and the theft of their gold, and he would make them pay.

They fled to the Río Dulce in Guatemala, and far up in the jungle, they found an old boatyard with a marine railway. The yard's owner hadn't had any business in a while, and he was drunk every day by noon. They settled in, sobered up the owner, hauled the boat, and went to work. While Theo recuperated, Cole modified *Shadow Chaser*, changing her superstructure, repainting her, and renaming her the *Bonhomme Richard*.

Meanwhile, as Theo grew stronger and his bones mended, his sight did not improve, but his spirits did. He figured out how to make his computer speak the text on the screen, and with the weak local cellular Internet Theo was soon back to his old self. At night when Cole was finished working on the boat, the two of them began their online search for those responsible for the events in the Cayman Islands.

That was when they discovered the Black Eagle Trust and the Enterprise.

"Hey, Greg," Theo shouted, "you fall in and drown?" He chuckled. "Now that would be funny. A dive master drowning in the toilet."

Cole heard the sound of a toilet flushing and a door opened in the back of the shop. A young Filipina woman wearing very short nylon shorts and an overflowing sports bra stepped through the door and walked barefoot across the concrete floor toward them. She had a tribal tattoo on one bicep and Cole saw the glint of some sort of piercing in her navel.

Cole spoke softly. "Uh, Theo, I don't think that looks like Greg."

The girl wore her long black hair in a braid that fell over her shoulder when she bent down to pat Princess Leia.

Theo's mouth stretched into a wide smile. "So, tell me, skipper. What does Greg look like? I'm a blind man and I keep telling her that I see with my fingers, but she won't let me touch her."

The girl punched Theo in the shoulder.

"Ouch!" he said. "Skipper, I'd like to introduce you to Gregoria Santos—Brian's new mechanic and dive master."

"Uh," Cole said as he looked from Theo to the stunning young woman.

She stuck out her hand. "Nice to meet you, Mr. Jones. Theo has told me lots about you." She spoke in a strong alto voice with very little accent.

He was surprised at the strength in her grip, and he saw the spark of challenge in her eyes. This was not someone he should underestimate.

"Uh, nice to meet you, Greg. I, uh, hear you are a welcome addition here at Gama's."

"Brian's mostly glad I don't drink, and I can keep the dive boat and the compressors running."

"And get this," Theo said. "She rides a Kawasaki crotch rocket to work and she won't even let me take it for a spin."

"Smart woman," Cole said.

Theo slapped his palms down on his thighs. "Greg, I think my skipper wants to get out to the boat. He's been traveling all day." Theo felt around the workbench for his laptop bag and began packing up his computer and his Bluetooth Braille reader and keyboard.

Greg shot Cole a look. "You're lucky to have this guy. He's brilliant at designing these ROVs."

"Hey, that's not all he can design. You should see his work space on the boat. One time he even designed a machine for peeling pineapples."

"So I like pineapple," Theo said. He slung his laptop bag over his shoulder and said, "Leia, let's go." The yellow Lab at his feet stood up and brushed against the side of his leg. Theo grabbed the metal bar attached to her harness and said, "Let's go to the dinghy." He raised his hand and waved. "Later, Greg."

Cole shouted, "See you tomorrow, Brian!" as they passed the side of the dining room and went down to the wharf where the Boston Whaler was tied up.

As they climbed into the dinghy and settled themselves for the ride out to the boat, Cole said, "Do you have any idea how hot that woman is?"

"Yeah. We blind guys can measure how hot a woman is by the way other guys stutter when they meet them. You just proved she's at the top of the stutter scale."

The noise of the outboard prevented conversation on the way out to the boat, but once aboard, they settled in the galley and Theo started a pot of coffee. He set a fresh bowl of water down for Leia, and then slid onto one of the bench seats at the Formica table.

"So, Riley. How is she? How did she take it?"

"I don't know. The fact that she left me in the middle of the night gives me a clue she's not all that happy with me."

"Wow. You figured that out all by yourself, did you?"

"I wish you could see the look I'm giving you."

"Sometimes I consider my condition a blessing. So, what happened over there in Thailand? What made you decide to show yourself to Riley this time?"

"Okay. You know about what she wrote on her blog. How she was contacted by this guy?"

"Yeah, some old guy who said he was a friend of her grandfather's. Peewee. She was supposed to meet him in Bangkok."

"She did. She met with him and all hell broke loose." Cole told Theo about Benny, the blowgun, and Peewee's story about the USS *Bonefish* in the Philippines.

"So this Peewee guy wanted her to have those documents in some Tibetan gold prayer thing. He just gave them to her?"

"Yup."

"Why?"

"Theo, I've been puzzling over that all day."

"Those pages with the odd-looking hieroglyphs—you do realize what they are?"

"I know what I hope they are."

"You're right. One page is a key of some sort. I think the other is a map that we'll figure out using that key."

"And the letter?"

"It says the *Teiyō Maru* was sunk by US bombers in the Babuyan Islands to the north of Luzon. That's a pretty big area, but I'm hoping the map will give us the exact location."

"Do you think it's legit? It's not some forgery made by a Filipino looking to score big off some treasure hunter?"

"No, Cole, I think it's the real thing. I had Brian help me run some tests on the paper of that letter, and we compared it to other letters from the Japanese military here in Luzon during the same period. It's a match."

"Well, they say the Dragon's Triangle stretches from north of the Philippines up to Japan. The Babuyan Islands would be inside the tip of that triangle."

"And there's something more."

"What?"

"I did some research into this Lieutenant Colonel Miyata. I checked through the National Archives database of Japanese documents that were collected during the war. I found one document that gave the military names for several members of the royal family. Lieutenant Colonel Miyata was also known as Prince Kaya Masako."

"You're shitting me. The architect of Golden Lily?"

Theo nodded, his teeth white in a wide grin.

"How soon can we be ready to go, you think?"

Theo laughed. "We've been looking for more than two years, and that ship's been down there for almost seventy years. I don't see what the hurry's all about."

"There's something I didn't tell you about Peewee."

"What?"

"He knew who I was—not John Paul Jones, but Cole Thatcher. Theo, they know I'm alive."

CHAPTER FORTY-THREE

Aboard *Bonefish*
Malacca Strait

November 22, 2012

The small open fishing boat changed heading and began motoring in her direction on an intersecting course. Riley pulled out the binoculars. Through the glasses, she saw three fishermen. There were no weapons evident but that didn't mean there wasn't an arsenal in the boat hidden from view. The word in the sailing community was that ever since the 2004 tsunami, piracy in the straits here had ceased. But Riley wasn't about to let her guard down.

The decision as to whether or not to carry a firearm aboard had been a difficult one for her. She often longed for a gun in situations like this one, but most foreign countries had made it extremely difficult for transient yachts to carry firearms. They made the captain surrender the firearm when you entered through customs and they only returned it to you when you got your clearance to leave. And the time you were most likely to need a gun was when you were in port. Yes, there were those yachts that had devised very well-hidden compartments and they never declared their guns. The problem with that was that it left you vulnerable to losing your boat or imprisonment if caught. It was a risk Riley decided she did not want to take.

So Riley had come up with her own weapons that wouldn't run her afoul of customs regulations in some third-world country. Her primary weapon was a Barnett Ghost 400 crossbow with an upgraded Nikon 3X scope, which rested on the port settee below cocked and ready to go. In addition, she had her dive knife on the bulkhead next to the binoculars case, the 26.5 millimeter German-made Geco flare gun in the sheet bag, her speargun just inside the seat locker, and several cans of hornet spray (which was far more caustic than pepper spray and would shoot farther) in the galley cabinet.

It was still a bit early to be attempting this passage, as the southwest monsoon season would not end for another month—when December brought with it the dryer winds of the northeast monsoon. Thus far, she had been lucky with squalls. She'd only been hit by one during the last three days, and though the winds got up to over forty knots, she had seen it in time to take in her sails. Now she was motoring with only her main up and a whisper of wind off her starboard bow. The sea was flat and glassy.

Riley moved into the companionway as the boat pulled alongside and matched her speed. The biggest man in the group stood up and hollered, "Cigarette? Whiskey?"

This wasn't the first time Riley had been approached and asked for these items. It seemed a bit odd coming from a devout Muslim populace, but she supposed the items sold for lots of money because they were scarce. She shook her head and held up empty hands. "No, sorry. No smoke, no drink."

The men waved at her and smiled. The helmsman started to turn off, but the big man called out, "You! Where husband?"

Riley put her hands together and placed them next to her cheek. "Sleeping." She pointed down into the cabin.

The big man nodded slowly and as the boat pulled away, he kept staring at her. She didn't like his look at all. When the boat had receded far enough away, she went below and grabbed her logbook and a pencil from the chart table. She brought them topsides and settled behind the wheel to make her entry.

She copied the longitude and latitude off the GPS chart plotter mounted in the helm. Then she added boat speed, course, wind speed, and wind direction. Her boat was making just over eight knots now thanks to some push from the tidal currents in the strait, but when the tide turned, her speed would drop considerably. It didn't matter. She would press on. She didn't have time to stop and anchor to wait out the unfavorable currents.

When she'd finished describing the incident with the fishing boat she returned to the cabin to put her logbook away in the chart table. Spread out on the other table in the main salon were many sheets of paper, her iPad, and her laptop. She'd been working on the CAD drawings for the musician's house in Nashville. He had a guitar collection worth over a million as well as original artworks, a recording studio, and a car collection. It was the biggest job she had ever taken on.

Before going back to work, though, she connected her satellite phone to her laptop and checked for email. Nothing more since the email last night from Cole. He'd said he would call her on the single-sideband radio this afternoon at 1:00 p.m. her time. She checked her watch. It was later than she thought. Only ten minutes to go.

She threw the switch on the panel, turned the radio on, and tuned it to 8104 megahertz. She put the volume all the way up so she'd be sure to hear his call over the noise of the engine, then went to the fridge to get a bottle of water.

"*Bonefish, Bonefish,* this is *Bonhomme Richard.*"

She looked at her watch. Three minutes early. She grabbed the mike. "*Bonhomme Richard,* this is *Bonefish.* How do you read?"

"Loud and clear. And it's great to hear your voice."

"Likewise. It does get a little lonely out here sometimes."

"You've only got yourself to blame for that."

"I seem to remember you wanted me to run off and leave my boat behind."

"I was ready to get back to work. How has the trip been so far?"

"Everything's good. I'm not happy about burning so much fuel, but I'm hoping to have more wind soon. I imagine you're chomping at the bit for me to get there so you can do some paperwork." When she'd made her plan to leave alone, she hadn't thought about the fact that she was taking the prayer gau with her. Cole would have to wait for her arrival to start work on the other documents.

"I have plenty to keep me busy," he said.

She wasn't sure what to make of that. He sounded like he didn't care whether she got there or not. "It's going to start getting really hairy tonight. There are fish traps in close to shore, but the middle of the channel is for shipping, and the traffic will get heavier as I approach Singapore."

"I don't know how you do it. How you stay awake."

"I've got alarms on my radar and on my AIS system. And then I just catnap."

"Well, listen, you be safe. I'll call you again on Sunday, same time, okay?"

"Sounds good," she said, although she didn't really want the call to end. "Say hi to Theo for me."

"He's standing right here and he says ditto. You be safe."

"Roger that."

"This is the *Bonhomme Richard*, clear."

CHAPTER FORTY-FOUR

Aboard the USS *Bonefish*
A Cave in Luzon

June 25, 1945

Ozzie saw comprehension transform the faces of the two Japanese sailors on the stone quay—this was not a Japanese submarine. The two men looked at each other and Ozzie knew they were about to run.

He cocked his pistol and pressed the barrel to the side of Prince Masako's head. "Tell those men not to do anything stupid."

The prince spoke aloud, but none of them had any idea what he was saying. The two sailors bowed deeply and then each went to stand by a bollard.

Westbrooke gave the order for the deck crew to proceed with mooring.

"Skipper, I think we'll need an armed detail to accompany us ashore."

"Right, ExO. Issue the orders to organize a shore party. I'd sure like to know where the rest of the Japs are."

As would we both, Ozzie thought.

The monkey's fists flew both forward and aft. The Japanese sailors on shore pulled across the heavier hawsers and secured them fore and aft. The winch motor started and slowly the sub narrowed the gap of aqua water until the hull was snug against the big black tires that hung along the rock face.

The chief of the boat organized a crew of half a dozen men with rifles to stand along the deck. The gunner held his position on the fifty-caliber deck gun as the gangway was being rigged.

"Listen, Your Highness. I know you don't think I'm going to shoot you because you are my best bargaining chip. You're absolutely right. But I won't hesitate to shoot Ben here."

The prince turned and met Ozzie's gaze with a hard look Ozzie hadn't seen before. So, there was a warrior under the professor façade. "Lieutenant, you do not have to worry. We are cooperating. We understand each other."

"Good. Let's keep it that way. Tell the men on the dock not to leave."

The prince spoke again and the two men stepped back against the far cave wall and stood at attention.

Up on the bow a sailor rigged another light and more of the cave became visible. The cavern was oblong, stretching back from the opening what looked like a good six to eight hundred feet, while the width was perhaps three hundred feet. The stone quay they had tied to had been carved into the cave wall. On their side of the chamber there were no stalactites, but on the far side of the water the spires stretched down from the ceiling like long dark icicles. Some reached down to the level of the water.

"What can you tell me about the layout here?" Ozzie pointed to the back of the cave where the light did not penetrate. "How far back does this cave reach?"

"This is an underground river, Lieutenant. We have followed it back for twelve kilometers."

"What? That's not possible."

"Oh, yes, there are many such caves here in Luzon." The prince smiled. "Trust me, I know."

"Where are your men encamped?"

"After the lake here, the river narrows and so does the passage. But it opens again into several large chambers. When the sea is rough, docking like this is not possible and this whole chamber floods. My men are camped in the third chamber, about one kilometer back."

"And what about another opening? Is there another way out back there?"

"Yes. That is why we camp there. We call it the back door. It is a small opening, not big enough to bring cargo through, and it is far from any road. But the cook's hut and the latrine are outside through that exit."

"Okay. You ready, skipper?"

"Let's go," Westbrooke said.

They assembled on the dock. One man was left behind on the quay to guard the two Japanese sailors, while Ozzie, Prince Masako, and Ben, flanked by two armed guards, led the way. Westbrooke, the chief, and four more armed sailors followed.

Two of the sailors carried flashlights, at the front and the rear, as well as both officers, but the ground was wet, slippery, uneven clay, so the going was slow. As the prince told them, the cave grew smaller at the rear and eventually the walls closed in around them. They found themselves in a high-ceilinged tunnel about twenty feet across with a fast-moving stream flowing down the middle of the passage. Overhead, stalactites dripped water on their heads and the passage walls shone with dampness in the light. There was still room on the right-hand stream bank for about three men to walk abreast, but the going was slow as the ground was slick with mud.

On their side of the passage, wires had been strung, and every twenty feet or so electric lights were affixed to the muddy side wall.

Ozzie considered asking the prince how to turn them on but he didn't want to warn the men ahead.

The air filled their nostrils with a damp, boggy smell. To Ozzie, it felt like trying to breathe through a muddy kerchief. The temperature was cool enough, but due to the humidity, his shirt was already drenched with sweat and the water that dripped on them from the cave.

One of the sailors at the rear of the patrol slipped and went down hard. He cursed and Westbrooke shushed him even more loudly. Ozzie halted the group while one of the other sailors helped the man who had fallen. It appeared only his pride had been injured. Ozzie waved them onward. The prince stepped along the passage with confidence, not even looking at the ground. Of course, he knew what was ahead. That was what worried Ozzie most.

Because they had been watching the ground, they came on the second chamber without warning. The lead man's flashlight lit up the wood of an enormous crate. They were all marked "UO2." The man shifted the light and there was another and another. They all had Japanese writing on them in addition to the symbol.

"What does that say?" Ozzie whispered. He pointed at the writing on one of the crates.

"It's the name of the ship," the prince said. "It says *Teiyō Maru*."

The lead sailor took another step and shone the light up into another huge chamber with fantastic dripping spires reaching down at them. But what made Ozzie gasp out loud was the sight of an enormous golden dragon perched on top of a huge pile of gold bullion, the front end of his serpentine body raised into the air as though he were just about to take flight. As the others caught up to them and the beams of the two flashlights danced around the cave, they saw dozens of wooden crates and barrels covering almost every bit of the space in the chamber that must have been one hundred feet across. Prince

Masako walked over to one of the barrels and lifted the lid. The flash-light beams glinted off the mound of colorful gems inside.

"Welcome to Golden Lily," the prince said.

CHAPTER FORTY-FIVE

Sukhumvit Cryonics Lab
Bangkok, Thailand

November 23, 2012

In the end, the old man made it easy.

Benny's contact at the Enterprise had access to all sorts of electronic information. A world-class hacker, he could provide anything from bank statements to satellite photos. Benny had used him many times before.

The old man Irv had worked for the Enterprise for years, so they had all his information on file. It took all of two days before his name popped up. He probably thought he was being cool by not using credit cards, but this outfit where he had his appointment today had run a credit check on him. Once his name popped, Benny's contact had hacked into this company's computers. Benny got the call the night before, reporting that the old man had an appointment at 9:00 a.m. at the Sukhumvit Cryonics Lab.

Benny sat inside an Au Bon Pain café across the street from the lab. A bottle of water and an uneaten pastry sat on the table in front of him. Very few people passed through the doors he watched. He was not surprised.

He had visited the place earlier that morning. When he'd first gone inside, he had no idea what cryonics was. He just wanted to check the place out to make sure that there wasn't a back entrance that the old man could use to slip out. Benny pretended he was a lost tourist, and he asked for directions to the Terminal 21 mall. The woman behind the desk was very patient with him. He asked more questions, and then she had explained to him what their business was.

Freezing people. Benny had never heard anything like it. These people believed that by freezing themselves now, someday in the future there would be technology that would cure their bodies of old age and they would live on. Benny thought it was crazy and unnatural. And expensive.

So that was what was going on. The old man had sold the goods to the woman on the sailboat so he could get enough money to freeze himself. Benny shook his head. He'd heard of some weird things in his life, but this one topped them all.

The old man's military side cap was always a giveaway. It made him easy to spot. The medals glinted in the sunlight. He came from the direction of the Chidlom SkyTrain station and walked more slowly than the upscale Thai crowd on this street. Benny checked his watch. The old guy was right on time.

Benny slid back his chair and threw some bills on the table. He figured Irv would be in there for a while, but getting across Sukhumvit wasn't easy, so he wasn't going to wait.

Once across the busy street, he positioned himself in a doorway next to the lab. Irv would probably return to the same SkyTrain station. Benny didn't need a gun to coerce him. He didn't need any weapon other than his bare hands with such a weak old man. He could simply threaten to break one or two of his old bones.

The old man walked out sooner than Benny had expected, but then he turned right instead of left as Benny had assumed. He was so short he disappeared into the crowd in an instant.

Benny darted onto the sidewalk and began pushing his way forward. Several women shrieked when he pushed them. He didn't care. If the old man heard him, it wasn't like he could run faster.

Where was he? He should have caught up to him by now. That was when he saw the old man climbing onto the back of a motorcycle taxi. The driver wore the required bright pink vest and a black ski mask. He pulled on a full face-covering helmet and kick-started the bike as the old man gripped his waist.

Benny saw that he wasn't going to make it, so he jumped on the nearest unattended bike and fired it up. The drivers were standing on the sidewalk smoking and one of them yelled as Benny shoved it into gear and took off in pursuit.

The motorcycle taxi driver darted and dodged through the traffic like a bat in the treetops. The driver had disappeared from sight when traffic came to a halt at a red light. Benny worked his way to the front of the pack and found the old man sitting on the back of the motorbike. He didn't turn around when Benny pulled up.

When the light turned green, they were off again and Benny found his navigation through the traffic was improving. He was able to keep the motorbike in sight this time. In about a mile, the bike pulled over and the old man slid off. While he was paying the driver, Benny parked the bike he was riding on the sidewalk and walked up behind the old man as he was positioning his garrison cap on his head.

"Hey, Irv."

The old man turned around with his mouth open. Then he smiled. "Hello, Benny. How'd you find me?"

Benny shrugged. "That place back there. You really planning to freeze yourself, Irv?"

"Just looking at all my options, you know."

"So, I guess you sold the Enterprise property. Not so smart, Irv."

"Naw." He waved his hand through the air. "I didn't sell it. I loaned it to a friend."

"Right." Benny grabbed Irv by the forearm. "And now you're going to help me get it back."

"How you gonna find her?"

"Don't worry. That's my business. But Hawkes told me to be sure to bring you along. We've got a plane to catch."

CHAPTER FORTY-SIX

Changi International Airport
Singapore

November 23, 2012

Elijah sipped his scotch and surveyed the crowd that hurried through the terminal. Benny was late. Elijah had specifically told him Harry's Bar in Terminal 3 at 2:00 p.m. It was now quarter past.

When Benny called a couple of days ago and explained his plan, Elijah decided it would be best if he accompanied Benny on this one. The old adage was proving to be true. If you wanted something done right, you had to do it yourself.

Elijah had secured his reputation by doing things right. It had once been a survival mechanism but he had turned it into his brand. He had been born into a poor Quaker family, and one winter day when he was five years old and his sister was sixteen, his parents had gone to take food and old clothing to a struggling parish family that lived high up in the mountains. When Elijah and Sarah awoke the next morning, they were surprised to learn their parents hadn't returned. They never knew for certain what happened, but they believed their parents' car must have gone off a cliff on the icy roads. If the crash hadn't killed them, they never would have survived the night's freezing temperatures.

Sarah didn't call the police. She was afraid they would take her brother away and put them in separate foster families. She was already working at a fast food place in the afternoons, and with their free school breakfast and lunch program, they survived and kept their status secret for the year and a half it took for his sister to turn eighteen. Then she filed to become his legal guardian. As his sister matured, she became more and more fanatically religious. Whenever he displeased her, he was forced to kneel in his bedroom and pray for hours. He learned to do things right the first time.

The men he worked with now expected it of him, and he would be reporting to them in three days. They were expecting good news on the Dragon's Triangle project, and he'd better have something for them.

When he saw Benny and the old man approaching down the corridor, he didn't like how memorable they looked. It was best in this business if you didn't stand out. Benny was wearing some kind of motley-colored indigenous jacket over his blue jeans and carrying his tooled leather case for his blowpipe in addition to a fat old military-surplus green canvas rucksack. His long, thick hair was tied back in a ponytail held by a leather thong. The old man was wearing a white long-sleeved shirt with a string tie, green slacks that were pulled up almost to his armpits, and his old army garrison cap covered with medals and ribbons. They looked like a pair of costumed extras off a movie set.

Benny had a tight grip on the old man's arm, and steered him over to an empty stool one seat over from Elijah. Benny sat between them.

The old man waved at the bartender, then leaned forward and pointed at Elijah's glass. "I'll have one of those," he said in a too-loud voice.

"Tell him to keep it down," Elijah said.

"Irv," Benny said, and he raised his hand to his ear and made a twisting motion.

The old man bent down and, while working his lips over his teeth, concentrated on a small black box attached to his belt. Elijah flinched when the piercing squeal of electronic feedback erupted from the old man's hearing aid.

"Irv," Benny said again, but this time he dragged his finger across his neck in a chopping motion.

Surprise registered on the old guy's face and he went back to fiddling with the box.

"He can't hear a damn thing," Benny said. "Not even when he makes it scream like that. The good part is we can talk freely. He can't hear us."

"Did you get us a boat?" Elijah asked.

"It's all set. I've even got an ETA. My buddy got me a satellite photo of her boat entering the channel off Singapore yesterday. She should pass within ten to fifteen miles of Natuna Besar tomorrow."

"It's such a big ocean. How can you be so sure?"

"The South China Sea is full of rocks and reefs. This is the route that's recommended to avoid ending up on those reefs. Don't worry. We'll find her. I've got two boats. They will be out searching for her starting at dawn. She won't get by us."

"Okay. Our flight's in a little over an hour. We should head out to the gate."

CHAPTER FORTY-SEVEN

Aboard *Bonefish*
South China Sea

November 24, 2012

Riley climbed up into the cockpit, sat on the high seat, and braced her bare feet on the fiberglass seat opposite. She leaned her head back and looked up past her dodger at the graceful curve of her mainsail's leech, the brilliant white sail contrasting against the cloudless sky. At the top of her mast, the black wind vane pointed at a slight angle back over her shoulders.

"Sweet," she said aloud as a wave lifted the aft quarter of her hull and she heard the *whooosh* as the white water broke around her, and her boat surfed on a diagonal down the wave. The south-southeast wind had her sailing on a broad reach, and it was her favorite point of sail. The Caliber 40 was not designed to be a racing boat, and her boat wasn't ever going to break any speed records, but she was fast enough and especially comfortable. Riley reckoned *Bonefish* had been averaging seven knots since she'd left the Middle Channel, and yet she was only heeled over about fifteen degrees, if that.

Riley patted the teak-topped coaming she was leaning against. "You go girl," she said aloud.

It was great to be sailing again after the windless trip down from Phuket to Singapore. She'd motorsailed the majority of those first three or four days, meeting many fishing boats and dodging ships in the straits off Singapore. The flat water and dry cockpit had allowed her to work long hours and she'd been able to get her draft proposal sent off that morning.

Now it was pure bliss with the engine off and a relatively empty ocean. No more noise and heat from the engine room or worried calculations as to whether or not her fuel would last. She could hear the creaking of the lines stretching in the puffs of wind, the rushing sound of the water sliding past her hull. In the distance, she saw three or four white birds circling over a spot in the ocean, and occasionally she could even hear the sound of their cries. They were hunting fish, no doubt.

Birds, fish, all were signs she was approaching land.

She slid back behind the wheel and checked her instruments. The chart plotter told her she had twenty-one miles to go to her waypoint off Natuna Besar, an island that belonged to Indonesia. The plotter showed an ETA of two o'clock. She would pass within eleven miles of the island, and since it had a mountain over three thousand feet high, she should be able to see it in the next hour or two. She'd read in one of her cruising guides that lots of sailors broke up their trip by stopping here, but that there wasn't much on the island. The people fished and farmed, and the capital city, Ranai, had some stores, fuel, and provisions. Stopping wasn't in her plans, though.

Riley checked the other instruments. Her autopilot was humming right along, doing a great job of keeping the boat on course. The boat did tend to slew around a bit in these long six- to eight-foot swells, making her compass do a drunken dance under the plastic dome, but the course averaged out. She knew she couldn't steer any straighter.

The wind-speed indicator showed the wind was maintaining the steady sixteen to twenty knots. And the sea beneath the boat was so deep it did not register any depth on her fathometer.

For the moment, the conditions couldn't be better, and she hoped to sight land soon to confirm her position. In the meantime, she should rustle up something to eat. She slid across the seat toward the companionway stairs.

Riley moved around her boat with ease, often not even aware of the fact that she was holding on in a bouncing, swaying environment. It usually took her a day or two to get her sea legs, but once she got over that initial queasiness, she got her appetite back.

She checked her sprouting jar. The alfalfa sprouts were bright green. She'd have her salad for lunch. She groped her way to her canned-food locker behind the port settee and dug around inside. Water chestnuts, black olives, and a jar of artichoke hearts. Add to that a slice of the bread she'd baked two days ago and a bottle of cold water and she would be set.

Thirty minutes later Riley had plugged her iPhone into the stereo, and she had some tunes playing from a CD that Billy had given her. It was by a bluegrass group called the Mountain Girls and Riley appreciated the intimate voice of the lead singer. She climbed into the cockpit with her food and settled on the low seat to enjoy her meal.

As she munched her salad, Riley thought about Cole. Once she got past Natuna Besar, she'd have about a thousand miles left to go. If she kept winds like this, she'd make it in a week.

When she finished her lunch, Riley stood in the companionway and examined the horizon through the window of her dodger. There were some low clouds ahead, but she was pretty sure she could make out the hard shape of the island. She was only fifteen miles off now.

She descended the steps, dropped her dishes in the sink, grabbed the binoculars off the chart table, and headed back topsides. She stood on the top step with her elbows resting on either side of the hatch and searched off her port bow. It was definitely the sloping sides of the island with the mountaintop shrouded in clouds. She lowered the binoculars and scanned the horizon for ships.

That was when she saw it. A small fishing boat appeared on the top of a swell and then disappeared into the trough. For a minute or so she had trouble spotting it again, but when she did find it, the boat was quite a bit closer. It wasn't as small a boat as she had originally thought. When she'd first sighted it, the boat looked like it would cross her bow, but then they changed back onto a converging course. The boat had the high bow typical of all the boats she'd seen in Southeast Asia, and it was painted with bright yellow, blue, and red stripes. Set back toward the stern there was a small deckhouse.

Undoubtedly this was going to be another attempted shakedown for booze and cigarettes or anything else she might have to share. Through the binoculars, she saw at least two men standing out on deck. There was probably at least one more in the deckhouse at the steering station. Though she had been approached by half a dozen boats already on this trip, and none of them had proved menacing, her training wouldn't permit her to do nothing as they approached.

Riley went below and collected her dive knife, the Geco flare gun, and the can of wasp and hornet spray. The steel flare gun shot twenty-five-millimeter flares that would probably kill a man if shot within a certain range. It was beefier and more accurate than the American plastic-variety flare gun. The insect spray was designed to take out a whole nest, and it shot a stream up to twenty-two feet away. She'd never had to use it, and she hoped today wouldn't be the first time. As a last precaution, she pulled her crossbow out of the forward hanging locker and nocked an arrow into it and cocked it. She slipped it under the covers on the forward cabin bunk.

When she emerged back on deck, she was surprised to see how close the boat had drawn. It was approaching at ten o'clock off her port bow and only a thousand yards separated them. One of the two men standing on the foredeck had a line coiled in his hand. It was attached to a grappling hook that he held ready to throw in the other hand. This was no ordinary fishing expedition. The sea was too rough for them to pull alongside her boat. One or both of the boats would be damaged. These guys were pirates.

She had to prevent them from boarding her, to scare them off. It was the first time she had ever fired the flare gun. She'd intended to put one across their bow, but the orange ball of fire passed very close to Mr. Grappling Hook. He dodged it and shouted something, and then motioned to the boat's driver. Riley could see the man through the windows on the front of the cabin. He wore a red bandana as a headband and he was shoving the wheel over as their boat passed hers going in the opposite direction. Then they slowed, turned across her wake, and then began to overtake and move up alongside her boat.

She reloaded and raised the flare gun to fire again. This time she would aim more carefully. There were no more than fifty feet separating the two boats as the pirates matched her speed. It was a wooden boat and from the sound of the engine, it sounded like an old gasoline one-cylinder. She wanted to scare them, not kill them. She was sighting down the barrel of the flare gun when she felt a sting in her upper arm. She looked at her bicep and saw the feather tail of a dart. The grappling hook thudded aboard and caught on one of her turnbuckles. The flare gun dropped out of her hand, and her arm dropped to her side, numb, lifeless. She felt dizzy.

Then she saw him step out of the deckhouse. Black hair streaked with gray, Fu Manchu mustache, the blue ink of tattoos on his forearms. He was holding the blowpipe in one hand and smiling at her.

With her good arm, she lifted the can of insect spray, aimed it at the grappling hook man pulling the line attached to her boat, and sprayed. She heard him scream just before she passed out.

CHAPTER FORTY-EIGHT

**Aparri, Luzon
The Philippines**

November 24, 2012

Cole watched the depth sounder as he brought his boat up the Cagayan River so as to avoid the shoal patch in the center just inside the river mouth. It was late in the evening, and he was losing the last of the day's light. The river water was a dark muddy brown, though, so even with good light he wouldn't have been able to spot any shallows. He dropped the anchor in sixteen feet and felt satisfied when he backed the boat down and the anchor set well. He was ready for a good meal and some rest after the 350-mile trip up from Subic Bay.

The town of Aparri advertised itself as a jumping-off spot for trips out to the Babuyan Islands, which lay some thirty to fifty miles offshore, but considering what Cole could see from the river—wood shacks, unpainted cinderblock buildings, trash, and stray dogs—the place didn't look like a tourist mecca to him. Cole wasn't getting a good vibe about the place. But after having no luck whatsoever with figuring out the map and key on their own, Brian had suggested they visit an old friend of his in Aparri, so here they were. They'd head ashore in the morning and locate the man Brian referred to as the Norwegian Psychic.

After making certain they were securely anchored, Cole shut down the engine and went to the galley to find Theo. He found him sitting on one of the settee bench seats with Leia asleep at his side. The table was covered with papers, Theo's laptop, and his special Braille machine. Theo had designed a machine that embossed raised areas of the page like Braille writers do, but he made his dots much sharper pixels. He said it took four of his pins to create one Braille dot. The end result was that he was able to emboss papers with two-dimensional designs. This enabled him to read maps and charts, to read schematic diagrams, and to work on the map and code key that Cole had sent him while Riley was sleeping. He was able to connect his embossing graphics machine to his laptop via USB and then he could print out a copy he could read with his fingers.

"So what do you say, Theo? Tell me you've had a breakthrough."

"Not really. This thing we're calling a map—it's more like a children's drawing. I've graphed it and run it through a program that is trying to match it to the nautical charts of the Babuyan Islands, but one of the problems is that we don't know what the scale is. And, of course, it is hand-drawn so it's bound to be inaccurate. Even the computer's drawing a blank. There are five major islands and dozens of smaller ones out there. That's way too big an area to search."

"We'll go ashore in the morning. Hopefully this friend of Brian's will be able to help us out."

"I don't know," Theo said as he started to clear off the table. "Brian didn't exactly effuse with his recommendation."

The next morning Cole used the crane to lower the Boston Whaler dinghy into the water. When they rebuilt *Shadow Chaser* and turned her into the *Bonhomme Richard*, Cole designed the transom so that it could fold down and create a swim platform and workdeck aft. It was easier for getting in and out of the dinghy and for loading and off-loading gear. He and Theo climbed in. Leia followed and lay down at Theo's feet. She was the only dog Cole had ever seen who didn't insist on riding up on the bow.

It had rained hard earlier that morning, but the day remained overcast and so humid Cole's shirt was soaked through before he even started the outboard engine. Theo wore a small messenger bag with the strap crossing his chest, and he put his arms over the bag to shield it from any rain or spray.

The way to the town was up a smaller tributary river. The buildings were pretty sparse at first, but about half a mile in they got to the downtown marketplace and there the riverbanks were solid with buildings. They saw lots of boat traffic around them and most of the people smiled and waved. Cole tied up the Whaler at the market where concrete steps led from the water up to the busy marketplace. He got out the cable and lock and secured the dinghy to a rusty iron ring set into the concrete wall.

As they passed through the food vendors in the market, Cole kept up a running commentary describing what he was seeing to Theo, who kept one hand on Cole's arm, the other on Leia's handle.

"The ground is muddy and there are puddles everywhere. Can't avoid them; try not to slip. We're passing through the local fruit and vegetable market. It's inside a courtyard of sorts. There's no roof overhead, but each vendor has slung some sort of plastic tarp over his or her space with another tarp on the ground that marks the outline of the stall. Some of the produce is stacked in little pyramids, like the potatoes, tomatoes, onions, and garlic. Several women have flats of fresh eggs, too. Now we're heading through an entrance gate and out to the street."

"Are there any full-sized taxis?"

"Nope, just tricycles."

Theo sighed. "I'm not taking the dog on my lap this time. It's your turn."

Cole motioned to the driver of one of the tricycle cabs—which were really motorcycles with a small aluminum pod of a sidecar. Dozens of them were parked along the street outside the market. The driver jumped up and mounted his bike.

"The Ryan Hotel?"

The driver nodded.

"I think he knows where to take us. Time to climb in."

Theo was a six-footer and slender, while Cole wasn't as tall, but stocky. He always felt like an idiot when they stuffed themselves and the seventy-pound Lab into this favorite mode of Filipino transport. The seat was only four to five inches higher than the floor. Their knees were at the level of their ears, and the ceiling was so low Theo couldn't straighten up his neck.

Aparri was a bigger town than Cole thought. The driver dodged through traffic on roads four lanes wide, his bike's engine groaning with the unaccustomed weight. The roads were full of potholes and the tricycle had the shocks of, well, a tricycle. Cole saw a cluster of young girls giggle and point at them as the bike slowed for a stop sign. Whether it was the dog, the black man (unusual in this country), or the sight of them all stuffed into the tiny sidecar, he wasn't sure. But after several turns and a couple of traffic signals, the driver pulled up in front of a green two-story building with a neon sign and shut off his engine.

Cole and Theo tumbled out of the sidecar. Theo straightened up to his full height and rubbed the back of his neck. "Every time, I swear I'm never gonna do that again."

"Not to worry," Cole said as he paid the driver. "Once this guy leaves, it doesn't look like there will be any other choice than to walk back."

Inside the door, Cole asked the woman behind the desk if she could help them find Skar. She pointed to the stairs.

When they reached the top, Cole saw a large room full of tables with a bar along one side. A lone man sat hunched over the bar. He had dark blond hair that fell to his shoulder in long, greasy-looking clumps.

Cole spoke quietly. "There's only one guy in here. Must be him. What in the hell is Brian getting us into?"

"That bad, huh?"

They crossed the room and Cole stopped behind the man hunched over his drink.

"Nils Skar?"

The man did not turn around. "Who wants to know?" His English was strongly accented.

"My name's John Jones. Brian Holmes sent us."

The man's head swung around and Cole saw from his profile that his eyes bulged grotesquely out of his eye sockets. "You're friends of Brian? Then have a seat."

"Actually, would you be willing to sit at a table with us? We have something we'd like to show you."

The man tipped his head back and drained brown liquid from a shot glass, which he then slammed on the bar. The noise raised someone in the back room, and a man came hurrying out from a door at the end of the bar.

Nils pointed them toward a four-top table. Even when the man stood, his shoulders remained hunched over, his chest concave. He staggered over to the table, pulled out a chair, and appeared to notice Theo and Leia for the first time as he collapsed onto the chair. He opened his mouth to speak, but instead launched into a fit of wet, gargling coughs that caused his whole body to convulse.

"Are you all right?" Cole asked.

Nils nodded and gradually the coughing subsided. He reached into his back pocket and pulled out a dirty-looking handkerchief and a leather pouch.

"Sorry about that," he said, wiping at the corners of his mouth. "My health is not good." Then he unzipped the pouch and the smell of cannabis engulfed them as he took out a package of papers and began to roll a joint.

Theo said, "Am I smelling what I think I'm smelling?"

Nils looked up at Theo with his bulging eyes. "And you are . . . ?"

"Theo," he said, and held out his hand toward a point about twelve inches to the right of where Nils was sitting.

"You're blind."

"Really?" Theo said with his hand still hanging in the air as an offer. "I hadn't noticed."

Nils grabbed Theo's hand and shook it heartily. "Ha! I like you. And I may be like you, soon. It's a brain tumor." He picked up the joint and licked the paper to seal it. "This is for the headaches. They don't mind here. They know me."

Cole spoke up. "Nils, the only reason we are here is because Brian told us you are very familiar with the Babuyan Islands. We need your help with a map."

Nils fished a lighter out of his pocket, lit the joint, and inhaled a lungful. After holding his breath for several seconds, he exhaled. "So," he said, "you are treasure hunters. And I was just starting to like your blind friend here. Listen to me." He leaned across the table, his bulging eyes staring at Cole. "*There are no authentic maps.* You have been cheated by some Filipino who has filled your head with stories of Yamashita's Gold and sold you a fake map. Do you really think if there was gold around here these people wouldn't have found it already?" He brought the joint to his mouth but another coughing fit stopped him from taking a drag.

"Brian told us you already ran one salvage operation of a Japanese submarine out in the Babuyans."

"And did he tell you that I also found two other wrecks and between the three we didn't even recover enough to pay our costs?"

"He didn't go into detail."

"I've spent enough of my life chasing after Filipino gold. I get a dozen guys a month contacting me with the same story. I guarantee you in a few months you'll be broke, and you still won't have found any gold."

Cole turned to Theo. "Let's show him the map."

Theo pulled a sheet of paper out of his messenger bag. "This is just a copy, of course, but we do believe it is authentic," he said.

Nils took a deep drag on the joint, then said, "A blind guy can read a map."

Theo ran his fingers over the map. "Feel it. The lines are embossed."

Nils tentatively touched the surface and nodded. "Nice. I could use something like that already. How'd you do that?"

Cole said, "Look, man, we didn't come here to show you how to make embossed maps. Brian said you might be willing to help us. He said we could trust you."

Nils held up his hands. "Okay, okay. You know, in this business, it gets to be habit. There are so many amateurs that come to the Philippines looking for Japanese gold, for Marcos's gold. This country is full of scammers, and I'm in the habit of pushing everyone away. Especially people with names like John Jones."

"Blame my mother. She was a patriot. It's John Paul Jones." Cole held the man's stare. "We didn't buy this document."

"Where did you get it then?"

"From an old man. An American. He served over here, and he claims he got it during the war."

"Describe him."

As he described Peewee for the Norwegian, Cole saw a flash of something in the man's face. Was it recognition? Then Nils closed his eyes. He started rocking and humming. "Yes," he said. "*I know!* I will."

Leia whined softly under the table.

"It's okay, girl," Theo said as he reached down to pat his dog. "What's happening?"

"I don't know. He's sitting right here but it looks like Nils has left the building."

When the Norwegian opened his eyes, he looked disoriented. "Uh . . . um. What were you saying?"

"Are you okay?" Cole asked.

Nils shook his head, more to try to wake up than to say no. "I'm all right. Ugh. My head hurts." He lowered his head, put his elbows on the table, and squeezed his head between his palms. "It's been a while since that's happened."

"Since what's happened?"

His voice was muffled when he spoke. "I see things—hear things."

Cole looked at Theo. At times like this, Cole really missed the silent communication they used to share with looks. His friend looked puzzled. He was trying to figure out what was going on.

Nils sat up straight, his eyes wide and bulging out of the sockets. "I assume you have a chart with you," he said.

Cole was ready to throw in the towel and get out of there. Cole didn't believe in psychics and this guy was about as fake as they come. But Theo produced his tablet and showed Nils how to read the electronic charts. Once the Norwegian was acclimated to the device, he brushed his finger across the touch screen and located the spot he wanted. He turned the paper drawing to reorient it, then adjusted the electronic chart again.

"There," he said. "I did my salvage work off Camiguin. That's the area I know best. Your map doesn't give me much to go on, but if I had to guess, I'd say that"—he pointed to the enclosed figure near the center of the page—"is Calayan Island and this obscene-looking shape down here is Dalupiri Island. I don't know about the drawing of a little animal or what the hand or the star are all about, but there is an interesting note on the charts here." He pointed to the screen, which showed the nautical chart of the two islands he had named. "Most of the water between these two islands is over a thousand feet deep. But tell me what you see off the northeast tip of Dalupiri."

Cole leaned in to examine the screen. "There's an area marked with a dotted line and it says 181-foot depth recorded in 1996. Interesting."

"Exactly."

"You know," Cole said, "there are always weird anomalies like that on charts. Most of the time it was just something that went wonky on a ship or surveyor's equipment."

"Yeah. Most of the time. But *something* is telling me not this time."

Cole rubbed his fingers through his beard. "Something?"

"Or someone."

"Okay." Cole stood and Theo collected the map and the tablet. "Thanks for your help, Nils."

The man launched into another phlegmy coughing fit. The dog's nails clicked on the wood floor as she scrambled to her feet. Nils called out, "Won't you stay for lunch?"

As they walked back toward the center of town, neither man spoke for the first ten minutes.

Cole was the first to break the silence. "It doesn't make sense that the depth would go from like twelve hundred feet to a hundred and eighty feet in that one little area."

"No, it could be an underwater mountain, but it's more likely something down there caused a funky reading."

"Something really funky—like radioactive?"

"Yeah, something like that."

CHAPTER FORTY-NINE

A Cave in Luzon
The Philippines

June 26, 1945

One of the enlisted men was the first to break rank. He lowered his gun, walked over to the barrel of gems, and thrust his hand inside. His fist rose into the air, spilling a showering cascade of colored stones that glittered in the beam of Ozzie's flashlight.

"Jesus!" the man said.

"Sailor!" Westbrooke shouted. "Back in line."

One of the men at the rear of the party took off at a trot, headed for the mountain of gold bullion. The chamber opened up like a half circle on their right. The golden dragon was against the far wall and the crates were stacked in such a way as to leave several walkways radiating out from the dragon. Ozzie shone his flashlight around the chamber. About one hundred feet ahead on the far side he saw a black opening. The beam of his light wasn't strong enough to see beyond the far wall, but Ozzie assumed that was the tunnel that would lead on to the next chamber. The one where Masako's men now slept. He wished Westbrooke would lower his voice.

The skipper continued to shout orders, but it had no effect on the men. One by one they wandered off through the aisles between the crates toward the center structure of gold bricks that appeared to support the dragon. Westbrooke followed them, but his orders did not seem to register.

Prince Masako touched Ozzie's sleeve. "That dragon is early Qing dynasty. You cannot blame your men for being drawn to it. Even though the statue is hollow, it is made of more than three tons of pure gold."

The snakelike body of the statue was about five feet in diameter, and it stretched back, rising and falling in an S curve. The beast's huge head reared up, fangs bared in his gaping mouth. The forelegs reached outward with razor-sharp talons. "How did you get it here?" Ozzie asked.

"Our soldiers discovered it in a temple in Thailand. It was transported here on a ship, then off-loaded by crane out in the cave where your submarine is. It rests on a wood cart behind the bullion. When it is safe to transport it back to the homeland, it can be hauled back out to the dock."

"And these other crates?"

"Let me show you." The prince walked over to one of the smaller crates and spoke to Ben. The young man pried up the lid.

"Precious metals and gems are not the only treasures." The crate was filled with straw-like packing material, but Ben dug down about a foot and pulled out a porcelain jar that stood about one foot tall. The paintings on it depicted a fierce stylized dog along with whiskery fish and pale blossoms. "Many of these contain this Chinese porcelain like ginger jars and vases from the Ming dynasty." He pointed at other crates. "Some contain paintings or ancient scrolls. There are jade and stone carvings, jewelry, tapestries. Whatever our men believed was of value."

Ozzie walked over to one of the larger crates. "And what about these big crates with the writing on them?"

The prince grinned and Ozzie turned away with a shiver.

"Just more valuables, Lieutenant." He called for Ben to return to his side.

Westbrooke returned without the sailor guards. "They won't listen to me. They're trying to stuff gold bricks into their pockets. It's mutiny." His voice sounded whiny, petulant. It was little wonder the men didn't give him more respect.

Ozzie shook his head. "No, sir, it's just greed. Give them a few more minutes. Let them explore. They'll be back."

Westbrooke stepped between Ozzie and the prince and spoke in a low voice. "We may not have a few more minutes, ExO. How long until the soldiers back there wake up?"

"I doubt your shouting just now helped, Westbrooke."

"Come on," the skipper said. "Let's go round them up."

The man might as well admit he can't control his own men, Ozzie thought. He followed him to the far side of the cave and stood staring up at the dragon's gaping mouth. The workmanship was extraordinary. The value of the statue would go far beyond its weight in gold.

"H2O. Try your hand," the skipper said. "See if they'll listen to you."

One sailor had taken off his shirt, spread it out on the cave floor, and piled gold bricks on it. He was now tying the cloth around it to make a bundle he could carry in one hand while he held his flashlight in the other. He was just a kid, no more than nineteen years old.

Ozzie walked up and shoved his shoulder. "Sailor!" he barked.

The young man jumped up and saluted.

A loud bang echoed in the stone chamber, and a hole appeared in the kid's forehead. His flashlight hit the ground first and his body crumpled after it.

Ozzie drew his weapon and crouched, looking all around him, but he didn't see anyone other than their own men. The shot seemed to have come from very close by. The gold now forgotten, the other sailors grabbed their rifles. The skipper scrambled for cover behind one of the larger crates.

"Turn off your flashlights," Ozzie said.

The other lights clicked off except for the one lone beam that still lit the cave floor next to the dead sailor.

Jensen, a machinist first class, stood with his rifle to his shoulder and began advancing on the dragon. One of the others clicked a flashlight on. As he shone the light around the platform and the pile of gold bricks, a dragon-shaped statue danced on the wall.

Another shot sounded. The sailor dropped his rifle and pitched forward onto the pile of gold bricks. The flashlight clicked off, leaving the cave in the eerie half light from that single flashlight beam.

The shots seemed to be coming from somewhere on the other side of the dragon. The prince had said the statue was on a cart. Ozzie wondered if the shooter could be under it.

Ozzie began to crawl backward, staying as close as he could to the side of the walkway next to the wood crates. If he could just locate the prince he could get him to put a stop to this. He cursed himself for not keeping the man close to him when he went with Westbrooke.

He heard the skipper's hushed voice calling out to his remaining men. "Can anyone spot the shooter?"

Still on his knees, Ozzie lifted himself up to look over the top of the crates next to him. He saw some movement. One of the sailors had hung his shirt on his rifle barrel and then raised it up above the crate he was hiding behind. Ozzie shifted his eyes to watch the back of the cave wall. With another loud pop, a bullet tore a hole through the fabric. Ozzie hadn't seen any movement or muzzle flash, but he was certain that was where the bullets were coming from. Where the hell was the shooter hiding?

"Captain Westbrooke." Prince Masako's voice sounded loud in the silence following the shots. "Unless you want my men to kill you one by one, I suggest you order your men to lay down their arms."

Westbrooke stood with his hands in the air and issued the order.

Ozzie joined the others as they lined up and placed their weapons on the ground in front of them. Ben appeared and pointed at Ozzie's flashlight. He handed it to the boy. Ben walked over to the pile of weapons, picked up a pistol, and disappeared back into the darkness.

There was movement back where Ben had gone. It was the prince in his white uniform. He stepped out from behind one of the large crates and spoke what sounded like an order in Japanese. A flashlight clicked on, blinding the Americans lined up with their hands in the air.

There was a loud clank of metal behind them. Ozzie turned away from the light to look. A small door hung open in the raised belly of the dragon. A man dressed in what looked like white pajamas tumbled out. He reached back inside the statue and pulled out a rifle.

Ozzie smiled. Well played, Prince.

CHAPTER FIFTY

Aboard Indonesian Fishing Boat
Natuna Besar

November 24, 2012

Elijah ducked as the pirogue slapped into a wave and salt spray flew back over the occupants of the boat. Irv was sitting next to him on the wooden bench seat, and the old man swore as he wiped the water off his face and neck. Elijah kept his eyes on the ribbon of blue water between the overhanging green jungle banks. The wind was blowing straight down the estuary inlet, creating wind waves that hit them as soon as they'd left the dock. He was determined not to let the old man know how nauseous he felt.

Benny had left their hotel in Ranai before dawn to go out on the fishing boat they'd hired to intercept the woman's boat. He'd called over an hour ago to say he had succeeded and would meet them as planned at the anchorage on the west side of the island.

Elijah had spent the morning with Irv making certain that he would never again consider stealing property that belonged to the Enterprise. Elijah hadn't wanted to stress the old man's weak heart—especially when he knew how soft it was. Even as remote a place as Ranai had prostitutes. Turned out it wasn't even necessary to cut the woman. The threat had been enough to have the old man begging for another chance.

Elijah had put himself into this situation of being overreliant on someone. He would fix it as soon as they had the documents and the old man had provided them with the location. Irv said he had stolen the documents and sold them because he wanted to retire and disappear. It was time for Irv to train his successor, and then Elijah would be happy to make him disappear.

When the green banks fell away and the bay opened up, Elijah saw the brightly painted fishing boat towing a sailboat less than a mile away. The boat was much bigger than the pirogue. He guessed that the boat's driver was just inside that back cabin looking out the windows across the front. He turned around and motioned to their boat driver, a brown little man who squatted in the stern next to the pirogue's ancient motor. The driver nodded and pointed at a sheltered cove just ahead. It looked like the fishing boat was headed that way, too.

Elijah recognized Benny moving among the others on the deck of the boat. They were rigging an awning to cover the foredeck that was piled high with nets, equipment, and plastic fuel drums. As their pirogue closed on the fishing boat, Elijah could hear the loud *put-put* of the engine. He wondered how the fishermen could stand it.

The bigger boat slowed and as the sailboat coasted up to it one of the fishermen jumped aboard. He threw off the towline and prepared to anchor the sailboat. The pirogue driver pulled his boat alongside the fishing boat just as it dropped its anchor a hundred feet away from the sailboat. The fishing boat captain shut down the noisy engine.

Benny reached down to give Irv a hand as the two men climbed aboard. "Perfect timing," he said. "She's just starting to come around."

Elijah followed the older man, and he was struck by the overpowering stench of fish, gasoline, and body odor. And the heat. Now that he was no longer moving through the water, the air was absolutely still. He already felt his shirt was damp under his arms.

"What do you mean?" Irv said. He had already taken his hat out and was fixing it on his head. The odor didn't seem to bother him at all.

"I shot her with a dart," Benny said.

Irv's hands stopped moving. "What?"

"It's okay. Nothing deadly. Just something to knock her out."

Elijah saw the young woman lying on the pile of nets in the shade of the canopy they'd rigged. She looked like she was sleeping.

Irv walked up to Benny and stuck his chin up toward the Malay. "Was that necessary?"

Elijah put his hand on the old man's arm. "Irv," he said. "Enough."

"Yeah, it was," Benny said. "She got one of the men here with some kind of poison spray. He still can't see. They're going to take him to the hospital, so we'll be a man down."

One of the crew was helping the injured man into the pirogue that had brought them out.

Elijah pulled his bolo tie off and began to unbutton his shirt. He felt as though he couldn't breathe on the filthy fishing boat and the pirogue was his tie to the far shore. "That's our boat," he said, pointing at the pirogue. "How are we going to get back ashore?"

"Don't worry. He'll be back."

The young woman on the nets moved her bare legs and groaned. She was only wearing shorts and a white tank top and her skin looked tan and firm. Although Caucasian women usually did not interest him, Elijah decided he was going to enjoy this. He took off his shirt, folded it, and placed it on top of a fuel drum.

"Get a bucket of water," he said. "Wake her."

As the pirogue pulled away and headed back up the estuary, Benny took a white plastic bucket attached to a rope and dropped it over the side. He retrieved the full bucket and threw the water at the woman.

The response was immediate. She sat up gasping for air, her hair dripping around her face, her white shirt turned semitransparent. She glowered at Benny.

"Our common friend here sold you something," Elijah said, "and we need it back."

She swung her head to look at him. "Who are you?" she said.

"You don't ask questions here." He turned to Benny, making sure that the woman and the fishermen would be able to get a good look at the dragon on his back. "Again."

Benny refilled the bucket and threw the water on her. She pushed to her feet and lunged at him. Elijah pulled his boot knife, grabbed her by her dripping hair, and yanked her head back. Her eyes widened when she saw the knife.

"Hawkes! Stop!" Irv yelled.

Benny backhanded the old man, then said something to the Indonesian crew.

"I would advise you to cooperate," Elijah said, his face inches away from hers. He looked for fear in her eyes, but saw only defiance. He let go of her hair and shoved her down and she fell back half on the nets, her bare legs splayed across the wood deck.

At Benny's direction, the Indonesian fishermen dragged Irv over to a fuel drum, picked him up, and sat him on top. Benny reached into his pocket and pulled out a pack of cigarettes. One of the fishermen pointed to the drums and shook his head. He said a word that sounded like *benzine*. The Malay put the cigarettes away.

"I understand you had help when you evaded my friend Benny there back in Bangkok."

She looked away.

"Who do you work for?"

She didn't answer.

He threw the knife and it stuck into the wood deck a fraction of an inch from her bare foot.

Irv yelled, "Hawkes, enough!"

She lurched forward for the knife, but Elijah grabbed her wrist before she got it. He twisted her arm and she winced, but she didn't make a sound.

"You will tell me. You'll tell me who your friend is and how to find him."

Her head was turned away from him, her wet hair hanging down, now hiding her face.

"Look at me!"

"Go to hell," she said.

"You don't want to make me angry."

She swung her head around to face him, her wet hair flying out of her face, and stared at him. "I'm not afraid of you."

"You should be." He turned to Benny and nodded toward the girl.

The girl was still glaring at Elijah so she didn't see him coming. In seconds Benny had flipped her over onto her stomach and straddled her, holding her arms behind her back.

"Get her up." The sun shone on Elijah's back and he reveled in the burning, tingling sensation. He stretched his shoulders back and rotated his head until he heard his neck crack.

Benny dragged the girl to her feet. She struggled and the Malay yanked her arms higher, causing her to arch her back, thrusting her breasts forward. Elijah could see the outline of a white bra through the wet fabric of her shirt and the twin dark shadows of her nipples. He stepped closer and pressed the tip of his razor-sharp knife to her chin. He saw a droplet of blood appear on her skin. He pressed harder and the bubble grew.

"I want my property back."

She stopped struggling and stared at him with those fearless eyes.

"And I want to know who else knows about this. We know you bought it from the old man," he said, and he removed the knife from her chin. The blood ran down her chin, dripped into the crevice between her breasts, and disappeared inside her shirt.

"Where's my boat?"

"I told you not to ask questions."

He laid the knife flat against the bare skin of her shoulder and slid it under the straps of her tank top and bra. The skin on top of her shoulder was mottled with scar tissue. "And if you don't tell me where it is, you're going to have some new scars to add to your collection." He turned the knife and pulled and slit through the straps. The front of her shirt fell forward, exposing her breast almost to the nipple.

Elijah heard noise. He blinked and turned his head.

Irv yelled, "Hawkes! Put me on her boat. I'll find it."

"Shut up!" Elijah yelled. The old man was spoiling his concentration.

He laid the knife flat and slid it under the other strap. He would make her fear him. "After I am finished with you, no one who knew you before will be able to recognize you." He slit the other straps. When the other half of her shirt fell open, he saw a little more of the red line the blood had traced between her breasts. He lifted the knife slowly, his eyes locked on hers as he prepared to follow the trail of blood with his knife and slice open the front of her shirt.

He heard a thud behind him and then footsteps trotting across the deck.

Elijah whirled around and in two seconds he had his knife at the old man's throat. "I said shut up, you fucking fossil."

"Don't hurt him," she said.

"Give me an axe!" Irv shouted. "I'll tear her boat apart, and I guarantee you I'll find it."

"You don't shut up, you son of a bitch, I'll cut your tongue out."

"Stop it," she said.

Elijah turned back to look at her, but she hung her head. She wouldn't look at him.

"You can have it," she said. "I'll show you where it is. Just don't hurt him. Take me over there. I'll get it, and then I'll tell you what you want to know."

Irv said, "I'll go with her to make sure it's the real thing. I'm the only one here who's seen it."

Elijah turned to Benny. "Take them both. If she doesn't cooperate, cut the old man's tongue out."

Benny nodded and the corner of his mouth pulled up in a half smile. He grabbed the old man's arm and walked them both aft to get into the fishing boat's dinghy.

Elijah watched as Benny rowed them across to her sailboat. The girl sat huddled in the boat, her arms across her chest holding up what was left of her shirt.

He was about to get what he wanted, so why did he feel disappointed?

CHAPTER FIFTY-ONE

Aboard *Bonefish*
Natuna Besar

November 24, 2012

Benny, the man who had shot her with the blowpipe, sat on the center thwart of the dinghy at the oars. He told Peewee to get in the bow. Riley slumped in the stern with her arms crossed to hold up her top. She knew she could take him while he rowed and she wanted nothing more. But on the fishing boat, one of the local men stood on deck with a rifle, watching them.

Ever since she'd awakened with water in her face, she'd been reacting, trying to figure out what was going on. That muscular monster with the dragon on his back was a madman. She was doing her very best right now to appear conquered and cowed. Let this guy think she was terrified, broken. Maybe he would drop his guard. It was time for her to stop reacting and figure out how she was going to get out of this mess.

Benny was much stronger than her. She'd learned that on the boat. And he wore a nasty-looking knife in a sheath on his belt. The handle looked like it was made of bone, and from the shape of the sheath, the blade was more than seven inches long. She was certain, after her experience with the one they called Hawkes, that this one also knew how to use his knife.

If she leaned a little to one side, she could see her boat anchored not far from the fishing boat. She wondered how they'd got it there. Had they sailed it? Judging from the mess the mainsail had been left in, they weren't sailors. Perhaps they'd towed it. Her eyes searched her vessel from stem to stern, looking for signs of any damage. She didn't see any.

These guys had a fast powerboat. Even if she did overpower Benny, she'd never outrun them in her sailboat. If she was going to escape, she would need to disable their boat somehow. But how?

Benny told Irv to get out of the dinghy and climb aboard first. She followed.

"Stay where I can see you," he said.

She climbed into the cockpit and stood still. She saw the flare gun lying on the cockpit floor. She considered picking it up, but the rest of the flares were in the ditch bag in the aft cabin. The gun was no good without ammunition.

While Benny was tying off the dinghy, Peewee whispered, "I'll help you. I'm on your side."

She acted as though she had not heard. She didn't know whether or not to believe him.

She looked down into the cabin and it took some effort not to react. It was a mess. They'd searched her home and torn her things up. Books, clothes, food, and pots and pans were strewn across the cabin sole. But they hadn't found what they were looking for or she wouldn't be here. There were so many places to hide things on a boat.

When Benny climbed into the cockpit, he said, "Where is it?"

"In the forward head."

"Okay, go down slowly. Keep your hands where I can see them."

"I'll need to get a screwdriver," she said. "It's behind an access panel in the head."

"Okay, wait till I'm down, too."

Riley went down the companionway stairs. She pointed to a drawer by the chart table. "There's a screwdriver in there."

He descended the stairs. "Okay."

Riley got the screwdriver out of the drawer just as she had said. He was all ready for her to try something. When it didn't happen, she hoped he'd relax just a little.

Walking below was difficult with all her belongings scattered on the floor. "I need to go up there." She pointed toward the bow. "I might stumble. It won't be on purpose."

Benny pulled the knife from its sheath. "I'll be right behind you," he said.

He stayed less than a foot behind her as she made her way through the main salon and into the forward cabin. She could smell cigarettes on his breath. "There's not room enough in the head for both of us."

"You know I won't hesitate to kill you."

She nodded. "I do. I'm going in here now."

She stepped into the head, slid open a locker, and removed the vitamins, cough syrup, and aspirin. That was all that was left in the cabinet. Then she unscrewed the panel that provided access to the ship's wiring. The prayer gau was there, wrapped in the piece of silk. She unwrapped it and placed the gold object in the center of her palm.

"I'm coming out now. I have it in my hand." With her hand in front of her she stepped out of the head.

Benny snatched the object from her. Then he turned around and stepped into the main salon. "Irv, is this it?"

While his back was turned, Riley felt under the pillow for the crossbow. It was right there where she'd left it. In their search, they'd lifted the mattress, emptied the drawers, but they hadn't looked under the pillows. She pulled out the crossbow, spun around to be free of the door, and aimed it at Benny's back.

"Yeah, that's it," Irv said.

Then she saw Irv lean over sideways and peer around Benny. She saw his Adam's apple twitch as he swallowed.

"Uh, Benny?" he said, and he pointed at Riley.

"Don't move," Riley said, "or you'll take an arrow through the heart." She saw Benny angle his head and look at her out of the corner of his eye.

"You know this is never going to work," he said.

"Drop the knife and put your hands in the air."

"All right. I don't need a knife." The knife fell onto a pile of clothes and disappeared into the folds of cloth. He raised his arms. "I'll enjoy it more with my bare hands."

"Irv, you'll find ropes in the cockpit locker."

The old man climbed the steps and began searching the seat locker.

"Now, turn around slowly," she said. "And put it on the table."

He turned around to face her. His mouth was smiling, but his dark eyes were humorless. "Put what?"

"You know. The gold artifact I just gave you."

Peewee came back down with one of her fifty-foot dock lines. Benny just stood there staring at her.

"Put it on the table," she said. "I know that you and your friend Mr. Hawkes do not plan to let me live, so shooting you right now would be an act of self-defense. And that way we won't have to bother with tying you up. It's your call. Give it to me, I'll tie you up and you live; don't give it to me, and I'll shoot."

Benny reached into his pants pocket and pulled out the prayer gau. He set it on the table.

She nodded at Irv.

That was when Benny made his move. He spun around to grab Irv. He planned to get the old man between him and the crossbow.

What he hadn't counted on was the heavy stainless-steel winch handle Irv had brought down with the dock lines. Benny deflected the full force of the blow that probably would have cracked his skull, but even the glancing blow made him stagger and fall. Irv had let go of the winch handle and Benny was pulling him down, going for his neck. Riley set the crossbow aside. She couldn't get a clear shot as the two men wrestled. From the floor by her foot, she lifted up her cast-iron Le Creuset rice cooker and swung it at the back of Benny's head. He collapsed on top of Irv.

Riley couldn't even see the old man. "Irv, you okay?"

She saw movement in the carpet of her belongings and when she pulled up on a shoulder of the unconscious man, Irv squirmed out from under him. She reached a hand and helped him up onto his feet. Riley looked down at the inert form. "I'm glad you were counting on him making a move."

Irv brushed off his sleeves and said, "Benny's that kind of man."

Riley peered out the galley window at the fishing boat anchored a couple of boat lengths away. "Okay. Now we just have to figure out how to incapacitate their boat." She stepped back. "Excuse me a second while I go grab another shirt." She found a bra and a T-shirt on the floor in her cabin and quickly changed.

When Riley came out of her cabin, Irv was finishing tying Benny's hands behind his back. He sat back on the bottom step and said, "You know when they sat me on top of that plastic fuel drum?"

"Yeah."

"While you were doing such a good job of distracting all those men," he said with a wink, "I took out my pocketknife and I wiggled the tip into the plastic until it punched a small hole all the way through. It's been leaking gasoline onto the deck for half an hour now."

Riley smiled. "And it's a wood boat."

She waved her hand at Irv. "Scoot over." She stepped over Benny and crawled up the steps and into the cockpit on her hands and knees.

The guy with the rifle would still be keeping watch. She grabbed the flare gun, then retreated back into the cabin.

Riley kept a ditch bag in the aft cabin whenever she was at sea. It was there in case she had to abandon ship. The waterproof bag contained everything she would need in the life raft, like food, water, flares, and a signal mirror. The fishermen had emptied the contents out of the bag, but the flares were easy to spot in the mound of stuff. She discarded a couple of smoke flares. She wanted only the rockets.

Out the galley window she looked again at the fishing boat. She saw the man named Hawkes gesturing at her boat. He suspected something wasn't right. They had to move fast.

"Listen," Riley said, "I don't want you to get shot. Stay below here. I can crawl out there and start the engine without raising my head. I have a remote button at the helm to raise the anchor chain, too. They'll hear the engine start, but they don't have another boat, so there's not much they can do about it."

"Be careful, sweetheart," Irv said. "I don't want you getting shot either."

Riley crawled out into the cockpit, set the flare gun on the seat, and reached for the key at the engine controls. She hit the start button and heard a single *click*. This had happened a few times before. "Come on, baby, start for me now."

She hit the start button again. *Click.*

"Irv, go to the electric panel and turn off the refrigeration and the radio and anything you see that might be drawing juice from the batteries."

"Okay." The hum of the refrigeration system stopped. "Try it now."

Riley silently asked her brother Mikey to put in a good word with whoever might be listening. She hit the start button again and heard the sweet roar as the engine turned over, caught, and revved up. She inched the throttle back a little, then flicked the switch to start raising the anchor. Nothing happened.

"Irv! The switch for the windlass."

"I got it!" he yelled.

She tried it again and she could hear the sound of the chain rattling into the chain locker below deck.

Crack! She heard the shot at the same time the safety glass in one of her portholes fell in pieces inside the boat. That gave Riley an idea. She crawled below and grabbed the signal mirror. She handed it to Irv.

"Keep your head away from the window, but wave this around inside and try to distract the shooter."

He moved to one of the forward portholes, and Riley watched the shooter. She saw the man shift his stance when he saw the movement. He raised the rifle to aim. She stood, sighted down the barrel of the flare gun through the broken porthole, and pulled the trigger.

The red ball of flame flew right over the top of the fishing boat and landed in the water on the other side.

About a half mile off up inside the estuary, she saw the long dugout canoe returning. For the moment, the only way they could reach her boat would be to swim. The canoe would change that.

The shooter saw the canoe, too. He turned his head to look. One of the fishermen started waving his hands at it, encouraging it to hurry up.

Riley aimed again, planning to lob it up in an arc this time. She fired.

The flare landed in the middle of the blue plastic tarp they had spread for shade. The flare burned straight through and fell onto the nets, but the plastic tarp caught fire. Pieces of curling flame fell to the deck. She watched as two men ran over toward a patch of flame and began stomping on the deck. The nets smoldered. More pieces of burning plastic rained down.

Hearing her anchor hit the bow roller, she shut the windlass off at the electric panel. She saw no sign of the shooter through the porthole, so she climbed out and slid behind the wheel. She crouched down, put the engine in gear, and pushed the throttle forward. As the boat picked up speed she turned the wheel to put them on a course for the sea.

The first explosion was small. It just sounded like a soft *whomp*. Maybe that was the gas-soaked decks catching fire. That was when she saw the man called Hawkes jump overboard. He started swimming away from the boat. Riley couldn't see where the fishermen were. Probably in the water on the other side of the boat. She set the autopilot.

"Irv, help me with this guy." Between them they dragged Benny out into the cockpit and onto the side deck. Riley pulled a life jacket out of her seat locker and tied it to him. The wooden dinghy was rubbing against the side of her hull. She slowed *Bonefish* and they rolled Benny over the side. He fell with a thud into the dinghy. The small boat shipped water and Benny started to come around.

"Untie the dinghy, Irv. Let's get out of here."

CHAPTER FIFTY-TWO

The Red Dog Ranch
Virginia City, Nevada

November 26, 2012

Elijah hollered, "Caleb!" when he reached the bottom of the stairs.

Tess came trotting out of the kitchen, her tail wagging. He stopped and scratched her ears, then patted her on the neck.

His hired man poked his head out the kitchen doorway. "Welcome home, boss." He disappeared back inside the kitchen.

"Why the hell did you let me oversleep? It's after ten o'clock." Elijah rounded the corner into the kitchen and headed straight for the coffeemaker. The pot was full and his mug was on the counter.

Caleb stood at the sink washing up a pile of dishes. "You didn't get in until two in the morning, and I could hear you moving around up there until after four. I figured you'd be jet-lagged."

"I've told you before, the best way to get over jet lag is to ignore it. Get on local time immediately." Elijah dumped two large spoonfuls of sugar in his cup and stirred. He didn't like Caleb noting his movements, and jet lag was the least of his problems. The last forty-eight hours had been brutal, and Elijah had much on his mind. After the

Indonesian fishing boat had burned to the waterline, Elijah and the fishermen had climbed into the pirogue and their weight nearly sank the boat. There was no way they could pursue the sailboat. By the time they reached Benny, Elijah wanted to kill him. That woman had eluded them for the last time. Next time, he would not only get the information he sought, but he would make her pay for all the trouble she had caused him.

"Sorry, boss," Caleb said.

"We've got people coming today."

"I got your text, and I did everything you told me to. We got lunch if they want it and the place is clean as it's ever been."

"I'll be the judge of that. I'll tour the house and grounds first thing, then, assuming you haven't got something royally screwed up, I'll come back and grab a quick workout and shower."

Mr. Black was the first to arrive. Caleb buzzed him in through the gate and directed his driver to park the car in front of the freestanding garage. The security monitors were mounted in a utility room off the kitchen, and Elijah watched over Caleb's shoulder as the black Escalade drove up the drive to the house. When Black climbed out of the car, Elijah was surprised to see the man dressed in a suit instead of his usual tracksuit. Obviously, it was in deference to their other guest.

Elijah met Black at the door and ushered him into the game room. This was not his first visit to Elijah's home. The remote location had become a favorite for meetings that required deniability. But this was the first time Elijah had seen the man nervous about a meeting.

"Do you ever dress for an occasion, Hawkes?"

Elijah looked down at himself. This was dressed up for him. White Stetson Oxford shirt with matching bolo and belt buckle, black Circle S slacks and the Lucchese boots that Caleb had cleaned and shined. He decided to ignore the comment.

"Can I get you a drink?" Elijah asked.

"Fuck yeah," Black said. Then he raised his hand palm out. "Wait. I don't know. These fucking Muslims don't drink, do they?"

"Some do," Elijah said. He'd spent time in the Middle East back when he worked for the CIA. "Who is this who's coming?" Elijah reached for a bottle of mineral water. He would need a clear head.

"I didn't tell you?"

"No. You just said he was a possible buyer."

"He said we're supposed to call him al-Habib, which is some kind of nickname. But the word is he's an honest-to-God fucking Saudi prince."

Elijah looked up from the ice bucket. "Interesting," he said. *There are only a few hundred of those,* he thought.

Black laughed. "You can say that again. He shouldn't have any trouble meeting our price."

From the direction of the kitchen they heard a soft chime. Elijah said, "That should be him at the gate now."

The man at his front door did not look anything like what Elijah had expected. There were no robes or head cloths. He was dressed in an exquisitely tailored charcoal suit that matched his graying hair and beard and wore a navy tie. The eyes that greeted him behind the rimless gold spectacles sparkled with humor at Elijah's surprise.

"Welcome to the Red Dog Ranch." Elijah extended his hand. "I'm Elijah Hawkes."

"Pleased to meet you. You may call me al-Habib, or just Al if you prefer."

The man's English and manners were perfect. "Please, follow me, Al. Mr. Black is in the game room."

After the greetings were complete, the new visitor turned in a circle, admiring the heads on the walls all around the room. "These are all yours?" al-Habib asked.

Elijah looked around at the animals' heads and images flashed through his mind of the hours he had spent hiking, tracking, and waiting, bow in hand. "Yes."

Al-Habib turned to Black. "I like this man."

"Would you care for some lunch?" Elijah asked. "My man Caleb has it all prepared."

Black said, "I'm starved."

"I understand you have horses," al-Habib said. "Would you show them to me?" He turned back to Black. "You go on ahead and eat. Mr. Hawkes will show me the horses and we'll join you soon."

"This way," Elijah said. He saw Black scowling at al-Habib's back as they left the room.

As they walked toward the paddock, Elijah explained to his new Saudi friend that the hills of northern Nevada were home to herds of wild horses, as well as deer, bobcats, and coyotes. One of his own horses was a mustang that he had adopted from the Bureau of Land Management. The other two were an Appaloosa and a palomino. Al-Habib told Elijah about the horses he owned back in Saudi Arabia. On the whole walk, they only discussed their common love for animals.

The two men stood with their arms resting on the top fence rail admiring the three horses munching hay on the far side of the paddock. The silence stretched out.

Finally al-Habib spoke. "You have a beautiful home and life here, Mr. Hawkes."

"Yes, I do love this ranch."

"But I understand you spend a good deal of time in the Philippines."

"That I do. I'm a mining engineer and Brightstone Security owns the Benguet Gold Mine. That's where my work is."

"Yes, gold. Your specialty, as I understand it, is in figuring out ways to defeat gold fingerprinting technologies."

"You certainly know more about me than I do about you."

The prince smiled. "And I understand you might have located another mineral?"

Elijah laughed. "We haven't located it yet, but we are hot on the trail."

"Can you tell me about this trail?"

"During the Second World War, the Japanese had their own atomic bomb project. My work in the Philippines concerns what the Japanese did in those later days of that war."

"I am aware of the Black Eagle Trust."

Elijah shook his head. There didn't seem to be much this man didn't know. "Okay. A German U-boat, *U-234*, surrendered to the US shortly after Germany surrendered in May of 1945. She had been en route to Japan with a load of uranium oxide. Most think that was the only instance of Germans sending uranium to Japan."

"It wasn't?"

"No. You see, my firm does research to determine if and where more gold can be found in the Philippines. There is a man who works for us, an expert in cryptography and a World War II veteran, who has been responsible for most of our finds after Marcos left. When the Purple decrypts were declassified—"

"Purple?"

"Yeah, that was the name of one of the Japanese diplomatic codes. Our fellow went through these archives, and he found signals in July of 1943 from a General Kawashima requesting uranium from the Germans. When he told me about it, I decided to see if there had been any earlier shipments of uranium. I made it a side project for him. He determined that there was a load of eight hundred kilograms of uranium oxide aboard each of the two U-boats, *U-219* and *U-195*, that arrived at Batavia, Djakarta, in December 1944."

"That is eight hundred kilos each?"

"Yes. We found evidence both of the U-boats off-loaded the uranium in Batavia onto a hospital ship called the *Teiyō Maru.*"

The Saudi laughed.

"Yeah. That was one of their favorite tricks—loading weapons and men aboard ships that the US could not bomb. The *Teiyō Maru* then headed for the Philippines to take on an additional load of gold. She was supposed to sneak the whole lot past the US sub patrols that had virtually created a blockade around Japan."

"I take it she never made it."

"No. And our flyboys had become more aware of the Japanese tricks. There was one instance where they sank a real hospital ship carrying Allied POWs, thinking it was flying the Red Cross as a ruse."

"So you think she was sunk by American planes?"

Elijah nodded. "Recently at a dig site near Tuguegarao we found some documents that we believe will lead us to the location of the wreck."

Al-Habib took off his glasses, removed the handkerchief from his breast pocket, and began to clean the lenses. When he was finished he threaded the curved backs around his ears and positioned the lenses on his face. Two of the horses across the paddock whinnied and took off at a playful gallop in the dusty open space.

"Some of us in my country believe it is time for us to join the nuclear club. We find ourselves with Israel on one side, and Iran on the other. The problem is, there is not agreement. Pakistan has offered to sell us weapons, but as you have seen in the headlines, they are unable to keep secrets." The Saudi prince turned to face him. "Can you keep secrets, Mr. Hawkes?"

Elijah held his stare. "Yes," he said.

Al-Habib smiled. "Good. And would you be willing to deal with me directly? Your organization has too many close ties to those still in the intelligence service. I am willing to pay you two million dollars in untraceable funds for this untraceable uranium."

"Let me get this straight. If I locate this uranium, you want me to keep quiet about it and then sell it to you without informing my employer. You know they would kill me for doing something like that."

"Yes. But I also know they underpay you and you have expensive tastes. What I am proposing would remain a secret. When my countrymen reveal to the world we have joined the nuclear club, no one will know where the uranium came from. Do we have a deal?"

Elijah looked across the paddock at his favorite mare, the palomino with the blaze of white on her face. Her head was turned and her big brown eyes stared at him expectantly. "Underwater salvage is expensive," he said.

"Of course I will pay for all expenses."

"Make it four million and we'll have a deal."

Al-Habib smiled and slapped Elijah on the back. "We have a deal then."

CHAPTER FIFTY-THREE

**Aboard *Bonefish*
South China Sea**

November 26, 2012

That first day at sea she had cleared the quarter berth bunk and told him to get in it and stay out of her way. Riley wasn't accustomed to having anyone else on board her boat, and she didn't know what to do with a ninety-three-year-old crewmember. She certainly didn't want him to die on her.

He started to tell her that the men they were running from had resources beyond her imagination. They would find a bigger, faster boat, he said. But she assured him she was not sailing the rhumb line. It might take them a little bit longer, but they wouldn't be where Mr. Hawkes might expect them to be, either.

As it turned out, no one had followed them. She figured Peewee was feeling a little green the first twenty-four hours because he stayed put in his bunk. Riley cleaned up the mess they had made of her home, and some items she never did find—like her satellite phone. Seemed the fishermen who had searched her boat had helped themselves to her phone, some jewelry, and her stash of a thousand US dollars in her underwear drawer. Fortunately, that wasn't all her cash. The larger amount was better hidden.

She had missed her scheduled radio connection with Cole due to the fact that she had been shanghaied by Benny and the pirates, and now that the phone was gone she couldn't email him either. She would continue to try him on the radio and hope that they would be able to connect eventually.

By sunset on the first day, she was back into her seagoing routine. She had the autopilot steering, the AIS system keeping an eye out for ships, and her various alarms set. She made herself a dinner of canned stew and biscuits, but when she opened the door to Peewee's cabin, his back was to her and he grunted at her offer of food. That was fine with her, she thought. She hadn't asked him along on this trip. She set a couple of bottles of water inside the cabin and left him alone.

The next morning Peewee finally emerged from his bunk with a little color in his cheeks. He said he was hungry, and she was relieved that he didn't look ready to die on her. In fact, he looked so well rested and fit she wondered if he had been sick at all. He was one remarkably vital ninety-three-year-old man.

Peewee climbed the stairs and sat on the cockpit seat like a man who knew his way around boats. This morning he had taken off his white long-sleeved shirt, and he was wearing only his white undershirt tucked into his belted khaki trousers. Riley noticed that while his skin was wrinkled, the muscles in his forearms looked mighty firm. Amazing.

He stuck his face in the companionway opening. "Beautiful day! I see you've cleaned things up. Sorry I wasn't much help. Upset tummy."

Riley looked at him and narrowed her eyes. "Irv, if I were the suspicious sort, I might think you faked seasickness just to get out of work and night watches."

He opened his eyes in shock. "Me?" Then his mouth stretched wide and she saw most of his too-perfect dentures. "You got any more of that coffee I smell?"

Riley reached for the thermos she had wedged in the sink. "How do you take it?"

"Just black, sweetheart."

She prepared pancakes for the two of them and since they were sailing on a broad reach and the boat wasn't heeling too much, she spread a towel on the table in the main salon and served the food below. When they had both finished eating, she stood to clear the table and said, "Irv, it's time for the truth."

"About my seasickness?" He reached up to adjust his hearing aid.

She set their plates in the sink. "You know what I mean. Who are you really, and what have you gotten me into?"

He folded his paper napkin in half and wiped his mouth. "I have told you the truth," he said. "Just not all of it."

She retrieved the gold prayer gau from the bowl where she'd left it the night before. "Who was that Hawkes guy and"—she set the gau on the towel in front of him—"why is this 'trinket' you gave me so important?"

Peewee picked it up and pulled off the top. He slid out the documents and separated them into two piles. On one side was the page with all the hieroglyphs and on the other was the maplike document and the one that Cole identified as a Japanese letter.

"It's true that Ozzie got this from a Japanese prince, but only this one document was in it." He pointed to the single page of hieroglyphs. "It turns out it's sort of a key to some encrypted maps the Japanese left behind."

"You knew this when you gave it to me."

"Yes. I realized what it was after the war when I took a look at what Ozzie had given me. I decided to stay on in the Philippines. I went to work for some Americans who were looking for Japanese gold. I used that"—he pointed at the paper with the symbols—"and I made my living interpreting maps the Japanese left and selling them information."

"And did they call themselves the Enterprise?"

Peewee's lips worked furiously over his dentures. "How do you know that name?"

"Cole. He went on and on about some guy named Andrew Ketcham who was at Corregidor. And another guy named Lansdale. He said they started the Enterprise at the end of the war and they're still around today. He said the Enterprise used me to find him."

He closed his eyes, reached up with both hands, and began to massage his temples. He opened his eyes and said, "You could say that, because I did work for them. But they don't know about him. Only I do. I haven't sold them that tidbit of information just yet."

"Why not? Did you use me as bait to lure him out of hiding?"

"Yes and no. The Enterprise is aware of both your efforts on the *Surcouf.* When I first heard about it I couldn't believe it. I'd found Richie's daughter. I never told them that I knew your granddad. As for Cole, time passed and they haven't had any more trouble from him. He is no longer important. But me—I never believe a man's dead until there's a body."

"The *Surcouf* was four years ago, though. Why contact me now?"

"You know about the Japanese gold in the Philippines. About Golden Lily."

She nodded.

"For years, the Enterprise has had tons of gold sitting in vaults in offshore banks around the world. They couldn't flood the market for fear the gold might be traced back to the countries of origin. Thailand, Indonesia, Malaysia, or wherever would demand they return the gold that was stolen from them by the Japanese."

"And it should be returned."

"Ha! Fat chance now. In the last few years, with the global financial crisis, the price of gold has gone through the roof! These guys ramped up their operation. But they needed to find a way to launder their gold. That's where Hawkes comes in."

"How so?"

"That's his thing. He's a metallurgist. He's been perfecting this method to defeat gold fingerprinting. The new technology has allowed them to introduce more and more gold into the international market. Combine that with the changes in the laws in the US that have allowed them to channel money into super PACs, and they're now cleaning out their vaults. And they've been pouring money into all their private intelligence and security contractors in the Middle East that hire up all their buddies when they leave government service and want to start making the big bucks."

"You haven't answered my question."

"I'm getting to it. For the last sixty years there have been rumors about the mother lode of all the Japanese sites. I'd gone through all the maps they had, but there was this rumor that the map to the mother lode was still out there."

"You're talking about the Dragon's Triangle."

Peewee smiled. "I knew I was right about you."

"What do you mean?"

He pointed to the other documents on the table. "These other documents. They were found in the Philippines a few weeks ago. Maybe they point to the *Teiyō Maru*, so I decided to give it all to you. I'm an old man. I've spent my life working for these fools. They haven't made the world a better place. We're just as close to Armageddon as ever, probably closer."

"That's what Cole thinks."

"Sweetheart, this time, I wanted to get some of the treasure for me. There's this place in Bangkok where I want to be laid to rest when I die. It costs more than I got. So, I figure I'll kill two birds, right? Give you your gramps' gift and you can figure out the map and find the wreck. You two seem pretty good at that."

"But you said you were the one who could decipher all these old maps. Why not just tell us where to look?"

"Where's the fun in that?"

She rolled her eyes.

"Listen, all the maps I've dealt with were of locations in Luzon. This time it's a shipwreck. I know bupkes about nautical charts. I knew if I didn't find this wreck soon, they were gonna kill me anyway. Figured it was time for me and the Enterprise to have a falling out. Time to go into business for myself, and I had a pretty good idea where I could find a treasure-hunting ship and crew."

Riley reached for the document Peewee said could be a map to the location of the *Teiyō Maru*. "I know charts, but this doesn't look like any nautical chart I've ever seen."

"Have you got charts of the Philippines aboard?"

"I have the electronic charts on my iPad."

"Then let's get to work."

CHAPTER FIFTY-FOUR

A Cave in Luzon
The Philippines

June 26, 1945

Ozzie stared into the bright light of the flashlight. He wondered if the prince intended to shoot them all then and there. He closed his eyes and thought about praying, but he didn't know what to say.

A high-pitched whistle echoed through the cave and the bare bulbs on the walls came on and illuminated the chamber. A contingent of about a dozen men came running into the cave from the far tunnel. They were a ragtag lot. Some of them bare-chested, others barefoot, some with white headbands sporting the red rising sun emblem. They all wore parts of what had once been Japanese Army uniforms. And they all carried rifles with bayonets attached. The men lined up in formation in front of the prince.

Either the other chamber was not far or they had been waiting in the darkness for the prince's signal. The prince issued orders and some of the men collected the weapons from the ground while two of them disappeared down the tunnel in the direction of the submarine.

Ozzie found it interesting that when Prince Masako spoke to the Americans or to Ben, his voice was soft and almost singsong, but when he spoke to his men, he shouted.

After shouting in Japanese to his men, the prince turned and spoke to the group of American Navy men. "Now we will return to your submarine, and Captain Westbrooke, if you do not want my men to shoot all of you, you will command all your men still on board to surrender. Do you understand?"

Westbrooke nodded.

The prince swung his arm through the air, smiled, and said, "After you."

Four of the Japanese soldiers moved behind them and prodded them with their bayonets. Ozzie followed along with the others, wondering if the prince was going to honor their agreement.

When they got close to the original chamber where the sub was docked, their party caught up with the two men the prince had sent ahead. The men were keeping watch on the submarine as well as their two companions, who were being held under guard by an American sailor. The prince sent Ozzie and Westbrooke ahead. Westbrooke nodded at the guard and then ordered all hands on deck. Once the entire crew was mustered, he explained their situation. The Japanese had already killed two of their men, and they still held four of them at gunpoint in the tunnel. He ordered the men to surrender and Prince Masako arrived right on cue.

The prince told Westbrooke to select half the men to stay on board to keep the submarine running and then to assign the remaining sailors to a work detail. They would start loading the crates onto the submarine.

"I have no desire to harm any of your men," Masako said. "But I need this submarine to transport some critical cargo back to Japan.

Once we arrive at the home island, you will be held as prisoners of war. However, I will not tolerate any insurrection. Any man who does not follow orders or who attempts to escape will cause one of his fellow sailors to be shot," the prince said.

The skipper and Ozzie were among the men who were to stay on board, and they were allowed full run of the boat. They both headed for the captain's cabin and slid the door closed.

Westbrooke sat on the bunk and held his head in his hands. "What are we going to do?"

Ozzie paced two steps, turned, paced two more steps, and turned again.

"This prince might be saying he's not going to hurt anyone, but I don't trust him."

Westbrooke looked up. "There's still the fifty-caliber deck gun and we've got the last two torpedoes."

"First off," Ozzie said, "the only torpedoes left are in the stern of the boat—not exactly pointed in the right direction—and second, firing either the fifty-caliber or a torpedo in here would be equally likely to cause a cave-in. We might kill the Japs, but we'd bury ourselves in the process."

"You have any better plan?"

"Let me think about it." The prince had only told him that he and Ben needed a ride to the Philippines. Ozzie had assumed he would be able to take the prince and Ben ashore in a boat and disappear, leaving the *Bonefish* free to head on out when he didn't return and make her way back to Guam. In his wildest dreams he hadn't figured on them docking inside a cave.

"You know we outnumber them," Westbrooke said.

"Are you sure of that? Who's to say there aren't a hundred more of them back in that cave? Like I said, I don't trust him."

There was a knock at the door.

"Yeah?" Westbrooke said.

"The Jap officer wants to talk to Lieutenant Riley."

Ozzie sighed. "Tell him I'll be right out." He turned back to West-brooke. "I'll go see what he wants."

Ben was waiting for him at the bottom of the gangplank, and he motioned for Ozzie to follow him. Now that the lights were on throughout the caves, walking through the passages was easier. He and Ben made good time. Prince Masako was overseeing the loading of one of the large crates onto a wagon just inside the treasure chamber.

He turned when Ben spoke to him in Japanese. "Lieutenant. Here you are."

"What's that say on these crates, anyway?"

The prince and Ben exchanged a look. "I told you. It is the name of the ship that brought them here. It says *Teiyō Maru*."

"No, I mean the letters and numbers—'UO2.' What's that mean?"

"I cannot tell you all my secrets, Lieutenant."

Ozzie started toward the crate, but Ben stepped in front of him and cut him off.

Then the prince said, "You are wondering if I am going to keep my promise to you."

"Yeah, when you started shooting my men, I did start to wonder."

"They are no longer your men. You are a free man and a rich man now. Follow me."

Ozzie considered protesting, but decided to wait and see how the prince intended to play this out. He followed the two of them into the passage on the far side of the treasure chamber. After a half hour of fast walking, they entered another chamber not as large as either of the others. There were no stalagmites—it looked as though the Japanese had removed them to level the floor—and the stream bed that had flowed along one wall of the treasure chamber seemed to have almost dried up or gone underground here. The dirt floor was covered with cots, equipment, tables, boxes of ammunition, and clothing. Three men stood at a table where they were working with wires and batteries and what Ozzie recognized from his work with the OSS in Europe as blocks of plastic explosive material. Aside from those working, a few men were resting on the cots. They all looked up when the prince entered. They all quickly stood at attention and bowed from the waist. No one said a word.

Off on one side of the chamber, a tent had been erected enclosing an area about twenty feet square. Ben lifted a flap to open the door and Prince Masako entered. Ozzie followed.

Inside were two cots, a table and a writing desk with paper, writing instruments, and a small lamp with a fringed shade. On the table he saw books, candles, and a square of what looked like white silk fabric.

The prince turned to Ozzie. "I spoke to my men and the news from here in the Philippines is not good. We must leave this place soon and close this chamber quickly. I will not be returning to this country for some time. In a few hours, the sun will rise, and I would like you to help Ben find his way safely home to his father's farm near Tuguegarao. Then you will be free to join the American soldiers. Will you do that for me?"

"We had a deal, Prince."

"Yes, and I will pay you before you leave. But now, before you leave on this long journey, Ben will take you to eat some food and rest until daybreak."

"Okay," Ozzie said, though he wasn't sure the Jap food would be any good for his stomach.

"Before you go, though, I must ask you for your sodium bicarbonate. I will return it to you before you go."

It was a strange request, but Ozzie didn't see any reason to refuse. He reached into his pocket and handed over the bottle.

He and Ben ate some plain white rice and boiled fish, and then Ozzie stretched out on a cot. He didn't sleep, though. He kept thinking about what the prince had said about closing up the cave and what he'd seen those men building back there. Somehow, he had to figure out how to find his way back here—before they set off those explosives and buried the entrance to the cave for good.

One of the Jap sailors shook his shoulder. Maybe he had just dozed off. Ozzie got up and saw Ben standing with the prince outside the tent. The sailor who had awakened him motioned for him to go join them.

On the far side of this third chamber there was another passage-way, and Ozzie followed them out that way. Shortly they took a much narrower route that branched off to the right. There were no electric lights in this tunnel and both the prince and Ben switched on flash-lights. After about fifty yards, they came to a narrow opening, and Ozzie was surprised to see daylight filtering in through the bushes that concealed the entrance.

Ben held the bushes aside and they stepped out into a small clear-ing on the side of a mountain. An old man was stirring a pot hung over an open fire while another chopped vegetables on a table. High trees shaded the clearing and protected them from being spotted by passing planes.

Ben walked over to the table and collected a heavy backpack. He opened the flap and pulled out a burlap sack the size of a grocery bag and handed it to the prince. Masako turned to Ozzie.

"As promised, you are now free to go. Ben is going to lead you out to the road." He held the burlap bag out to Ozzie. "This is the payment I promised you. There is more than a kilo of gold in here as well as diamonds and rubies."

"Thank you." Ozzie shook the prince's hand. He should've been glad to be getting away with his life—he wasn't sure the others would—not to mention the gold, but Ozzie had got into this whole thing with the bigger goal in mind. "There is one more thing, though, Prince Masako. On the sub you spoke about the maps to all the other

Golden Lily treasure sites. You said you had to come back to get them. What happened with that? Where are those maps?"

"They are gone, I'm afraid. Much of the treasure you have seen here arrived on the *Teiyō Maru* after I returned home to Japan. There was a small gold dragon, a miniature version of the large statue you saw. I had placed the maps inside that dragon. My remaining men were not disciplined, and the crew of the *Teiyō Maru* stole many items before they left—including that dragon. They took it when they sailed. I came all the way back here only to discover the maps are gone."

Something about the prince's statement was off. Why was he explaining this? "What do you mean?"

"My men heard on the radio that the *Teiyō Maru* was bombed. The ship sank. So you see, the maps really are gone."

"Are there other copies?"

The prince smiled and touched the side of his head. "Here only. Good-bye, Lieutenant," the prince said.

What happened next took Ozzie by surprise. The prince turned to Ben and embraced him. They stood like that for so long, Ozzie began to wonder if he should start down the mountain on his own. When Masako finally let the young man go, they both had tears in their eyes. Masako spoke softly in Japanese, then he reached into his pocket and removed the small piece of white silk Ozzie had seen earlier. Ben extended his hands, palms upward, and the prince spread the silk cloth on his hands. He reached into his pocket again and removed the gold prayer gau this time. He placed the object in Ben's hands, folded the silk around it, and closed Ben's fingers over the bundle. The boy bowed his head. Then the prince grabbed Ben by the back of the head, and they pressed their foreheads together. They said something in Japanese in unison. Then Prince Masako turned briskly and walked back into the cave.

Ben's back was to Ozzie. He was fussing with his shirt and pants—probably hiding the gold object. They started off. As he followed Ben through the forest on the downward slope, Ozzie tried to spot some sort of landmarks so he could find his way back one day, but all he saw were trees.

After they had been walking for over an hour, Ben was so far ahead, Ozzie could barely see him.

"Ben!" he called out, asking him to slow down and wait up. Then he heard something in the bush behind him. It sounded like breaking twigs. He half turned and it felt like a blinding blast exploded on the back of his head.

CHAPTER FIFTY-FIVE

Aparri, Luzon
The Philippines

November 26, 2012

"Can you take the con?" Cole asked once they had cleared the river mouth and the depth sounder showed the bottom was more than a hundred feet beneath them and dropping.

He wanted to take another look at the copy of the map and the charts of the Babuyan Islands, and he needed a clear head. He was glad to be leaving Aparri behind and headed for the Babuyan Islands, but he didn't feel very confident about the information they'd got from the Norwegian. There was something about the man that made Cole not trust him. Brian seemed to think he was all right, though.

"Sure," Theo said. "I've got it." He reached up and switched on the radar and the AIS. Cole turned back toward their living quarters aft of the wheelhouse, but he paused in the doorway for a moment to watch his friend.

Theo had modified all the electronics on board their vessel so that they gave audio signals. The AIS system gave him a readout of the name and type of commercial vessel approaching them and the vessel's speed, course, and their closest point of approach. The more likely scenario in these islands, however, was that the boat crossing their bow would be a small wooden fishing vessel called a *bangka*, a sort of canoe with a single outrigger, and they hoped the radar would pick it up and the fisherman would have the good sense to stay clear. If the radar detected a target, a tone would sound—high-pitched meant it was to starboard, low-pitched was to port—and the frequency of the ping told Theo how far off it was. If the target worried him, Theo could fetch Cole to take a look for whatever was ahead.

Cole watched as his friend slid a big set of headphones up onto his head and flipped open his laptop with the Braille reader. Theo's fingers danced across the keyboard. Cole watched the screen he knew his friend could not see. In a matter of seconds, he had connected his laptop to a satellite network, used a VPN logon, connected to Spotify, and was playing his favorite soca and reggae tunes through the headphones.

"I know you think you're being sneaky, mon," Theo said.

Cole chuckled and shook his head. "No way you can hear me with those headphones on," he said.

"I might be blind, but the eyes in the back of my head aren't."

"Amen, brother," Cole said.

Cole turned around and headed for the stove to make himself some coffee. He needed some time alone. Time to think. He didn't want to say anything to Theo, didn't want to burden his friend, but Riley had missed their scheduled radio chat yesterday. He'd tried raising her boat again this morning, but still no luck. Where the hell was she? He was afraid to even consider the many possible things that could go wrong on a small sailboat in the South China Sea. If he thought about them, maybe it would make one of them true. He had to put thoughts of her out of his mind. There was nothing he could do.

The thing that most bothered Cole about this location off the island of Dalupiri was, what had the hospital ship been doing there?

He couldn't come up with a single reason why the *Teiyō Maru* would be in that location. Her last known port of call was Djakarta down in Indonesia. Though they had no record of it, they assumed that the hospital ship had then put in someplace in the Philippines close to this mythical megasite. There she had taken on a cargo of gold that she was supposed to transport back to the homeland. So, if she was headed home, why would she go up around the northern end of Dalupiri Island? It didn't make sense.

For the next hour Cole studied the page he had got from Riley's prayer gau. Not the map, but the other one with the symbols. He assumed it was some sort of key. The Japanese had wanted to be able to come back and find the treasure, but they didn't want anyone else to be able to figure it out. Cole was lost deep in thought when he heard Theo call his name.

"Yeah?" He stood up and stretched. His back hurt from sitting for so long.

"Come here. There's something I want you to look at."

From habit, as soon as Cole entered the wheelhouse, he searched the horizon outside the windows. He didn't see any ships or small boats, and the islands weren't visible yet. "I don't see anything out there."

"No, not out there. Here." Theo had pulled his big black headphones down around his neck. He pointed to the iPad he had affixed to a mount beneath the SSB radio. The tablet was connected to the radio by a cable.

"What is it?"

"I got a call on the SSB from Greg back in Subic Bay. She'd been watching the TV in the bar with Brian. She said the Japanese met office has just upgraded an area of low pressure southeast of the Philippines and named it Tropical Storm Bopha. Conditions are good for it to strengthen. I downloaded the weather fax charts from the SSB. I want you to take a look at them."

"How far away is it?"

"It's way out there now, like south of the Marianas and close to the equator, but it's generally heading west."

"Is it likely to come this way?"

"No, but this one is an odd storm. It's late in the season and it keeps growing in spite of that."

"So you're worried that the storm is going to stray from the forecast path?"

"Not really."

"Then what is it?"

Theo pointed to the screen image of a chart of the islands of Borneo and Palawan. "I reckon Riley is probably right about here, and that would put her directly in the forecast path of this storm."

CHAPTER FIFTY-SIX

Aboard *Bonefish*
South China Sea

November 28, 2012

Riley pressed the button on the side of her wristwatch and the dial lit up the cockpit with a bright greenish glow. Ten more minutes until Peewee was supposed to relieve her. This business of being able to sleep for more than twenty minutes at a time was something she'd be willing to get used to.

Her watch went dark again, and the night was restored. She still saw faint spots in her eyes, though, when she looked out into the inky night. Just that one small flash could ruin your night vision on a night like this. The low clouds hid the stars, and the only light outside the cockpit was the occasional flash of bioluminescence when one of the big swells broke into a frothy crest.

The wind had been building steadily since noon. She'd put a second reef in the main just before dark and rolled up the jib entirely a few hours ago. They were now doing better than seven knots under reefed main and staysail. The seas were growing, but they were taking them on the quarter so there wasn't much spray.

The clunk of the aft head door closing told her that Peewee was up early for his watch. Light poured onto the side deck from the port.

Again, she was impressed by how well he was doing for a guy his age. No, she thought, for any guy. He now maneuvered around the boat at sea, swinging from one handhold to the next like a monkey in the trees. It was clear he'd spent time at sea before.

They'd passed most of their afternoons sitting at the settee table, poring over the charts of the Babuyan Islands. Peewee had taught her what some of the symbols on the sheet meant. Most pertained to land, but they'd begun to translate some of the symbols, and they were working on a hypothesis at the moment.

The head door opened and the light poured out. She turned her face aside. The light clicked off.

His face appeared in the companionway. He was wearing the black wool watch cap she had given him. "How's it going, sweetheart?"

He smiled his crooked smile and Riley realized she had stopped seeing the scars on his face. She saw *him*, not the surface of his skin.

"It's a little bouncy, but we're making good time. We'll be in Manila in no time if we keep this up."

He started to climb on up the steps, but she stopped him with her palm in front of his face like a traffic cop. "Oilskins and harness, buddy. Nobody enters the cockpit at night without them."

He looked up at her. "You know, you're a bossy broad," he said, then he disappeared below.

A few minutes later, Irv climbed into the cockpit wearing her second yellow foul-weather jacket and the big bulky safety harness with a built-in inflatable personal flotation device. He attached his carabiner hook to the big pad eye bolted to the side of the cabin, then looked at her and winked. "You happy now?"

"Very," she said. "When I sail solo, I never get to climb into my bunk at night." She lifted her shoulders and hugged herself. "It's gonna feel good."

"Hey, just because it's easy to kick a man when he's down, it doesn't mean you should."

She opened her mouth and aped an exaggerated look of shock. "Look around you, Mr. Peewee. You're not down. You're surrounded by the beauty of nature!"

He laughed. "Yeah, right. But truthfully? It's been a good day."

"Yeah, it has. You taught me lots about those symbols the Japanese used. It's interesting. We're pretty sure we know which island now. We'll have the location pinpointed by the time we get to Manila."

He nodded. "You may be right."

"I am indeed." She stood up and patted the old man's shoulder. "And in the meantime, there's a warm bunk down there with my name on it." She pointed at the wheel. "It's all yours."

Instead of heading straight to her bunk, though, once below, Riley put a kettle of water on the stove and prepared two mugs with powdered hot chocolate mix. While waiting for the water to heat, she slid onto the seat at the chart table, leaned her head back against the bulkhead, and closed her eyes for a minute. It was comforting to go below into the safety of the cabin and to listen to the whooshing noise made by the water flowing by outside the hull and the creaking of the woodwork inside as the hull flexed. There were some sailors she knew who hated long passages, but she wasn't one. She enjoyed this life where the world shrank down to her little ship in the middle of the big wide ocean.

She clicked on the red-tinted light, grabbed a mechanical pencil from the rack holding her nav instruments, and opened her logbook. Much as she loved her electronics, Riley still found great pleasure in recording her observations in her ship's logbook by hand. She knew there were apps for her phone that would record her latitude and longitude via GPS with the click of a button, but this was how she had been taught to do it by her father all those years ago when she and her brother had sailed on their first sailboat named the *Bonefish*. Change was okay, and she usually embraced new ways, but this was a ritual she was loath to give up.

When she'd finished, she closed the leather-bound notebook and replaced it inside the chart table. Then she glanced at the SSB radio. Should she try again? Ever since she had missed the scheduled radio call she and Cole had set up, she had been listening and calling and trying to reach him. Was he sending her emails, wondering what had happened to her? If so, she wasn't able to receive them. The same men who had held her prisoner so she couldn't make their radio "date" had also stolen the satellite phone she'd connected to her computer to send emails. She wished now she had bought herself a Pactor modem that would enable her to send emails via the single-sideband radio, but she had decided the sat phone would suffice. She'd overlooked the cardinal rule of cruising: redundancy.

The kettle whistled and she got up and made the hot drinks for herself and Irv. After handing him his, she returned to the chart table and eyed the radio again. It couldn't hurt to try while she drank her chocolate. She flipped the breaker on and pushed the radio's power button. Static exploded from the speaker, followed by a high-pitched whistle. She pushed buttons to jump between the various preset frequencies. Whenever she heard voices in the ocean of static, she stopped and tried to tune them in. She found an Aussie cruiser talking to a Dutchman, but other than that, every other voice she heard was speaking a language she did not understand. After running through the presets, she went back to 8104 megahertz and almost fell off the seat when Cole's voice came through loud and clear with almost no static.

"*Bonefish, Bonefish*, this is the *Bonhomme Richard*."

Riley fumbled for the mike.

"This is *Bonefish*, do you read? Over."

"Roger, roger. Holy crap, Riley. Is that you?"

"Roger. It's me."

"God! It's great to hear your voice! I've been so worried about you."

"Good to hear you, too."

"Is everything okay?"

"Yeah, we're fine."

"You missed our last scheduled call."

"Roger that. It was unavoidable." She considered explaining more, but she didn't want to worry him. "Everything here is A-OK now. We're currently"—she flipped open the logbook—"located at nine degrees, nine minutes north, one hundred sixteen degrees, fifty-eight minutes east. We're off the southern tip of the island of Palawan—only about thirty-five miles offshore, so technically we're in Philippine waters."

"You keep saying 'we.' Did you pick up a hitchhiker or something?"

Cole thought he was being funny. Little did he know. "Yeah, well, just habit, I guess. The 'we' is me and my boat."

"Have you been watching the weather?"

"Negative," she said. "Had a malfunction with my satellite phone. Can't download any weather info."

"You need to know that there is a tropical storm forming south of Palau. Conditions are favorable for it to build. Might be a typhoon soon, and it's heading toward the southern Philippines."

"Thanks for the info. We should be okay. That's still a long way off and we're making good time. Should arrive in Manila in three to four days."

"Great. You keep moving and get out of the way of that thing. Does your cell phone still work?"

"Affirmative."

"Okay. I'll send a plane for you when you get in. I'll text you where to meet the pilot."

She rolled her eyes at that. He was pretty confident she wanted to join him. "Where are you?" she asked.

"We're up in the Babuyan Islands anchored in the lee of Dalupiri Island. Think this is the location of the *Teiyō Maru* marked on the map. We've been searching a grid with the magnetometer, but no luck. Too deep."

"What map?" she asked. As far as she knew, she was the only one with a map.

The silence on the other end dragged out.

"*Bonhomme Richard*, are you there?"

"Roger. Back in Phuket. At the Shanti Lodge? After you fell asleep I sent pictures of all the documents to Theo. I assumed you wouldn't mind."

Riley stared at the radio. She lifted the microphone to her face, opened her mouth, then stopped. The hand holding the mike dropped into her lap.

"*Bonefish, Bonefish*, this is the *Bonhomme Richard*, do you copy?"

She heard the clank of Irv's safety harness, and she looked up to see him leaning through the companionway to look at her.

The voice called again from the radio speaker. "Riley, come on, this is Cole. Do you copy?"

Irv said, "Your phone is ringing. You gonna answer that?"

She shook her head. "I don't think so. It seems Mr. Thatcher thinks he's the only one who can figure out where this shipwreck is." She reached out and turned off the radio.

"You thinking what I'm thinking?" he asked.

She nodded. "They're looking in the wrong place."

CHAPTER FIFTY-SEVEN

Corregidor Island
The Philippines

November 29, 2012

Elijah ran his hand along the barrel of the huge gun mounted on the steel swivel plate set into the concrete. He tried to imagine what it had been like back when they had originally brought these guns up to the batteries. It certainly hadn't been the parklike setting that surrounded him today. American boys had fought and died for their country on this soil, and it was now up to men like him to make sure that America remained the superpower she should be. Elijah checked his watch again. Benny was late.

The damned savage excelled only at the most basic skills—tracking and killing people—but lacked the finesse required to do anything that required an intellect. If only he could just let Benny kill them both and be done with it. Elijah hated all this waiting.

He lifted the binoculars that hung round his neck and focused them on the freighter that inched past the island. Through the lenses he could make out the tiny men on deck. These glasses would suit his purpose.

Where was Benny? Surely he didn't get lost. There was a big sign along the roadway that identified this place as Hamilton Battery. Corregidor was nothing if not well marked and all the drivers knew every landmark. The Filipinos had turned the entire island into one big museum. He took a couple of steps over to the edge of the cliff and looked out across the bay toward some other small islands to the south. Any boat entering Manila Harbor from the south would pass by here.

He had come out here a couple of days earlier with Esmerelda, and they had taken a private tour. She explained to him that some of the locals eschewed the ferry and instead came out on their own boats. There was a jitney bus service to get around on the island, and they went to the beach on the south side. But no one was supposed to stay on the island overnight.

Riding around on the jitney bus with mobs of Filipino tourists was not going to work for him. He had hired one of Esmerelda's friends who worked on the island as a guide to be his driver for the day. Elijah had sent him away while he waited for Benny.

The crunch of footfalls on the rocky surface of the battery made Elijah turn. Benny was strolling over to the edge of the cliff like he didn't have a care in the world. As always he carried that leather satchel of his, a constant reminder of his ability to deliver a quick death. Elijah was surprised he had not heard the vehicle that had dropped Benny off out here.

"You're late."

"You chose the meeting location. It's not so easy to get to." Elijah wondered if he had walked from the boat dock.

"Have you ever been out here before?"

"No."

"Hmm," Elijah said. He wasn't surprised. People like Benny had no intellectual curiosity. History meant nothing to them. They lived only in the present. "Well, perhaps you'll learn something. You are going to have a chance to get to know Corregidor very well."

"Why?"

"You want to know why? Because you screwed up, that's why. A girl and an old man, and you can't even handle them. They leave you tied up on your back in a rowboat. Like a trussed-up hog."

Elijah looked at the savage, but Benny's face was turned toward the sea. Elijah continued. "The only reason I choose to do business with a man like you is because you are supposed to be good at what I need you to do. How many times does that make now that they got the drop on you?"

Benny continued to stare out across the water, but now Elijah could see the muscles of his jaw working.

"How'd they do it anyway, Benny? Was it because her tits were hanging out and you were thinking with your little head instead of taking care of business? Men like you just can't leave that alone when it's right there for the taking, can you? And she's a white girl, too."

Still, he didn't acknowledge Elijah.

"Listen, boy. You answer me when I'm talking to you."

Benny swung his head in Elijah's direction, but the rest of his body remained rigid. "What do you want me to do?" His black eyes screamed hate but the features of his face remained stiff and calm.

"You're going to stay right here on this island until you see her boat come sailing past right there." Elijah pointed out at the band of blue water. "Then you are going to call me."

Benny turned and took a step toward him, continuing to stare with those hate-filled eyes. "You could have told me. I'd have brought my gear."

"This is going to be your chance to go native. I thought you'd like that. You can fashion yourself a loincloth if you want. Catch rabbits or something and cook them over the open fire."

"And if they find me staying out here?"

"I would be very disappointed in you. You're supposed to be the great tracker and outdoorsman. Besides, if you are starving, there is the restaurant on the other side that serves lunch. But I would think that would be the coward's way. Are you a coward, Benny?"

Benny's face was now only inches from Elijah's. "I'm not afraid of you, if that's what you're asking."

Elijah laughed in his face. "You are so predictable. My dog is smarter than you, Salim. It's no wonder this girl keeps outsmarting you, but alas, you're all I've got. So here it is. Be my watchdog." Elijah lifted the binoculars so the strap slid up off his head. He held them out to Benny. "Her boat is slow, but you won't be able to sleep the nights through. Nap. Then wake and check. Don't let her get by you this time. Do you understand?"

Elijah could almost see the slow movement of the gears inside the man's head. His jaw muscles flexed again. Then his eyes lowered to the binoculars. He reached out and took them.

"That's right," Elijah said. "You find her and this time, call me. I'll take care of her myself."

Benny didn't walk back to the road. He took off into the trees, following the ridgeline. In less than a minute, he had vanished.

Elijah checked his watch. His driver would be returning in twenty minutes. He leaned against the barrel of the big gun and resigned himself to wait.

The heat from the black-painted metal passed through his shirt and into the muscles of his back. He felt some of the tension begin to drain out of him. He probably should go wait in the shade, but there was something about the power of the big gun that drew him to it. It was nothing more than a museum piece now. It probably hadn't fired in more than sixty years, but the aura of its destructive power was still there and it drew him like a magnet. He wondered how many men had died from its firepower.

Elijah felt let down that he hadn't been able to get Benny to strike. It had been a while since he had made it to training at the dojo in Sparks and Elijah wanted to hit somebody. He needed to blow off some of his own power. He'd studied karate and ninjutsu, but the philosophical part of those martial arts bored him. He didn't want to meditate. He wanted to inflict pain. Recently he'd taken up the study of Krav Maga. He believed he had finally found a martial art that was teaching him something about real fighting. Of course at the dojo one had to hold back all the time. Elijah wanted the opportunity to try out some of the new moves without worrying about the damage.

Elijah was startled by the sound of crunching gravel behind him again. He looked over the top of the gun expecting to see Benny returning, but instead he saw a lone man standing there staring at him wide-eyed.

"Excuse me," the man said, and then he began coughing a deep wet cough that shook his entire thin frame.

Elijah turned away. He had no desire to talk to the stranger. The man looked like a drug addict. He had long stringy blondish hair and his huge eyes were too big for his face.

When the coughing fit stopped the man spoke again. "Mr. Hawkes?"

That got Elijah's attention. He turned around, then stepped out and around the big gun emplacement. "Who are you and how do you know my name?"

"My name is Nils Skar. I wouldn't expect you to remember me. I worked on one of your projects about five years ago. They call me the Norwegian Psychic."

Yes, he did remember something. "That project. Where was it?"

"In Santiago City. My appearance has changed some since then. I've been ill."

He looked so different Elijah never would have recognized him. "Did you follow me here?"

"I came to Manila to find you because I have information for you."
So he was selling information. "Go on."

"I met a man in Aparri who has a map. He claims to have got it from an old man—a World War II vet."

Elijah ran his hand over the black paint on the big gun. He didn't want to appear interested. "That is not a very original story around here. You know that."

"But I saw this map—or at least a copy. It looks genuine. And I understand you have recently lost such a map?"

Elijah's head snapped up and he stared at the man. "Who told you that?"

"Mr. Hawkes, remember, I've been employed as a contractor for you and your organization. I know many people. And besides"—he smiled—"I am a psychic."

"So what are you proposing?"

"The man I met in Aparri is on board an excellent salvage vessel. He appears to be operating under a false name. I thought that might interest you."

"Go on."

"I can be your eyes and ears on this—if you are willing to compensate me for my time."

A dark car drove up and pulled off to the side of the road. Elijah recognized the car that had driven him out here.

"There's my car," he said. "Would you like to join me for the ride back to the ferry dock?"

CHAPTER FIFTY-EIGHT

Aboard *Bonefish*
Manila Bay, Philippines

December 2, 2012

Wouldn't you know it, the wind died just as they were ready to make their turn toward Luzon and Manila Harbor. Riley watched the sun set behind them as *Bonefish* ghosted past the lighthouse on Cabra Island, and the wind dropped away to almost nothing. Most likely it was some sort of land effect that was stifling their breeze. But they had been lucky with the wind until now, so if they had to motor the last seventy miles or so, she figured she had no right to complain about it.

"So close and yet so far," Peewee said as he set his dinner bowl down on the cockpit cushion. He picked up the binoculars to look at the lighthouse. A tall, white, modern-looking tower stood next to the old Spanish ruins of the previous lighthouse. They were no more than two miles offshore, and they could smell the scent of an open fire on shore.

The boat rolled in the swell. The headsail spilled the light breeze and snapped back and forth from one side of the boat to the other, making a loud *thwack* each time the sail was whipped to the opposite side of the boat. Other than the noise from the sail, though, it was quieter than it had been in days. No wind, no rushing water, no creaking rig or boat. Riley wasn't in too big a hurry to start the engine.

She scraped the last of the chicken pilaf from the bottom of her bowl and stuck the fork in her mouth. She had to force herself to swallow. It would be nice to get into port and eat some fresh fruits and vegetables for a change. She'd run out of ideas for ways to make canned chicken and tuna look edible.

"So Irv, we need to talk."

The old man rolled his eyes and playacted a melodramatic shiver. "Those are the four words men fear most. 'Honey, we need to talk.'"

"I know you pretty well after sailing with you these past few days. When you want to avoid something, you joke about it."

"Me?" he said, again with the exaggerated look of innocence.

"Yeah, you." She picked up his bowl and stacked the dishes. "First, I want to make sure you're not planning to disappear again."

Irv tried to make a long face, but the side of his face that was scarred only drooped halfway. "Sweetheart, would I do that?"

"Peewee, you've done it twice."

He grinned and pointed his finger at her like it was a gun. He pulled the trigger and said, "You got me there."

"We need a plan. I'm pretty sure they'll be expecting us in there."

"Knowing Hawkes, he's got people keeping watch on all the ports of entry."

"He's that good, huh?"

Irv worked his lips over his teeth and nodded.

"So, we've got to be better," she said. "From this point on, we need to be on full alert."

"Your boyfriend said he would send a plane."

"Don't call him my boyfriend." Her voice was louder than she had meant it to be.

"Okay, okay. Cole. Any idea what he meant by that remark about a plane?"

"No. Not really. You don't suppose he's rich, do you? He only recovered a ton of gold."

Irv cocked his head to one side and looked at her. "Riley, you know this isn't fun and games. These Enterprise guys are really dangerous."

"Believe me. I know the type."

"They're fanatics. They started out political—they were rabid anti-communists during those Cold War years. But now it's just about money and power. This thing could end badly for all of us. I'm sorry I got you involved. I mean, what do you get out of this?"

She sat up a little straighter and swiveled her head to look all around the horizon. "Oh, boy. That is the big question. What do *I* want?"

"Is Cole Thatcher the answer to that question?"

She took a deep breath, then exhaled. She'd been so angry at Cole for leaving her alone all those years. Then he'd taken *her* documents and was trying to locate this wreck without her. She *wanted* to stay mad.

But when she thought of him, she heard his laughter and saw the sunlight dancing in those sea-green eyes. The muscles at the corners of her mouth tightened. "What can I say? I know he's crazy and he drives me crazy, but I'm also crazy about him. The thing is, Peewee, I'm not sure the feeling is mutual."

"Crazy, huh? That's a unique way of putting it."

"Well, Cole is one of a kind. You know, I joined the Marine Corps after my brother died because I didn't want to have to think anymore. I wanted someone to tell me the right thing to do."

"That's what being in the military is about. Following orders."

A strip of coral-colored light lay on the western horizon. A single star shone in the navy sky. "You see, what makes Cole so different is he follows his own path—always. He decides what's right and wrong. When you start letting others make decisions for you, things can go terribly wrong. As they did for me in the Corps. I hate to think I'm like my father in that, but I suppose it's true. I don't think Cole can stomach that."

Irv leaned forward and narrowed his eyes. "What was so terrible about your father?"

"Oh, God. Have you ever heard of an organization called Skull and Bones?"

Riley was surprised by the startled look on his face. "I've heard of them."

"I suppose you have. Cole thinks they're affiliated with the Enterprise. My father was one of the head honchos. He was willing to sit back, follow orders, and sacrifice his own son for the organization—so believe me, I know something about fanaticism."

"I'm sorry."

"Irv, tell me about my grandfather. He was a Bonesman, too. What kind of man was he?"

"Ozzie? He was a swell guy. We were best buddies as kids. He would've done anything for me. Give me the shirt off his back."

"Really? I'd like to believe that, but I haven't seen much evidence of that in the family so far."

"Sweetheart, trust me. Your grandpa was a real American hero."

"You told me in that letter you sent that you would tell me what really happened to him."

"I'm afraid I'm not as good a man as Ozzie was. I lied to you to get you to come meet me. It was bait for the hook. I don't know what happened to your grandpa."

Riley leaned back on the cockpit seat and looked up at the sky. A handful of distant stars were visible now. Without looking at him she said, "You know, Irv, you asked me why I'm on this crazy quest—what I want. I remember when I was a kid when my folks were still married and my brother was still alive. We were all so close. We were a family. Now, we're like those stars up there that may or may not exist anymore. Where there once was a family, now there's nothing but residual light and cold empty space. See, that's it, Irv. That's what I really want. I want to be part of a family again."

"Riley, I'm sorry. I—"

"Well," she said. "Enough of that." She stood, slapped her hands on her thighs, then rubbed at her eyes. "Let's get back to the plan for tomorrow. Assuming we get to the dock safely, we'll be in quarantine until the Manila Yacht Club gets the customs and immigration people to the boat. I'll plug my iPhone in now so it will be fully charged, and we'll wait for the text. Cole only uses burner phones, so we can't call him."

"Listen, sweetheart. I know Manila. It's my town. I got friends there. Once we're cleared, we don't wait on your boat. We can get lost in this city. You just follow me."

"Okay. Hey, remember your complaint this morning about the dried egg on your fork? Well, now it's your turn to wash the dishes."

"Be the labor great or small, do it well or not at all."

He was starting to drive her nuts with these sayings of his. "Okay. I'll fire up the engine and take in the headsail. With the engine running we won't have any problem running the radar all night. If either one of us sees an approaching vessel, we wake the other. Hopefully, whatever surprise they have planned for us is supposed to take place on land, not out here, and we'll be on the dock by the time the sun rises.

CHAPTER FIFTY-NINE

**Northern Luzon
The Philippines**

June 26, 1945

Ozzie sputtered and spit the water out of his mouth. He shook his head. The water continued to drip onto his face. He tried to turn away and blink the water out of his eyes. He saw an olive-drab sleeve and a dirty brown hand holding a canteen. Water warm as piss dribbled out of the mouth of the canteen.

"Cut it out," he said. "I'm awake already."

He started to sit up but the butt of a rifle slammed into the center of his chest, knocking him back and snapping the back of his head onto the ground.

"Ow, shit," he said.

The pain at the back of his head was blinding. He squeezed his eyes shut again.

When he opened his eyes a dirt-covered face with black eyes hovered six inches above his face. He smelled hot breath that stank of cigarettes. The eyes blinked and he couldn't help but notice how long this guy's eyelashes were.

"What's your name?" The voice sounded like a kid's. Filipino accent.

"Who's asking?"

The guy answered with another blow to Ozzie's sternum from the rifle butt.

"Okay, okay." Ozzie coughed and tried to catch his breath.

The sunlight burned into his eyes as the breeze waved the feathery leaves high up in the tree canopy. "Lieutenant Harold Oswald Riley, United States Coast Guard."

The face was back. Ozzie welcomed the shade. He'd take anything to block that sunlight.

"Why'd the Japanese let you go?" The eyes were taunting him.

Ozzie blinked, trying to clear the sunspots out of his eyes. He wanted to get a better look at the face. This guy must be one of the Filipino guerrillas in the resistance movement. So they were recruiting kids now. Must be getting pretty desperate.

"Look," Ozzie said. "I'm an American. I'm on your side. If you'll let me sit up, I can explain."

He was surprised then when his interrogator stepped back and grabbed one of his arms. Another person grabbed his other arm. They dragged him over to a tree and propped him up against it.

There were two of them then squatting in the dirt in front of him. His interrogator, the smaller of the two, was dressed in raggedy old US Army uniform castoffs with a web belt that cinched the blouson tight at the waist and another web belt that crossed from shoulder to waist carrying extra ammo and a couple of grenades. He wore a broad-rimmed hat with a string cinched up under his chin. The other man was shirtless, though he wore a red cotton scarf round his neck. A leather belt held up his pants and the machete he wore. They both wore dusty high boots and their faces were streaked with mud and sweat. They were speaking to each other softly in their own language as they studied him.

Ozzie reached back and felt the back of his head. He felt dampness and his hand came away bloody. Must have landed on a rock. He was wondering if he had a concussion when he heard movement in the brush behind him. With a half turn of his head, he saw that there was another body on the ground not far from him. Then he recognized it was Ben. The boy was tied up and gagged, and he was struggling against the ropes.

The shirtless one stood, walked over, and delivered a vicious kick to the boy's ribs. He said something in Tagalog and then spit.

"Hey," Ozzie said. "That's not necessary. I'll tell you whatever you want to know. Leave him alone."

The shirtless one looked over at his companion.

Ah, Ozzie thought. *Only the kid speaks English.*

His interrogator stood and walked over to Ben, then turned to look at Ozzie. There was something about the way the man walked. Then it hit him.

"You're a woman," he blurted out.

She walked back over to him and squatted in front of him again. Now that he knew to look, he saw the swell of her breasts beneath the shirt, under the ammo belts. "Yes. And why should that matter to you? Don't think it means I'll be sorry if I decide to kill you." She laughed a deep, throaty laugh. "You keep saying you will explain. I'm waiting. Why were the two of you set free with all this gold?" She pointed to the bag the prince had given to Ozzie.

"I can explain that."

From far up the mountain on the other side of the valley, Ozzie heard the loud screeching sound of an animal or a bird. His captors exchanged a look and spoke a few words in their language. The woman turned to him.

"It looks like the others have made it back to the camp already. You can explain to them."

They untied Ben's feet and used the rope to bind Ozzie's hands. Once they'd pulled both of them to their feet, the woman led the way while the man brought up the rear with his rifle pointed at their backs.

The noise they'd heard had sounded close by, but they had to walk all the way down to the bottom of a deep valley and then traverse a stream. And though Ozzie prided himself on his fitness, he had never realized just how difficult it was to walk without one's hands and arms for balance. It wasn't so bad at first and he was enjoying watching the woman's ass. But then he stumbled and fell several times, and the bare-chested man seemed to get perverse pleasure out of yanking him back to his feet. Ozzie's head ached and his mouth was parched. The going didn't get really difficult until they started up the other side. The trail led them back and forth in switchbacks and across rock outcroppings where it was almost impossible to climb without his hands. Or without a rifle at his back. It was quite the motivator. By the time they arrived at the camp it was late afternoon, and Ozzie was starting to think he would prefer to be shot than to have to walk another step.

At first he didn't even see the camp. The woman held up her arm and stopped walking. There was a clear space on the jungle floor ahead, but Ozzie didn't see anything other than trees. Then he noticed movement above. When he looked up, he saw a man's head appear in the leaves of a tree. The head was bare, the hair a light brown. He dropped a rope ladder and it wasn't until he started to climb down that Ozzie made out the roof of the tree house, or more accurately, tree hut. The walls and roof were all made out of leafy living branches and it would take a very sharp eye to recognize that the tree was anything other than how nature had made it.

When the man reached the ground, the woman dropped her weapon and ammo belt to the ground and ran over to him. She nearly knocked him over when she leapt at him, throwing her arms and legs around him, embracing him before he even had a chance to turn around. When they kissed, her hat fell off her head and hung down her back by the string round her neck. Thick black hair fell past her shoulders.

Must be nice getting a greeting like that, Ozzie thought.

Above him in the branches of the trees, he began to make out other faces appearing amid the leaves. One man slid down a vine, another dropped a second rope ladder from a different tree.

When the two finally let go of each other, the woman led her lover over to inspect the two prisoners. The man wore a ragged and torn US Army uniform with sergeant's stripes on the shoulders. When they were about fifteen feet away, the man stopped, raised his arm, and grabbed his own forehead.

"Well, I'll be damned," he said. "Riley?"

Ozzie blinked, trying to focus. He knew the voice, but he wasn't sure he would have recognized the man without it.

"Peewee?" he said. "What the hell are you doing out here?"

CHAPTER SIXTY

Corregidor Island
The Philippines

December 3, 2012

When his watch started beeping, Benny's eyes blinked wide open. He threw off the green army blanket he had stolen from one of the diorama displays in the Malinta Tunnel, stood, and stretched. He had grown accustomed to snatching his sleep in these two-hour stretches. He didn't mind waking and making his rounds anymore. He picked up the binoculars and headed for the edge of the cliff that overlooked the sea and the entrance to the bay.

He had chosen this campsite on the hill above Corregidor's public beach because it offered a fantastic view of the channel and there was close access to bathrooms and showers. During the day there were often tourists on the beach with their picnics, and he'd been very successful at getting invited to eat with them. The moon was directly overhead and only one night past full. When he stepped out of the shadows of the trees, he felt exposed in the bright light.

There were lights from three different vessels visible. Nearly every time he looked, there was some kind of boat passing by. The biggest was clearly a large ship. He could see the squarish shape of the containers stacked on deck. The other two vessels were mere pinpricks of light. Through the binoculars, he made out the bigger of the two. It looked like a Filipino long-liner fishing boat, headed out to search for the elusive huge tunas that feed the local demand for sushi. He shifted the glasses to the third and felt his pulse speed up.

The moonlight reflected off the single white sail. This was the second time in four days he had spotted a sailboat. The previous time it soon became apparent that the boat was leaving Manila and heading south. He thought back to the boat he had seen in Phuket. The details seemed to match. Long low cabin. No pilothouse. White hull. Single mast.

Benny checked his watch. It was twenty minutes past one. From abreast of the island Corregidor, the sailboat had to cover about twenty-five miles in to the Manila waterfront. He did the calculations and decided they would probably arrive at sunrise. They would be kept under close watch until they could clear with the authorities, and on a Sunday that would probably take a while. The first boats would start arriving here at dawn, ferrying the employees out for the day. He could arrive shortly after they did.

Over the last several days, Benny had reached a decision. Hawkes had said to call when they arrived. The man had said Benny was no longer fit to intercept them, and from experience Benny suspected that meant he would not pay, either. Benny would call Hawkes when he had the girl and the old man in his custody, and then they could renegotiate his fee.

Yesterday Benny had called his support source at the Enterprise. He explained the situation and said he needed the number to the woman's personal phone. He knew her website from the information they had gleaned off the computer the old man had used to contact her. Two hours later, Benny had got a call from his contact. He had her number. He had already composed the text in his mind. He needed the location, though. The earlier he got back to the city, the sooner he could scout for a quiet spot where he could take them.

He lifted the glasses one more time to check the boat. The timing was right and the boat fit the description. There were not nearly as many sailboats traveling into Manila as there were in Thailand. Yes, that must be hers. He turned and headed back to his campsite. He buried the charcoal wood and ash from his fires as well as the blanket. He swept the ground clean, then started out on the long walk to the ferry dock on the other side of the island.

CHAPTER SIXTY-ONE

Aboard *Bonefish*
Manila Yacht Club

December 3, 2012

The customs and immigration officers didn't show signs of wanting to leave. She had filled out all the paperwork and the officers had stamped the passports, but the man and woman were looking at each other and speaking in Tagalog.

The four of them were seated around the table in the main salon of *Bonefish*. Even though it was only a little after 9:00 a.m., the cabin was hot and stuffy. Riley had turned on the fans, but the thick, humid air in that tight space barely moved.

"Here it comes," Irv whispered.

The woman customs officer avoided looking into Riley's eyes when she asked for five thousand pesos as a clearance fee. "If you don't have pesos, you can just pay one hundred US dollars," the woman said.

At that moment, Riley's phone vibrated in her pocket. She pulled it out and looked at the screen. She saw the message: *Meet me at 11:00 in the San Agustin Church in Intramuros.*

Riley showed the phone to Irv. "Do you know where that is?"

He nodded.

She turned back to the officials. "If I pay you, I will need a receipt with your names on it." Both officers had ID badges on lanyards. Riley started writing down their names on the corner of her clearance papers. "Sir, could you spell your last name for me?" she said to the man.

He spoke to the woman in Tagalog again, and then he slid out of the banquette seat and rose. He offered Riley his hand. "Thank you and welcome to the Philippines," he said.

As they climbed up the steps and out onto the dock, Riley could hear the plaintive notes of the woman's voice. She did not seem happy about her partner's decision to give up on the bribe.

When they were gone, Riley said, "You ready?"

"Yeah. You want I should call us some transportation? I've got an old buddy from the Scouts who runs a cab service."

"That sounds good." She handed him her phone. "Hey, do you know if there's a back way out of this place?"

"Through the boat dry-storage area. There's a gate back there. I can loosen up the chain so we can squeeze through."

"Okay, have your friend pick us up in front of that gate."

He nodded and dialed. He spoke in Tagalog and when he disconnected he said, "It's all set. He'll be there in about twenty minutes."

"Give me a minute to throw some extra clothes and things in my backpack, and then we'll get out of here." She tossed him a small duffel. "Here. Feel free to pack your old clothes and any stuff that I've loaned you."

Up in the forward head on her boat, she pulled out the compartment behind her toiletries and removed the prayer gau. When she had returned it to the hiding spot here, she had wrapped it again in the silk cloth. She unwrapped the silk and looked at it. Since Cole had already copied the documents, they probably wouldn't need this. On the other hand, back in the Caribbean, the answers they sought turned out to be not in writing on the page, but in the design of things. Maybe the little gold prayer box had its own story to tell. She wrapped it back up and slid it into one of the plastic bags she used for taking liquids onto airplanes. She buried it under her clothes in the backpack.

When they were ready, she got two towels out and told Irv to drape one around his shoulders. "Let's make it look like we're just moseying up to take our showers." She wasn't sure how effective it would be, since he already had his damn garrison cap on his head. She didn't think guys usually wore their battle ribbons into the shower.

After she locked up her boat, they walked up the finger pier and into the main yacht club building. The receptionist was a large woman whom Riley thought looked disturbingly like Imelda Marcos. The woman focused on Irv. "Are you the captain of *Bonefish*?"

He turned to Riley and winked.

Riley said, "No, that's me."

"Oh? All right. A young woman telephoned a few minutes ago. She asked if your boat had arrived yet. When I told her it had, she asked for your cellular number. I told her giving out phone numbers is against policy. She was not happy. I hope this won't inconvenience you."

"No, it's quite all right. Really. Thank you." Riley leaned across the counter. "I'm going on a little sightseeing trip. Could you please alert your security to take extra care watching my boat? I don't know who this woman is, and I fear she may try to break in."

"Don't worry, miss. I'll tell them."

"Thanks. The showers are back this way?"

"Yes, at the end of the hall."

Riley had already seen that there was a side door across from the showers that led out into the boat dry-storage area. They headed down the hall and slipped out the door.

"A woman," Irv said once they were outside. "I've never known Benny to work with a woman."

"It would be smart, though. We'd be less likely to suspect a woman."

"Come on. The gate's over here."

Irv was right about the chain on the gate. How he'd come by this piece of information, she didn't know, but since the chain was looped around the gate a couple of times they were able to pull tight all the slack, and because they were small they both managed to squeeze through the gap.

Outside at the curb, an old-fashioned horse and buggy waited while the traffic on the wide boulevard lined up behind it trying to get around. The cart had two big wooden-spoked wheels and a small seat in back for passengers. The cart itself was made of wood, but it bore a roof of what looked like leather. The driver, who had thick white hair, dark wrinkled skin, and a hunched back, sat on a little seat just ahead of the passenger seat. He held a long whip in his right hand.

"What the hell?" Riley said.

"Jump in," Irv said. "It's called a *kalesa*. This is Manila, sweetheart." He walked up to the front and shook the driver's hand. "Good to see you, Pedro," he said. He continued in Tagalog, but Riley understood when he said San Agustin in Intramuros. Then Irv hopped in back with Riley.

The horse took off at a trot. Pedro waved his whip in traffic like a turn signal and managed to get into the center lane, from where he could make a U-turn. Riley saw another *kalesa* traveling in the opposite direction with a couple of smiling Japanese tourists in the carriage. And there were crazy painted stainless-steel buses that looked like they belonged in a Mardi Gras parade.

Irv noticed her looking at one with the name "Ruby" on a big signboard above the windshield. "That's called a jeepney," Irv said. "You'll see them all over the country here."

Riley turned back to face him. "Irv, I don't like that business about that woman on the phone. We need to be extra careful."

"You're right, sweetheart." He scooted forward on the seat so he could speak into the ear of the driver. After they conversed, Pedro turned right onto a side street.

There were lots of women on the street, and Riley suspected they were prostitutes from their dress. "Where are you taking us, Peewee?"

Pedro stopped the horse and turned to look at Riley. Irv reached over and picked up several strands of her hair and the two of them chatted on in Tagalog.

Riley swatted his hand away. "What are you doing?"

Pedro whistled and pointed at one of the girls. She strolled over to their carriage.

"Do you speak English?" Irv said.

The woman nodded and Irv scooted closer to Riley and told the young woman to climb in.

"She's about your size and build, but her hair's too dark," Irv said. "Do you have a hooded sweatshirt in your bag?"

She understood his plan, then. "Great idea," Riley said, "as long as she doesn't get hurt." She dug into her backpack and pulled out her favorite navy hoodie.

"It's a church," Peewee said. "If it's not your friends, they'll be out to snatch, not to hurt."

It was crowded in the *kalesa* now with the three of them in the back. Pedro flicked the reins and the horse took off, his hooves making a lovely clip-clopping sound as they made their way through the city traffic.

"What's your name?" Riley asked when she handed the sweatshirt across to her.

"Consuelo," she said. Worry lines appeared on her forehead as she looked back and forth at them. "What do you want me to do?"

"Don't be afraid," Riley said. "I won't let anything happen to you. We're going to a meeting at a church. I will pay you one hundred US dollars if you will walk into the church with us, wearing that." Riley indicated the hoodie. "Once I see who is there, then you can go."

Consuelo stuck out her lower lip as she considered the offer. Then she said, "One hundred twenty dollars."

"Deal," Riley said.

As they passed Rizal Park, Irv told Riley a little of the history of the Intramuros section of Manila. The name, he explained, translates to "within walls," and the old city was built in the 1570s by the colonizing Spanish ruling class, who chose to build their walled enclave by the mouth of the Pasig River. They built the fort, churches, government buildings, schools, and fine homes inside while the walls, gates, and drawbridges were designed to keep overseas intruders as well as the native people outside. Irv said he had visited the city when he first arrived in the Philippines before the war broke out. He had seen Intramuros before it was nearly destroyed along with the rest of Manila by the retreating Japanese at the end of the war.

They entered the walled city through a large gate and the street under the horse's hooves changed to cobblestones. The narrow one-way streets wound between the stone buildings and wrought-iron balconies. Riley thought it was remarkable the way they had rebuilt the place. There were still remnants of the ruins, but many of the buildings looked like they were centuries old when in fact they had been rebuilt in the last sixty years.

They had Pedro take them past the church once. When he turned his horse onto General Luna Street, the church loomed into view. Irv said it was the only building in Intramuros that was left intact after the bombing. It was a Sunday and they saw that there was a mass under way. A sign said the service was from ten to eleven.

Irv explained the plan. Once most of the people had left the church, Consuelo would walk in the front door and walk up the aisle to the altar. Meanwhile, Riley and Irv would enter through a side door and stand in the shadows to watch.

Riley said, "Somebody is expecting me after the mass. When everyone has left the church you'll go in. You're about my size. But if anyone approaches you, Consuelo, push the hood back and show who you really are. And I'll be right there watching, okay?"

The young woman nodded.

Pedro positioned the *kalesa* around the corner from the church. He would wait there and direct Consuelo to head for the front door in five minutes. The service must have ended early as people were flowing out the door.

Irv led Riley around through a garden to a courtyard and the side door into the cathedral. They hung back in the shadows of the alcove. Within their small side chamber there was a life-sized statue of the Virgin Mary on one side and a glass display of what looked like bones on another. A table by the statue was covered with flickering votive candles, and out by the main cathedral there was a carved stone font of holy water. With their backs to the wall of the alcove, they inched their way closer to the church.

The main cathedral was breathtaking. It was difficult not to be distracted by the painting on the ceiling, the chandeliers, and the magnificent carved wood furnishings. They couldn't see back to the front door of the cathedral, but they should see Consuelo once she was halfway to the altar.

Riley heard Consuelo scream before she saw her.

"Let's get out of here," Irv whispered.

"We can't just leave her."

"That was the whole point of this. She's the canary."

"You go on. Get Pedro to pull up right in front and get his horse ready to run."

"You're nuts," Irv said, but he turned and left out the side door.

She peeked around the corner. It was Benny and he had Consuelo's neck in the crook of his arm. She was whimpering and he was yelling in English. "Where are they?" he shouted.

Farther back in the alcove, red velvet ropes were strung between steel posts to keep people back from the wood and glass case with the relics in it. The posts had wide, round metal bases. She lifted one up. It wasn't attached to the floor. She unclipped the rope from the end post, carried it to the edge of the alcove, and set it down.

She stepped out into the main sanctuary and said, "Are you looking for me? If you want me, come get me." Then she made as if to take off running out the side door. She picked up the post and tucked herself back inside just around the corner. She heard his footsteps and brought the post up over her shoulder like a baseball bat. She wished she could see. Timing was going to be everything.

She swung and the moment she made her move, she knew she had gone too soon. When Benny came round the corner, the end of the post missed his head, but he ran right into the end of it and it poked him in the shoulder. His momentum drove the base back and it hit Riley in the chest. The impact knocked her off balance. She felt herself going down on the stone floor and she knew it was going to hurt.

CHAPTER SIXTY-TWO

San Agustin Church
Intramuros, Manila

December 3, 2012

Riley landed on her tailbone first, then the back of her head bounced off the stone floor. Her vision went black and then it was like watching fireworks for a second. The impact felt like an electric shock to her spine, but her butt didn't hurt as much as her head. She was vaguely aware of Benny standing over her.

Something slammed into her ribs and all the air in her exploded out of her mouth in a low moan. He'd kicked her. She rolled over onto her side and tried to curl up into a better defensive position. She felt dizzy—she couldn't get enough air.

"Where's the old man?" he said.

She wanted to tell him to go fuck himself but all that came out was something between a cough and a moan.

She saw his feet on the stone floor not far from her body and she noticed he was wearing cloth espadrilles. That was certainly better than the cowboy boots that Hawkes guy wore, and she suddenly thought it was funny that she was critiquing his shoes at a moment like this. But when she saw the foot swing back in preparation for another kick, she didn't think anything was funny anymore.

His foot slammed into her arm where she was trying to cover her midsection. Her arm deflected the blow, but it still knocked her breath away. It didn't take much at this point. She tried to focus on his feet, thinking if only she could grab them and pull him down, trip him somehow. Where were the other people in the church? Surely somebody must be around to see what was happening. Tears blurred her vision. She wasn't crying. She was too mad to be crying. It was the pain in her ribs and her butt.

"Where's the gold you stole?" He leaned over and grabbed her backpack. She hugged her arms tight to her body so he couldn't get the backpack off her.

He lifted half her body off the floor by the backpack. The straps cut into her underarms. He was yelling at her in a language she didn't understand, but she knew it was profanity from the way he spit the words at her.

From the corner of her eye, Riley saw movement behind Benny. Thank God. Someone was coming. She turned her head so she could see better. At first she thought it was Consuelo returning, but then she saw this was a much younger Filipina woman wearing baggy green camo pants and a tight tank top. She came trotting into the alcove. Her shiny black hair fell in a long braid down the front of one shoulder and an elaborate tattoo circled one of her firm biceps.

Benny was so intent on wresting the backpack off Riley's back, he hadn't noticed the woman. She pulled a string off one shoulder and a little backpack purse swung around in front of her. Her hand plunged through the drawstring opening and pulled out a little canister. Opening her mouth wide, she pantomimed holding her breath and pinching her nose. Then she kicked Benny in the thigh.

With a loud groan, he let go of the backpack and swung around to face the young woman. She lifted the canister, pointed it at his face, and before he knew what was happening a stream of liquid hit him in the eyes and across his face.

Riley was holding her breath and trying to cover her face, but some of the burning spray landed on her bare forearms.

Benny roared and held his hands up in the air over his head. Like Riley, he obviously had been trained in what to do when hit with pepper spray. He knew the worst thing he could do just then would be to rub his eyes.

The Filipina woman ran over to Riley and extended her hand. She pulled Riley to her feet. Then she held up her hand to signal stop.

Benny was swinging his arms, trying to connect with one of them. He was like a blinded bull snorting and coughing and trying to get some revenge for his pain. When he couldn't connect with anyone, he staggered over to the wall, felt his way to his right, and located the font of holy water. He plunged his face into the water.

"Let's go," the Filipina woman whispered. She took Riley by the hand and pulled her toward the back of the church. Every step sent pain shooting out from her tailbone. She wondered if she had broken her coccyx. It hurt so much it almost made her forget the pain in her ribs and her head.

The other woman pushed open the heavy wood door, and the sunlight was so bright both women stopped and held their free arms up to shield their eyes.

"We can't stop," Riley said, her voice still hoarse. "He's coming. Get out of here and don't let him find you." She blinked to clear her eyes and then she saw the *kalesa* parked at the curb. Irv was standing up motioning for her to hurry. "I've got to go. Thank you so much." Riley gritted her teeth and walked as fast as she could down the walkway to the street.

As she was climbing up into the *kalesa*, Irv said, "Hurry up. Here he comes." Then he patted Pedro on the back. "Go, go!"

The driver flicked the reins and the horse stepped away from the curb.

Riley eased her sore body down onto the seat and turned to look.

Benny was standing outside the wood doors, his arms raised to shade his face. His long hair hung in dripping strands down either side of his face.

The young woman ran up to the rolling *kalesa* and jumped onto one of the shafts alongside the horse just as the driver snapped his whip and the horse broke into a fast trot down the narrow cobblestone street.

She was panting from the run, but as she clung to the side of the carriage she said, "Riley, I'm here to take you to the plane."

Riley was stunned. She sat unmoving, just staring at the woman. Irv reached across, offered her his hand, and with Pedro's help they pulled her into the *kalesa*. Once she was safely seated, Riley said, "How do you know me?"

"I'm a friend of John's," she said. "He asked me to look out for you."

Riley's face must have looked a complete blank as it took her several seconds to remember that Cole was going by an alias here in the Philippines.

The woman continued. "He told me to watch the Manila Yacht Club. When I called this morning, they said you'd arrived, but wouldn't give me your phone number. I took a cab down to find you, but as we were going south on Roxas Boulevard, I saw the two of you just outside the yacht club fence climbing into a *kalesa* headed north."

Riley turned to look at Irv. That would explain the mysterious phone call to the club. He was being uncharacteristically quiet and just staring at the woman. Granted, she was a knockout in her tank top.

Riley guessed it didn't matter how old the guy was, he could still be struck dumb by cleavage.

Riley turned back to the woman. "How'd you know it was me?"

"John described both of you, and hey"—she gestured toward Irv—"there aren't many couples around the yacht club that look like you two. We made a U-turn but we lost you for a while when you turned off Roxas. Then we found you again along Rizal Park and followed you into Intramuros."

Irv turned his body halfway around in the seat to check the traffic behind them. The back of the *kalesa* had a cutaway window with a rolled-up cloth that could be dropped to keep out rain. "Riley," he said. "We got trouble."

She looked back and saw two taxis behind their carriage, but behind the taxis was one of the strange three-wheeled vehicles she'd seen all over the streets. It was a motorcycle with an enclosed sidecar and a little roof over the motorcycle driver. Benny was hanging out of the passenger sidecar, motioning and yelling at the driver. He held his blowpipe in his hand.

"We've got to get out of here," Riley said. "Out where there is more room."

"Those tricycles can be fast," Irv said. "He'll catch us if there's more room." Then Irv said something in Tagalog to Pedro, who turned his horse right at the next street.

Riley thought they were headed back for the same Intramuros gate where they had entered. Unfortunately, only one of the two cars followed them around the corner and now Benny's tricycle was even closer. It looked like he was urging his driver to try to pass the taxi that separated him from the *kalesa*.

Irv yelled, "Duck!"

The three of them bent forward at the waist just as they passed through the gateway.

"What is it?" Riley asked.

"That damn blowgun."

The *kalesa* had turned toward the harbor onto the street that passed between the park and the walled city. Traffic was bumper to bumper, moving very slowly. Probably the only thing preventing Benny from getting out and running was the residual effects of the pepper spray. He needed the driver's eyes.

The carriage jerked to a stop. Pedro cried out and jumped to the ground.

"What's happening?"

Their horse's front legs had buckled. Pedro was trying to free the animal from the front shafts of the *kalesa* so it could roll onto its side without overturning the cart.

"Shit," Irv said. "He hit the horse with a dart."

Riley glanced behind them and saw that a truck now blocked Benny's tricycle, but traffic in his lane was moving. "We've got to get out of here."

"A dart?" the woman said.

"He's got a blowgun and he shoots poison-tipped darts. It's probably just knocked the horse out temporarily. He hits you or me, it's a heart-stopper."

The woman said, "Follow me then," and she jumped down out of the *kalesa*.

Peewee beat her out the other side of the carriage. Riley eased her way to the ground.

They darted between the cars, putting distance between them and Benny's vehicle. Then the woman cut over to the sidewalk. She ran up to an empty tricycle and climbed onto the motorcycle. "Climb in," she yelled.

Riley pushed Irv inside the small aluminum pod and crawled in after him. The owner of the vehicle, who had been talking in a group of men a distance off, came running over, hollering.

The motorcycle roared to life and the woman took off, driving them down the sidewalk and sending locals and tourists scrambling to get out of the way.

Irv turned around and looked out the tiny window in the back of the sidecar. "Benny's got his driver on the sidewalk too, now. They're not far behind us."

When they reached the intersection with the big coastal boulevard, Roxas, the light was red for them but they bounced down off the curb, causing Riley to see stars again when her butt bumped down onto the hard seat. The little tricycle charged out into the traffic.

Horns blared and tires squealed as the cross traffic swerved to avoid them. Somehow they made it across without getting hit. Their driver continued another couple of blocks, then turned left and drove down a street and into the parking lot of a restaurant. She pulled the bike to a stop and yelled, "Come on!"

Riley tumbled out but Irv was taking longer. The two women lifted him out and set him on his feet just as the other tricycle pulled into the parking lot. The strange woman led them through the restaurant out to a ramp that led down to a long finger pier. Tied alongside the pier was a seaplane.

The woman put two fingers in her mouth and let loose an ear-piercing whistle as they pounded their way down the dock. Riley's body ached in places she didn't know she had, but now Irv was going even slower than she was.

And Benny was gaining on them.

The engines fired up and the props started turning on the seaplane. A hatch opened up on top and a man poked his head out. He reached down into the plane and pulled up a long rifle. He took aim and let fire. Riley heard the pop and saw the recoil. Then he disappeared back down the hatch just as they arrived alongside.

Riley looked back and saw Benny peering out around the side of the restaurant door. Riley guessed the pilot was shooting over the top of the restaurant, but it had slowed Benny well enough.

The woman swung open the door on the side of the plane and motioned for them to get in. Riley helped Irv climb up and they each took one of the three seats behind the cockpit. The woman who had brought them here ran forward and untied the one line that still held the plane to the pier, then jumped in and closed the door.

As the plane taxied away from the pier she made her way forward and sat in the copilot's seat. Before she put on the big headphones that she'd picked up off the seat, she turned around and smiled a broad, white smile. She had to shout to be heard over the noise of the engine. "Whew! That was fun. By the way, I didn't introduce myself back there." She wiped her hand on the camouflage fabric of her pants and held it out toward Irv. "My name is Greg."

Riley noticed Irv was staring at her hand. Then, like he was waking up from a trance, he took her hand in both of his, shook it, and shouted, "Another pretty girl with a funny name."

Greg shrugged, then shook Riley's hand. "And this guy"—she pointed to the pilot—"is Brian."

The pilot lifted one hand briefly to wave, but he didn't turn around. He was busy taxiing the aircraft out into the bay.

"Buckle up, folks," Greg said as she slipped the headphones over her ears. "Next stop—Subic Bay."

CHAPTER SIXTY-THREE

**Northern Luzon
The Philippines**

June 26, 1945

The woman standing next to Peewee brushed one side of her long black hair behind her ear as though she needed to be able to hear better. "What? You know this man?"

"Well, I'll be goddamned." Peewee walked up and placed his hand on the side of his friend's face. "Ozzie Riley. And you're a looie now. Big-man officer. You haven't changed a bit."

Ozzie wanted to be able to say the same to his friend, but it wasn't true. Not that lying had stopped him in the past. But he was sure Peewee would know it was a lie.

Gaunt. That was the best word to describe him. As his name suggested, Peewee had never been a big guy. Even at twenty years old, he'd only been about five foot four and maybe a hundred and twenty pounds. Not that Ozzie was much bigger—he only had a couple of inches on his friend, but he'd always have a bulkier build. Right now Peewee would be lucky to tip the scales past a hundred.

"I'm surprised you're alive," Ozzie said. "Last I heard you were a prisoner in Bataan."

His friend smiled and Ozzie saw gaps where teeth should have been. Peewee patted Ozzie's cheek and stepped back. He slid an arm around his girl. "Naw, the Japs didn't keep me for long. I escaped and joined up with my buddies here. I've spent most of the war here in the mountains with the guerrillas." He indicated the several Filipino men who had gathered around them. Most of them wore bits and pieces of uniforms or civilian clothes that looked torn and mended and then torn again. "That's Manolo over there," Peewee said, pointing to a bare-chested man with shoulder-length frizzy black hair, a cigarette in his mouth, and a Thompson submachine gun in his hands. "This here's Rafi." The older man wore a once-white peasant's shirt and a straw hat. A long machete hung from his belt. "That pretty boy over there is Ferdinand." The man he referred to wore a clean-looking Filipino Army uniform with lieutenant's stripes, a very white smile, and pomaded black hair combed back into a wave reminiscent of Clark Gable's. Judging from the man's eyes, he was part Chinese.

"You've already met Gregoria, here." Peewee kissed her on the cheek and she smiled back at him. "And her partner on patrol there is Danilo."

"My backside got to know the barrel of his rifle quite well on the way here."

Peewee translated the comment and the men laughed.

"So, buddy, what do you say you untie my hands?"

"Most of these guys here don't speak English. They don't know what we're saying right now—they only know that Greg and Danilo brought two prisoners to camp who were released by the Japs. Lucky for both of you, they also don't know about the gold Greg found on both of you. Normally, these guys shoot collaborators."

"Peewee, I'm not a collaborator."

"Ozzie, this is me you're talking to. I know you'd sell your mother if they offered you enough. And what about your friend over there?" He pointed at Ben.

"No, he isn't a collaborator either. That kid got kidnapped by the Japs, and he was made to work as a valet for a Japanese prince. The prince took a shine to him. Now the Japs are getting ready to head back to Nippon, and it didn't make sense to take Ben with them, so the prince decided to let him go."

Ben was a problem. Ozzie was starting to see his encounter with his old friend Peewee as a way to get another chance at the treasure in the cave, but if he spun a yarn for them here, and Ben got to talking, he could mess up Ozzie's plans.

"So he was waiting on some damn Jap prince?"

"Peewee, he's just a kid. He was more like a slave, a POW just trying to stay alive. Make sure he gets back to his family, and you'll never hear any more from him."

His old friend turned then and faced Ozzie. "Did you know they found this on him?" Peewee held up a dagger. "Are you sure he was on your side?"

Ozzie looked at Ben, but the boy had his eyes on the ground.

Peewee continued. "So what about you? What's your story?"

"I was assigned to a submarine, the USS *Bonefish*."

"But you're Coast Guard."

"Let me finish. We were on patrol and we picked up some prisoners, survivors from a sunk ship. It was nighttime. Turned out they were a decoy. There were others—frogmen in the water. They overran us and took the captain and first lieutenant prisoner. They took over the ship and brought her into a cave on the coast here."

"Yeah, I know about the cave," Peewee said.

"Well, right now there's an American submarine in there with all her crew."

"Still don't see how you got out."

"Like I said, the prince had taken a shine to that kid." Ozzie point-ed at Ben. "He wanted someone to guard him to make sure he made it home safely. The skipper suggested me."

"And why was that?"

"Like you said, I'm Coast Guard. I wasn't part of his regular crew."

"So what were you doing on the sub?"

"I'm OSS, Peewee. I'm a spy."

CHAPTER SIXTY-FOUR

The Makati Shangri-La Hotel
Manila, Philippines

December 3, 2012

Elijah slipped his key card into the door lock and pushed open the door. He felt great after his late-morning workout in the hotel's health club followed by a steam in the sauna. When he walked into the suite's bedroom, he saw Esmerelda was still there in his bed. Not surprising. Even though it was well past noon, he hadn't paid her yet. She appeared to be fast asleep, though she'd kicked off the sheets and was displayed in an especially alluring pose—on her back, thighs parted, arms above her head, her breasts sweet, firm mounds. Elijah stopped to admire the girl and his body reacted just as it had several times the night before. She was probably no more than seventeen years old, but she already knew more than most American women about how to treat a man with respect and do as she was told. He knew when it came to sex, he could ask her to do anything. He dropped the thick white robe he'd worn back from his steam. He wore only shorts beneath it.

He took a step toward the bed, then stopped. No, there was no time for that today. His Saudi friend was expecting a progress report this afternoon, and Elijah only had a few hours to come up with something to tell him. He walked over to the big picture window and drew open the curtains, revealing a deep blue sky over the city skyscrapers. He looked straight down twenty-seven floors at the tiny people walking the sidewalks along Ayala Boulevard. No more important than a train of ants leading back to their hill.

He turned from the window and spoke to the naked girl. "Time to go," he said. "Get up and get dressed."

She opened her eyes and formed her lips into a pout. "You come to bed?" she said.

"Got to disappoint you this time, honey. You go on home." He held up one hand with his fingers pointing downward, making like legs walking.

She hopped out of the bed and came up behind him. She ran her hands over his back and made a sort of purring noise. "Your tattoo is very sexy."

Her warm hands on his sweaty back made him start to grow hard again. He thought of the massive dragon tattoo on his back as a source of his strength, and when women touched him there it went straight to his dick.

"Come here," he said.

She walked around in front of him, her lovely naked backside to the glass. Fresh from the bed, her skin looked a rosy pink in the sunlight pouring through the window.

He put his hand under her chin and tilted her up so she had to look him in the face. "That dragon you like so much? It's there because I was born in the Chinese year of the Wood Dragon. That means I am a very powerful man."

She made that pout again and stood on her tiptoes, trying to kiss him. He had a better idea.

He shoved down his shorts and kicked them across the room. Then he put his hand on top of Esmerelda's head and pushed her down to her knees.

Elijah reached forward, put his palms flat on the warm glass, and watched the ants crawling around on the street as the girl worked on him. He flexed the muscles in his shoulders and knew that it caused the skin beneath his dragon to ripple, bringing the beast to life. He would collect his dragon sword and make the blade razor-sharp once more.

He came just as he imagined swinging the dragon blade, causing all the ants to scatter.

Elijah walked out to the suite's living room, lifted the phone, and called room service. He ordered a late lunch for himself and extra coffee and cups. He asked that it be delivered in half an hour. Then he went to the room's safe and removed his wallet. He knew better than to leave it in the room with a Filipina girl. He suspected she'd conducted a search the minute he left for his morning exercise.

Esmerelda walked out of the bedroom wearing the low-cut mini-dress and platform shoes she'd had on when she'd arrived at his door the night before. He pointed to the table where he'd left the money and turned back to the window. She left without saying a word.

After a shower and shave, and dressed in his best jeans and boots, Elijah stood in front of the huge bathroom mirror and tightened his bolo tie. He reached up and patted his hair, making sure not a single black hair was out of place, and stared into his own blue eyes.

He was taking a tremendous risk by agreeing to Al's proposal to cut the Enterprise out of this deal. You didn't fuck with these guys without knowing that if they caught you, you'd be dead. But four million dollars? Some men wonder what their price is. Elijah now knew his. Maybe he'd take Caleb and Tess and head down to Argentina or Peru or South Africa. With the price of gold today, he knew his knowledge would be welcomed anyplace they were pulling the shiny stuff out of the ground.

A knock on the door meant his lunch had arrived.

Elijah had just started eating when the house phone rang and the desk told him that a Mr. Nils Skar was asking to see him. He told them to send him up, though Elijah found the man physically revolting. One would think that a true psychic would know better than to interrupt a man's meal.

He opened the door and told Skar to help himself to coffee while he finished eating. But when the man settled himself into the chair opposite and ran his hands over his long, stringy hair before grabbing a coffee cup, Elijah found his appetite gone. He pushed away the rest of his omelet and toast.

"What have you found out?" Elijah asked.

The Norwegian had just finished putting three sugars into his coffee cup and he held up his hand as he took a sip to test it. Elijah blotted his mouth with the cloth napkin and kept his eyes trained on Skar.

After he swallowed, Skar nodded. "They make good coffee here," he said.

Elijah continued to stare without speaking.

"Okay, okay. I just needed some coffee to get my brain working." He rubbed his hands together, then placed them palms down on the table. "I've learned a few things about this John Paul Jones and his boat the *Bonhomme Richard*."

"That's really his name?"

"It is what he calls himself. As to his real name? I think not."

"Go on."

"He's been in the Philippines just shy of two years. He befriended Brian Holmes, the wreck diver over in Subic Bay. He's tried to keep a low profile while doing research on the sly on something called the Dragon's Triangle."

"And how do you know that?"

"I bought drinks for some of the regulars at Holmes's bar. They overheard Jones talking to Holmes about it. They said it was an area of ocean north of the Philippines that's like the Bermuda Triangle."

"What about before he came to Luzon?"

"That's the thing. His boat was registered in the Cayman Islands a few years ago, but before that I can't find much record of him or the boat. Both seemed to appear out of thin air."

Elijah pushed his chair back and stood. He crossed over to the window and stared out at the city. "And what about the woman? What did you learn about her?"

"That's where it gets interesting."

"Spare me the commentary, Skar. Just give me the information."

"There's plenty about her out there. I got her name from the US Coast Guard documentation database. There was only one sailboat named *Bonefish* listed. She served for seven years with the US Marines. There are several old news articles from 2008 when she was involved with a boating accident off Guadeloupe in the Caribbean. There was an explosion and two men went missing and are presumed dead. One of two was a maritime archaeologist who was apparently looking for the wreck of a World War II submarine called the *Surcouf*."

Elijah's head swung around slowly. "She's that woman sailor?"

"You know this story?"

Elijah said nothing.

"Well, unless she has some sort of fetish for male treasure hunters, there's a good chance that our Mr. Jones might be the guy who went missing four years ago. If only we can establish some connection between the two of them."

They were interrupted by a knock on the hotel room door. Elijah assumed it was the room-service attendant returning to clean up. He crossed to the door and opened it.

Benny stood outside.

"What are you doing here? You're supposed to be out on Corregidor." Elijah stepped aside so the man could enter.

"My phone died. I saw her boat pass by last night. I waited until morning and took the ferry back to Manila so I could report to you. But by the time I got to the yacht club she and the old man were leaving."

"I assume you followed them."

Benny nodded. "But I lost them."

Elijah leapt forward and grabbed Benny by the front of his shirt. "You fucking stupid savage." He pulled Benny close. "You were outsmarted *again* by this girl?"

Elijah wanted to see fear in the man's eyes. Instead he saw a blank face, and those dark, almost black eyes were trying to burn a hole right through him.

Benny said, "They went straight to the docks by Rizal Park and they got on a seaplane. There was no way I could follow. The plane headed north."

Nils Skar interrupted. "Can you describe the plane?"

"Just a seaplane. It did have a name on the side. It said 'Gama's Resort and Dive Center.'"

Skar grabbed Elijah's arm. "That's Brian Holmes's plane. *There's* our connection."

CHAPTER SIXTY-FIVE

Subic Bay, Luzon
The Philippines

December 3, 2012

Greg opened the door to the room, stepped back, and handed Riley the key. "There you go. You'll be in here and"—she pointed down the open corridor—"Irv, you'll be right next door."

Irv gave Riley the thumbs-up sign and said, "*Constant togetherness is fine—but only for Siamese twins.*"

Riley rolled her eyes at him.

"This is a dive resort so the rooms aren't fancy, but they're clean," Greg continued.

"It looks great to me," Riley said. "After almost two weeks at sea, I'm heading straight to the shower."

"Okay. Let me know if there's anything you need."

"I can't thank you enough."

"Whenever you're ready, come on down to the restaurant and we'll talk about tomorrow. I know you are anxious to join the *Bonhomme Richard*, but there just wasn't enough time to refuel and make it up there in daylight today."

• • •

Night had fallen by the time Riley left her room and headed to the bar. It was more crowded now than it had been when they'd arrived and Brian had taxied the seaplane right up to the floating dock in front of the restaurant and dive center. There was a flat-screen TV above the bar and though the sound was muted, Riley saw the headline "Typhoon Bopha takes aim at Mindanao with winds of 250 km/hr."

The crowd was mostly Caucasian men, a few with Filipina wives or girlfriends. They all seemed to know Brian, who was holding court behind the bar. He was in the middle of a story when he spotted her.

"Riley, welcome to Gama's!" he shouted. His Australian accent was even thicker than it had been earlier.

She leaned over the bar. "I have a favor to ask."

"Anything," he said. "Just ask."

"Have you got any way to contact the *Bonhomme Richard*?"

"Sure. I've got a radio in my office and we usually chat in the evenings about this time."

"Could I—"

"Follow me." Brian came out from behind the bar and led Riley from the room and down a hall. He opened a door and switched on the light.

What he referred to as his office looked a lot more like a workshop to her. There was a long table in the middle of the room on which were several artifacts in various stages of restoration. One piece looked like a blob of coral, while another was a perfect blue-and-white porcelain Chinese jar. The design on the jar was of frothy waves at the bottom and several winged dragons flying around above the waves.

Brian sat at a desk along the wall of the room and turned on a single-sideband radio. "Those boys are frustrated. This ought to cheer them right up." He only called their boat name a couple of times before Cole replied. Riley smiled when she heard his voice.

"*Bonhomme Richard*, I've got a young lady here who would like to talk to you. I'll leave you two alone."

Brian handed her the mike and closed the door on his way out.

"Hey, Cole."

"You made it. I was getting worried about you. The southern islands are getting slammed by this typhoon."

"Yeah, I'm pretty glad to be here, too. My boat's at the Manila Yacht Club. How are things with you?"

"Frustrating. We know it's here somewhere, but we're having no luck."

"Well, I've spent some time with an expert. Remember Irv?"

"Yeah. The old guy from Bangkok?"

"Right. He and I have been going over some things."

"Please tell me you're not sharing information with him. Riley, I don't trust him."

She wasn't sure how she was going to explain to Cole that she'd been sharing her boat with him. "I know that. But Brian is going to fly us up tomorrow afternoon. Can you meet us off the island that is to the southeast of you? If you head out in the morning, you could be there by noon, right?"

"What's this about?"

"I'll explain when I see you."

There was a long silence. Riley was certain Cole understood the need for camouflage. They had no idea who might be listening.

"So I'll see you tomorrow," she said.

"Okay. We'll be there."

"Good. Trust me on this, Cole. You'll be happy you did."

She shut down the radio after they had both signed off. Businesslike. From this point forward that would be how she would deal with him. It was foolish to think their six days in the Caribbean meant as much to him as it did to her. If it had, he wouldn't have stayed away from her for four long years.

She was tired and she wanted to get some much-needed sleep. She hurried to the door. When she stepped out into the hall, she saw a man with shoulder-length hair hurrying off toward the bar. Where had he come from? She walked to the door a few steps away in the opposite direction. It was locked. He hadn't been in there. There was only one other logical explanation. He'd been outside the door to the office. She followed him.

When Riley stepped into the bar she couldn't see a man with long hair in the crowd at first. Then she saw him on the other side of the bar—at least she assumed it was him because she hadn't seen his face in the hall. It was a face you wouldn't forget. His eyes bulged out of his head to such an extreme degree it had to be some physical ailment. On the bar in front of him was a half-finished beer and a cigarette burning in the ashtray. He certainly didn't look like he'd just been lurking down that hall.

"Riley, come here!" Brian shouted. "I want to introduce you to some of my mates here."

She walked over to the bar and one of the fellas gave up his stool for her. She slid onto the seat and found herself directly across from the long-haired guy. Brian went around the bar, telling her names. When he got to the bug-eyed fellow, he said, "This guy's got experience working up in the Babuyan Islands. We're in luck. He just flew in from Manila. You might want to talk to him. Nils Skar, meet Riley."

The guy nodded at her and lifted the hand with the burning cigarette.

Brian continued. "Folks around here call him the Norwegian Psychic on account he hears voices. The good part is the voices tell him where to dig!"

There was good-natured laughter around the bar.

"Since he knows the area up there, I've invited him to come along with us tomorrow." Brian set a beer in front of her and he lifted his own glass in the air.

Riley raised her glass.

"To good hunting!" he said.

CHAPTER SIXTY-SIX

Camiguin Island
The Philippines

December 4, 2012

Cole stood on the bow of his trawler with his forearms resting on the steel bulwark. He had just dropped the anchor in thirty-five feet of clear water and watched it hit the white sand bottom before letting out a little more than a hundred feet of chain. The four-hour trip over from their anchorage off Calayan Island had been rough, with twenty- to thirty-knot winds on the nose and fifteen-foot seas. Here in the anchorage off the west side of Camiguin Island they had found excellent protection, and the water was calm, with a pleasant cooling breeze off the land. Cole didn't know why Riley had asked him to come to this place, but he hoped her reason was sound. He didn't want to have to retrace his route across that channel anytime soon.

Ashore was a white sand beach backed by a fringe of palms with assorted structures that mostly looked like homes. Just back from the village, the island rose up at a steep incline toward the jungle-covered mountains. He could count at least two volcanoes, the southernmost of which actually had steam rising out of it. On his chart that one was called Mount Camiguin. After what had happened to him in the Caribbean, being this close to active volcanoes made him uneasy.

He turned at the click of dog's nails on the deck to see Theo and Leia walking toward him.

"Hey, boss," Theo said, "what does it look like ashore?"

"You'd like it, my friend."

Theo rested his arms on the bulwark next to Cole and they both turned their faces toward shore.

"It looks a bit like Dominica. It would remind you of home. Two volcanoes in sight. There's a small village and I can count at least five good-sized fishing canoes pulled up onto the beach. So far nobody seems to be paying too much attention to us, but if I know small islands like this, that won't last for long."

"No, I imagine the village is all abuzz already about the new boat that just dropped anchor offshore. The coconut wireless is humming."

"Just wait until a seaplane drops out of the sky. That will really get the gossips started."

Theo chuckled. "You're right there. Is there plenty of open water for them to land?"

"Yeah. You could bring an aircraft carrier in here."

Theo nodded. "Judging from the number of wrecks marked on the chart, this harbor has been used by ships quite a bit. I wonder how many of those wrecks are from the war."

"Most, I suspect. But I hope Riley asked us to bash our way over here based on something more concrete than the number of old wrecks marked on a chart. If the wrecks are charted, they've also been well picked over."

"You'll be able to ask her yourself soon enough."

"Yeah—if she's speaking to me."

"Hey, all you did was steal her treasure map. Why should she hold that against you?"

Cole opened his mouth and started to protest, but he saw his friend grinning.

Theo said, "You know what, mon? You make it too easy. Come on, Leia, let's leave Cole to his misery and go get this boat ready for company."

Misery was right, he thought after Theo left. When he'd decided three years ago that he couldn't risk contacting Riley and endangering her, he thought he had lost her forever. Now he'd been offered this second chance, and he was afraid he may have blown it already.

Cole didn't know how long he'd been standing out there when Theo called out to him from the wheelhouse.

"I just heard from Brian on the VHF. They're about twenty minutes out. He says it's him and four passengers."

"What the hell?" Cole walked back to the door to the bridge and the boat's navigation center. Theo sat in one of the two raised chairs that faced an impressive array of electronics. "We've got five guests coming?"

"That's what he said."

"Where are we going to put everybody?"

Theo laughed. "I see what you're getting at. We don't have enough bunks. I guess somebody is going to have to double up. Like maybe Riley can bunk with you?"

"That's not what I was thinking."

"*Right*. You keep telling yourself that."

"I'm going to go launch the Boston Whaler. Somebody is going to have to ferry this lot from the plane to the boat."

Cole headed to the afterdeck to use the crane to lift the boat out of its chocks on the cabin top. He'd just splashed the boat into the water and was releasing the lifting harness when he heard the distant sound of an aircraft engine. He looked up and searched the sky to the south.

After several seconds, he finally located the tiny dot in the sky. He stowed the dinghy harness and returned to the wheelhouse.

"I don't like this, Theo. It's too many people."

"Relax, boss. I know being paranoid is your thing, but this time, just focus on the girl."

"No, seriously. There is a reason why we have survived and been left alone for all these years. My paranoia has served a purpose and kept us alive. I never should have contacted Riley. You know how much they want this Dragon's Triangle. And we've got to stop that from happening."

"Cole, can you see the plane?"

"Yeah. It's about to touch down on the bay."

"Okay, mon. Focus on the plane. Get in the dinghy and go pick them up."

Cole sighed as the floatplane splashed down on the sparkling blue water. He guessed there wasn't much he could do to change the situation now. Brian and the others had no idea what they were getting themselves into.

"While you're gone," Theo said, "I'll put together some lunch for everyone."

"Okay," Cole said. But inside he was thinking, *Great, now we've got the blind feeding the blind.*

Brian's was the first face he saw when Cole pulled his Whaler alongside the floatplane.

"G'day, mate," the pilot called out through the open window after he shut down the engines. "I see you've shaved all that hair off your face for this great occasion."

Cole waved and rubbed his hand across his freshly shaved upper lip and chin. "Yeah, I figured the beard wasn't worth putting up with a leaky face mask."

Brian looked back over his shoulder into the plane, then back at Cole. Brian gave him the thumbs-up. "Right," he said.

Then the door in the body of the plane swung open, and Cole saw Riley's gray eyes smiling at him.

Unfortunately, that moment of elation was short-lived as he next saw who the two additional passengers were: Nils Skar and the old man, Peewee. The needle on his paranoia meter was suddenly pegged.

It only took two trips in the dinghy to get all the passengers delivered to the trawler. They got the seaplane tied off on a long line trailing behind his anchored boat. Riley and Brian were the last two off the plane.

"How was your trip?" he asked.

Brian said, "The weather was pretty good. No thunderstorms, anyway. But we will want to get back first thing in the morning if we can. I'm worried about that Typhoon Bopha. You heard the news?"

"Not much. What's happening?"

"They say it's causing massive devastation down in Mindanao. It's not likely it'll come this far north, but you never know. I'd like to get back home."

"I can certainly understand that," Cole said.

They were approaching the swim step of the trawler and Riley grabbed the dinghy's painter. "I'd never have recognized the boat," she said as she climbed out of the dinghy.

"Yeah, well, I've done a bit of work on her since the last time you saw her." As soon as he'd said it, Cole wished he could take the words back. The last time Riley had seen his boat, she believed that he had just died and been entombed in the submarine *Surcouf.* Seeing his boat again must be bringing up those old memories.

Brian said, "You got any cold beer on this tub?"

"See Theo in the galley."

Brian climbed up the ladder to the afterdeck and Riley followed him.

"Riley, could you hold up a minute?" Cole said.

She turned and waited as he climbed up and joined her.

"I'd like to have a few minutes to talk to you alone. I want to apologize to you. I overstepped. I get so—" He stopped. There was always so much to tell her but when it came time to do it, he felt like a tongue-tied schoolboy.

"Cole, I get it. It's just as well it happened this way. It's clarified things. Made your priorities clear. I've had a little taste of the way these Enterprise guys operate, and you're right. We've got to stop them."

She turned and walked away from him.

What the hell just happened? he thought.

As Riley approached the door to the galley he heard her call out, "Yummy, I smell something cooking. Where is that Theo?"

Cole thought, *Theo! Oh, shit! She doesn't know.* He called out, "Riley. Wait up!" But he was too late. She turned and disappeared through the doorway. He trotted up to the opening fearing the worst.

He stepped through the oval metal door and saw Brian, Greg, Peewee, and Skar all jammed onto the tufted vinyl bench seats at the dinette. They were chowing down on pizza, drinking cans of San Miguel beer, and chatting. But there was no sign of either Riley or Theo.

The sound of her voice caused him to turn his head, and he saw her standing in the wheelhouse facing forward out the front windshield. Cole walked up to join her, and it was only when he reached the threshold into the wheelhouse that he saw Theo was there with her. Riley's back was facing Cole and of course Theo, standing opposite her, couldn't see Cole either.

"I don't understand," she said. "Theo, what happened?"

"Riley, it's been more than two years now. It no longer matters how it happened. They tried to kill me and they didn't succeed. That's the good news." He shrugged. "Anyway, I've learned to live with it."

"Cole didn't say a word to me about it. I can't believe he didn't tell me."

Cole eased slowly back into the passageway, but he could still hear their voices.

"Go easy on him, Riley. In some ways, it's been harder on him than on me."

"I don't see how—"

"He blames himself. And because of what happened to me, he decided he had to stay away from you—to keep you safe. I know these past four years have been painful for you, but believe me, he was suffering, too."

"Oh, Theo," she said.

Cole peered around the corner of the bulkhead, and he saw her slide her arms around his waist and embrace him.

"Enough of this mushy stuff," Theo said, pushing her away. "Let me introduce you to the newest member of the crew." He leaned down and rested his hand on the head of his yellow Labrador retriever. "This is Princess Leia, or just Leia for short. Go ahead. Shake hands."

Riley dropped to one knee. "Hey girl, shake." Leia lifted her paw. "I'm Riley," she said as she shook the dog's paw. "I'm glad to discover these guys have another female in their lives."

"So, Riley, you think what we're looking for is here at Camiguin?"

She stood and looked at the array of instruments and screens. "Yeah. You guys have really outfitted this boat with all sorts of new toys, haven't you?"

Theo reached up and touched a screen. The image of the map from the prayer gau appeared.

Riley looked at him. "Okay, I can see that. But what about you?"

"In this case, I've studied this map for so long, I don't need to see it. But here." He reached up on the dash and grabbed a stiff piece of paper. He handed it to her. "I developed a tactile printer that does for images what Braille does for letters. It can't do color and it's difficult to read very intricate designs, but I've been reading nautical charts with this for over a year now."

"You really are amazing."

"I know," he said. "So are you going to tell us what you figured out about this map?"

"Okay."

"Here you are," Cole said, stepping into the wheelhouse as though he hadn't been skulking in the passageway listening.

Riley turned to look at him, and he saw the dampness on her eyelashes before she tried to rub it away. She shot him a look that told him he would have more to explain later.

Theo said, "Riley was about to show me what makes her think Camiguin is the place."

"Before we get to that," Cole said, "I'd like to know more about what Irv and Nils Skar are doing here. I don't trust either one of them."

"I wondered about that, too," Theo said. "The old guy was pretty funny when I served them the pizza, but I thought Cole said he was a member of the Enterprise."

"*Was* is the key word there," Riley said. "I guess we've all had our secrets. About a day out of Singapore, I was intercepted by our friend from Bangkok. Remember Benny?"

"Intercepted? What happened?"

"He pulled alongside in a fishing boat that was a lot faster than my boat, and he shot me with one of his darts."

"What?" Cole said.

"Yeah, the next thing I knew I woke up aboard some pirate boat at anchor off Natuna Besar, and this weird American guy named Hawkes was trying to get me to give him the prayer gau and to tell him your name."

Cole turned away from her and swore. This was all the old man's fault. He'd started all this. "Then what happened?"

"Irv was there with them. It seems he's an expert crypto-analyst, and he has been working for them."

"I knew it."

"But listen, it's thanks to him that I got away. We went back to my boat supposedly to fetch the prayer gau, and Irv and I managed to escape. We've just spent more than a week on my boat together. It was a pleasant change having company at sea."

"You mean when we talked on the radio—"

"Yeah. He was right there next to me." The look on her face told him she was back there in her memory. "A man his age, even a man in great shape for his age like Irv, he's got to know his time left on this earth is short. The way I caught him looking at me sometimes—it gave me the feeling there's more to his story than he's letting on. I haven't figured it out yet, but I believe him when he says he's done working for the Enterprise. And it was thanks to his help that I figured out the map."

Theo said, "So explain it to me. What did you figure out?"

"Hang on, now. We still haven't heard what she has to say about that freaky Norwegian."

"I don't know anything about him," Riley said. "First time I saw him was last night. I think he was eavesdropping outside the door to Brian's office when I called you on the radio. Then he somehow got himself invited along. I can't figure out why Brian trusts him."

"I didn't like him the first time we met him," Theo said.

Riley grabbed Cole's arm. With her other arm she pointed out the window at the front of the pilothouse. "Look. There's a boat coming out."

"Great," Theo said. "That's all we need."

"I'd better get back to the galley quick," Cole said, "to make sure we have our story straight.

• • •

A few minutes later the entire party was standing on the aft deck. Brian was acting as spokesperson and Greg was translating. Of the four men in the boat that came alongside, one said he was the mayor of the village, and he wanted to know what they were doing in his bay.

Technically, Theo was the owner and skipper of the *Bonhomme Richard*. Cole was just a crewman. They had all agreed that their cover story was that they were an environmental group there to take samples of the sand on the bottom of the bay. Cole had heard on the news that the Chinese had recently sent a ship to Camiguin to do some mining of the mineral-rich black sand on the bottom. The Full Fathom Five Maritime Foundation, an organization Cole and Theo had once set up and could trot out when needed, was there to make sure the Chinese did not rob the Filipino people. Brian explained all this, but the mayor still demanded they come ashore and fill out the required paperwork.

"Ask him if there's a pub in the village," Skar said.

The others laughed, but when Greg spoke at length in Tagalog and the mayor answered, she told them there were actually two.

Brian offered to take Greg as translator and Theo as captain into the village in the dinghy, but Peewee and Skar both wanted to go, too. In a matter of minutes, they had all piled into the Boston Whaler and pushed off for shore.

Cole turned to Riley. "It looks like it's just you and me left behind," he said.

CHAPTER SIXTY-SEVEN

**Northern Luzon
The Philippines**

June 26, 1945

"So you're in the OSS? We've been working with those guys for years. Funny we never crossed paths before."

"I was in Europe up until Germany surrendered. Worked as a frogman doing underwater demolitions. Then they sent me on this sub. Even though we got captured by the Japs, I still can't tell you what my orders were. The skipper and I both hoped that if I could get out with Ben here, I'd be able to come back with reinforcements, and we could get our sub back. There are a hundred and eighty American prisoners in that cave. Are you and your men up for that?"

"Okay, Ozzie. I've heard your story, and I need to convene a council to explain it to the others."

Peewee spoke in Tagalog to Danilo and the young Filipino poked Ozzie again with his rifle.

"What did you say to him?"

"Danilo's going to take the two of you to the stream where you can wash up. After our council, we'll eat."

The Filipino jabbed him again and Ozzie nearly fell.

It was more than two hours later when the others arrived. The valley had fallen into deep shadow. Earlier, Danilo had escorted them to the small creek where they washed and drank their fill of water. Then he had taken them to this place on the hillside where a rock overhang made a sort of small cave. A hunchbacked old woman stood over an open fire stirring the contents of a pot and turning sticks with small birds strung on them. Under the rock ledge, the daylight was nearly gone and the faces of Ben and Danilo were tinged with the reddish-gold light from the fire.

When Peewee and Gregoria arrived, Ozzie looked to their eyes to see if they could give him any clues as to what his fate might be. Peewee was running around acting all self-important, but he saw Gregoria was sneaking glances his way.

He wasn't too worried about it. His friend might have toughened up a lot while in the Philippines, but Ozzie was certain Irving Weinstein would not order his old friend shot as a collaborator.

Meanwhile, Gregoria came over and sat on the ground next to Ozzie. Ferdinand, Rafi, and Manolo made themselves comfortable, too, and they all formed a semicircle around the fire as they sat staring at the glowing embers.

Peewee said, "Who wants some chow?" and then he spoke in their language. His men spoke back to him with laughter and affection as he helped the old woman serve the food. They passed the plates around.

Gregoria watched Peewee as he worked and talked with the other men. Then she said, "What was he like as a boy?"

"Irv? I'd say he was bookish. He was always reading his adventure books, but he wasn't very strong, so his mother never let him go out and have adventures. Only with me. I watched out for him. Irv and I used to build small boats in the woods behind our parents' houses. He always liked building things."

She smiled. "Bookish. Yes, I can see that. He still tells me stories at night when I have trouble sleeping."

Ozzie watched the firelight on her face. She had opened a few buttons on her shirt and he could see the rising swell of her breasts.

"Why do you have trouble sleeping?"

"This war has brought many terrible things to my country."

Ozzie liked listening to her voice. Her English was very good and her accent only made her seem more exotic. "What happened to you?"

"Three years ago, the Japanese came to my village. I was only seventeen."

"I have heard terrible stories of the things the Japanese have done to the Filipino people."

"Yes. They came to our house and took my mother and me for the officers. When my father protested, they shot him."

"I'm so sorry," he said.

"It was not you. I am very thankful to the Americans. When my mother tried to stop them from touching me, they raped her—over and over until she hemorrhaged and died. After one week, I wanted to die, too. Ozzie, Rafi, and Manolo came to our village. It was three against twenty or more. They killed all the Japanese and freed us. The other villagers ran and hid in the jungle. They feared more Japanese would come. My family was gone, so I asked to go fight with the guerrillas. They laughed at me at first, but then they have found I am very useful, as I can walk into any Japanese camp and pass as a comfort woman."

Peewee sat down with his plate of food on the other side of her. "And she's become a hell of a fighter. She might be small, but I'd wager she's killed more enemy than you have, Ozzie."

Ozzie hadn't been with a woman since he was back in Pearl—maybe four months back. With her long, soft hair and flashing dark eyes, Gregoria fascinated him.

"This is quite a camp you all have set up here. Those tree houses—what made you take to the trees?"

"Mostly poisonous snakes, spiders, and scorpions," Peewee said.

"Ah. Those sound like good reasons to me."

"So, my friend," Peewee said, "the council has met and this is what we've decided. Lieutenant Marcos over there"—when he heard his name, Ferdinand gave a jaunty salute over his dinner plate—"he's going to escort Ben to his home in Tuguegarao. He's still regular army. He joined us for a while when things got too hot up in Bessang Pass, but he's decided to go back to his unit. They're going to scram on out of here soon as they've finished eating."

Ozzie was pleased at the news. That was one problem solved.

"And the rest of us are going to do as you asked. We are going to free that submarine."

"Excellent."

"Rafi over there says he can get us a fishing boat. We'll go in by sea."

"Have you got the weapons and the ammo to take on the Japs?"

"Hell yeah."

As Peewee went through the logistical details, laying out the plan first in English and then repeating it in Tagalog, Ozzie couldn't concentrate on what he was saying. He kept sneaking glances at the woman next to him and he convinced himself that half the time, she too was watching him.

When the men got up and walked to the edge of the rock overhang to smoke, Ozzie stayed next to Gregoria.

"You don't smoke?" he asked.

"No," she said. "My parents disapproved."

"I see," he said.

"I really should go help Rosa with washing up."

She stood and went to the wood bench where the old woman was washing dishes in a big metal basin. Gregoria took the bucket and headed off into the jungle in the direction of the stream where Ozzie and Ben had washed up earlier.

Ozzie stood. Seeing that Peewee was still deep in conversation with his men, he followed her. No longer hobbled by having his hands tied, Ozzie was able to move through the bush almost soundlessly. When the noise ahead of him went silent, he slowed.

Gregoria knelt at the side of a little pool and cupped her hands in the water. She drank and washed the clean water over her face. The droplets on her skin shone like silver in the moonlight.

Ozzie stepped out of the bushes. "Can I help you with that bucket?"

"Oh," she said. "You startled me. I didn't hear you coming."

"Sorry," he said. He moved close to her. "I didn't mean to frighten you. I can't help but notice how beautiful you look in the moonlight." He touched her wet cheek. Her eyes met his and she didn't look away.

He admired her wet lips, partly open as her breath quickened and her chest rose and fell. He started to reach for her, but she turned her back to him.

"Please," she said. "Stop."

Ozzie had seen the way she looked at him. He placed his hand lightly on the curve where her neck met her shoulder. Her skin was so soft.

"Hey, buddy, what's going on here?" Peewee came charging through the bushes and Ozzie stepped back from the woman.

"I came to the stream," Ozzie said, "to wash up after eating, and I was just offering to carry the bucket for the lady here."

"I'll get the water." Peewee picked up the wooden bucket and dipped it in the stream. "Gregoria, I'll see you back in my quarters."

The woman slipped into the trees without a look back.

Peewee left the bucket on the ground and stood. He walked up to Ozzie and put his face bare inches away. "You haven't changed a bit, like I said. You always were a selfish son of a bitch—thought you were better than me. Back home, if there was a girl I liked, you'd set your eyes on her and take her away just for the sport of it. This isn't high school, asshole, and I'm not that scared little shit who let you walk all over him. You get near her again, and I'll break your neck."

Peewee turned, picked up the bucket, and walked slowly into the trees.

CHAPTER SIXTY-EIGHT

Camiguin Island
The Philippines

December 4, 2012

"In that case, we'd better get to work," Riley said. She didn't want Cole thinking she had anything else on her mind. She turned away from him—it was too dangerous to look at him right now—and she started across the deck. "I'll show you what I've figured out with the map."

"Riley," he said. "Wait a minute."

She stopped and turned around. Her heart rate had jumped into the danger zone when she heard the change in his voice.

He didn't say anything for several long seconds. It looked like he was struggling to find the right words. Then he said, "Before we do that, can I show off the changes I made to the old *Shadow Chaser* to turn her into this state-of-the-art salvage vessel?"

"Sure," she said, and it took every ounce of determination in her not to sound disappointed.

"When we hauled out down in Guatemala, we cut away all the old cabin aft of the wheelhouse, which included the entrance to the old hold." He showed her how they had made more interior room for three sleeping cabins and turned the old fishing hold into a divers' paradise.

"We got rid of the old shrimper outriggers and placed this crane on the aft end of the trunk cabin." He bent over and pulled back a large hatch cover on the aft deck to reveal the diving gear area.

He was wearing khaki cargo shorts with a tropical print shirt, which she guessed he had even ironed for the occasion. She felt the corners of her mouth turn up when she thought how much more she appreciated the view of the muscles rippling in his legs as he lifted the hatch cover than any creases on his sleeves.

"That's the compressor for filling the tanks," he said, pointing into the hold, "and the helium tank for heliox deep dives. We've got built-in tank racks and lockers for all our other gear. And that monster on the cradle there is the latest version of Theo's ROV, still named the *Enigma*. She's got hi-def video now, and we've got a couple of these GoPro little video cameras that divers can wear as headgear. Over there we've got a couple of DPVs."

"I remember ROV is remote operating vehicle, but what's a DPV?"

"Diver propulsion vehicle. It's like an underwater scooter with a little propeller. That's Theo's design, too. There are commercially designed ones, but Theo's uses some new nickel-metal hydride batteries, and it goes faster and longer on a charge than any of the others."

"Looks like you've got all the toys."

"Come on, I'll show you the changes inside the main cabin." He led her to the port-side watertight door into the galley.

"By removing the outriggers," Riley said as she ran her hand over the outside of the door frame, "you've transformed her from old fishing boat to modern salvage yacht."

"That was the idea. Not much is original anymore except the hull and the classic old wood wheel and pilothouse." He motioned for her to go on into the galley. "Here we found we could enlarge the seating area without losing counter space due to more modern appliances. The stove is now propane and the fridge is a more efficient twelve-volt holding-plate system. The entire roof area of the wheelhouse is now covered with solar panels, and with the new lithium-ion house batteries Theo can use all the electronics he wants."

"This galley looks like a cook's dream," she said, running her hand over the new Corian countertops.

"And down in the engine room, there's a washer/dryer combo and a thirty-gallon-per-hour reverse-osmosis water maker so we don't have to take short showers, either."

Aft of the galley a welded steel staircase descended about four feet to a companionway with two doors on each side. The first on the port side led to a head with a real stand-alone shower. On the opposite side of the hall was a sleeping cabin with a nice full-sized berth and warm wood cabinetry. Riley noticed the dog bed on the floor and the massive array of computer gear, so it was no surprise when Cole told her it was Theo's cabin. Aft of Theo's was a cabin with nothing much more than four bunk beds. Cole told her it was for when they needed extra crew.

The last cabin opposite the crew's quarters was the master stateroom. When Cole opened the door he kept his hand on the latch, and Riley had to brush against him to squeeze through the doorway. She kept her eyes lowered, but her stomach felt like a popcorn popper on high heat. The cabin featured a walk-around queen-sized berth covered with a navy-blue spread. To one side of the door was a desk with a laptop computer and beyond it were several wood cabinets for clothes. Reading lights were mounted on the bulkhead at the head of the berth, and above them a bookcase stretched across the full width of the cabin.

"Home sweet home," Cole said.

She walked around, keeping her back to him, admiring the fine woodworking and cabinetry. "Very nice work, Cole. It's not just a yacht. It's a home."

"The original captain's cabin on the old shrimper was meant for one man. I redesigned this as a double. See? Two hanging lockers, two sets of drawers for clothes."

"Yes," she said. "It's beautiful."

Though it was the largest cabin on the boat, it was starting to feel exceptionally small and far too warm. She tried to get to the door to get out, but he stood there blocking the way. "Aft of this I saw two sets of stairs—one going up on deck, the other down into the engine room, I guess."

"Right."

"Shall we go take a look?" She attempted to slip past him, but instead she bumped her tailbone on the chair at his desk. She winced.

"What's wrong?"

"Oh, it's nothing."

"Riley, you're hurting. I saw that look."

"It's just that back in Manila, you said you were going to text me where to meet the plane. So, when I got a text, Irv and I assumed it was you. Only when we got to Intramuros, I found Benny there instead. He got a few licks in before we got away."

"But I sent Greg and I told her to text you."

"Thankfully she saw us leaving the yacht club and followed us or I'm not sure how we would have ditched Benny. She was great. Anyway, I took a fall, and I'm still a little sore on my backside."

He made a fist and started to strike the surface of the desk, but then he slowed and just pounded his fist like a gavel on the surface. "I'd like to take that guy and beat his face to a pulp."

"Cole, stuff happens to people you love, and it's not your job to protect them twenty-four/seven. What happened to Theo—that wasn't your fault. You're not his keeper. This business with Irv and Benny would have happened whether you were around or not. Irv did know my grandfather, I'm sure of it. You can't protect me from my own family. Now let's get out of here and go look at the rest of your boat."

He didn't move. Instead, he reached up and ran a finger down her cheek. His touch was so light she wondered if she was imagining it, as she had so many other times.

"I'm sorry," he said.

She turned her head aside. "For what?"

"For being an idiot. I wanted to protect you. My heart was in the right place, but I really mangled it, didn't I?"

She nodded, her throat too tight to speak.

"I couldn't bear the thought of losing you, so instead I put you through the very thing I feared. And now they're after you anyway."

He reached up and stroked her hair. When his palm slid down to her cheek again, she closed her eyes and tilted her face into his palm. Then she stepped back.

"I can't," she said. She took another step back and her backside bumped into the chair at his desk.

"What's wrong?"

"I've had to compartmentalize my feelings just to keep moving. To get to this place. Now you want me to open that box. I don't know if I can."

He stepped closer. "Riley." He reached out and touched her arms just above the elbows.

"How do I know you won't disappear?"

"I don't blame you for not wanting to go through that again. But there is nothing that will ever make me leave you now."

She wanted to tell him then—the truth about Lima. To find out if what he was saying was true. But when his arms slid around her and he pulled her body to his, she tilted her head back and met his kisses with hungry lips.

Riley closed her eyes and lost herself in the pleasure of his mouth on hers, their tongues dancing, tasting, caressing. His hands slid up her neck and into her hair, grabbing handfuls, his kisses going deeper still. She knew she should stop, that she would not survive having him and then losing him again, but all she wanted at that moment was more. More of his mouth, more of his hands on her body.

He framed her face with those hands and leaned back. "I can't believe you're really here." He extended his leg behind him and nudged the door closed with the toe of his boat shoe.

She smiled at him. "And I can't believe your boat-tour-as-foreplay gambit actually worked."

He placed his hands on the waistband of her shorts and began steering her toward the bed. "Yes, Magee. Very clever, no, ending the tour in my cabin?"

"Oh yeah," she said as the bed touched the back of her knees and he eased her down. "And I do appreciate a clever fellow."

He sat next to her on the bed, took her in his arms, and kissed her again, slipping his cool fingers under her shirt onto her hot bare skin. A shiver rose at the base of her neck and swept down her spine as she arched her back. He took hold of the hem of her polo shirt then, leaned back, and lifted it over her head.

Riley reached back to unhook her bra, but his hands were on hers, gently pushing them to one side.

"Allow me," he said. "I spent too many nights alone in my bunk fantasizing about undressing you."

When her breasts were free he kissed his way down her neck to her collarbone, and she groaned aloud when he finally arrived, his tongue teasing first one and then the other nipple until both were pebble-hard.

"Cole," she said, running her fingers through his sun-bleached hair and grasping handfuls of it in her fists, "if this is all a dream, don't wake me."

After some delicious, maddening minutes he sat up, and began to unbutton her shorts. "I don't know about your dreams," he said, wetting his lips, "but mine are never this good."

He slid her free of her remaining clothes and she stretched out before him, naked on his bed.

He stood for several seconds slowly unbuttoning his shirt and shorts, taking a long look at her. She half smiled at him, wishing he'd hurry and stop torturing her. Her world had been reduced to the aching hollow need between her legs.

When he shrugged off his shirt, she enjoyed the sight of his hard chest and the washboard shape of the muscles across his abdomen. The years had changed his body, erasing any vestiges of softness. When he'd stepped out of his shorts and crawled up the bed to her, she slid her leg between his, wanting to connect her soft skin against the hardness of him.

What *was* it he did with his fingertips? They danced over her skin. By the time he kissed her neck, her whole body was trembling. Again she was arching her back, and pushed her hips against his. Her throat, her breasts, her lips—he seemed to be kissing her everywhere at once, his mouth on her skin sending white-light explosions of electric pleasure through her body. More powerful than all of this was the bone-deep connection she felt to him, as though the waves of pleasure were silk filaments wrapping them in their own cocoon. When at last he pushed inside her, she felt like gravity itself had released them, and together they burst free and took flight.

CHAPTER SIXTY-NINE

**Benguet Gold Mine
Baguio, Philippines**

December 4, 2012

The only four-wheel-drive vehicle Elijah could find to rent in Manila was a Mitsubishi Strada, the turbo-diesel crew-cab pickup truck. He didn't mind the truck so much except that he couldn't relax in the backseat like he could in a limo or a luxury SUV. He had to sit up front next to Benny. But since he didn't know what to expect over the next few days, and he wasn't going to have the resources of the Enterprise at his disposal, he thought the truck bed might come in handy.

By the time they pulled up in front of the main office at the mine in Baguio, Elijah was sick of Benny's odor of sweat and cigarettes. As usual, Jaime Belmonte had appeared on the porch as the building came into view, and he fluttered around like an obsequious moth drawn to the light when Elijah climbed out of the truck. Elijah ignored him.

"Listen, Benny," he said to the savage. "Until further notice, you are now my driver. That's your job. So don't go wandering off. I won't be long. I have to go down to see Wolf in the lab. Then you can take me to my hotel in town." Elijah turned to Belmonte. "Jaime, find a room for Benny for tonight."

"Yes, sir, I'll be happy—"

"Shut up, Jaime. You don't speak unless I ask you a direct question."

Wolf was waiting at the door when Elijah approached the lab building.

"Good afternoon," the German said.

"Same to you, Wolf." Elijah knew the man was not happy to see him. Wolf had to know why Elijah had come.

"Are you getting any closer to finding this Dragon's Triangle site? I complain when I have too much work, but too little work is just as bad. In fact, I think it is worse. I'd rather be tired than bored."

"Yes, my people are at the site now. But salvage work takes time, as you know," Elijah said.

"They say it will be bigger than anything we have seen since the days of Marcos."

"I hope so." Elijah walked over to the cabinet where Wolf stored the sword. "You know why I've come."

"Yes. It's in the same place. I haven't touched it."

Elijah bent down and removed the velvet-covered parcel. He set it on the table, then opened the cloth. The sword was even more spectacular than he remembered. The intricate gold work of the dragon's face on the hilt and the jagged, teethlike spikes along the outer curve of the blade surpassed the images in his imagination. He could feel the power from the sword flowing into him. He had been right to make this side trip into the mountains to get it. Having the sword with him would change his luck now.

Wolfgang said, "Swords from this period have sold for several million dollars at auction recently. I am not an expert, but it is possible this one is as valuable. And to think Belmonte wanted me to destroy it."

Elijah had no idea it was worth that much. But it didn't matter. He couldn't sell it. He patted Wolf on the back. "Ulrika would be proud of you for saving it."

Wolfgang looked like he was going to be sick. He spoke in a low whisper. "Even though I couldn't save her."

"What did you say, Wolf?"

The German stood on the opposite side of the table, staring down at the gold hilt of the sword. "I thought of taking it, you know. Like the old man did."

"What are you talking about?"

"The sword. I thought about taking it and leaving this godforsaken place."

Elijah shouted, "Forsaken? God has blessed us. Look at all the gold he has given us."

Wolf moved around to the end of the table. "God didn't give you anything. You took it. Just like you took my wife. She killed herself because you raped her."

"Rape? I didn't rape her. You were there. You watched and you got off on it."

"You had a knife."

"I fucked your wife because you couldn't. She needed it. She wanted me. You heard her screaming. She loved it."

Wolf made his move then, grabbing the sword with both hands and swinging it back. Elijah was ready for him and threw a punch straight to the man's abdomen. The sword clattered to the floor when his fist buried in the doughy flesh, and Elijah heard the *whoof* of air when Wolf doubled over. Elijah clasped his hands together and lifted them over his head and brought them down hard on the back of the man's neck. He crumpled to the floor.

Elijah walked over and picked up his sword. He laid it down on the velvet cloth and folded it into a tight package.

"You shouldn't have dropped my sword, Wolf. You have no appreciation for beautiful things." He tucked the package under his arm and turned to look at the body on the floor. He swung back his boot and delivered a hard kick to the man's ribs. Judging from the satisfying depth his boot sunk into the body, Elijah broke more than a couple of them.

"Wolf, maybe your bad luck with women has to do with your ugly face." He drew back his leg and kicked the toe of his cowboy boot right into the German's nose and blood gushed from the mangled flesh.

"Oh, Wolfie, now you've made me really mad. You just got your blood on my Lucchese alligator boots. You're going to have to pay for that, my friend."

As Elijah was walking back up to the office, his phone rang. He held the sword tight under his arm and reached into his jeans pocket for the phone.

"Mr. Hawkes, it's Nils."

Elijah stepped away from the building and into the shade of the pine trees. "What do you have for me?"

"I joined the party in Subic Bay and this morning we flew up to Camiguin Island."

"That's a different island than the one you mentioned before."

"Yes, the woman seems to think the map leads here. She hasn't had a chance to explain why."

"Okay, so what have they found?"

"Nothing so far. We just got here. Right now they are trying to sort things out with the local officials. They've always been very touchy up here about treasure hunters."

"I want to know everything they know as soon as they know it."

"That's a problem. There is no cell service up here. I came ashore with them, and I've borrowed a satellite phone from some campers. I don't know when I will be able to call you again."

"Figure it out, Skar. That's what I'm paying you for."

"Yes, sir."

Elijah disconnected and hurried back to the front of the camp where they had left the truck. He didn't see the savage around, so he bounded up the steps.

Both men were sitting inside Jaime's office drinking whiskey.

"Belmonte, did you do the research I asked for on the phone this morning?"

"Yes, sir, and I had a difficult time finding a contact—"

"Jaime. I don't care about what you did to get the information. Just give me what I asked for."

"The man Cole Thatcher was no longer being actively pursued because he was presumed dead; however, the bounty from the Patriarchs remains intact. It's five hundred thousand dollars."

"Do they want to talk to him?"

"No, sir. They want him dead."

CHAPTER SEVENTY

**Camiguin Island
The Philippines**

December 5, 2012

Riley had been awake for a while when she felt Cole stir, slide his arm off her waist, and roll out of the bed. She admired the view as he walked naked to the door. He opened it a crack, then quickly eased it closed again.

"Shit," he whispered.

"Good morning to you, too."

He whipped his head around. "Oh, you're awake. Sorry. It's just—"

"There's a line at the head?"

"Three deep," he said as he rummaged in a drawer for clothes. When he'd pulled on a pair of swim trunks, he sat on the bed and took her in his arms. "Let me say a proper good morning." He kissed her in a manner that wouldn't be considered "proper" at all. "But I can't tarry. Nature calls and if the head's not available, the aft deck will have to serve."

"Unfair male advantage," she called out as he slipped out the door.

Much as she would enjoy spending the morning doing more of what they'd spent most of the night doing, Riley knew Cole would be eager to see if her interpretation of the symbols on the map was right.

It had been well after dark the night before when they'd heard the sound of the outboard and realized the others were returning from their trip ashore. Cole had gone out and fetched her backpack from the galley before the rest of the crew got back aboard. Then they'd heard Theo sorting out the sleeping arrangements for the extra four guests as Riley lay half on top of him with one hand on his chest and her head tucked into the curve of his neck. He stroked her hair and they both chuckled at the wisecracks slung their way from the other side of the door.

Riley climbed out of the bunk and picked up Cole's shirt from the floor where it had ended up the night before. She slid her arms into the sleeves and buttoned a couple of buttons. Through the windows she could see that it was a gorgeous morning outside. The sun had already heated up the decks enough to cook an egg and there was very little breeze. She picked up her backpack and peeked out the door. It looked like the coast was clear. Just as she reached for the handle, the door opened and Greg smiled when she saw Riley before her.

"I'm glad to see somebody's got her glow on this morning," she said.

Riley started to mumble good morning, but Greg quickly switched places with her. As she was closing the door, Greg said, "Hop in the shower, girlfriend. I'm the one bunking with three guys, so I don't need you going around smelling like sex." She closed the door.

When Riley entered the galley a half hour later, there was a chorus of "Good morning" from Brian and Theo, who were seated at the table. Cole was standing at the counter pouring himself a cup of coffee from an institutional-sized percolator. He grinned at her.

"Get ready for comments from the peanut gallery," he said with a nod toward the fellows at the table.

Brian said, "I certainly wouldn't make any off-color comments to such a beautiful young lady. I'd only question her sanity at hooking up with a crazy bloke like you." He winked at Riley.

Riley swatted Cole on the behind and said, "I like my men crazy."

Cole picked up another cup and poured one for her. "Yeah, crazy enough to drive my boat over here in the hope that you've figured out where our wreck is."

She looked at him over the rim of her cup. "Is that a challenge?" She took a sip of the hot liquid. Theo must have made the coffee. It was excellent.

Cole shrugged. "Call it what you will, the time has come to lay it all out there."

Brian said, "I thought that was what she did last night."

Theo started coughing. "I think I just snorted my coffee," he said.

"Listen, boys, that's enough," Riley said. "Time to put away your inner twelve-year-olds and get down to work. Where's everybody else?"

Theo slid out of the dinette and said, "Greg asked to go take a closer look at the *Enigma*. As to those other two guys, I don't have a clue."

"Forget them," Cole said. "Riley, what do you need?"

"Have you got an iPad with charts of the area?"

"Sure," Theo said. "I'll go get it." He walked forward into the wheelhouse and they all heard his voice when he said, "Hello, I know you're there. Is that you, Nils?"

The reply was muffled.

"Come on back to the galley. Riley's about to explain where she thinks this wreck is."

When Theo returned, Nils Skar was right behind him. Riley wondered what he'd been doing up there.

Theo handed Riley the iPad. She said, "Don't tell me you've figured out a way to use this, too."

"Sure," he said. "Music, audio books, and I can make some pretty crazy tunes in GarageBand."

Riley kissed Theo on the cheek. "You are amazing."

"I know," he said, and he sat back down on the dinette. He spread out his own tactile representation of the map, and slid a paper copy of the map they'd found in the prayer gau onto the table in front of Riley.

Riley hollered out, "Irv, are you in your cabin? I need you out here."

From down the aft corridor she heard Irv's voice. "I'm coming."

When he appeared in the doorway to the galley adjusting his hat on his head, Riley asked, "You getting extra hours of beauty sleep?"

"How do you think I keep this physique in such good shape?"

On the iPad, Riley opened up the iNavX app and accessed the charts for the South China Sea.

"When comparing this Japanese map to the Babuyan Islands charts, at first blush one would assume that this phallic-looking thing in the corner is the northern tip of Dalupiri Island."

Brian said, "She's got phalluses on the brain."

Cole started to open his mouth, but Riley was faster. She swung on him, pointed her finger at his mouth, and said, "Don't even think about it."

"Well, darling," Brian said, "after what you did to him last night, he wouldn't be a man if he wasn't thinking about it."

Riley rolled her eyes. "You guys are impossible."

Cole put his arm around her waist. "We're guys. It's in our jeans."

Riley looked at the men around her, then closed her eyes for a minute. The others seemed to be having good fun, but Peewee looked extremely uncomfortable with the sexual innuendo. She opened her eyes and sighed. "Look, guys, we can play word games, or we can find this wreck."

Cole kissed her on the cheek. "Did you know you get red spots on your cheeks when you're really irritated? It's quite fetching. Okay. We'll be good now. You were about to tell us what other island looks rather like a man's penis."

"It's not exactly another island. It's part of an island. You see, I was looking at the chart of the Babuyan Islands on the iPad like this." She held the tablet up in the portrait-viewing mode. "My boat was bouncing around because we were at sea and the image changed orientation to landscape view, like this." Riley moved the device to show them.

"It makes me crazy when it changes on its own like that," Brian said.

"But when the chart changed the view—see, here—the island of Camiguin became visible in the corner of the screen. I guess it was the way I was sitting, but it was like something clicked. I saw this area not north up like we always think of charts. Instead, I saw the island on a forty-five-degree angle." Riley turned the sheet of paper so the lower left corner pointed downward. Then she slid her fingers across the tablet screen and enlarged the view. She set the paper on top of the glowing screen and aligned the images.

"It's a very smart way to disguise a map—draw it on the diagonal," she said. "See, this is Magasasut Point off the southwest side of Camiguin, and this is the little Pamoctan Island in the center of the bay. It all started to fit with some of the other symbols that Irv had shown me on the key list."

"Like what?" Cole asked.

"See these three lines here? That's the symbol for a river. And this weird thing that looks like a hat down here? That's a volcano, and while the scale's a bit off, the volcano called Mount Camiguin is down at the south end of the island."

"What are these arrows? I thought they were indicating the currents in the channel."

Irv spoke up. "In all the work I'd done on Japanese treasure maps, I'd never seen that symbol either. I didn't know what they were. It was Riley who explained to me how to read the symbols on the nautical charts. She pointed out that there are lots of wrecks off the main village there."

Riley said, "I did some research then and I discovered they estimate that there are more than thirty known World War II wrecks around Camiguin. I think those are marking other wrecks, but not our wreck. See this weird duck-like symbol? I think that marks the site of the *Teiyō Maru*. That symbol is on the other sheet, and Irv told me what it's meant in his experience. I'll let him explain."

"When the Japanese sealed up the caves and tunnels where they stored some of their treasure," Irv said, "they often made various types of traps for others who might try to dig it up before the Japs returned to get it. They used bombs, poisonous gas, and various types of booby traps. Sometimes, after they set off explosives and buried the entrance to a cave, they would then flood the area above the entrance and create a man-made lake. In my experience, that?" He tapped the duck-like mark on the map. "That's the symbol for an underwater treasure."

"Whoo-hoo!" Brian shouted. "I like the sound of that." He clapped Cole on the back. "What are we waiting for, mate? Let's go get it."

CHAPTER SEVENTY-ONE

**Camiguin Island
The Philippines**

December 5, 2012

Cole couldn't have asked for better weather. They'd only been search-ing their grid for a little over two hours, motoring through glassy calm water and towing the new dual-frequency side-scan sonar system they had recently installed, when Cole thought he saw something on the screen. It was off to their starboard side.

"Did you see that?" he asked Riley, who was standing behind the helmsman chair. He pointed at the screen, but the image was already gone.

"No. But I'm having a hard time making out what's what. The picture isn't very clear."

"The problem is the depth. It's varying between one eighty and over two hundred feet. Our cable isn't long enough on the sonar tow-fish. Let me circle back."

Cole turned the boat around and attempted to retrace their path by following the bubbles left by their wake. On the second pass, they saw something that looked like a mound on the bottom.

Theo said, "I wish I could be of more help. One of these days somebody is going to figure out how to get computers to help humans read sonar like dolphins."

"Theo, I wouldn't be surprised if that somebody turns out to be you." Cole throttled back to slow the boat way down until she was barely drifting and he made another pass. "There, see that coming up on the screen?"

"Yeah," Riley said. "It looks like the bow of a ship. Definitely."

Theo stuck his head out the side door and hollered back to the crew on the aft deck. "Hey, guys, we may have something. Bring the sonar towfish alongside. Greg, are you ready to launch the *Enigma*?"

"Ready when you are, Theo," Greg yelled back. "I can't wait to drive this baby."

Cole said to Theo, "You told her she could drive it?"

"Sure," Theo said. "Better her than me."

Cole watched the sonar screen in the pilothouse to make sure they weren't going to drop the anchor on top of the wreck. The *Bonhomme Richard* carried three hundred and fifty feet of anchor chain, but the chain would be running almost straight up and down when anchoring at that depth. He dropped about one hundred feet away from the wreck. That should keep them from drifting, since there was little wind or current.

With Theo issuing directions, Greg and Brian were able to launch their ROV, the *Enigma*, with the new crane. On the starboard side aft, Brian turned the reel to feed out the cable that delivered the power and brought back the data. Greg worked the controls of the ROV from the laptop's keyboard while sitting cross-legged on top of the cabin aft. The video feed from the camera on the underwater vehicle was being broadcast on the screen. Theo leaned against the cabin next to her and used Greg as his eyes. He had his tablet tucked under his arm.

Cole stood outside on the side deck leaning his hip against the bulwark, his arms crossed, and watched his crew working together. Over the last couple of years, Brian had often worked on their boat, so he knew it well, and watching Greg's enthusiasm, Cole understood why Brian had hired her as his new dive master. He looked around the deck. Two of his passengers were missing. He wondered what Nils Skar and Peewee were up to and why they weren't out there with the rest of them peering over the side.

"There it is," Greg called out.

"Describe for me what you see," Theo said.

"It's pretty dark down that deep, but the ROV's light is starting to reveal some detail. It looks like she's pretty far over on her side. We're approaching from the angle where most of what we see is her bottom."

Cole and Riley both walked over to watch the laptop screen over Greg's shoulder.

"Even from this angle I can see a gaping hole in the middle of what would be the port side reaching well below the waterline."

Theo handed Riley the tablet. "You should be able to find the photo of the *Teiyō Maru* on there," he said.

Riley touched the screen and there was an old black-and-white photo of a merchant vessel. "Found it."

"That photo was taken shortly after she was launched in Holland in the 1930s. The Japanese bought the Dutch merchant vessel and turned her into a troop carrier and hospital ship."

"Greg," Cole said, "check out some of the distinctive characteristics, like the porthole up in the bow. We've got some other photos of her that also show the name was written on the bow in kanji characters on top and the Roman alphabet underneath."

"Okay, I'm climbing up toward the bow now. It looks like there is a lot of growth on the outside of the hull. There's thick, brownish-beige algae and some red-colored plants."

"She should have the red-and-white crosses of the hospital ship painted on her, too. Probably on the stacks."

"There is an anchor, so we must be all the way forward. I'll start back now. There. Look. Those dark circles look like portholes."

"I see them, too," Riley said. "Go back down under the ports."

Cole looked at the photo of the ship and then looked at the screen again. "There, stop," he said. The screen was filled with what looked like a brown wall covered with algae. "See—it's hard to make out because it's so covered with growth, but that looks like a *T*." He drew with his finger on the screen. "And just next to it, that's the straight up and down of what looks like the vertical stroke of the capital letter *E*."

Greg said, "I think I see it."

"I've set the laptop to record this on video," Theo said. "We can look at freeze frames later."

Greg continued to move the ROV so as to pan the video camera across the deck of the ship. Considering that it had been underwater for more than sixty years, it was amazingly well preserved. Then one of the stacks came into view and there it was, a very clear image of a cross.

"Okay, Brian, that's it. You ready to dive?"

"Let's go, mate."

Brian had spent the morning preparing their gear. They would be using heliox-filled tanks due to the extreme depth and the DPV scooters would help them to descend quickly. Cole was checking over his backpack and tanks when Nils Skar appeared on deck and approached him.

"Could I speak with you a minute?"

"I'm preparing to dive here, Nils. What do you want?"

The man pushed in too close and focused his huge eyes on Cole's. "The voices have been talking to me." The odor of cigarettes and days-old sweat wafted off his thin frame.

"Nils, what are you talking about? What voices?"

Brian walked over and looked at the Norwegian as though examining a museum exhibit. "You'd ought to listen to him. This is why I brought him along."

Cole looked at the greasy, stringy hair that fell straight down from the crown of his head, parting around the ears. He couldn't believe that Brian took this freak seriously.

Nils put his hands over his ears. "They're getting louder. They're saying you need to look in the master's cabin. There is a small golden statue of a dragon. You will find what you are looking for inside the statue."

"Okay, man. Okay. We'll look."

The Norwegian nodded, turned, and walked back to the cabin and disappeared.

Cole looked at Greg. She burst into a fit of giggles. Then she raised her shoulders and shook her head. "That was totally weird."

Then Cole turned to Brian. "You believe that nonsense?"

"I tell you, he has been right more often than not. The map says there's treasure here, and I'm hoping for lots more than one gold statue. I say let's get wet."

"I don't believe in psychics," Cole said. He picked up the head strap for his GoPro underwater video camera.

"Uh, guys," Greg interrupted. "You're going to want to take a look at this."

Cole stepped around so he could see the screen. "What?"

"I just took the *Enigma* through that hole in the hull. Look at this."

The light from the ROV shone on the steel frames of the inside of the hull. Greg tapped at the keys and the vehicle turned ninety degrees. The ROV was shining the light all around from the sides of the hull to the bulkhead and back to the gash in the hull.

"That can't be," Cole said. "The hold is empty."

"Hey, mate, I thought you said this Dragon's Triangle wreck was supposed to be the mother lode."

"That's what everyone thought. I've traced the documents back to Djakarta. Brian, this ship was supposed to be carrying gold—and uranium."

Brian stared at him open-mouthed. It was the first time Cole had seen the Australian speechless.

Greg looked up at him. "So, I guess you're gonna want me to show you where the master's cabin is?"

Cole cleared his ears continuously as the DPV carried him downward at a speed of about two knots at a semi-steep incline. The wetsuit had felt like overkill in the warm water at the surface, but every few feet, the water around him grew both colder and darker. He glanced over his shoulder to make sure Brian was still there off his flank. They wouldn't have a whole lot of bottom time, and they needed to be as economical as possible with their movements. Theo had designed the DPV with a removable high-intensity LED light that worked like a headlight when attached, but could be pulled off to use as a flashlight. Cole carried a second light in a pocket of his buoyancy compensator.

Before getting into the water, they had watched as Greg navigated the ROV up over the deck, past the lifeboats still hanging in their davits, and up the face of the bridge structure, which appeared to be intact. All the glass had been blown out of the bridge windows, but by shining the light through the forward openings, they were delighted to see the wheel and engine telegraph, though encrusted with growth, were both still visible. The corridor that led aft from the bridge would certainly lead to the master's cabin, so Cole told Greg to back the *Enigma* out of the opening before she got hung up on something. He and Brian would head down.

When they passed the hundred-foot mark he checked his watch out of habit. Then he looked at the band he wore on his other wrist. Theo had a friend at FEMA and he had sent them a couple of micro-electronic personal dosimeters that measured any radiation in the environment. These new models had been designed for work at nuclear reactors and they were supposedly waterproof to three hundred feet. So far, so good.

He could see the light from the ROV on the wreck down at the end of the cable he was following, and he felt both excitement and dread. Cole had spent some time in a decompression chamber in Gua-deloupe, and he had become a much more cautious diver as a result.

The two divers hovered over the deck and Cole saw the remains of a deck gun on its side. Some of the covering for the hold must have been made out of wood because he could also see into the empty space and out the jagged hole where the sea floor was visible. Could the bomb that sank her have dropped into the hold and blown her cargo out to be spread across the sea floor? Surely there would be something left to show that had happened. No, Cole thought, there hadn't been anything in her hold. The boat that had been reputed to be the treasure of all treasure ships was empty.

At the surface, they had agreed that Cole would enter the wreck while Brian would stay outside and enter only if Cole signaled for help. Cole had a safety line with one end attached to his buoyancy compensator, the rest coiled and tucked into his weight belt. When they reached the bridge, they discovered an open doorway on the star-board side. Cole parked his DPV on the deck, handed Brian the coiled safety line, and gave his friend a thumbs-up signal. He reached up and pushed the button to start his own video camera. With the light from his vehicle in his hand, he swam into the bridge. He checked his wrist. Still okay. If there was any uranium aboard, he was feeling confident that it was still well sealed.

He swam through the doorway into the dark corridor and the beam of his light showed two closed doors. Because the ship was lying partway on her side, everything inside was tilted over about thirty degrees, creating a funhouse-like sensation of disequilibrium. The first door broke loose when he pushed it and beyond he found only a small compartment with a hole in the floor. There must have been a steel toilet there that had since rusted away. The second door farther down the passageway would not yield to his pressure. He knew he mustn't exert himself too much and use all his air. Then he spied what looked like a rusty steel bar on the floor of the bridge. He retraced his path, grabbed the bar, and finally he was able to force the door wide enough to get his arm and flashlight inside.

The first thing that surprised him was an almost intact gas mask that looked half-buried on the floor inside. As he panned the light across the floor, he saw more dishes poking out of the debris. He could not see the far side of the cabin so he braced his fins on the opposite wall and pressed his shoulder to the door. Slowly, the gap widened until it was wide enough for him to get through with the backpack and twin tanks.

Cole checked his watch. Six minutes remaining. He checked the radiation dosimeter. Zero. Still good. He swam through the narrow gap.

The master's cabin had remained closed all those years. When he rounded the door, just his movement through the water stirred up the organic soup that lined the floor. The beam of his light caught all the specks of floating debris and the once-clear water turned opaque. Cole held still and waited, knowing that he was wasting time and precious air.

Slowly, the matter in the water began to settle. As the visibility cleared, Cole could make out a shape against the bulkhead. He tried to control his breathing and his heart rate, both of which had doubled. Despite the wetsuit, he felt a shiver that seemed to start in his bowels and raced to the back of his neck. Emerging from the layer of putrefied organic matter on the floor were algae-covered bones and a human skull. If he had not been alerted by the Norwegian psychic, Cole never would have recognized the brown lump the skeleton had once cradled in his arms as the statue of a dragon.

CHAPTER SEVENTY-TWO

**Camiguin Island
The Philippines**

December 5, 2012

By the time Greg announced that Cole had exited the wreck carrying something, Nils Skar and Peewee were already at the transom peering over the side of the boat. Greg had been giving a running account of what she saw on the screen so Theo could "see" what was happening below.

"Theo," Greg said. "We don't need video of the two of them decompressing down there, do we?"

"No, let's bring up the *Enigma*."

Riley tended to the cables while Greg brought the ROV back to the surface. She then jumped down onto the aft dive platform and attached the lifting cables.

Riley joined Peewee at the bulwark. "So, what do you think Cole found?"

He stared down at the water and worked his lips over his teeth for a long while before he spoke. "*A false tale often betrays itself,*" he said.

"What do you mean by that?"

"Riley, I'm an old man. At some point, the lies catch up with you."

She remembered what he'd told her about his hopes to afford a final resting place. "You talk about being old, Irv, but when I'm with you, it's easy to forget just how old you are. You're in great shape."

He made a dismissive grunt. "Being here, looking at that wreck in the video—it's making me remember the war. I was in the mountains just a few miles thataway"—he pointed toward the southwest—"when this ship went down."

"I hadn't really thought about that. You must have lost good friends in the war."

"Yeah," he said, and he started coughing to clear his throat. "There was this one gal."

Riley smiled. "I knew there had to be a story about a girl."

The old man looked up at her and waggled his eyebrows. "You bet. She was a firecracker. A local girl with the guerrillas. She could handle a Tommy gun like nobody's business. Probably the only woman I ever loved."

"What happened?"

"She died."

"I'm sorry to hear that. Did she die in action?"

"No," he said. He had been about to say more when they both heard splashing at the stern. Theo called out in a voice like an old-time radio announcer, "The divers return from another brush with death."

"Somebody want to help me with this?" Cole said. "Damn thing's heavy."

At the sound of his voice, Riley rushed down the short ladder to the aft platform.

Nils Skar appeared at her side. He bent down and reached for the statue. "Could that be because it is made of gold?" he said.

Riley saw the look on Cole's face and quickly stepped between Nils and Cole. "I'll take it," she said.

Cole was right. The statue was damn heavy, and though it was completely overgrown with aquatic plants and crustaceans, the head, forearms, and tail made it plenty clear what it was. She climbed back up the ladder and set the heavy object down on the back end of the cabin. Greg appeared at her side with a plastic wash basin half filled with water. Riley set the artifact in the basin.

"Look," Greg said, "where you touched it there. You knocked some of the nasty brown slime off."

The color of the metal beneath shone through.

"Just like that freak said," Greg whispered.

Riley looked around for him. Nils was standing back at the stern, leaning against the bulwark. He nodded at her when their eyes met. She turned away. Peewee was leaning on the cabin on the other side of Riley and he stared at the statue with a faraway look on his face.

"Should we clean it up?" Riley asked.

"Whoa," Cole said as he bounded up the ladder from the swim platform aft. "My find, my cleanup job."

He was still wearing his full wetsuit and his face bore the red, round circle from where his face mask had pressed into his skin. His hair was dripping wet. He leaned in and kissed her with his chilled lips. "It's not what I'd hoped for, but at least it's something." He squinted up at the sun overhead, then unzipped the front of the wetsuit. "Damn, it's hot out here."

Behind him Brian was peeling off his own wetsuit. "That's your fault for kissing your girl when you're still kitted up."

Cole grinned at her and said, "It's worth the risk."

Theo said, "You know, I get nervous when it gets this quiet with no wind. I'm going to go check the weather."

Irv reached over and touched the statue almost reverently. "Where did you find it?"

"In the captain's cabin, just like he said. The captain was in there, too. I almost had a heart attack when I saw the skeleton on the floor with the arm bones scattered around this thing. The guy must have drowned closed up in his cabin holding onto it. Wait till you see the video from my head cam." Cole tossed his wetsuit onto the deck and took the brush and cloth from Greg. The growth washed off easily in most places.

Irv said, "The *Teiyō Maru* probably went down in four or five minutes. They had this honor code called *bushidō*. A captain who lost his ship was disgraced. He knew he had to go down with the ship and he wanted to take his stolen treasure with him."

Cole had brushed off most of the algae, and though it would need to be polished and restored, the head with the open mouth, the clawed forearms, and the rippling scaled back were clearly exquisite. He paused in his cleaning and turned to look at the old man. "What makes you think it was stolen?"

"That's why the *Teiyō Maru* got the code name Dragon's Triangle. That *is* the treasure."

"What are you talking about?"

"Look on the bottom of it. The statue is hollow. You should find a door."

Cole turned the statue over and Riley saw the thin outline of what looked like a crack in the metal. "There," she said.

"Somebody get me my dive knife!" Cole yelled.

Brian jumped down to the aft platform and handed it up to Riley. She passed the knife to Cole.

"Irv, if you know so much about this, what's supposed to be in here?"

"That's why this is considered the mother lode. Hidden in there are maps to all the Golden Lily sites in the Philippines."

Cole got the tip of the knife wedged into the crack, and with an effort the door popped open. Brown water flowed out. Cole looked up and said, "Maybe it's not so bad. I see what looks like oil-soaked canvas. If the maps are there, maybe they're still okay."

He pulled out a corner of the parcel and gently wiggled the rest loose. The oilskin parcel was wrapped with some kind of string that fell apart when he pulled on it. Cole set the parcel down on the cabin top and flipped it over once. Then he turned it again. At the last turn, brown pulpy water sluiced out across the white paint.

Cole tried to pick up one of the bigger lumps of paper pulp but it broke apart in his hand. "Well, shit," he said.

"You can say that again, mate," Brian said. "Salt water plus paper equals shit."

Peewee took off his hat, sighed, and rubbed his sleeve across his forehead. He looked terribly old and tired, Riley thought. Whatever it was that had been burning inside him just seemed to flicker out. He turned around and leaned against the bulwark for support.

"Hey, guys," Theo called from just outside the wheelhouse. "We need to get out of here and find some kind of shelter. Typhoon Bopha, which was heading away from the Philippines, has started to curve back. If it keeps turning, it will be headed straight for northern Luzon."

CHAPTER SEVENTY-THREE

Northern Luzon
The Philippines

June 27, 1945

By the time Ozzie returned to the rock overhang, only Danilo was still there waiting for him.

"Ben and Lieutenant Marcos?" Ozzie asked.

Danilo made a sweeping motion with his hand to indicate they were on their way. At least that had been taken care of. Then Danilo motioned for Ozzie to follow him.

They walked back through the trees. He never would have guessed they had arrived at the tree houses, but suddenly there was a rope ladder there. Danilo grabbed a dark wool blanket that was hanging from one of the rungs and he threw it at Ozzie. The Filipino pointed at the ground.

Ozzie pointed at himself and then at the ground. "You're saying I'm supposed to sleep down here on the ground?"

The man grunted and started to climb the ladder.

"What about the spiders and the snakes?"

The man didn't answer. Ozzie reached out to grab Danilo's boot and got a glancing kick at the side of his head in return. Then the ladder was gone, pulled up into the trees.

He wrapped the blanket around him, sat on the ground, and leaned against the trunk of the tree. The noises of the forest around him grew louder the longer he sat there. He'd slept no more than a couple of hours at most in the last forty-eight hours, but his eyes remained wide open. It was going to be a long night.

A hand grasped his shoulder and shook him. Ozzie tried to move his head, but his neck was so stiff he could barely move. Then a boot connected with his ribs.

"Get up, princess." It was Peewee's voice, but it came from too far away to be connected to the boot. "You sleep on the ground too long, you'll get crud up your ass."

"Okay, okay," he said. He glared at Danilo, who stood over him wearing a half smile. Ozzie threw off the blanket and tried to stand. It was going to be a process. He rolled his head around and stretched out his legs.

The sky was already gray with the coming dawn. When he got to his feet, he saw they were working to bring down equipment from the tree house he'd been sleeping under. There were four rucksacks and the men were filling them with ammunition belts, magazines, and grenades. It looked like they were planning quite a party.

"We've got a long hike ahead of us," Peewee said. "It's going to take us the better part of the day to get to this village on the coast. Rafi's going to meet us there with the boat. Head on over to the kitchen now. We'll eat first, and then we'll take off."

Breakfast consisted of strongly garlic-flavored rice washed down with a hot dark liquid that was supposed to pass for coffee. The day had already turned hot, and it was only an hour after sunrise.

When they returned to the campsite, each of the four men took a backpack.

"What do you want me to carry?" Gregoria asked.

"This is not your mission. Somebody's got to stay here and watch over the camp."

"Why? You're taking every last bit of ammunition we have."

"There's still the radio. And all that gold we got off him and the kid," he said, pointing his thumb at Ozzie.

Ozzie shrugged, but inwardly he was glad to know for certain they had taken the prayer gau from Ben.

"If we don't come back," Peewee told Gregoria, "we need you to call and let somebody know the sub coming out of that cave has Japs, not Yanks, in charge. Whatever it is they want to get back to Japan must be pretty damn important for them to send a royal prince to highjack a US submarine. We can't let that cargo make it back to Nippon."

Peewee put his arm around her shoulder and walked her a short distance away. They spoke in soft murmurs. Ozzie saw Peewee lift his dog tag chain over his head and he slid it down her dark hair. He tucked the dog tags into her cleavage and then the two of them embraced. When they separated, Gregoria climbed up into one of the trees and disappeared.

By Ozzie's best account, they had four M42 machine guns and the Thompson. Peewee told him they had the most ammo for the M42s because they were able to use captured Jap ammo in those. The plan was to head into the cave in the dark and try to join forces with the Americans. Hopefully, with their firepower and by outnumbering the Japanese, they would be able to retake the submarine.

They hiked up and down more mountains than Ozzie could count. Aside from a brief stop along a stream to eat their lunch of now cold rice, they kept up a steady pace. The other men conversed in Tagalog, but Peewee never said a word to Ozzie during the trek.

It was close to sundown when they first spotted the village. They had been able to see the ocean through the trees off and on all day, but they never got any closer. Ozzie reckoned they had been traveling south parallel to the coast. The houses they first saw on the outskirts of the village looked abandoned. They saw no livestock and the fields looked overgrown.

Late in the afternoon the sky had clouded over and they had been cooled off by a thunderstorm. They were all drenched to the skin now.

Before entering the main part of the village, they stopped behind an abandoned house and stood with their backs to the wall. Manolo made that same birdcall Ozzie had heard when Gregoria first captured him. A similar call came back in return.

"Rafi," Peewee said. The men didn't lower their weapons, but they walked more confidently into the street that ran through the few houses that made up the small village.

"Where is everybody?" Ozzie asked as they walked past house after empty house.

"The Japs came through here over a year ago and scared them all off. They didn't want people living too close. That's how we found out about the cave. When we heard they'd forced out the villagers, we started nosing around to see what was going on. Coastal lookouts said they'd seen boats head north up the coast from here and then disappear."

When they reached the beach, they saw a forty-foot fishing boat anchored offshore. Ozzie could make out the name *San Pedro* painted on the bow. Rafi was standing next to a small canoe that looked like a smaller version of the big boat. Both had outriggers, but the fishing boat offshore was planked, not a dugout, and it had a small wheelhouse in the back. What looked like a smokestack came up through the roof of the wheelhouse.

Peewee looked oddly nervous as he eyed the canoe.

"Don't tell me you still can't swim?" Ozzie said. It was something he had razzed his friend about every summer of their childhood. Peewee had loved to sail in the small boats they built, but he always wore a life jacket. Ozzie told him he'd never get any girls if he was the one wearing the Mae West.

"I like being on the water, not in it. That's what I got you for."

"Oh, really? You didn't fill me in on that part of the plan."

"Yeah, well, you might want to grab something that floats before we take off. You're going to be in the water for a while."

CHAPTER SEVENTY-FOUR

The Babuyan Islands
The Philippines

December 5, 2012

With the weather about to turn bad, Brian said he wanted to get to Subic Bay to get his plane locked down. Cole told Riley they didn't have the speed to make it all the way back to Subic, so he thought they should take the *Bonhomme Richard* back to Aparri.

While Greg ran Brian back to his anchored plane, Cole and Theo gave orders to the rest of their passengers to get all the dive gear stowed and make the boat ready for an overnight passage at sea. Typhoon Bopha could be on them in forty-eight hours if it stayed on its present course.

When Greg returned, Riley helped her hoist the dinghy into its chocks on the aft end of the cabin and tie it down while Cole and Theo lifted anchor. The sun was nearly setting when they turned away from Camiguin Island and set a course for Dialao Point on the northwest corner of Luzon. Cole said if they continued to make eight knots all night, they should be at Aparri by dawn.

Cole called a crew meeting in the galley and assigned the watches for the night. With two to a watch, he would have eyes on Nils and Irv, since he didn't trust either one of them. Greg and Theo took the first watch and offered to make dinner as well. When the crew scattered, Cole took Riley by the arm.

"Could I interest you in a glass of wine?" he asked.

"That sounds good. I was going to stand outside for a while to enjoy the sunset."

"I'll meet you on the aft deck."

When she stepped outside, it was that time of the evening when the sun is about to set and the light has a golden cast to it. She walked to the aft deck and leaned on the railing, her hair whipping around her face in the wind.

She heard him walk up behind her and stop. Turning her head, she looked at him over her shoulder. He had a glass of pinot noir in each hand and his teeth were blazing white against the coppery glow of his skin.

"What are you up to?" she said.

"I'm taking mental pictures of you on my boat in this magical light and storing them for when we are old and gray."

"For when I get old and ugly, you mean?"

He laughed and handed her a glass. "No, you'll never be ugly. When we're both in our nineties, I'm sure you'll still be the most beautiful woman I know."

She clinked her glass against his. "Keep this up and I might just stick around until I'm ninety."

They stood then in a comfortable silence watching the waves and the seabirds. The sun kissed the horizon and sank into the sea.

"Are you terribly disappointed?" she asked after a while.

"About the dive?"

She nodded.

"No, it's still out there. I'm certain of it. I'll find it eventually—before they do."

"Ah. It's *them* again."

He chuckled. "One of the many reasons I like having you around, Magee. You keep me on my toes. *They* aren't just shadows for you anymore, are they?"

"Their Mr. Hawkes is a particularly nasty piece of work. I'm all for making sure he doesn't get what he wants."

Cole took a long sip of wine. After he swallowed, he said, "Being inside that ship this afternoon certainly did feel creepy."

"I guess. Seeing those bones?" She shivered. "I'm glad it wasn't me."

"I'm not a superstitious type, but there was something down there that felt, I don't know. Ominous. That's not quite the right word. Evil, maybe?"

"Knowing some of the atrocities that both sides engaged in, I think *evil* is a word that would fit."

"After that business with Nils telling me what to look for and then finding it—it felt spooky."

"How did he know?"

"I intend to have a nice long talk with him and your buddy Irv in the morning before we reach land. I want to know how both of them know what they know. Say—later tonight when you're on watch with the old man, why don't you see what you can learn?"

"I'd be happy to."

Greg appeared out the side door of the wheelhouse. "Hey, captain. Sorry to bother you. Theo's got a question for you."

Cole's eyes met Riley's and she saw disappointment. "Duty calls."

"It's all right. It's getting chilly anyway. I'm going to head into your cabin."

"Our cabin," he said, and he turned and walked forward.

. . .

When Riley closed the door to the cabin, the boat was starting to pitch and roll in the swells. She was afraid to set down her wineglass, but she wanted to look again at the prayer gau and the documents within. Maybe she would be able to figure out something to help Cole find this Golden Lily treasure mother lode site.

With her glass held tight in one hand, she searched through the pockets of her backpack until she felt the silk cloth. She pulled out the artifact rolled up in the cloth covering and took it over to the desk. She sat down in the chair, unrolled the silk, and set it aside. She was struggling to keep the gold tube from rolling off the desk without letting go of her wineglass when she heard a knock at the door.

The noise startled her and her hand jerked. A splash of red wine hit a part of the silk and made an oblong pool across the desk.

"Shit," she said as she looked around for a box of tissues or paper towels or anything to clean up the mess before it rolled onto the floor.

The knock came again. "Coming," she called. She pushed back the chair and stood. She tilted back the glass and drained the rest of her wine. *I can't spill any more if my glass is empty,* she thought.

She reached for the door handle. Peewee stood outside with his hat in his hand.

"Can we talk?"

She laughed. "I thought those were the words men most hated. Come on in. Excuse me while I clean up here." She left the door open and returned to the desk.

The old man came in and sat on the edge of the bunk while she rummaged through the drawers. She found a legal pad and tore off several sheets of paper to mop up the wine. It wasn't the most absorbent material, but she finally had the desk clean. She blotted the piece of silk between two sheets and was sad to see the fabric had discolored to a strange brown in some places, while the rest was pink from the wine. The brown tint was probably due to age.

Riley sat back down in the chair and faced the old man. "So what's this about?"

"I haven't exactly been honest with you."

"Gee, Irv, I'm shocked."

He took in a deep breath and slowly exhaled.

"Okay, I'll help you out a little," she said. "It was you who put Nils up to that psychic business with the voices, right? You were the one who knew the dragon would be there."

His mouth was working feverishly at his dentures as he nodded.

"Do you want to tell me how you knew?" she said.

He nodded. "That's why I'm here. Nils Skar and I have known each other for years. But there's more."

"Go on."

"Has your boyfriend told you about the uranium?"

"What?"

"He was expecting to find uranium on the *Teiyō Maru*. And he was part right. The Japanese had their own atomic bomb project under way. The *Teiyō Maru* did pick up uranium from a German sub in Djakarta and bring it to Luzon. But she unloaded it before going up to Camiguin."

Riley was startled by the sound of a voice behind her.

"And how do you know that?"

Cole was standing in the open doorway. Riley stood and moved next to Peewee on the bed. "Come on in and listen, okay?" She turned to the old man. "You all right with him hearing this too, Irv?"

"If we're going to find this mother lode site, he'll need to know this, too."

Cole closed the stateroom door and sat in the desk chair. He hiked it up close to the knees of the other two. "So, what do you know, Irv?"

"When I was in the mountains with the Philippine Scouts, we heard the Japs had found a huge sea cave and they were using it to off-load equipment. By this time, the Americans had retaken Manila and

Yamashita was still holding out with an estimated ten thousand troops in the mountains of northern Luzon. The Japs were having a hell of a time getting supplies and ammunition past the Americans. Any ships anchored in a cove were likely to get bombed."

"But they could take all the time they needed if they were inside a cave. I get it."

"The cave was primarily used as a sub base, but a small ship like the *Teiyō Maru* was able to fit inside as well. The cave was huge. It went back for several kilometers following an underground river. There were several large chambers and they were using it as a Golden Lily treasure site, too. From what I've heard through the years, and what I've seen, it's the biggest of all the Golden Lily sites. The only map to the location of the cave was inside that dragon."

"And it's now pulp soup," Riley said.

"How do you know the uranium was off-loaded there?"

"The Japs' plan was to bring the uranium to the cave and then load it onto a sub to take it back to the homeland. After that, they intended to blow the entrance to hide their treasure, probably leaving the few troops still there to die inside. They did that a lot with Golden Lily so no survivors other than the royal family would know the locations. Then they'd get away back home in the sub. The problem was they were even losing their subs at an unacceptable rate. That was when this royal prince came up with the plan to hijack a Yank sub. That way they'd be assured of a safe passage." Peewee looked at Riley. "We're talking about the *Bonefish*. That's how I know all this. Your gramps told me."

Riley noticed the boat's roll was getting worse.

Cole said, "We're starting to feel some swell from the storm, I think."

"Feels like it," she said. Then she faced Irv again. "So where is this sea cave?"

"All I know is it's somewhere south of Vigan. You've got about fifteen miles of mountainous coastline there. Today, the mountains inland are part of a national park. You know, we didn't have GPS in those days, and I never actually saw the cave. When the Japs were placing the charges to blow the entrance, something went off accidentally and they buried themselves and the front cave entrance."

Riley caught something in the tone of his voice. "You said *front* entrance. Was there another way in?"

He nodded. "That's how Ozzie got out. After the war, I went back and I searched, but it's hundreds of square miles of very difficult terrain. It was Ozzie who told me there was a map that was inside a dragon statue on the *Teiyō Maru*. The captain stole it, never knowing what it contained."

"So you focused on trying to find the map."

"Yup. I came up with the code name Dragon's Triangle. That gold and the uranium are still in there. And you aren't the only one after it."

"My *friends* back at Natuna Besar." Riley's eyes met Cole's and they nodded in silent agreement.

"Right. And it's not just that they want to sell it to the highest bidder. They already have a buyer. The Saudis are pissed that Iran is getting a bomb, and they want one of their own."

"That's what I was afraid of," Cole said.

The bow of the boat rose up on an especially large swell. Riley remembered the glass she'd left on the desk and jumped up to grab it. The prayer gau rolled off the desk onto the cabin sole. She picked it up and went to roll it back up in the silk, then stopped.

"Cole, come here a minute." She spread the piece of silk out on the flat surface. The piece was about eighteen inches square. Half of it had been wetted by the wine and the more she looked at it, the more she thought it wasn't just age that had turned the fabric brown. "When I was a kid, my mother taught me how to do silk painting. You use something called resist to stop the dye from spreading across the fabric. See how this brown coloring stops here?" She pointed at the fabric.

"Yeah," he said. "It looks deliberate."

Peewee got up and crossed to the desk. "Well, I'll be," he said. "That son of a gun. That's invisible ink. It's an old OSS trick. I've only ever seen it used on paper. You dissolve sodium bicarbonate in water and use it as ink. Put grape juice"—he looked up at Riley—"or in this case wine on it and it will 'develop.' He used something as a resist—probably wax."

"He?" Riley said.

"Yeah, Prince Kaya Masako."

Riley turned to Cole. "You got any more of that wine?"

Cole disappeared for a minute and returned with a plate and the wine bottle. He spread the dry part of the cloth out on the plate and then poured the wine on it. They watched as the edges of the cloth turned pink but a distinct shape formed in the center.

Riley took hold of the edge of the plate and gave it a quarter turn. "Does that look to you like a pretty good map of northern Luzon?"

"Sure does," Cole said. "And just south and a little inland from where Vigan would be, that sure looks to me like a little X."

"As in X marks the spot?" she said.

Riley turned to Peewee. His head was up, facing the bulkhead, but it was clear from the look on his face he was a hundred miles away.

"You okay, Irv?" She touched his arm and he flinched, then gave his head a shake.

"What?" he said. "Oh, sorry. I was just thinking about the path this piece of silk took to get here. So while we've been spinning our wheels trying to decode the map to the location of the *Teiyō Maru*—"

Riley smiled and nodded. "We had the map to the treasure site with us all along."

"I'll go tell Theo to change course. If we turn now, we could be entering the Abra River at Vigan by late tomorrow afternoon." Cole disappeared out the door.

"Doesn't that mean we'll be heading toward the typhoon?" she asked aloud, but he was already gone.

CHAPTER SEVENTY-FIVE

Camp John Hay
Baguio, Philippines

December 5, 2012

The Manor at Camp John Hay was the closest one could find to a five-star hotel in Baguio, and Elijah was pleased that they had offered him a suite. Those were usually booked up far in advance, especially as the holidays were approaching. Camp Hay had been built in 1903 as a place where American troops could enjoy a little R & R. Even after the end of the Second World War when the Philippines became independent, Camp Hay had remained under the control of the United States Air Force. The property had been turned over to the Philippines in 1991, and it remained a favorite of the military, corporate, and intelligence communities for meetings and holidays. At an elevation of five thousand feet, the cool, dry air was a welcome respite from the heat and humidity of Manila.

When they drove through Baguio City, Elijah had directed Benny to stop at a hardware store. He had found the tools he needed: a metal file, a fine whetstone, light oil, and a few sheets of four-hundred-grit sandpaper. Then they had driven out to Camp Hay and Elijah had dismissed the savage and sent him back to the mine.

In spite of all his failings, Wolfgang had done an excellent job of cleaning up the gold work on the ceremonial sword, but he had made no attempt at sharpening the blade. That was just as well, since working the blade was an art. Elijah had been taught to sharpen swords by a master swordsmith in Kyoto. He had explained that you could not force an edge onto the blade. Rather, one had to be patient and allow the edge to reveal itself.

His suite at the Manor provided a sitting area complete with a couch and a low coffee table. He'd had room service bring him a glass of scotch when he returned from a late dinner, and now Elijah took a towel from the bath and placed it on the table. He arranged his tools on the towel. Starting with the file, he took off the heavy layer of corroded steel along the edge. Then he dribbled a layer of oil onto the stone and began the tedious process of sliding the blade across the stone. When the oil turned too black, he cleaned the stone and re-oiled it with clear, golden oil.

For nearly an hour he worked the edge. Slow and steady. It was important to hold the blade at no more than a thirty-degree angle and to remain consistent with every pull across the stone. Elijah found the work soothing. It recharged him after the energy he had expended at the mine and gave him time to think.

Benny had failed repeatedly, but now his failure could turn out to work in Elijah's favor. Rather than salvaging the wreck himself, Elijah would let this Cole Thatcher do it for him. Nils would tell him when Thatcher had brought the uranium to the surface, and Elijah could then hijack the salvage boat and dispose of the crew at sea. Al-Habib would then send one of his yachts to rendezvous at a remote location, and once they transferred the cargo, Elijah could sink the salvage boat in deep water and proceed with the Saudis to their next port of call.

No trail. A clean operation. God helps those who help themselves. And he intended to help himself to whatever Cole Thatcher found.

Elijah considered himself a devout man, but his God wasn't the peace-loving God that his Quaker parents and sister believed in. His was a lightning-bolt-throwing, vengeful God. The fact that Elijah succeeded and excelled at everything he did was proof of his God's love.

His thoughts were interrupted when his cell phone rang. He recognized the number. The day was dawning in San Francisco and the Philippines situation was first on their agenda.

"Elijah, I want an update. Now. These delays are unacceptable."

He was beyond caring what Black thought now. The Saudi was his new boss. But he didn't want Black to come looking for him until he'd had time to disappear.

"I was hoping to be able to give you better news. We've made progress, but the results are not what we hoped. I got our property back from the old man and we deciphered the map. My men have located the wreck in the Babuyan Islands, but the cargo isn't there. Either someone got to it before us, or it never existed to begin with."

Elijah held the phone away from his ear as the stream of curse words exploded from the phone.

When the other man slowed, Elijah said, "I was very disappointed, too. I was hoping the promised gold would keep me employed awhile longer."

"You sound too calm about this, Hawkes. How do I know you're telling me the truth?"

"You don't."

"What kind of game are you playing?"

"You don't know if I'm telling you the truth or not—but at the end of the day, you've got to trust somebody unless you want to do everything yourself. That's your call. You know where I live. I know you can have me killed at any time."

"Well, I don't suppose you'd take that stand if you were trying to double-cross me. So what's next?"

"Back to the archives, I suppose. We know the gold is there. We've only found fifty percent of what the Japanese stole."

When he disconnected the call, Elijah hurled his phone at the couch cushion. He got up and with his fists balled up at his sides, he paced the length of the sitting room, pivoted, and strode back. *How dare he accuse me?*

His phone chirped again. Certain it was Black calling back with more accusations, he barked into it. "Hello?"

"Mr. Hawkes, this is Nils." The voice was very soft.

"Skar, I can barely hear you."

"I can't speak any louder. I stole their sat phone and I'm in the head. They dove on the wreck today and the hold was empty."

"What? That's not possible." In an instant he wondered if somehow his lie to Black had been turned to truth. Was God punishing him for lying?

"The old man told me to tell the divers to look for a gold statue of a dragon. There was supposed to be maps to all the treasure sites inside."

"So, did they find it?"

"Yeah, they did, but the maps had turned to mush from the seawater."

"Shit. Shit. Shit."

"Wait. There's more. Just now they found out there is something written on the silk cloth that was wrapped around the gau."

"What do you mean 'something'?"

"Like maybe another map."

"I'm getting tired of these damn maps."

"The old man says what you are looking for is in a sea cave close to Vigan. The Japanese sealed the front entrance, but there is another entrance in the mountains."

"Are you still at Camiguin?"

"No. They say there's a typhoon coming. We're running for cover—but we just changed course for Vigan."

"I'll drive there tomorrow and meet you. Skar, if you can't steal this cloth, at least get a photo of it. Then call me."

When Elijah picked up the sandpaper and returned to the sword, he had to force himself to be gentle. Why couldn't things have gone according to his plan? And how dare Black show him that kind of disrespect?

Stop, he told himself. Feel the power of the blade. Make her as beautiful as she was the day the swordsmith made her. He polished the rest of the blade, removing all corrosion on the fine steel. Using a washcloth, he wiped the excess oil off the blade and buffed the sword to a glistening shine.

Unable to help himself, he touched his finger to the edge, and a thin line of red split his fingertip when he pulled it away. He smiled at the line and watched the blood seep out the cut. A hot tingle of excitement traveled down his spine to his scrotum. He reached for the edge again, but drew his hand back. He looked around the room for something to cut. The bed, wood furniture, a television. Nothing that would satisfy his need to cut.

He placed the sword on the towel and slid down the couch toward the end table. When he picked up the phone receiver, he pushed the button to ring the front desk.

"Yes," he said, "I'm in room 426. Could you have someone bring me up some fresh towels, please?"

The knock came sooner than he expected. He tossed the velvet cloth across the sword on the table and went to the door. The maid looked no more than eighteen years old, a petite little Filipina with her shiny black hair pulled back in a girlish ponytail. She smiled shyly at him as she offered him a stack of white fluffy towels.

He turned his back to the door and walked across the room. "Just put them in the bathroom for me."

When he heard her in the bathroom, he picked up the sword and strode across to the entry door. He closed it, turned the dead bolt, and added the chain. He was standing in front of the door with the sword in his hand when she returned.

She stopped and her eyes grew large when she saw him. "Don't scream," he said. "I promise, I'll hurt you if you scream."

He walked closer to her and touched the tip of the sword to her chin. He inhaled and he was pleased she wore no perfume.

The girl blinked her big brown eyes and a single tear rolled down one cheek.

"Are you frightened?"

She nodded and he saw her shoulders tremble.

"Do just as I say. Take off your dress."

A sob convulsed her body, but she did as she was told. Not like the American woman.

When the loose-fitting dress fell to the floor and she stood in her white bra and underwear, he was pleased to see that while she was not much more than five feet tall, she had large breasts for her small frame. He slid the tip of the sword off her chin and down to her chest. He tickled the tip up under her bra strap. When he turned the blade flat against her skin and slid it under the slender strap of fabric, the blade made a thin red line on the curve of her breast. She whimpered as a small drop of blood rolled down the inside of her breast. He inhaled the intoxicating scent of her blood before he turned the sword edge up and sliced through the other strap.

He felt that hot tingle again between his legs, and he clenched as he felt himself grow stronger. Yes, he thought. He deserved this. God helps those who help themselves.

CHAPTER SEVENTY-SIX

South China Sea
Off the Philippines

December 6, 2012

Cole had made hot chocolate for them before he went off watch at midnight. Riley wished that she could have had Cole as her watch partner, but she understood why he wanted to pair himself with the Norwegian while she got paired up with Peewee. Cole didn't trust either one of them.

She had tried to use the head right after Cole went to try to get some rest, but the door was locked. She returned to the helm.

The old man was seated in the helmsman chair, so she had wedged her body into the corner where the dash met the side of the wheelhouse. The seas were running twelve to fifteen feet now and the trawler was twisting and rolling in the wild swell. It sometimes took all her strength just to stay upright. The wind instruments showed a sustained thirty knots, with frequent gusts much higher. The motion of the trawler was quite a bit different from her sailboat, and there were too many open spaces with too little to hold on to.

Riley checked the radar screen above the helm. Still no sign of any traffic, but that was hardly surprising. It was no time to be heading out fishing. Theo had hooked up the iPad to the single-sideband radio, and using a special app, he was receiving GRIB charts that showed the typhoon was continuing the curve. Before he went off watch, Cole told her that the death count in the southern Philippines was at five hundred and climbing. In the Philippines they had renamed the storm Pablo and they were calling it a super typhoon.

All the motion was sloshing the contents of her bladder rather uncomfortably.

"Irv, you're in charge for a bit. I'm going to try to get into the head again. Somebody's camped out in there."

Moving from handhold to handhold, she made her way slowly through the galley and down the steps to the head. When she turned the door handle, it was still locked.

"Damn," she said in a whisper. It was too difficult to return to the bridge, so she decided to wait. The boat was on autopilot, so Peewee would be fine.

Riley knew that time moved slowly on night watches, but she kept checking her watch, and when it had been five minutes she rapped on the door. "Hey in there, somebody's waiting out here."

A couple of minutes later, the door opened and Nils Skar staggered out. "Sorry," he said with his head down. He was hunched over and he didn't look her in the face. He was clutching his stomach and supporting himself with one arm along the bulkhead. She wondered how seasick he really was. He'd been fine at dinner the night before.

When Riley returned to the bridge, she was surprised to see Greg there talking to Peewee. She overheard Greg say something about her grandmother.

"Everything okay here?" Riley asked.

"Sure," Greg said. "That Nils Skar guy creeps me out. He came back into the crew quarters and woke me up. I wasn't keen on being alone with him, so I thought I'd come keep you guys company."

"I know what you mean," Riley said. "Sorry to send him your way, but he'd been parked in the only head on the boat."

Greg turned back to Peewee. "Like I was saying, my mom never got to know her mom, but she named me after her—my grandmother."

"What do you know about your grandma?" he asked.

"Not a lot. I know during the war she was a member of the Katipunan."

"What's that?" Riley asked.

"It's a Filipino secret society," Greg said.

Riley thought, *Great. Conspiracy nuts in the Philippines, too.*

"The Katipunan Society was started during the first Philippine Revolution against Spain in the 1890s. Bonifacio and Rizal. Our country's great heroes started it. Then the guerrillas resurrected the organization during the Second World War when the people revolted against the Japanese occupation."

"I heard something about that when I was with the guerrillas."

Greg's face lit up. "You were there? You might have met my grandmother."

Peewee shrugged. Riley could tell he really liked Greg, and she wondered why he wasn't launching into more of his stories.

"My grandma died when Mom was little, so she was raised in orphanages. Because of her and my features, Mom always thought her father was probably an American GI. Later in life, Mom was told she couldn't have kids of her own. I came as a surprise when she was in her late thirties. She never married my dad. It was just her and me. We were close, but she died when I was seventeen, and I've been on my own ever since."

"How long ago was that?" he asked.

"Ten years ago now."

From the time she had spent on the boat with him, Riley could tell when the old man was zoning out, searching for something in his overflowing memory banks.

Peewee turned away from her and looked out the front windscreen. "What did you say your mother's name was?"

"Honoria," Greg said.

Late the next afternoon, Riley was wedged into the dinette reading a guidebook about the city of Vigan when Cole came into the galley and slid onto the bench opposite her. He reported the good news that the typhoon was losing strength after turning around to head for Luzon.

"We're still going to have a hell of a ride getting through the mouth of this river," he said.

"Riding the swells coming in and meeting an outgoing current— that sounds like it could get ugly real fast."

"That's one of many things I'm worrying about."

Riley reached across the table and took his hand in hers. "Tell me about the others."

"Well, first off, I can't wait to get rid of that nosy Norwegian. Seems he's always skulking around but he never contributes anything. I'm looking forward to spending another four-hour watch with him like I look forward to a root canal."

"When you were off watch last night, he was spending a lot of time in the head. Seasick, I assume. I mean, even the dog's seasick. She hasn't come out of Theo's cabin all night."

"Nils didn't act sick on watch. He ate all the snacks Theo and Greg had left for us. And the guy's a thief. On our morning watch I caught him trying to steal my satellite phone. He had it under his shirt."

Riley pinched her nose. "He stinks, too. You can get rid of him as soon as we get to shore. Kick him off the boat."

"I intend to. My other worry is that map. It's crude, to say the least. If we believe your friend Peewee, this Japanese colonel or prince or whatever found out that the maps had been stolen and the *Teiyō Maru* had sunk. He had to blow the sea entrance to the cave to hide the gold, but he wanted to leave behind some indication of where the entrance to the back door to this cave was. So he made this crude drawing in invisible ink." Cole shook his head and squinted at her. "I don't know, Riley. Doesn't that sound far-fetched to you?"

She laughed. "Cole, you of all people? Talking about far-fetched?"

"Well, I admit it's a bit out of character for me to be a doubter. But it's not like they had GPS back then. That's a lot of jungle to search. And I've got a problem with your friend Irv. His stories seem to change as the situation changes."

"I know."

"We're going to be counting on his memories of what a jungle valley looked like sixty years ago. Hell, I don't even know if he can make the hike to get up there."

"I'm remembering a guy who made a speech not too long ago about how important it would be to find this hoard of war loot and return the national treasures to the countries from which they were stolen. Does that not matter just because these treasures are going to be hard to find? And what if there really is uranium? You ready to take a chance on that going to the Saudis?"

"They can buy a bomb if they want to."

"That's true. But exposing this plan of theirs will make that much more difficult. Look what happened after you exposed what the Patriarchs had done."

Theo appeared in the doorway that led to the bridge. "We're getting close. We're about four miles out. If you want to prepare the boat, the time is now."

"Thanks, buddy," Cole said. "I'm calling a crew meeting in the galley here now. Spread the word." Then he stood up, leaned across the table, and kissed Riley on the forehead. "And thank you—for being so amazing."

He slid out of the dinette and made his way aft, calling out to the crew to join them in the galley.

Irv and Nils Skar slid onto the seat Cole had vacated. Greg stayed at the helm on watch and Theo braced himself in the doorway. Cole anchored himself by leaning one denim-clad hip against the galley counter.

"Okay, listen up. It's probably going to get very ugly going across the bar at the mouth of this river. The swells we've been seeing all day are nothing compared to what we're likely to see. The current coming out and the waves going in create an effect like the rapids in a river. There's a very real possibility that we'll start surfing and lose steerage. We may broach or get rolled over by one of these waves. Of course, that's the last thing we want to have happen. I sure as hell don't want to lose my boat, but everyone is to put on life jackets right now. Theo?"

"I'll bring them."

He disappeared for a minute and returned with an armful of bright orange life jackets.

Cole said, "Put them on and be sure to use the crotch straps. I don't care how uncomfortable it is. We'll need to make sure all watertight doors and windows are shut tight and nobody, and I mean nobody, is to go out on deck. Find a spot where you can hold on tight and make sure there is nothing that can fly if we take a roll. Theo and I will be on the bridge. The rest of you, go make yourselves secure for the ride of your life."

Riley helped the others get their life jackets on. Greg and Riley decided to stay in the galley while Nils and Peewee headed for their cabin. They double-checked all the doors and made sure no pots and pans or knives could come loose.

"Greg, have you ever entered the Abra River by boat?"

"No. I think it's usually an easy entrance, but with these conditions, Cole is right to be careful. It's been raining for a while and the river will be running."

Riley tugged at the life jacket. "Geez. I hate wearing these things."

"And I hate being back here where we can't see what's happening."

"Shall we go join the guys?"

"Absolutely."

When Riley came through into the wheelhouse, the view outside the windows was terrifying. The water was no longer the gray-green of the deep sea under gray skies. The sea around them was mud-brown. The mountains were visible in the mist just beyond the coast, but between their boat and the coastline were row after row of breaking waves. Then they were plunged into a trough and Riley couldn't see anything but the white foam as the breaking wave rushed past the hull. Then the boat climbed up the back of another wave and rode the breaking sea down into the trough.

The muscles in Cole's arms stood taut beneath his skin as he wrestled with the wheel, determined to keep the boat straight and not let her turn sideways to the swells. "What are you doing up here?"

"I have to watch. I can't just sit back there."

The boat climbed up an extra-large wave and then tipped teeter-totter-like at the top and started to slide down. "Well, hold on tight. We've got a ways more to go before we're through this."

When they reached the top of the next wave, it looked like the rows of waves stretched on forever, but the banks of the river mouth were not far. The opening looked narrower than it was. Still, it shallowed rapidly on either side. Cole didn't have much margin for error. Riley shivered and braced herself for the next downward slide.

From the corner of her eye, she caught a glimpse of movement behind her. When she turned her head to look, she thought she saw a crack of light around the door to the captain's cabin. Then it was gone.

Had the door come open? Maybe the latch wasn't holding and it was banging as the boat twisted and rolled in the waves.

"Looks like something came loose aft. I'm going to go check on it." She had to yell to be heard above the noise from the wind and the waves.

"Okay," Cole yelled back. "Be careful."

She nodded and started back through the galley. She descended the steps and passed the door to the head. When she got to the cabin door, she pushed on it and it held. She tried the handle and it unlatched the door right when the boat rolled. The door swung inward and Riley did, too. She lost her balance and stumbled into the room. As she was falling, her mind took a quick snapshot of the scene.

Nils Skar was leaning over the desk. He had Cole's GoPro camera in his hands and he was holding it over the desk. On the surface of the desk, the piece of silk was spread out flat so the map was visible.

Riley hit the floor on her bad shoulder. Pain shot up into her neck. Nils jumped over her and she reached out to grab his foot but he pulled free and slipped out the door.

She was on her feet in seconds. When she emerged into the hall, she saw Nils at the top of the aft steps opening the watertight door that led to the deck.

"Nils, stop!" she yelled.

He got the door and the overhead hatch open as they headed down into a trough. Through the opening she saw only sky. She pulled her way back and up the steps. When she pushed the door open, water as high as her ankles poured in from the deck. She saw Nils standing at the bulwark in his bright orange life jacket. He was looking at the riverbank.

Riley pulled the hatch closed and secured the door behind her. As the boat rose up again, she held on to the handle to keep from sliding toward the stern. Nils held on to the bulwark with both hands. The swell was not as high as the one before it. The boat leveled out.

When she stepped away from the hatch and started toward him, he turned and saw her. He swung one leg up over the bulwark.

Riley tried to run, but the tilting, slippery deck slowed her down and she reached the rail just in time to see his head disappear into their wake. She watched to see if he was going to get sucked under the boat, but his orange life jacket brought him right back up to the surface. He began stroking toward the riverbank.

She fought her way forward, hugging the bulwark, and pounded on the door to the wheelhouse. When the door swung open, Greg's mouth opened in shock.

She heard Cole shout from inside. "What are you doing out there?"

"Binoculars." She pointed aft. "Nils went overboard."

"What? How?"

Riley shouted, "He jumped!"

Greg turned around and Theo was handing her the glasses.

Cole called back to them, "There's no way I can turn around. It's calmed down a little, but if I turn sideways to these swells, I still might roll."

"I know," Riley said as she braced her hip and tried to steady the glasses. She saw the orange life jacket in the water. Then he stood up. The water came only to his thighs. He began walking toward shore.

Riley motioned for Greg to go back inside and she followed. She closed the door behind her. "He made it ashore," she said. "And he stole one of your underwater cameras."

"Shit," Cole said as he wrestled the wheel.

"You can say that again. Because he took a picture of the map just before he jumped overboard."

CHAPTER SEVENTY-SEVEN

Vigan City
The Philippines

December 6, 2012

Elijah directed Benny to the Hotel Salcedo de Vigan in the downtown section of the old Spanish colonial city. The Salcedo was the only decent hotel as near as he could tell, and while he didn't care to be in the touristy center of the city, he found himself enjoying the horse buggies, the cobblestone streets, and the Western feel of the place as they drove in. Vigan reminded him of Virginia City, except for the fact that it was raining. He wondered if he would ever go back there to his ranch. Certainly not if he found the uranium and made this deal with the Saudi. He would miss Tess.

When Benny pulled the truck up to the front of the hotel, Elijah directed him to get their luggage out of the truck. Elijah carried his own laptop bag inside when he went to the front desk. He was able to secure a suite for himself and space in a dormitory for Benny. Elijah used a different passport than the one he had used in Baguio. That one he'd tossed into a river as they'd driven the winding roads down off the mountain. He didn't have an unlimited number of IDs, but last night had been worth it.

He told Benny to follow him to the suite. Elijah went straight to the desk in his room, unloaded his laptop, plugged it in, and pressed the start key. He told Benny to put his suitcase on the bed. He opened the desk drawer and found a hotel pad and pen. He handed them to Benny.

"I'm going to send you out to get us some gear."

"What kind?"

"I'm about to tell you. Sit down and write what I tell you to write."

Benny made himself comfortable in a big leather chair and balanced the pad on his knee.

"Like I told you in the truck, we're going to be looking for an entrance to a cave. See if you can find one of those folding spades. Do you know what I'm talking about?"

Benny nodded.

"We'll need about one hundred feet of rope. And a handheld GPS. If you can't find one in a store here, see if you can find a phone store and buy a smartphone that has maps and GPS."

Benny wrote it all down on the paper.

"Food and water. We may end up in the mountains for at least one night. Flashlights. A couple of rain ponchos and some insect repellent. We'll each need a backpack to carry our gear, too."

When Benny had the list complete, Elijah gave him money. "Don't take the truck. Give me the keys. I want you to ask downstairs for someone to find you a cabdriver who really knows his way around the area. It will be much more efficient than driving around trying to find this yourself."

When Benny was gone, Elijah called downstairs and asked them to bring a full bottle of scotch to his room. He poured himself a drink and set to work at the computer trying to learn as much as he could about caves in Luzon and the local geology. Just south of Vigan was the broad alluvial plain formed by the mouth of the Abra River. For several miles south of that, the mountains came right to the coast. Given that Luzon had hundreds of caves and there was another underground river upstream as a tributary to the Abra, it was not inconceivable that a river had passed underground and found its way to the sea by going through the mountains there and forming a cave accessible from the ocean side.

It was late. Benny had been gone for a couple of hours. Elijah was considering going down to find a meal when his phone rang. He looked at the readout. He didn't recognize the number.

"Mr. Hawkes? It's Nils Skar."

"Where are you?"

"Somewhere close to Vigan. Just a minute." There was a muffled sound like someone handling a phone in the wind and Elijah heard voices talking. "They say this place is called Fuerte. It's on the coast just outside Vigan."

"How'd you get there?"

Nils recounted the story of getting caught in the captain's cabin and jumping overboard at the mouth of the river. "I don't know how far I walked. I was at it for several hours. Then I met these fishermen and they gave me a ride in their boat to this town. I'm using a cell phone that belongs to a guy they know here. I've got the camera here for you, and I sure hope there's a photo on it."

Nils told him the name of the bar he was calling from. Elijah said he'd be there within the hour.

Elijah knew that type of camera. It had no screen. He would need the laptop. It had an SD card slot. He shut the computer off and slipped it into the sleeve. He could leave the power cord in the room. He put the sleeve into his laptop messenger bag. There was still room in the bag. He crossed to the bedroom and unzipped his suitcase. Buried under the top layer of clothes was the sword wrapped in the cloth.

He slipped it into the computer bag. Part of the hilt stuck out the top of the bag, but covered as it was, no one would know what it was.

The directions he got at the hotel desk were impossible to follow, and he drove around in the dark peering through his wipers. As he searched for the bar, he remembered the first time he'd had to field dress a deer. It was winter and there was a light dusting of snow on the ground so he wasn't worried about the meat going bad. He took his time and discovered the thrill of cutting flesh and watching hot blood spill steaming onto the snow. For years after, he fulfilled his needs through hunting. And what now if he could never return to the ranch?

Elijah pulled the truck to a stop in front of a small bar with a red neon sign that simply said BAR beneath a lit-up San Miguel beer sign. It was noisy inside and the place reeked of fish and stale beer. Filipino pop music was playing just loud enough to make the men inside have to shout to be heard.

When he spotted Nils in the center of a group of men who obviously had been buying him drinks, Elijah motioned for him to leave.

The Norwegian waved back at him, then wobbled and nearly toppled over. The little prick was drunk and didn't want to leave.

If it were possible, he looked even worse than he had before. His clothes were still damp and his hair was matted with bits of seaweed and sand. Elijah didn't want to touch the man, but he wanted to see the photo. Now.

He walked over, grabbed Nils by the elbow, and steered him out of the bar as the Norwegian kept up a tirade in the high-pitched, whiny voice of a child throwing a tantrum. Elijah threw him into the front passenger seat.

"You want to get paid, you'll stay put and come with me. I'll buy you a drink back at the hotel."

Elijah drove back down the dark road toward Vigan. "So where's the camera?"

Nils reached into his pants pocket and produced the boxy camera in its waterproof case. "Here. I can't tell how the pics turned out 'cause it doesn't have a screen."

Elijah saw a break in the trees on the right side of the road. It probably led to the river, which he could see through occasional breaks in the foliage. He slowed and pulled off the main road.

"I've got my laptop in the back. Let's just get out of traffic and have a look."

Of course, they had not passed another vehicle since they left the bar. He swung the wheel hard over and parked the truck at the river's edge.

He rolled the windows down before shutting off the ignition.

The night was quiet aside from the occasional whirring noise of insects in the grass. Far out in the river, they heard a plop as a fish jumped. The sky remained overcast, and though the storm had let up for the moment the night air still smelled like rain.

Elijah reached into the back of the truck and grabbed his computer bag. "Let's see what we have." He slid the sword onto the floor of the backseat and lifted the laptop out of the bag.

Nils struggled to open the camera's waterproof case. "Sorry. It's my eyes," he said. "I don't see well in the dark."

"Give it to me." Elijah opened the case and retrieved the SD card. He slid it into the side of his computer. When the machine was fully booted up, he opened the last image on the card.

It was perfect. "Well done," Elijah said.

"If you're happy with that, I'd like to be on my way tonight. You won't need me anymore, right? If you could pay me, then I'll be headed back home to Aparri."

Elijah closed the laptop and looked at the man sitting next to him. "I could manage that," he said. "It's a long ride back to the hotel, though. I'm going to take a piss before we get back on the road."

"Good idea," Nils said, and he opened his door.

Elijah reached into the back and slid the laptop into the bag. He glanced up as he unwrapped the sword. The Norwegian was walking toward the river.

Sliding out of the truck, Elijah held the sword tight against his right leg in case the man finished too soon. He needn't have worried. After all the beer, his stream was still splashing into the river when Elijah stopped a few steps behind him.

As he raised the sword over his head, he felt the ink on his back tingling. He took a deep breath of the rain-washed air, anticipating the rich scent he would soon smell. Then Elijah swung the sword in a downward cut at the side of the man's neck in a move he had practiced hundreds of times at the dojo. Only this time he did not pull back at the last moment.

He was astonished when the head splashed into the water before the legs crumpled.

CHAPTER SEVENTY-EIGHT

Northern Luzon
The Philippines

June 27, 1945

The sky remained overcast as the night drew around them, and the darkness appeared impenetrable. Ozzie wasn't sure they'd be able to find the boat out in the bay, much less the entrance to the cave. While they had been waiting for nightfall, he'd wandered around the village and come upon a fisherman's net with float buoys attached. With the help of Rafi's machete, he fashioned himself a string of buoys that he could either trail behind him as he swam, causing minimal drag, or use to support him if he needed to rest during the swim.

They paddled out to the fishing boat in the canoe and Rafi started up the engine. Rafi then changed the anchor line over to the canoe before they climbed aboard the fishing boat and pointed the bow of the boat out to sea. Soon it was impossible to see the shore behind them.

Ozzie knew little of this northern part of Luzon, but he had spent time in Manila before the war started. Manila was a lively, vibrant city and he was surprised that there weren't more lights along this coast.

He wondered if there really were no people living close by or whether they were observing a blackout.

The boat chugged along for more than an hour across a flat sea. Peewee and Rafi had a chart back in the wheelhouse and from time to time a light would flick on and they'd mark the boat's position based on their knowledge of dead reckoning. Ozzie hoped they knew what they were doing. Finally Peewee came out of the wheelhouse carrying what looked like a thick belt.

"Here," he said, "put this around your waist. There's a couple of flares in here as well as a waterproof light and compass."

"I take it I'm going to swim from here?"

"Yeah. I reckon we're about a thousand yards off the rocks. To get to the cave entrance, you have to go through a channel of rocks. The Japs use range markers, but we can't do that, so we want you to swim in and put flares on the rocks—one on each side of the channel."

"It's going to be hard to find this channel."

"When you get in closer, you should be able to spot the cave entrance. There are some lights on in there, but they're positioned so they don't shine out and can't be seen very far offshore. Use the compass. Follow a bearing in. The cave should be due east of us."

"Don't worry. This isn't my first night swim."

Ozzie stripped off his shirt, but decided to keep his pants on. They'd make swimming a little more difficult, but they were dark in color, unlike his Skivvies. He checked out the pouch in the belt, tried the flashlight, and steadied the compass. Then he sealed it up again to keep the flares dry and tied the rope connecting him to his floats round his waist.

There was a warm layer of water on top, but when he slipped all the way into the water, his feet reached down to the cooler temperature.

"Listen, buddy," he said to Peewee. "Don't take any wooden nickels, you hear?"

Ozzie pushed off from the side of the boat and began to swim.

. . .

So much for Filipino navigation. Ozzie had been maintaining a strong, steady crawl stroke. He stopped swimming and, while treading water, reeled in the fishing floats that trailed behind him and tucked one under his arm to keep him afloat. Then he pulled the compass out of his waistband. There was quite a bit of bioluminescence in the seawater, so he wiggled his hand and splashed around to create enough bluish light to check his bearing. He was still on course and he'd covered at least two thousand yards by now. The island of Luzon had to be up ahead somewhere. It wasn't like he could miss it. He tucked the compass back into his waistband and faced forward, switching to the breaststroke. Only a few strokes farther, and he sensed the darkness ahead was more solid. At last, he began to make out the outline of a large rock.

He changed course slightly to his left to swim around the rock, then peered into the darkness, trying to see the main island. If it was out there, he still couldn't see it. Squinting into the black night, he stroked his way onward and then all of a sudden, like he had just figured out an optical illusion, he saw the dimly lit oval shape of the cave opening. Just to make sure he wasn't imagining it, he swam closer until he could make out the submarine tied up to the dock.

No men were in sight. Ozzie figured it was late and he was certain there was some kind of guard. Hopefully it was only one or two men.

Turning back seaward, he could make out the two rocks that framed the entrance to the channel. It was time to set his flares.

Climbing onto the rocks turned out to be more difficult than he thought. The stones' surfaces were covered in a light slime that made them slippery as heck. If he tossed the flares onto the rocks, though, they'd be too likely to fall into a crevice and then become invisible. He wanted to place the flares so they were easily visible from the seaward side, but nearly invisible from the cave.

He pulled himself onto a ledge and lit the first flare. Stepping up on the rock so he could reach a dry spot, he just managed to wedge the burning flare into a crevice before he fell and cut open a gash along his forearm.

Ozzie tried not to think about the blood and sharks as he slid back into the water and pulled hard for the rock on the other side. From the other side of the channel, the rock had looked as big as the first one, but when he arrived, he saw it had been an illusion. Ozzie had thought it was farther away. In fact, the channel was only about one hundred feet wide. He tried to pull himself up onto a ledge, but he slipped. He had to light this flare before the other one burned out.

He lit it and this time when he tried to wedge it into a Y-shaped crevice, the flare rolled off and landed in the water. Luckily it didn't burn out, but when he grabbed it and lifted it out of the water, he was in full view of the cave. He stroked one-handed back to the rock, but from the direction of the cave he heard the submarine's Klaxon horn sound.

By the time he'd wedged the flare securely on the rock, the horn had stopped but he heard a voice shouting orders in Japanese. The mouth of the cave seemed to work like a megaphone, amplifying the sound.

Then from seaward, he heard the sound of the *San Pedro*'s engine roaring at full tilt.

Ozzie didn't want to miss out on the action, so he slipped into the water and began stroking toward the cave entrance, making sure he was clear of the boat channel. The last thing he wanted was to get run down by the prop on the *San Pedro*.

He had covered half the distance to the cave when the fishing boat was suddenly almost on him. He was surprised by the speed she was traveling when she passed him. It was crazy to be careening along at full throttle toward a small opening in a cliff.

No sooner had the *San Pedro* passed him and bounced him around in her frothy wake than Ozzie saw another shape streak past, traveling in the opposite direction and moving even faster. It didn't register until he saw the bluish bubbles and the long luminescent trail in the water. He turned his head in time to see it porpoise up out of the water and then dive back in. The *Bonefish* had just fired a torpedo!

Ozzie heard the *ack-ack-ack* of gunfire as the *San Pedro* neared the cave entrance. It was impossible to tell which side was firing—probably both. Certainly Peewee and the Filipinos must have seen the torpedo as it passed under their boat. That would have been more than enough to make them trigger-happy. Ozzie stopped swimming and pulled the buoys close to him. No sense in swimming too close with all those bullets flying.

Then he saw it out of the corner of his eye.

It all happened so fast he barely had time to register the absolute terror that paralyzed his body. To seaward, the comet-like trail was streaking through the water just below the surface, leaping free like a wild animal and making a gradual turn round to the left. Ozzie had heard of this happening before. The right rudder had jammed. The thing looked like it would head down the coast, but it kept on turning through 180 degrees until it was headed straight back at him. The torpedo flew past not more than twenty feet away. The water rose up in a pressure mound as it passed, leaving Ozzie gently rocking in its wake. The last sight he had of the *San Pedro*, it was in the embrace of the cave mouth. He watched the silhouette of a man jump up onto the fishing boat's bulwark and leap into the air before a bloom of fire exploded against the cliff, just to the right of the opening. Then there was another explosion, and another. The last thing Ozzie remembered was all the rock and debris raining down into the water all around him.

CHAPTER SEVENTY-NINE

**Vigan City
The Philippines**

December 7, 2012

When the alarm went off Cole felt like he had just closed his eyes. He reached over and slapped at the top of the clock to silence it. Riley stirred where she slept on her side, her firm body curved against his, her skin soft and warm. She made little humming sounds of contentment as she wiggled her ass and pressed against him. That woke him faster than any alarm. He burrowed his way through her hair and nibbled at the side of her neck.

"Good morning, Magee," he said. He liked the way her body fitted against his and his enthusiasm was showing.

"Good morning, Thatcher. You're up and at 'em mighty early."

"That's one way of putting it. It would be a shame for my efforts to go to waste, don't you think?"

He felt her ribs bounce as she laughed softly. Cole wanted to be sure to remember everything about this moment, the smell of her skin and hair, the warmth of her body, the joy he felt waking to find her in his bed. "Riley, I never knew loving someone could feel this great."

She pulled out of his arms and rolled over. Worry lines streaked her face. "Who said anything about love?"

"I did. I love you, Marguerite Riley, and I want to spend the rest of my life with you."

She was shaking her head and frowning. "No, no. You don't know me, Cole. There's so much you don't—"

"Nothing could possibly change the way I feel."

"You say that now. But Cole, I know you. You have such rigid beliefs about what's right and wrong. How you feel—it is going to change."

He drew back from her and faced her squarely. "Riley, you can trust me. You have something to tell me, you can tell me."

She rolled onto her back and stared at the overhead, and he could see all the conflicting emotions playing out in her face as she struggled to find the words. He wanted to take her in his arms and wipe all that fear and worry off her face. But he knew the best thing he could do at that moment was to wait. Maybe, if he gave her enough time, she'd figure out how to tell him what was wrong.

When she started to speak, her voice was quiet, but strong. "That last day in Guadeloupe just before you disappeared, Diggory Priest told me the real story behind what happened down in Lima. I think part of me had an inkling, but I had buried it deep inside. Dig confirmed it.

"See, he was with the CIA and working undercover as an attaché at the embassy in Lima. I was a Marine Security Guard. It was against regulations for us to fraternize, and yet we did it anyway. I wasn't myself when I was with him. I can't explain it.

"Anyway, that morning he asked me to deliver a radio to another Marine. He knew I could get it past security. Only it wasn't a radio. After I delivered it, I ran out to a little local bodega to pick something up, and the bomb exploded while I was gone." Her face tightened and her eyes filled. "Cole, it wasn't terrorists. The Shining Path had nothing to do with it. It had something to do with mining rights and making the Peruvians do what the Patriarchs wanted. I delivered that bomb. I killed my friends."

He held her until the tears slowed. It was his turn now to struggle for words. Whatever he said next she would remember for the rest of their lives together. He wanted to tell her that she wasn't to blame for what had happened, that she'd just been used. But he knew just having him tell her not to blame herself wasn't going to do her any good. In the end, he didn't say anything fancy, he simply told her the truth.

"I love you, Marguerite Riley, and I want to spend the rest of my life with you. Nothing is ever going to change that."

When Cole and Riley walked up the steps into the galley, the rest of the crew was already assembled. Theo was at the stove stirring a pan of scrambled eggs and Greg was buttering toast.

"Glad you decided to join us," Theo said.

Cole headed straight for the coffee pot. As he poured a mug for Riley, he said, "Doesn't sound like the weather has cleared up any out there." The rain hammered away at the cabin roof.

The Abra River had many different channels at the mouth, and the evening before they had followed a returning fishing boat around several islands until they came to a channel that was lined with fish traps. They could see a dock and a road ashore, so they dropped the hook. Greg hailed a passing fisherman and they'd learned the town of Vigan was several miles inland.

Theo said, "Fortunately, the storm has been downgraded to a tropical storm, so I'm not worried that the boat will drag while you're gone, but it's not going to be fun climbing those mountains in thirty- to forty-knot winds."

"For a while last night, it looked like it was calming down," Greg said.

"Tropical storm weather comes in bands," Theo said. "It will rain like the gods opened all taps, then it will go calm and dry for a spell before the next band hits. A calm spell doesn't necessarily mean it's through."

"So," Cole said. "Are we ready? Let's go over it all one more time."

"Again?" Peewee said. "At my age my memory's like a sieve, but even I can remember last night."

"I printed up some topographical maps I found online," Theo said.

"Talk about the blind leading the blind."

"Shut up, Irv. I had Greg help me to make sure I wasn't printing up ads for Viagra—which was possible, since you'd just been using the computer."

"Children, please," Riley said. "Let's take a look at these maps."

Greg handed her several sheets of paper and together they spread them out on the dinette table. Greg said, "From comparing these maps to the nautical charts, we've been able to narrow down the location. There's really only a small area along the coast here where the water is deep enough for ships to go right up to the shore. If there was a cave along this coast, Theo concluded it had to be here." She pointed to the chart. "Peewee said the cave was big enough for a freighter like the *Teiyō Maru*. That must mean the ceiling is quite high, so the underground river that formed the cave must have cut under a fairly high hill or mountain that reaches all the way to the coast. So, we know that the cave wouldn't have been under the valleys, and we're thinking it's under this mountain here." She drew a dark line on the map. "As the cave goes inland it climbs, and the other entrance would likely be on the side of the hill here." She drew a circle.

Cole said, "And that's not that far from the Gabriela Silang Memorial Park, at the entrance to the Northern Luzon Heroes Hill National Park."

Peewee said, "Yeah, the mountains where the guerrillas were fighting is now a national park."

Greg patted his arm. "We honor our heroes who fought for our independence. Thank you for helping them."

"You make me feel like an old man."

Greg kissed him on the cheek. "You are an old man."

"Right," Cole said. "We figure we can leave the van along the road here, where there's a parking lot for the parks."

The night before, Cole had sent Greg ashore to rent a car, and she'd returned with a van. It was the only vehicle she'd been able to secure at that hour. It belonged to the owner of a local gas station. While she'd been getting the car, Cole had packed their gear and Riley and Peewee had worked with Theo at scanning the image off the silk and transposing it onto maps and charts in the computer to determine the location.

"Okay," Cole said. "We know we aren't going to be alone out there. Nils got away with the camera and we should expect company."

Riley said, "You mentioned that you thought he was stealing the sat phone last night? I'll bet he used it to call someone to tell them what we were doing. Hawkes and Benny were probably already here when we arrived yesterday. They've had as much time to prepare as we have."

"I doubt they have access to the computer help we have"—Cole nodded toward Theo—"but they won't be far behind us."

"If I were them, I'd hide and wait to follow us," Riley said.

"Let's hope they aren't that smart. Without the analysis Theo did, we'd be looking at about two to three miles of coastline and thinking it could be anywhere along there. They probably don't know the park is there."

"Fingers crossed," Riley said.

"So, I've packed four bags for us. Theo is staying with the boat as our tech support and backup. We'll take the sat phone in case we don't have cell reception up there. He can call in the cavalry if we need it."

Greg said, "Referring to the Vigan police as the cavalry might be an exaggeration."

"If we need help, I'm certain Theo can be very persuasive. In your bags, you'll find some food and water, underwater lights, headlamps, rope, et cetera. We don't have much in the way of weapons, but I do have two spearguns. They're pneumatic and small enough to fit into a backpack. I've put one in my bag and the other in Riley's. We'll buddy up—me and Greg, and Irv and Riley. Every bag has a knife."

"I've got my own, as well," Greg said.

Cole smiled. "I'd be surprised if you didn't. I've also brought masks and mini-fins in case we find this cave and it's flooded. It must have been formed by an underground river, which probably got dammed up when the Japanese buried the entrance."

"You guys need to eat fast and go," Theo said, putting plates of food on the table. "You want to start hiking while it's still dark."

The drive through Vigan and across the Abra River took longer than they thought due to the rain and wind. There were other cars on the road, people driving to work and big buses full of travelers. When the rain closed down visibility, the traffic slowed to a crawl. By the time they reached the turnoff for the Gabriela Silang Memorial Park, the dawn had turned their world a drizzly gray.

Before climbing out of the van, they pulled on their raingear. Cole had brought his foul-weather pants as well as the jacket, but he could tell already that he would be too hot under all that gear with his jeans on. Riley and Greg both wore their full foul-weather suits with shorts underneath while Peewee wore one of Theo's rain jackets. It came nearly to his knees. Cole had the topo map in a Ziploc bag, while Riley had dropped a pin in her phone's Google Maps app at the center of the area Theo predicted would be the probable location.

The going was easy at first. Though not as well traveled as an American park might be, still, there was a well-worn path up the mountain. The farther they went, though, the more difficult it became to find the trail. Soon they were forging their own path. In places the forest grew thick and some of the trees were huge, but at other times the growth on the ground had died off from lack of light, and the tree canopy gave them some measure of relief from the constant downpour.

Cole was glad he'd brought a machete. In places where the growth was thick, they would have had to walk much farther if they weren't able to cut through. Because he was cutting the trail, he was on point. Greg followed him, then the old man. Riley took up the rear.

The ground they covered in the first half hour was fairly flat, too, but when they started climbing, Cole knew Peewee was going to be a problem. No doubt about it, he was in great shape for a guy his age. But he was *ninety-three years old*. Most people his age were in wheelchairs, not climbing mountains in the rain. On the other hand, the old guy claimed that he had seen the location of the so-called back door to the cave. While things had changed in sixty years, no doubt, he would be invaluable if he recognized something.

Cole stopped and turned around. "Water break," he said.

"All you gotta do is stick out your tongue," Peewee said.

Cole ignored him. He'd been able to hear how hard the old guy was breathing. He didn't want him having a heart attack out in the middle of nowhere. "How's everybody doing?"

"What you really want to know is"—Irv paused to catch his breath—"is the old guy gonna croak on you."

"Well, you got me there, Irv. You aren't, are you? Gonna croak, I mean?"

"Not if I can help it. But you know what they say, *False confidence often leads into danger.*"

Cole cocked his head at the old man. "If you're trying to tell me something, just come out and say it."

The old man just opened his water bottle and took a long drink, and Riley stepped in. "That's just an endearing habit of his, Cole. Ignore him."

After another half hour, they came to a flat stretch, but the brush was thick and the rain came down in sideways-driven torrents. Cole's machete was losing its edge. The brush just bent under his blows. The rain was seeping in around his hood and he was drenched through and through. Water had filled his hiking boots, and even with thick socks his feet were sliding around and he knew he'd have blisters soon.

He stopped hacking at the bushes. He'd heard something odd, even with all the noise of the rain. Maybe they should wait for this rain band to pass. He should ask Riley to check on her phone how much farther they had to go. He turned around.

There was no one behind him.

How long had it been since the last time he'd turned around? He'd been so focused on trying to cut their way through the undergrowth.

"Riley?" he shouted. He saw the bushes dancing farther back. He started to step toward them when Greg came hurtling at him from around a large tree. She almost ran into him, but managed to pull back just in time. Bent over, hands on knees, she was panting. Water streamed off her yellow hood.

Cole reached out and put a hand on her shoulder. "Where are the others?" he shouted.

Greg stood up and put her hands on her hips. Her face looked pained. "I don't know," she said. "I turned around and they were gone."

CHAPTER EIGHTY

Mountains of Ilocos Sur
The Philippines

December 7, 2012

Riley peered out of the thick bushes. She still couldn't see anybody, but she was certain she'd heard a voice. Irv started to move, but she touched his shoulder with one hand and with the other held her finger to her lips. She knew he was hurting, but if he made a noise now, they might end up dead.

It had started when Irv slipped and fell. They had already fallen a bit behind the others. Poor Peewee just couldn't keep up, but he was too stubborn to ask them to slow down. The rain was coming down so hard that Riley was walking with her red foul-weather jacket hood cinched up tight around her face. She walked with her head bent forward so she could watch the ground, and so the water didn't run into her eyes.

She saw the odd movement in her peripheral vision and looked up in time to see his left foot had slid off a root and his ankle twisted. The old man toppled forward and hit the ground hard. Riley feared he might have broken a hip. She rushed forward and knelt beside him.

When she looked ahead, she couldn't see either Greg or Cole. Some instinct prevented her from calling out to them. She helped Peewee into a sitting position and she saw the way his face tightened when he moved. She pointed to his ankle and he nodded.

That was when she was certain she heard a voice. She'd probably heard something earlier, but it hadn't registered on her consciousness the way it did this time. The voice came from behind them and it wasn't that far away.

Riley turned her head and looked up the trail in the direction Cole and Greg had gone. With his machete, Cole was leaving a trail like a mini-bulldozer. Peewee had been slow before, but now with the twisted ankle they would never be able to stay ahead of their pursuers. She looked around, trying to decide what her alternatives might be.

There was the speargun in her pack. She could try to shoot at them. The problem was there would be more than one and she had only one spear. She was expecting all three: Benny, Nils, and Hawkes.

Then she noticed, about six feet ahead, a small animal trail that took off to the right. That direction eventually would lead to the very steep side of the mountain, but maybe it would get them far enough off this main trail to avoid detection by the men behind them.

With her thumb she motioned that they were going to stand. Peewee grimaced, but nodded. Riley stood first, then she squatted and got his arm over her shoulder while she put her arm under his waist.

He weighed so little. She wondered how he had managed to make it this far. She pulled him to his feet. He was shorter than she was, so she walked hunched over and practically carried him.

When she came to the spot where the trail branched, she stopped and pointed to show him what she planned to do. Then she took a very large step.

"Lift both feet," she whispered, and he bent his knees. He was surprisingly light. She swung her foot forward in another large step. "Now put your good foot down." Lifting his arm off her shoulder, she placed his hand on a tree for support. She picked up some wet leaves and scattered them over the two footprints. The rain pounded the leaves flat. Riley resumed her position supporting Peewee and they traveled another fifteen feet before they heard a loud crash in the bushes no more than fifty feet away.

She pulled Peewee down into a crouch. They crawled into a thicket of vines that grew over some waist-high bushes. They both wore bright red jackets, so they needed as much cover as they could find.

So now they lay there listening and watching, afraid to move.

Then she heard a voice again, but this time it came from the opposite direction and it was calling her name.

Peewee's head whipped around and looked at her. His lips mouthed the name, "Greg."

Riley nodded.

Then they heard a man yell, "Stop!" And there were footsteps. Running. Away from them.

Riley crawled out and pulled Peewee with her. She had to get the old man to a safe place. Then she could leave him and go help the others. She got him to his feet and hurried farther back away from the trail.

She was walking fast toward what looked like an open circle at the center of a patch of bushes, with Peewee's good foot hitting the ground on about one of every three of her strides. His arm across her shoulder was setting her old wound on fire. She gritted her teeth and pushed forward as fast as she could. She had to get back to help Cole and Greg, and she was almost there.

Her left foot must have caught on a vine. The next thing she knew her body twisted and her leg brought her to a fast stop and she fell to the ground in the patch of vines and bushes. Peewee kept right on going. She saw his arms fly up, then disappear. She heard his voice calling out for several long seconds. It sounded like he was falling. Then all she heard was the rain.

She unhooked her foot and crawled forward and then she heard the crack of green branches breaking, and she too was falling out of the gray rain, through the bushes into the dark. Her hands clawed at the vegetation and her right hand found a mat of vines, which she dug her fingers into. Her arm yanked straight, her shoulder screaming against the weight of her body, but she was hanging, not falling, about six feet down into a hole.

Riley looked down and tried to make out what was beneath her. The two bodies falling through the shrubbery had created a hole and allowed a shaft of weak light into it. She blinked, trying to get her eyes to adjust, and then saw the red jacket on the floor below her. The body looked very small. He was a long way down.

She reached up with her left arm to try to get another handhold on the matted clump of vines. Her shift of weight caused some of the roots above to let go and she was showered with rocks and soil. Her body dropped another three or four feet, but then the vines held.

"Irv?" she called out.

He didn't move. It was still a very long way down. Her fist and shoulder ached. She couldn't stay there forever. Should she try to go up or down?

The decision was made for her. She tried to grab the vines again with her left hand and this time some more roots let go and dropped her down another six or eight feet. Then she felt the roots breaking and she was calculating how far she was going to fall when the whole thing let go and she dropped the remaining twenty feet to the floor of the cave.

Riley bent her knees when her sneakers hit the floor and she rolled onto her side, doing her best to protect her head with her arms. She brought with her a mass of vegetation, which landed on top of her a second after she hit the floor. She pushed the plants off her, brushed off some of the dirt, and went to Irv. He was on his back and his eyes were closed.

She put two fingers on his neck and felt for a pulse. It was weak, but he was alive. She pulled his backpack out from under him, opened it, and got out a bottle of water. She put the pack under his head to raise it and poured a little water on his face.

His eyes fluttered, then opened. He tried to smile. "Maggie," he said. He'd never called her that.

"Irv, look," she said. She waved her arm in a half circle. "You found the cave." The cool, damp air smelled like wet clay, and droplets of rain continued to fall on them from the skylight at the top of the chamber above them.

"Guess I did, sweetheart."

Riley's eyes were gradually adjusting to the dim light. The chamber they were in was quite large and somewhat oval in shape. There were both stalactites and stalagmites, she wasn't even sure which was which, but the spiky spires that reached down from the ceiling were the longest.

"Come on. Let's get you up." She lifted his arm, but it was totally limp. He didn't move anything other than his face.

"That's not gonna happen. I'm all broke up inside. This is it for me."

Riley lifted the limp hand to her lips and kissed it. "No, Cole will be here soon with the satellite phone and we'll call for help. We'll get a medevac chopper and take you to Manila. They'll fix you up."

"Listen, there's nobody wants that more than me. The man upstairs must have a sense of humor to take me today."

"What do you mean?"

"Today's date?"

"Oh," she said when she realized what he was talking about. "December 7. Pearl Harbor Day."

"From then till now, I've been determined to cheat death. But now that it's here, I'm not afraid of it anymore. I did better than most."

Riley brushed at a tear that started down her cheek. She didn't want him to see it. "That you did, Peewee. That you did."

"About that nickname. Let me tell you this story while I can still talk. Where's that water?"

Riley held the bottle to his lips and he took a drink. He ran his lips over his dentures before he spoke. "Do you remember when I told you about a Filipina girl I once loved?"

Riley smiled and nodded.

"Her name was Gregoria and she fought with the guerrillas in these mountains. When we learned that the USS *Bonefish* was in the cave, we decided to stage a raid. Free the Americans. Gregoria stayed behind. We got a boat and went in at night. Only one of us could swim—Ozzie. He had to swim in. Light flares for the boat. The Japs saw us and fired the stern tube. Torpedo's rudder jammed, it turned a hundred and eighty degrees and came back. Japs didn't blow the opening to this cave. We did."

Riley touched the side of his face. "Is that how you got this?"

He closed his eyes and inclined his head. "Only one man survived, sweetheart. It was Ozzie."

"What?" Riley wondered if delirium was setting in. "I—"

"Shhh. Listen." He motioned for more water, but he barely swallowed any. He just moistened his lips. "I woke up on the beach. Gregoria had pulled me out. She was supposed to stay back at camp, but she followed. She saw it all. I was unconscious, burned and drifting away. Becoming Peewee was her idea. She had his dog tag. Hard to explain how Ozzie Riley was the only survivor from a missing submarine. Better to become Sergeant Irving Weinstein. We always looked like brothers. And now, with my scars . . ."

"You're—"

His head dipped but the answer was in his eyes.

"You've been living a lie all this time?"

Riley found herself looking at his face, searching for some resemblance to her own features. Was it possible? Could this man really be her grandfather?

He started coughing and Riley could tell his voice was growing weaker.

"Tell your friend Cole I knew Andrew Ketcham at Corregidor. We were both Bonesmen. What we did . . ." His voice trailed off.

His thoughts appeared to be jumping all over. How would she ever know what was true about Ozzie Riley and what was him pretending to be Irv?

He closed his eyes for several seconds, then opened them and spoke again. "Gregoria. She nursed me in the mountains, then in a village. Don't know where. We fell in love.

"The treasure room is that way." He moved his eyes to indicate where.

Riley peered out into the darkness. She couldn't see much outside the shaft of light they were in. She pulled the backpack off her own back and pulled the flashlight out of the side pocket. When she clicked it on, she was surprised to see there were mounds of stuff around them in the cave. It was all rotten and moldy looking, but she saw what looked like some wood crates and some piles of fabric.

"This is camp room. Treasure next chamber. Giant gold dragon. Hollow. Small one was replica. They caught us—hidden in dragon."

A dragon big enough to hide a man would be big indeed. And made of gold?

"What about this back door for getting out of here?"

He moved his eyes in the opposite direction. "That way. Keep right."

"If I can get out back there, maybe I should go and try to find some help. Get you a doctor."

"No, too late. Stay with me." He coughed again and it sounded like his lungs were full of fluid.

She lifted his hand again in hers. It felt so odd to hold that lifeless hand. He wasn't dead yet, but his hand appeared to be. It wasn't fair. She'd just found her grandfather in time to watch him die.

"Maggie," he said. His voice was barely more than a whisper. "I'm glad I got to know my granddaughters." He closed his eyes.

"Granddaughters?" She hadn't meant to say it out loud, but in surprise, she'd blurted it out.

When he opened his eyes, there was still a sparkle of humor there. She could see him summoning the strength to speak. "Gregoria got pregnant. Made me promise to name our daughter Honoria."

He closed his eyes again and his body grew still. If not for the barely perceptible rise and fall of his chest and the breathing that sounded like he was gargling water, she would think he was already gone. The rain was still falling on him, the drops collecting on his face and flowing like small rivers in the wrinkles in his skin. Riley took off her jacket and tried to make a little tent to cover his face. She took his hand again.

There was so much more she wanted to ask him. So much she wanted to know. Was it true? Was Greg her cousin? He had manipulated Riley into chasing after his Dragon's Triangle, so it stood to reason he might have done the same with Greg.

Riley loosened the hood under his chin and pushed the fabric back from his face. She combed his thin hair with her fingers. He took a deep breath and exhaled. She waited for the next breath. Just when she thought he wasn't going to do it, he inhaled a long, gurgling breath.

"I'm glad I had the chance to get to know you," she said. She didn't know if he could hear her anymore. "Maybe I'll never understand why you did what you did. Why you waited until now to find me. Why you never came to us when Michael or my father were still alive. You know, when you wrote in your letter that you would tell me what happened to my grandfather, I never imagined it would be this."

His eyes popped open, but they appeared to be focused on something over her shoulder. It was eerie enough to make her turn her head and look, but she didn't see anything there.

She turned back. His eyes were only half open now.

"Grandpa?" she said.

He exhaled another long burbling breath. Only this time, he did not inhale.

Riley sat there holding his hand, brushing her fingers through his hair over and over, and she cried.

CHAPTER EIGHTY-ONE

**Ilocos Sur
The Philippines**

December 7, 2012

"They can't have just disappeared." Cole put his arm around Greg to turn her around.

Greg resisted. "I saw two men coming up the trail. They'll get both of us if we don't get out of here."

He knew she was right. But he had to find Riley. "I've got to look."

She shook her head. "I didn't see any sign of them. They're probably hiding and we need to do the same."

He whipped off his backpack and dug out the satellite phone. "Can you make it back to the van on your own?"

She nodded.

He shoved the phone into her hands. "I'll distract them. You circle around and get back to the van. Call for help." He was worried that she would refuse to leave them, so he added, "I'll find the others. We're counting on you."

She took the phone and slipped off into the brush on the side of the trail. In seconds she had disappeared from view.

Cole already had his backpack off, so he unzipped his red jacket. While he was taking it off he was scanning the forest around him. He needed a tree with strong branches, but low enough for him to climb. He spotted what he wanted, and he was glad it was on the opposite side of the trail from where Greg had disappeared.

Beneath the big tree's canopy was a thick cluster of bushes. He jammed the red jacket deep inside, making sure that it could be seen if one looked hard enough. He spread the sleeves out, trying to make it look like a person facedown on the ground.

He slung the pack back onto his back and hid his machete at the base of the tree. Then he jumped up and grabbed one of the lower hanging branches. He walked his feet up the tree's trunk until he could loop one leg over the branch. He climbed higher. He was standing on a branch about twenty feet off the ground and reaching for a higher branch when he saw movement through the trees. He moved his body so the trunk of the tree was between him and the two men.

By moving his head a few inches to the right he could sneak a look around the trunk. It looked like there were two of them. Both wore clear plastic rain ponchos. Cole recognized Benny, and he assumed the other one in the jeans and boots was Hawkes. No sign of Nils Skar. No big surprise. Nils wasn't the hiking type.

Hawkes held a machete-like blade in his hand. Benny had his three-foot-long blowpipe.

They stopped a good distance back. Benny pointed to his own eyes with two fingers, then pointed ahead. He was communicating that he'd spotted something. Then he held his palm up flat, signaling Hawkes to stay put.

Cole wished he'd had time to get his speargun out of the pack on his back. That had been his plan. Now, he feared the movement would give him away. Right now his best weapon was surprise. Benny was coming as the advance man, which was good. Better to deal with them one at a time. Right now he had to take Benny out of the equation, and he'd only get one chance. He'd better be quick about it, too, because Hawkes would be there right on his tail.

Benny's movements reminded him of a big cat. He was stalking the bush, walking slowly, knees bent, body close to the ground, his blowpipe at his mouth.

At first Cole feared Benny was going to approach the bush from the opposite side, but he needn't have worried. It made sense to use the thick tree trunk as cover. And he was so focused on sneaking up on the man hiding in the bushes, it never occurred to him to look up.

When Cole jumped, he was totally focused on getting his hand on that blowpipe. Benny fell under the weight of Cole's one hundred and eighty pounds falling on his back, and Cole knocked the pipe loose from his grip. Both men rolled in the mud. The Bornean man was fast, but Cole's years of amateur wrestling paid off. It was only when he had Benny under control with his head in a half nelson, pinned facedown in the mud, that Cole saw the needlelike point of the dart clenched between Benny's teeth.

Benny jerked and started to turn his head, intending to smash his mouth against Cole's bare forearm. Cole released the half nelson and whipped his arm out of the way, and the dart plunged into the tattooed skin of Benny's own forearm.

Cole scrambled back in the mud still on all fours.

Behind him he heard Hawkes coming through the bushes. Cole rose, intending to run, when a knife flew past his ear and stuck into the tree.

"Stop or I will kill you."

Cole stopped.

"Put your hands on your head and turn around slowly."

Cole did as he was told. The rain had eased up and the man had pulled the hood back off his head. He pushed his wet black hair straight back from his forehead. The sky, the woods, and the rocks were all a rain-washed gray, but this guy's blue eyes seemed to burn with some kind of inner light. He pointed the blade at Benny, and Cole saw that it was a sword with an elaborate gold dragon designed into the hilt and blade.

"What's wrong with him?" Hawkes said.

"He stuck himself with one of his darts. From what I've heard, he'll be going into cardiac arrest soon." At the moment, he looked like he was sleeping. Maybe he was already dead.

Cole saw no emotion in the man's eyes. "And where are the rest of your friends?"

"I don't know," he said.

"And I don't believe that."

"Look, I was cutting the trail, then I turned around and they were gone. I'd like to find them as much as you. Let's backtrack and look for their trail."

"Where's your machete?"

Cole lifted his chin toward the tree.

Hawkes walked over and retrieved his throwing knife and the machete. He slid the machete under his belt, then he nodded once and waved the sword in the direction of the trail.

Cole kept his hands on his head and started back down the trail.

"I'm surprised at you guys. Blowguns and fancy swords? Isn't that a little low-tech?"

"Don't underestimate what I can do with a blade. Now shut up and find that trail."

It was difficult to see anything on the wet ground with the cut branches from Cole's own trail-making and the passage of so many people. They walked for about two hundred yards before Cole saw anything other than trampled shrubs.

He stopped. Where the large buttress root of a jungle fig tree crossed their trail he noticed a long muddy streak that cut through the leaves and headed off into the brush at the side of the trail. Cole's best guess was that a foot had slid off that root and made that skid mark through the mud. He looked more closely and saw where the person had fallen, where the forest floor of rotting leaves had been pushed into the mud by something bigger than a foot.

"What do you see?" Hawkes asked.

"Can I use my hands?"

The man nodded.

"See that mark where something dug into the mud? I think some-body fell here."

"Okay. I see that."

"Step back, will you?" When he didn't move, Cole said, "Look. I'm not going to run away. I'm seriously worried that Riley's hurt. I want to find her." He didn't add that if they could find the others, he, Riley, and Irv would then outnumber this guy by three to one. And wherever she was, she still had the other speargun. If he could make enough noise, maybe she'd hear them coming. Finally Hawkes took a couple of steps back up the trail.

"They would have been walking this way." Cole made like he was walking up the trail. "Somebody fell here. Then they heard you com-ing. They had to hide. Where?"

Cole examined the trail for several steps. Then he saw what looked like a barely discernible animal trail. He turned in that direction and took several steps off the main trail. He scanned the bushes until he found a broken branch at his waist level. "There." He pointed.

Hawkes walked over and looked where he was pointing.

"This is too high for any animal to have done this," Cole said.

Hawkes waved the sword. "Go on."

They walked another twenty feet and Cole couldn't find any other traces of a trail. Then he heard the muffled sound of a voice calling out. She was crying, "Cole! Help!"

. . .

If he hadn't been following a voice that was clearly coming from beneath the ground, he might very well have fallen into the hole. The thicket of undergrowth masked the cave's skylight completely. It was little wonder it had not been discovered before. The problem was it was impossible to know how firm the ground was around the edges of the hole.

Hawkes said quietly, "Don't tell her I'm here. Tell her you're coming for her."

"Riley," he yelled. "I'm here."

"Cole," she called. "Be careful. It's at least a forty-foot drop."

"Ask her what's in there."

"Riley, what do you see? Is it as big as the cave in Guadeloupe?"

She didn't answer right away—which wasn't surprising, given that they'd never visited a cave on that island. Cole hoped she would get the message that something was not right.

"It's bigger," she said. "There's gold down here. Lots of it. Come down and see."

Cole said to Hawkes, "She knows I have a rope in my bag." He could see the man's mind working. He was dying to get down there to see the gold himself.

Hawkes pulled the strap of his own pack off his shoulder and tossed it on the ground. "Get my rope as well. Tie each one to a tree with a bowline I can check. Make them both secure. We'll go down together so I can keep an eye on you."

While Cole tied off the ropes to two large trees, Hawkes took off his poncho and used Cole's machete to cut away the vegetation so they could walk to the edge of the hole. Both men put their packs back on and got ready to go down into the cave.

"You know I won't hesitate to kill you."

"Sooner or later, I figure that's your plan," Cole said.

"I promise you it will be very soon if you try to escape."

Cole gave him an injured look. "Here I am cooperating and you keep threatening me. You'll hurt my feelings."

"Shut up and go down that rope."

Cole picked up a rope.

"Not that one, the other one," Hawkes said.

"Not very trusting, are we?" Cole said. He switched to the other rope.

Cole sat on the edge of the hole that was only about fifteen feet across and still partially covered with the canopy of bushes and vines. He looped his leg around the rope. The roof of the chamber was thick and though soil slipped over the edge with him, the rock held. He slid off the edge and lowered himself hand over hand, aware that Hawkes had followed a few seconds after him.

His eyes were still adjusting to the light when his feet hit the cave floor. Directly beneath the skylight, he stood in a column of light. He saw Peewee flat on his back, his glassy eyes half open and staring. No need to check for a pulse. It looked like the fall killed him.

But the old man was alone.

"Where is the woman?" Hawkes asked. He pulled a strap off his shoulder and started to dig around in his pack.

"What? Are you the one with hurt feelings now? She wasn't here to greet you?"

Hawkes produced a small, high-intensity flashlight and directed the beam around the cave. "Go check out those boxes."

"Can I get my light out of a side pocket of my pack?"

Hawkes nodded and, flashlight in hand, Cole started around the chamber, looking at the material on the cave floor. The crates were empty. "I know what you're looking for and this isn't it. Looks like these crates were for ammunition. Some food. There are some rusting empty cans here. Bedrolls. Clothes. Looks like the remains of a campsite here."

In the center of the chamber where the pillar of light shone down from the skylight, they heard a thud and turned around in time to see the second rope fall to the floor with another thud.

From above they could hear the sound of laughter. It was Benny.

"Hawkes. Thanks for finding the cave for me."

Cole shut off his flashlight. He didn't want to present a target for the blowpipe. Then again, maybe those darts weren't as lethal as the old man thought.

"You're making a big mistake, Benny." Hawkes had turned his light off as well. He bent down and pulled something from his boot and began walking toward the center of the chamber.

"No, you made the mistake thinking I was dead, but you didn't stick around to make sure. You work around that poison long enough, it's like snakebites. You develop an immunity."

"You know I'll find a way out of here and when I do, first I'll make my fortune off all this gold down here. Then I'll come after you."

At the surface, a light clicked on and shone around down into the chamber.

Hawkes threw the knife and they heard the crunch as the Bornean fell in the bushes. Clods of dirt and rock tumbled to the floor. Then Benny appeared to slide down the pillar of light like a fireman racing down the pole to a fire. He hit the cave floor with a *whomp*. One leg was bent under him in a position even a yogi couldn't manage, and the knife hilt protruded from the center of his chest. He didn't move.

Cole said, "You know he was our last chance for getting out of here."

"I doubt that, Mr. Thatcher." Hawkes walked over, pulled his knife out of the body, and wiped the blood on a sleeve of the dead man's shirt.

Cole felt his stomach clench and he turned away.

"Now switch on your light. Let's go find that girlfriend of yours, and see if there really is any gold in here. We'll follow that water."

Hawkes shone his flashlight on the stream that trickled across the chamber next to the wall.

"All right," Cole said as he aimed his own light at what looked like a tunnel. "I guess we follow the yellow brick road. Get that? Yellow brick?"

"Shut up and start walking."

CHAPTER EIGHTY-TWO

The Cave in Ilocos Sur
The Philippines

December 7, 2012

The "tunnel" wasn't quite what it looked like at first. The ground was uneven damp clay and the ceiling varied from so low he had to duck, to twenty feet above their heads. It was clear that a path had been worn at some point in the past, but the evidence of it was wearing away from the constant dripping moisture. The ground in the tunnel was at an incline, and Cole could tell they were descending in elevation. The stream that ran alongside the path grew larger the farther they went and, probably due to the remnants of the tropical storm, the water level looked higher than usual. Occasional rapids and small waterfalls filled the tunnel with the sound of rushing water and in places it spilled across their path.

Someone had once strung wire along the left wall of the tunnel. Maybe there had been light fixtures. The wire was still there along the ground, but whatever they had provided current to was gone.

Cole didn't mention it, but he saw footprints in the mud in several places. The imprint looked like the familiar nonskid design of the soles of Sperry Top-Sider sneakers: Riley's shoes.

After more than half an hour of picking their way over the remains of the slippery path, the tunnel started to open up. Their flashlights only penetrated twenty feet ahead, but the walls were definitely growing wider apart and the sound of their footsteps and their breathing wasn't bouncing back off the close walls in the same way.

Cole said, "Looks like there's another chamber up ahead."

"Shhh," Hawkes said.

But Cole was certain if Riley was in that chamber, she had already heard his voice. She'd had the warning she would need to take cover.

The second chamber was half again as big as the first one they had dropped into, and this one was full of boxes. They played their lights over the first stacked crates they encountered and when they came to the end of the stack, Cole realized there was a corridor through the stacks leading to the other side of the cave. He shone his flashlight down the corridor and Hawkes, who'd arrived next to him, did the same.

"Holy shit," Cole said.

Their combined beams revealed a pile of bricks, which, though somewhat dull in color from the mineral deposits on them, were obviously made of gold. But the most startling vision was the dragon that seemed to be perched atop the pile of bricks. Its forelegs were raised in the air, talons spread, and its mouth opened in a wide snarl with fangs bared. It appeared to be identical to the dragon he found on the *Teiyō Maru*, only ten times bigger. Though it was streaked with stripes of varying colors from the relentlessly dripping cave, this dragon too was made of gold.

Hawkes stepped behind him and touched the tip of the sword to his back. Cole felt the prick as it cut his skin through his T-shirt.

"Put your hands on your head. Start walking."

Cole set his flashlight on top of his head and clasped his hands over it. He started walking toward the dragon.

"Miss Riley," Hawkes shouted, and his voice filled the cavern. "I know you're here. I have the tip of a very sharp sword ready to carve out your friend's kidney if you don't come out quietly and show yourself." He waited.

Cole heard nothing but their footsteps and the occasional *plop* as a drop landed in a puddle somewhere in the cave.

"Need I remind you how fond I am of playing with blades?"

Still no response.

When Cole got closer to the stacked gold bullion and the dragon statue, he saw that there were other aisles between the stacks of material in the chamber. They entered the clear area in front of the dragon, and they were at the hub with five corridors stretching out like the spokes of a wheel.

"Under normal circumstances, I'd be willing to take my time. Cut off, say, a finger at a time to coax you to reveal yourself. But I'm tired of your games. Come out now or your friend will die."

When the silence dragged on, Cole said, "Maybe she isn't here."

"Shut up." His voice was quiet but it sounded like he was barely holding back a torrent of rage.

"I mean, don't you want to see if the submarine is still down there?"

Hawkes yelled, "I said shut up, you imbecile!"

Something hard smashed into the back of Cole's head and drove him to his knees. When he touched the back of his head, his hair felt wet and sticky. "No need to get testy about it."

Hawkes's cowboy boot smashed into Cole's side. He heard the *whoof* as his own lungs emptied of air and he fell forward. Cole's arms collapsed, but he forced himself back up off the ground. He was on all fours, and by turning his head just a little he could see Hawkes holding a fancy ornamental sword. It was another dragon.

"Did you hear that?" Hawkes shouted. "It was the sound of your boyfriend's ribs cracking. Now show yourself or I swear I will kill him."

Cole wanted to come up with a clever line but he couldn't get enough air to speak. He hoped Riley wasn't there, wasn't watching him on the ground unable to stand. He hoped she was safe.

The man walked around to the other side of him and this time he stomped down with the heel of his cowboy boot on the underside of Cole's right foot. Cole groaned through gritted teeth. Even with his hiking boot, the man had broken at least a couple of toes.

"That groan you just heard was the sound of his toes breaking."

Cole saw the man twisting and turning around, searching the cavern for movement. If she was there, she was remaining very quiet.

"Miss Riley, this magnificent sword is quite capable of beheading a man. And so am I." Hawkes took a stance with one foot forward, the other back, and he began to raise the sword slowly in front of his body like a movement from tai chi.

Before the sword reached its apex, Cole heard what sounded like a whoosh of air and a short metal spear appeared through Hawkes's neck and lodged there. The sword clattered to the ground while the man clutched at the spear, then fell to his knees. Bright red blood flowed down the side of his neck and bubbles foamed around the shaft of the spear. His mouth opened and closed, making gargling noises.

Cole crawled to the sword and began to push it away out of the man's reach. Then he saw Hawkes fumbling for the knife in his boot. The man's fingers closed around the hilt and all the while he was making those horrid gagging noises.

Cole grabbed the dragon sword and swung it, meaning to knock the knife out of the man's hand as he pulled it from the boot. The sword's blade made a clean cut and both hand and knife fell onto the muddy cave floor. In spite of his own injuries, Cole scrambled back in horror until his back came up against the stack of gold bricks.

From behind him he heard a metallic clank. It was coming from the dragon statue. He pulled himself up to look over the top of the pile of bricks and saw what looked like a door drop open from the belly of the dragon. A pair of long brown legs emerged, followed by the most beautiful body he had ever seen. One hand held the speargun, the other her backpack. When her head cleared the beast's belly, she wore a headlamp on an elastic headband above a face lined with worry.

Riley jumped off the stacked bricks, bent down, and threw her arms around him. "Are you okay?" she said into his ear.

He kissed her, then pulled back and looked at her face, trying to memorize every inch of it. Then he smiled. "What took you so long, Magee?"

CHAPTER EIGHTY-THREE

The Cave in Ilocos Sur
The Philippines

December 7, 2012

Riley helped Cole to his feet, trying hard not to cause him further pain. She needed to put some space between herself and that thing on the floor. She wasn't ready to deal with the ramifications of what she had just done. She had waited, not wanting to pull the trigger on the speargun until she had no other choice to save Cole's life. She would focus on that.

They walked slowly down the aisle between the stacked wood crates, the canvas-wrapped bundles, and the fifty-gallon fuel drums. He had his arm across her shoulders and he was leaning on her for support, trying not to put any weight on his broken foot.

"You have to breathe," she said. "I can hear you're holding your breath."

"It hurts too much to breathe."

"I think the consequences of not breathing are worse," she said. She turned to look up at his face and the beam of her headlamp swung from the path ahead of them to the piles of material that formed the walls around them.

"Wait," Cole said. "Let's just take a peek."

The lid to the steel drum next to him was askew. Riley slid the steel disk to one side and bent her head forward. Her light shone on what looked like a drum full of beige rocks that varied in size from peas to a few the size of plums.

"Uncut diamonds," Cole said.

"Really? They look so ordinary," she said. She slid the lid closed but not before Cole pocketed one of the bigger rocks.

"Come on," she said. "None of this stuff will matter a bit if we don't find a way out of here."

"What about the 'back door'? Shouldn't we try that first?"

"I already did," she said. "Before you got here. Irv told me how to find it. I trotted back and came to a rock pile. I think the Japanese had time to blow that and bury the entrance before the guerrillas forced them to fire the torpedo."

"Torpedo? What are you talking about?"

"Oh, I'll tell you later. Once we get out of here. I'm almost afraid to ask, but what happened to Greg?"

"I think she's okay." He stopped, winced, and began to reach for his side, then thought better of it. "I gave her the sat phone and told her to go for help."

"Good. She'll call Theo. Cole, are you sure you're okay to walk?"

He nodded and started moving.

When they got to the stream that flowed along the wall of the cave, they turned to follow the water. Just before leaving the big cavern, they passed four big crates with writing on them. In addition to the Japanese kanji script, there were the letters "UO2." Cole pointed at the crates.

"Uranium dioxide," he said.

Suddenly Riley wished he'd worn his personal dosimeter on this trip. "Let's get the hell out of here."

At least it was downhill. They walked for so long, she had to pinch her nose and pop her ears a couple of times. Cole wasn't talking. Just listening to the hitch in his breath every time he had to put weight on his foot was making her ache for him. Because every step was on the irregular slippery terrain, she was afraid he was going to fall and perhaps even puncture a lung.

Eventually, the sides of the cave began to look different, smoother somehow. She wasn't sure what to make of it until she saw that there was a line and the wall above that line looked like the rest of what they'd seen, with crystalized mineral deposits on the surface of the mud. Below that line, the walls were a different texture.

She pointed and aimed her headlight at the wall. "Look at that line. I'm guessing it's a waterline. I think this cave flooded up to here."

"I think you're right," Cole said.

Soon their path appeared to level out more and the stream began to widen. Riley said, "This whole cave system was formed by this underground river. When they caused the entrance to cave in, it backed up the river and the cave flooded."

Cole finished her thought for her. "So it follows that if the cave is no longer flooded, erosion and the pressure from within helped the water find a way out."

"And all we have to do is follow the water."

Cole took another slow, labored breath. "Easy for you to say."

A few minutes later the walls of the cave opened up, and they walked into a cavern twice the size of the treasure cavern. Most of the floor of the cavern consisted of a huge lake. Riley reached up and covered her headlamp. A faint glow lit the water on the far side of the lake.

"Look at that," she said.

He squeezed her shoulder. "Light," he said.

Riley checked her watch. "It's four thirty. This coast faces west. If the storm clouds have cleared out, there might even be sun out there."

"Sun would be nice," he said. "Very nice."

Riley pulled her underwater flashlight out of her backpack. The light's intensity was stronger than her little headlamp. She passed the beam all around the cavern. It was magnificent, with a dome at least seventy-five feet high.

"This has got to be close to five hundred feet across," Cole said. "Unbelievable."

"Look," she said, shining her light on the wall on the opposite side of the lake. "The stalagmites hang down all the way up to there. Then they stop. That must be where the landslide closed off the entrance."

"Riley, those are stalactites."

"Okay, science guy. How do you remember which is which?"

"Easy," he said. "*Stalactite* has the letter *C* in it for *ceiling*. *Stalagmite* has a *G* in it for *ground*."

She rolled her eyes. "Okay, you win. Do you at least agree with me about the entrance?"

"Yes, dear."

"That's better."

To their left, she discovered a long, narrow dock that was certainly not a natural formation. It had been carved out of the side of the cave by men.

"This must be the dock they tied the sub to," she said. "So where is the submarine?"

She helped Cole step down onto the level surface of the dock and together they walked to the edge. When Riley pointed her powerful light at the water, it lit up the entire cavern with a pale turquoise light. There, just under the surface, was the long dark shape of a submarine lying on its side.

"Riley, say hello to the USS *Bonefish*."

. . .

"Cole, it's our only way out."

They had been arguing for ten minutes. He didn't think she could do it, and she was watching him grow more pale and sweaty by the minute. She was worried about other internal injuries, but even if he only had broken ribs and a broken foot, the pain must be agonizing.

"Riley, I don't want you taking that chance. If you try it and you don't make it, I couldn't bear it. Let me try."

"There you go again. Don't you see how that's the same kind of thinking that led you to stay away from me for four years? Cole, I'm a big girl."

"Actually"—he put his hand against his bicep—"you only come up to about here on me."

She glared at him. "This is not a joke."

They were sitting on the end of the dock with their feet hanging over the edge as they discussed their options.

"There's so little light coming through, I think that tunnel is very long and narrow."

"If so, you'll pull me out." She opened her backpack and took out the coil of rope. Cole had given them each a hundred-foot coil. She uncoiled the rope and spread it out on the stone dock so it would run freely, and Cole wouldn't get surprised by a tangle in the line.

She decided to keep the shorts on, but peeled off her shirt and shoes. From her backpack, she pulled out the mask and compact travel fins and adjusted the straps to fit.

She sat back down next to Cole, wearing only her shorts and her bra. She pulled on the fins. "Have you still got that topo map in a Ziploc?"

"Yeah, but the map won't do you much good."

"Hand it over. It's the bag I want." When he gave it to her, she pulled out the map and put her iPhone inside. The case it was in was supposed to be waterproof, but she didn't want to test it out today. She sucked the air out of the bag and closed the double seal. She slid the bag into her underwear and patted her belly. "If the phone works, I'll be calling Theo in about ten minutes."

"Riley, I don't like this."

She picked up the rope and passed it around her waist. "I know you don't, but you've got to trust me. Here's the deal. If you feel one pull on the rope, it's no big deal. Something just got hung up somewhere, okay?"

"All right."

"But if you feel two sharp pulls, like this"—she demonstrated two yanks close together—"that means trouble, pull me out."

"Two means trouble."

"And if you get three in a row like this"—she pulled one, two, three—"that means I made it through to the other side. Got it?"

"Two means trouble. Three and you're on your way."

She smiled, leaned in, and kissed him on the cheek. "No heavy good-byes, buddy." She picked up her mask and dive light and jumped into the water. "Give me a chance to warm up."

She swam around a bit, then took several deep breaths and dove down once for practice. Riley knew she was always better at breath-holding and free diving after she'd been in the water for a while. She swam over to the entrance to the tunnel and peered down. It did get tight in there. She surfaced after staying under for just over a minute. She treaded water for a while to get her heart rate back down to normal. She'd left her headlamp on the dock next to him. Maybe it was the light, but he really looked terrible.

"You're right," he said.

She put one hand behind her ear and grinned at him. "What's that you said?"

"In this condition, I couldn't stay down that long. Deep breathing's not my strong point right now."

"And I'm just getting warmed up. Are we ready?"

He stared at her for the longest time and didn't say anything. Finally he said, "Yup. I'm ready."

She nodded and speeded up her hyperventilating to super-oxygenate her system. She put her finger in the air and announced, "I shall return!" Then she took a deep breath and dove.

The little fins weren't super powerful, but she felt good cruising through the underwater tunnel. She could see the narrow space ahead, but she hoped it was just a curve and not too tight a space. When she got there, her shoulders brushed against both sides, but she could tell the space was taller than it was wide. She turned on her side and scraped though. Her lungs were starting to burn when she could see the end of the tunnel about twenty feet ahead. That was when the rope around her waist went tight and pulled her to a stop. The rope wasn't long enough. It was so tight in there, she couldn't see the bowline knot at her waist. There was no way she was going back now. She pulled at the knot and felt herself growing weak. One of the strands of rope loosened a bit. She got her finger into the gap and it loosened a little more. She pulled the loop and the line came free. She gave the rope three strong tugs, then swam for the light as the blackness closed in, and she fought to hold on to consciousness and not open her mouth.

When Riley broke through the surface and inhaled a lungful of air, she immediately flopped over onto her back and floated. She gasped air in and out in raspy breaths. She opened her eyes and saw a spot of blue sky showing through the clouds. That had been close, much too close.

When her breathing returned to normal, Riley pulled the bag out of her pants. The phone looked dry inside and the vacuum seal was still intact. She opened the bag and pushed the button to turn the phone on. Not only did it work, but she had service. She pushed the button to pull up her favorites and dialed the number Cole had given her for his sat phone.

"Hello?"

"Greg? It's Riley."

"Riley! Are you okay? Is Cole with you?"

"I'm okay, but I'm going to need your help. I just swam out of the cave and left Cole inside."

"We must not be far. When the weather calmed down, Theo decided to up anchor and move the boat off the coast closer to where you are. Give me your position."

"Hang on." Riley pushed buttons on the screen of her phone and read off the longitude and latitude.

"Got it. We're anchored in the bay off Sulvec, just over a mile away. We'll be there in a few minutes."

"Good, because I'm treading water, and I'm going to need two pony tanks with regulators to swim Cole out of there."

"No problem. I'll get the gear and meet you in the Boston Whaler."

Thirty minutes later Riley surfaced inside the cave and swam over to the dock. She handed Cole one of the pony scuba tanks. The little bottles were only fifteen inches long and could be held in the palm of one hand, so she'd been able to coax them in front of her body through the tunnel's pinch point.

"See, I told you I'd come back for you."

Cole grinned. "Hey, Magee. I never doubted you for a second."

"Right."

EPILOGUE

Manila Yacht Club
The Philippines

December 31, 2012

"May I come aboard?"

Riley was sitting in the cockpit of her boat, wearing a light and lacy summer dress and drinking a glass of chilled pinot grigio. The ice bucket and bottle were on the cockpit table along with another glass. She felt very self-conscious about the low-cut front and the little half sleeves, so she didn't get up. She simply called out to him, "Come on aboard."

When Cole stepped under the dodger, she let loose with a soft wolf whistle. He stood in front of the companionway and modeled the beige linen jacket, khaki pants, and blue checked shirt. "Can I take the jacket off now?" he asked.

"Sure." She laughed. "Make yourself comfortable."

But he didn't take it off right away. He stood in front of her with his mouth gaping open. "Riley, you know nobody is going to notice my sartorial splendor with you at my side in that dress."

She tugged at the front. "I'm not used to showing this much skin."

He sat next to her and pulled her close. "Your skin is gorgeous," he said before he kissed her.

When she came up for air, she ran her finger along his jawline and rested her head comfortably against the slight hollow between the muscles of his chest and his shoulder. "If you keep this up, Thatcher, we're going to be late for our own party."

"Magee, with you, I can keep it up all night."

She sighed with a little half smile on her face. "Promises, promises. By the way, speaking of promises, you were going to tell me about Washington. You've been avoiding the issue."

"For good reason. Are you sure you want to get into this tonight? Why ruin a lovely evening?"

"Now you have to tell me. Did they give you access to Ozzie's files?"

Cole sucked his lips in over his teeth. It was a habit of his. He did it when he was uncomfortable.

"Just tell me and get it over with. You're making it worse by hesitating."

"Okay. After you recounted what he'd said just before he died, and I passed that on to the folks who handled the *Surcouf* decrypts, I was permitted access to certain files. What your grandfather told you was true. Harold Oswald Riley was stationed at CAST Station Corregidor in the fall of 1941. Andrew Ketcham, whom he knew from Yale, was the one who broke the Japanese naval code. He knew what the Japanese were planning a couple of days in advance of Pearl Harbor. We can assume your grandfather did, too."

She reached across her body and slipped her hand under her dress onto the skin of her injured shoulder. Her fingers massaged the skin and she felt the familiar sharp flashes of pain.

"We know that Ozzie Riley left Corregidor in January on a Dutch ship. There is a record of that ship meeting a French submarine in the North Atlantic, so it appears that Ozzie was the one who passed the diplomatic pouch to the *Surcouf* in an attempt to get those message decrypts about the attack on Pearl Harbor back to the Patriarchs."

"So the secrets my father fought to protect involved the misdeeds of his own father."

"Right. And given how many Bonesmen have been involved in all branches of the intelligence community, it's a good bet that in spite of the top-secret designation, your father knew about what your grandfather had done."

"Since he named all his boats *Bonefish*, I expect that's the case." Riley looked across the harbor and watched a containership steaming out of the harbor. The early evening was clear and she could see the smoky blue outline of the island of Corregidor peeking over the breakwater. "I wonder if Ozzie really did change there at the end of his life, or if he was just using us to get the gold."

"I don't suppose you'll ever know for sure."

She turned to watch his face when she asked the next question. "Do you think it's possible to have evil in your blood? Like, does it get passed from one generation to another?"

Cole reached over and picked up her hand. "I think you'll find the answer to that question in your memories of your brother Michael."

She leaned in and put her head on his shoulder again. "And that's why I think I'm going to keep you around for a while."

They sat together in each other's arms, not speaking for several minutes.

Then Cole slipped away from her and pulled off his jacket. He fanned himself. "I think I'm getting overheated. Maybe we'd better stay home. Forget the party. We could stay here, turn on the AC, put on some nice music. We could make our own little happy new year." He poured himself a glass of wine and refilled hers.

Riley clinked her glass against his. "That is a tempting suggestion."

"I think I hear a *but* coming."

Riley sat up straight. Resting on the table next to the ice bucket was the embossed invitation to the night's shindig. She picked it up and read aloud. "'You are cordially invited to attend a New Year's Eve Party at the National Museum of the Filipino People and the Grand Opening of the Dragon's Triangle Exhibit sponsored by the Full Fathom Five Maritime Foundation.' That's you, remember?"

"Yeah, I know. I just hate parties."

From behind her, she heard a female voice call out. "Knock, knock. Permission to come aboard, captain?"

When Riley turned to look at the finger pier next to her boat, she saw Greg and Theo standing arm in arm.

"Permission granted," Riley said. "You both look fabulous."

"Thanks," Greg said as she stepped aboard. She was wearing a bright red silk sheath dress that accentuated her curves. It was the first time Riley had seen her wear her hair down. She was stunning.

Riley noticed Theo had stayed on the dock. "Aren't you going to join us, Theo?"

"No, I want to get to the museum to check over the preparations. But Greg has something she wants to give to you first."

Greg sat down on the cockpit seat, her eyes alight with joy. She was holding a white envelope on her lap. "I came right over because I thought you'd want to know and it's just not the kind of thing to discuss at some big party."

"What are you talking about?" Riley asked.

"When you first told me the story that Ozzie told you, I figured the old man had lied about everything else, so why should I believe him about that. But it bothered me, and I decided I needed to know for sure. So before we buried him, I asked the pathologist to take a DNA sample. I got the test results back this morning." She handed Riley the envelope. "He was my grandfather." She opened her arms and said, "Welcome to the family."

Riley sat there frozen for a moment, overwhelmed. Then she stood up and grinned. "Thanks, cuz," she said, and she threw her arms around Greg. She could tell from the young woman's grip on her that Greg was just as rocked by the moment as she was.

"Okay, Greg," Theo said gently, at last. "Come on, let's go. There are going to be dozens of dignitaries at this shindig and I have to make sure everything comes off as planned." Riley and Greg stepped away from each other, backhanding their tears from their cheeks and laughing sheepishly about the display. Theo rolled on: "Seriously, the vice president of the United States is going to be there. Not to mention the president of the Philippines. A princess from Thailand. A deputy prime minister from Vietnam."

"Yes, Theo," Cole said. "We know."

"Well, obviously you're not going to help. I'll bet you've been trying to talk Riley into staying home."

"Right again, Theo," Riley said.

"Cole, this was all your idea," Greg pointed out. "You're the one who said the only way you could prevent the Philippines from hiding all the treasure away in their government coffers was to convince them of the great international relations coup it presented. We'll make half the countries in Southeast Asia permanently in our debt tonight by returning all the identifiable gold, works of art, books, manuscripts, jewels to the countries from which it was originally taken. It's a brilliant idea and I'm going to be very proud to be a Filipina tonight." Greg kissed Riley on the cheek, and then jumped back onto the dock. "Of course, if you really don't want to go, Theo is going to be there, and you could just let him take all the credit."

"Okay, already. I know I have to go. Can't you just let me whine about it a little longer?"

Greg laughed as she and Theo started up the dock. Theo called out over his shoulder, "I guess that's up to Riley."

When they were gone Cole turned to Riley with an expectant look.

"What you've done here is a good thing, Cole Thatcher," she said. "I'm proud of you. Let's go. I have my old friend Pedro waiting with his *kalesa* out in the parking lot."

"Not just yet." Cole lifted his jacket, reached into the pocket, and drew out a long box. "I have a little present for you. It will go great with that dress." He opened the box and lifted out a gold chain necklace. Hanging from the chain was a golden dragon, and in its mouth was a very large diamond.

"Cole, it's stunning, but a diamond like this must have cost a fortune."

"Not necessarily," he said as he brushed aside her hair and hooked the clasp behind her neck. "Not if you happen to pick up an uncut diamond while sightseeing in the Philippines."

"But—"

"Shhh. Don't worry. They know. You don't think I struck this deal and got *nothing* out of it, do you? I'm going to need a lot of fuel."

"What are you talking about?"

"Well, I've been reading up on the Knights of Malta. Did you know that the Sovereign Order of Malta has its own constitution, passports, stamps, and public institutions, but it's not a real country? There are those who believe—"

"So I take it you're going to the Mediterranean."

"*We're* going to the Med. We can take the *Bonhomme Richard* and have the *Bonefish* sent aboard a ship."

"Why is it you always want to have my boat delivered?"

"Well, there are those Somali pirates between here and the Med."

"And you don't think I can handle them?"

ACKNOWLEDGMENTS

I would like to thank the following people: Terry Goodman, David Downing, Anh Schluep, Keith MacKay, Brian Homan, Rob Schwab, Tom Bennett, Cindy Gray, Bruce Amlicke, Kevin Foster, Jan Helge, Sharon Potts, Neil Plakcy, Christine Jackson, Miriam Auerbach, Kristy Montee, Mike Jastrzebski, Wayne Hodgins, and Tim Kling.

ABOUT THE AUTHOR

Christine Kling has spent more than thirty years messing about with boats. It was her sailing experience that led her to write her first four-book suspense series about Florida female tug and salvage captain Seychelle Sullivan. Christine earned an MFA in creative writing from Florida International University and her articles, essays, and short stories have appeared in numerous magazines and anthologies. The first novel in the Shipwreck series, *Circle of Bones*, was released in 2013, and *Dragon's Triangle* continues the adventures of Riley and Cole. Having retired from her job as an English professor at Broward College in Fort Lauderdale, Christine sails the waters of the Pacific, the Atlantic, and the Caribbean with her pup Barney, the Yorkshire Terror, and she goes wherever the wind and good Wi-Fi may take her.

Visit Christine at http://www.christinekling.com